The
LAST WAR
ORPHAN

JENNA NESS

The LAST WAR ORPHAN

bookouture

Published by Bookouture in 2025

An imprint of Storyfire Ltd.
Carmelite House
50 Victoria Embankment
London EC4Y 0DZ

www.bookouture.com

The authorised representative in the EEA is Hachette Ireland
8 Castlecourt Centre
Dublin 15 D15 XTP3
Ireland
(email: info@hbgi.ie)

ISBN: 978-1-83618-452-2
eBook ISBN: 978-1-83618-451-5

This book is a work of fiction. Names, characters, businesses, organizations, places and events other than those clearly in the public domain, are either the product of the author's imagination or are used fictitiously. Any resemblance to actual persons, living or dead, events or locales is entirely coincidental.

To my mother, Pam Briggs,
who never stopped loving me and believing in me,
even during my obnoxious teenage years.
You make the world a better place
with your warmth, kindness, creativity and love.
Mom—you're who I most want to be.

PART ONE

1

LUCIE

JUNE 1940

When I woke, bleary-eyed from sleeping with my cheek pressed to the side of the back seat, I saw the mid-afternoon sun, brilliant in the bright blue sky, over a Paris that was eerily recognizable.

But it was like meeting the evil twin of your best friend, in one of those silly movies that Josette loved. It still *looked* like Paris, with the soot-stained buildings and blue-gray rooftops, the green parks and cafés and sprawling, twisting alleyways. And yet it did not.

As we drove through the city, I gaped at the ugly red Nazi flags draped over our government buildings, at the energetic German soldiers goose-stepping across our squares. Even Parisians had changed. I looked at them on the sidewalk as we passed by. The stone-faced old man, staring at the Nazi soldiers with beady eyes from beneath his beret; the desperate young mother pushing a baby carriage, her shoulders slumped, her face furtively looking this way and that, as if trying to navigate through a nightmare. The two dirty children playing a game on the side of the road, their parents nowhere to be seen. Nazis were everywhere, lounging, smiling, arrogant in their assurance. They were the only men I saw in the city now who were older than me and younger than sixty.

Paris, home for all my life, had become a place where I no longer felt welcome or safe.

I heard a low-pitched whine. Sitting in my lap, Choupette looked up at me with anxious dark eyes, quivering.

"It's all right," I told her, petting her fur, trying to comfort both of us. "Everything's going to be all right."

My cheeks felt hot as I said it. I always blushed when I lied. But I didn't want my little dog to be afraid. She'd been through enough. We'd found her a few days earlier on the road to Marseille, when we'd still thought there was a chance we'd escape this war.

Choupette's curly fur was soft and shiny now, the color of pumpkins in October, after all the baths I'd given her. She was less scrawny too, fattened up on the treats I'd fed her, sometimes giving her my own meals. She'd been starving, her fur matted with dirt. When I thought of the awful men who'd mistreated her, it still made me seethe, so I tried not to. Thankfully, those men had been caught and thrown in prison. Justice had prevailed, as Sister Helen said it usually did—eventually.

I'd always believed her. Now, as I looked at the ugly swastika that had replaced the French tricolor flag, I didn't know what to believe. No more equality. No more fraternity. No more liberty.

Another whine. As we drove through the normally colorful streets of my former neighborhood, the Marais, the buildings seemed wan with curtains drawn and many shops still closed. I held my pup close. When I'd asked the Nazis where they were taking me, they'd said with a laugh they were taking me home. But I was scared. Why would they take me, a sixteen-year-old nobody, all the way back to St. Agnes's, when so many other French children were abandoned, lost, hungry?

We'd seen so much desolation on the road from Paris after it had fallen to the Germans ten days ago. Our headmistress, Sister Helen, had taken the last six orphans who hadn't found foster homes, including me and my older sister, Margot, and fled south, trying to reach Marseille.

But yesterday, she'd left me—just me—behind in the countryside, supposedly for my own good. I'd run away a few hours later, desperate to find them again. But within hours I'd been picked up by the Nazis. I still didn't know where Margot, Sister Helen and the other girls might be, or how we'd ever find each other again.

I shivered as we drew closer to my street.

"Here," one of the soldiers said in German, pointing, and we turned down the rue Commines. "Go slow." He pointed. "There. See it? Turn right."

The driver frowned, narrowing his eyes. "That's a street? Our truck will barely fit down that alley."

The first shrugged. "That must be why the *Reichsbevollmächtigter* chose it instead of staying in one of those fancy French hotels with the other officers. You know his purpose. To control everything from the shadows."

The driver snorted. "Schröder can do whatever he wants, since he—"

"Shh," the first soldier said warningly, nudging him in the ribs, looking at me in the rearview mirror. The driver followed suit, his expression a little bemused.

"You can't think she speaks German?"

"It's not impossible."

"She doesn't look like a criminal," he muttered, gripping the steering wheel. "She's just a kid."

"Even a child can be a criminal if she's foolish enough to defy the Reich."

The driver frowned again as our eyes met in the mirror. As we turned onto my street, I quickly looked away.

The ivy-covered arch led to the private cobblestoned alley where Le Refuge Sainte Agnès pour Orphelines et Filles Abandonnées had existed for three hundred years, back when this part of Paris had been farmland, owned by a convent. All of the rest of the neighborhood had grown up around it, leaving only St. Agnes's left as a reminder of those long-ago days.

My stomach clenched as we drove down the slender alley, with its green trees and gated garden. Golden sunlight filtered softly through the fluffy clouds above.

Then I saw my home—or what had become of it.

For all the days and nights since we'd fled Paris, I'd often dreamed of the large timbered house, with its bright pink paint and wisteria and ivy climbing its walls. I could almost smell the chalk on the chalkboard, hear the laughter of my fellow orphans playing in the yard, hear Berthe calling us to supper, or Sister Helen to our classes or to our prayers. Through the most terrifying moments of our journey, I'd clung to the memory of those days to steady the rhythm of my frightened heart.

Now I was back.

I'd once heard Berthe say that when God wished to punish us, He answered our prayers. And for the first time, I fully understood what that meant.

The wisteria and ivy had been hacked away. The bright pink color which Sister Helen had added when she'd first become headmistress back in 1925, trying to bring brightness and cheer to the old orphanage, had been sanitized with white paint.

St. Agnes's, instead of a profusion of creativity and comfort, now looked just like any other old, timbered three-story house. The shock of it so denuded was like seeing Josette without her lipstick, or my older sister Margot without her ferocity, or Sister Helen without her firm platitudes.

After seeing all those Nazi flags across Paris, this was the last straw, and it cut me to the quick.

"I still don't understand it." The driver had exited the truck and was scratching his head beneath his cap, looking up at the house with wide eyes. "What a dump. Why would he choose to live here? He could have his own mansion."

"It's not for us to understand," the other soldier said sharply, and he opened the back door for me and Choupette.

My knees felt a little weak as I slid out of the truck. My dog, for her part, bounded out in relief. She sniffed around, then relieved herself on a bush. Her boldness made me decide I must be brave too, though for me that meant merely taking one step forward, then another.

As the soldiers walked ahead to ring the front doorbell, I squared my shoulders, waiting behind them. Pretending I wasn't afraid.

2

LUCIE

The door swung open. I heard a gasp, then a profusion of French.

"*Ma petite!*"

I was enveloped in the embrace of Berthe Cochet, our plump, white-haired cook. Before we'd fled Paris, I'd brought flowers to her sickbed, as she was recovering from pneumonia. She'd insisted we must leave her, saying she'd lived through many wars in her eighty years and would not allow any mere Boche to drive her from her home.

Finding her still here, safe, still wearing her same dress and apron and old shoes, was enough to make me weep as she pulled me into her voluminous embrace.

"Berthe," I choked out and closed my eyes, clinging to her. She smelled of lavender, of freshly baked bread, of savory stews, of fruit pies and everything good.

"But what on earth?" Berthe drew back, her softly wrinkled face concerned. "What are you doing here, child?"

"The *Reichsbevollmächtigter* wishes to see her," the first soldier said in German, and when Berthe stared at him blankly, he repeated himself, more loudly.

"I got separated from Sister Helen and the others," I explained in French. There was no reason to alarm her with the whole story. "The soldiers found me alone in Boulins and brought me here. I guess... the German officer who lives here now wants to see me?"

Berthe's eyebrows rose as she gasped, "See you? Why?"

"I don't know." I bit my lip. "But don't worry. The others are still on their way to Marseille. Th-They must be."

My voice wobbled, in spite of my best efforts.

"Poor lamb," Berthe whispered and squeezed me one last time in a hug. "Don't worry. I would die before I let anyone hurt you."

Then after those shocking words, she stepped back, her wrinkled face blank as she beckoned us all into St. Agnes's.

Inside, everything looked the same—but utterly different. The inside walls had also been painted a fresh white, and the broken balusters on the staircase repaired. The wood herringbone floor shone with fresh wax. When we'd left, the rooms had been mostly empty, the best furniture sold for travel money and, before that, to cover our bills since charitable donations had dried up at the beginning of the war.

Now, the rooms were filled with new, modern furniture and young German men in uniform, not orphan girls and their teachers. The soldiers turned to stare at me as I passed by.

"He's in there." Berthe pointed at the door of what had been our main schoolroom.

I shivered again, looking back at the two soldiers who'd driven me from Boulins. They looked almost as scared as I was.

Finally, one adjusted his cap and led us inside the open door.

"Reichsbevollmächtigter Schröder?" he said nervously.

A middle-aged man in uniform sat at a glossy new desk in the center of the room, surrounded by several younger soldiers. He didn't look up. "*Ja?*"

The soldier seemed to gulp a little. He pushed me forward into the former schoolroom, now a study, with documents and posters spread across the large, stark desk. "Here is the Vashon girl. As you requested, sir."

The older man turned, then examined me with cold gray eyes. Beneath his peaked cap, he had light brown hair with gray fanning his temple.

"That is good, soldier. You may go."

With a relieved nod, the two soldiers from Boulins turned and fled. The man turned to the other officers in the room, including one chubby young man with wire-rimmed glasses. "You also."

They gave a sharp bow, clicking their heels, and left, the last one closing the door behind him. The last thing I saw before the door closed was Berthe's worried face.

The middle-aged man rose to his feet, reflexively straightening his jacket. After reaching for a nearby cane, he limped around the desk towards me. I stared at his cane, made of glossy wood, the brass handle with the head of a glaring eagle. The end of its beak looked sharp enough to really peck someone.

He was solidly built, wearing a close-fitting uniform in grayish-green, a bewildering number of silver insignia adorning his shoulders and collars, indicating that he was a powerful man not to be trifled with. He was in his late forties perhaps, with an aquiline profile and hard jaw. His face was handsome, in that doughy German way, or might have been, except for the coldness of his gray eyes, which didn't match the rest of his pleasant face.

Then he smiled, unexpectedly. "Mademoiselle Vashon." He spoke in heavily accented French, gesturing towards a nearby chair. "Won't you sit?"

I would have preferred to stand—as anyone would when cornered—but it wasn't really a question. Nervously, I sank into the cushioned leather chair. It was soft and new, in a modern style, industrial and sleek, so different from the hodge-podge of old furniture we'd had before. Biting my lip, I looked down at Choupette.

"And who's this?" Unexpectedly, the man turned to her. Gently, carefully, he lowered his hand for the dog to sniff. Tentatively, she did, then backed away, curling up beside my chair.

"Her name is Choupette," I said, waiting for him to order her out of the house, as the foster family in Boulins had. Instead, he just smiled.

"*Bonjour*, Choupette." His accent was atrocious, but I gave him credit for trying. I knew my accent in German wasn't much better. Margot was the one who spoke the language best, Josette the one who could write it with a flourish.

Still standing, he leaned back against his desk. "Mademoiselle Vashon, I am sorry to have dragged you to Paris in such a... high-handed fashion. I hope you will forgive me."

"That's all right," I said, unsure.

His smile broadened. "I am Reichsbevollmächtigter Otto Schröder."

"*Reichsbev...*" My mouth couldn't quite manage all the consonants, but then I'd always been the despair of poor Fräulein Mueller. I licked my lips and tried again, "*Reichsbevor...*"

Flinching a little, he held up his hand, still smiling. "It's quite all right, little *Fräulein*. You may call me Herr Schröder."

"Oh, *danke*," I said, relieved.

He switched to German. "You're no doubt wondering why you're here."

I tilted my head, looking at him blankly. He seemed friendly. But the soldiers had been afraid of him. Should I reveal I understood the language?

As I hesitated, he repeated the words in French. "*Vous vous demandez sûrement pourquoi vous êtes là.*"

Biting my lip, I gave a tentative nod. Better for him not to know. But even the unspoken lie made me blush.

"I need your help, Mademoiselle Vashon." Sitting companionably in the leather chair beside mine, he leaned forward. "I've been looking for your headmistress. Helen Taylor."

"You have?" I frowned. "Why?"

He tilted his head, leaning back. There was something tight in his posture, but he still held that easy smile. "It's a matter between the two of us. We're... old friends, you see. I hoped to find her here, but I arrived too late. A day too late."

We'd left Paris just before it had been declared an open city. Sister Helen, whose nickname made her sound like a nun but who'd actually gotten the name as an American nurse in the last war, had never mentioned a German man friend. I wondered if he was in love with her, like our longtime benefactor John Cleeton. That might explain why such a powerful German officer would requisition the orphanage, rather than staying somewhere more luxurious. He missed her.

I felt sorry for him. If he was in love with her, he, like Mr. Cleeton, was likely doomed to disappointment.

"Where is Helen Taylor?" he asked, smiling. "Can you tell me?"

I sighed. How heartbreaking it must be to love someone who didn't love you back. Though also very romantic, too, like that poem from Shakespeare about love not altering when it finds itself altered... Oh heavens, what was that line? I'd been rather a dunce at literature, too.

But one line from *Hamlet* suddenly popped into my head, clear as day: *One may smile, and smile, and be a villain.*

"I'm sorry, *monsieur*," I said slowly. "I don't know where she is."

It was true, but even if I'd known, why would I tell a Nazi officer? The man might be infatuated with her, but I didn't know him from Adam.

He looked disappointed. "You told the soldiers she's taking some orphans to Marseille, including your sister? But she left you in Boulins yesterday?"

I bit my lip. I'd been pleading with them to let me go. "Yes," I said reluctantly. "I was just trying to catch up with them when the soldiers accosted me."

"Accosted you?"

"Saved me," I corrected diplomatically.

He nodded. "I'm sorry you were separated from your family. That must have been very traumatic."

His sympathetic words caused a lump in my throat. "Thank you, *monsieur*."

"Traveling all alone. With no identity papers, I was told. No money." He tutted his tongue against his teeth. "I'm glad we got you back to Paris safely. I'll have to let Madame Taylor know you're here when I find her." His darkly gleaming eyes searched mine. "Is there anything else you can tell me? Something that might help me reunite you more quickly?"

At the thought of being reunited, my lips parted to tell him the name of John Cleeton's rented house in Marseille, the Villa del Mar. Then I heard the echo of my sister's warning: *You trust people too quickly, Lucie. They're not all kind and good, no matter how passionately you wish otherwise.*

Snapping my mouth closed, I shook my head.

Otto Schröder tilted his head, considering me. "Perhaps later you'll remember more." He rose awkwardly to his feet, grabbing his nearby cane. "In the meantime, I'll send my men to search south of Boulins, and wire a telegram to the American consulate in Marseille." He limped around his desk. Seeing my yawn, he added kindly, "Until we find them, you're welcome to sleep in your old room, if you wish."

"My room?"

"I left the dormitories in the attic untouched. Berthe can make you food, if you're hungry."

As if on cue, my stomach growled. "You'd really let me stay?" I said slowly. He wasn't locking me in some fearsome German prison? I looked down at my dog. "Choupette, too?"

"Of course. Dogs are like family, are they not?"

I swallowed hard. I could hardly believe a Nazi officer could show more kindness than that ghastly French family in Boulins. Biting my lip, I said, "You really want to reunite me with my sister?"

Sunlight came from the window, glinting off his silver eagle and the ghoulish skull medal on his cap. Picking up the receiver of the black phone on his desk, he looked at me. "You are safe here, Mademoiselle Vashon." His voice was gentle. "Until we find Madame Taylor, you'll be my guest. If you wish to earn money, you can help Berthe in the kitchen and I will pay you the same wage I'm paying her. But that is your choice."

Choupette looked up at me with a tentative wag of her tail. My forehead furrowed. Was it a trick? It didn't seem like a trick.

Maybe...

I looked up. Maybe he wasn't so bad. Perhaps it would be all right to trust him. Just a little. As much as any Frenchwoman could trust a Nazi invader.

And at least I'd be with Berthe, whom I loved. It had never felt right to leave her, no matter how many times she'd insisted.

The thought of making money sounded nice, too. Almost as nice as sleeping in my old bed in the attic and eating Berthe's cooking again. I reached down and gave my dog a comforting scratch behind the ears, then rose to my feet in decision.

"Thank you, *monsieur*. You are very kind."

His white teeth gleamed. "My pleasure."

He placed the phone to his ear, so I left the old schoolroom —now his study—and went to go find Berthe in the kitchen. As I walked down the familiar hall, the tight knot of despair in my heart slowly loosened.

Maybe I hadn't been lying earlier when I spoke to

Choupette. Maybe, just maybe, I told myself, everything was going to be all right.

But as I passed the cluster of waiting German officers staring at me with cold eyes, I felt a flash of warning, like the second before lightning, when your skin prickles at the electricity of the storm about to come.

3

MARGOT

"Stop fidgeting," I told Josette harshly, glancing to the right and left. "You're making people stare."

The redhead froze, looking at me incredulously. "*I'm* making them stare?"

Leaning forward, I hissed, "I told you to be inconspicuous. And look at you."

Clutching her half-empty glass of pastis in one hand, Josette looked down at her short-sleeved blouse, which highlighted a bosom far more generous than mine, down to her carefully brushed skirt, which showed off her bare legs to her bobby socks and saddle shoes. Her face had been powdered, dark kohl lined her green eyes, and her lips were ruby red. The only thing she was missing was blush, but her cheeks were red anyway as she glared at me, tossing her coiffed shoulder-length hair.

"What are you talking about? I'm inconspicuous."

"Like a giraffe surrounded by hyenas," I muttered under my breath, ducking my head. I could feel the eyes of the men on us in this little bar on the edge of a rough district of Marseille. Or, more accurately, on her.

I never should have let Josette out of my sight today. Last night, after my mother and John Cleeton and the little girls had sailed for America, Josette and I had vowed to head for Paris to save Lucie. Given the threatening telegram Otto Schröder had sent to the American consulate in Marseille, we had no choice but to return to occupied France.

We'd found a place to sleep in an overcrowded inn, where we'd given false names, just in case Schröder's men might still be looking for us. Since then, we'd bought a few travel supplies and packed them in our old school bags, then we'd separated to look for Roger Cochet, our former travel companion. He was crafty and tough, and we knew he could help us with the difficulties ahead—if we could find him and convince him to come with us. We only knew he was staying with some old friend somewhere along the rue du Panier. Josette had searched the north side of the street, I'd taken the south. After hours of looking, I'd started to despair, since I'd known we couldn't remain in Marseille another night.

I'd seen him almost by chance then, coming towards me on the street, a package under his arm, shoulders slumped. When he saw me, he'd sucked in his breath, halting flat on the sidewalk.

"Margot, what are you—" Joy had lifted to his dark eyes. As he'd come forward, for a breathless moment I thought he might kiss me—not just on the cheeks, in a typical friendly greeting, but on my mouth.

Then he stopped. His hands dropped back at his sides. "What are you still doing in Marseille?"

"I've been looking for you," I said casually, as if it hadn't been hours of knocking on door after door.

He clawed back his dark, untidy mop of hair. "I was sure you'd already left on the ship for America with the others."

We faced each other awkwardly in the street. Against my will, my gaze fell to his lips.

Kissing him to hurt Josette had been wrong. It had been childish, spiteful. I'd done it suddenly, right in front of her, just to win an argument two days before. It had been cruel—to both of them. No wonder he'd left us. I hated myself for what I'd done.

But that wasn't even the worst of it.

With a shiver, I forced my gaze upward.

"I told you. I couldn't leave Lucie behind. We just sent Helen with the little Jewish girls and Mr. Cleeton. It wasn't easy to... um... convince her." Some things were better left unexplained—like how we'd tricked Helen into drinking drugged brandy so she couldn't leave the ship. Even desperately sick, she'd still wanted to be the one to stay and sacrifice herself. I shook my head, remembering. "But we managed."

"Who's *we?*"

"Josette and me."

I waited for some sign that he was proud of me for doing the hard thing, the brave thing. But he only scowled.

"Of all the dumb ideas. Great time for you and Josette to decide to be friends again, just so you could remain in Europe in a war, instead of going off safe to America. You had the golden ticket, you know that? How dumb could you be!"

My cheeks went hot at his jibes, but he wasn't saying anything that hadn't already occurred to me.

"You did tell me to value Josette as a sister," I said, deadpan. It wasn't always easy. Six months younger than my own eighteen years, Josette Dubois had always been my rival. We'd grown up together in St. Agnes's orphanage, and aside from her cloyingly infatuated behavior with Roger, the girl was the biggest bossy boots in the world. She annoyed me to no end.

"*Now* you choose to actually take my advice?" He sounded exasperated.

"We couldn't leave Lucie in Otto Schröder's hands."

"Schröder? What are you talking about?"

His eyes widened as I told him Lucie had been taken to Paris, where she was being held hostage by the same Nazi officer who'd threatened Helen's life.

Roger let out a low whistle. "The man sure does hate Helen. Did you ever find out why?"

I hesitated. "She helped his wife escape a bad marriage."

"Recently?"

"Fifteen years ago."

"Seems like a long time to be sore at someone."

"She shot him so they could get away," I said reluctantly.

His eyes went wide. "*Sister Helen?*"

"Left him with a limp. It's one of the reasons I was determined to send her to America. As far as the Germans are concerned, she's a wanted criminal."

He laughed, then shook his head ruefully. "Just goes to show you can't trust anyone these days. Even matronly headmistresses can have shady pasts."

"It was self-defense!"

"Doesn't matter. They'll claim it's attempted murder." He sobered. "And now Schröder is holding Lucie hostage in Paris? He's powerful. Dangerous."

I shivered. "I know."

"You should have just gone to America, Margot. There's nothing you can do."

Squaring my shoulders, I lifted my chin. "Except go to Paris to get her."

He stared at me, then gave a low, almost admiring snort. "You're crazy. You'll only get caught."

"Not if we have the right help." I fluttered my eyelashes at him with an ingratiating smile that outclassed even Josette with its outrageousness. He stepped back, laughing in spite of himself.

"I told you I wanted to help liberate France. Not die in a hopeless mission."

"Oh, for heaven's sake, Roger, do you have a better idea?" I snapped, putting my hands on my hips. "My little sister needs us. Your great-aunt, too. Are you really just going to leave them there—his prisoners? You were at St. Agnes's when Schröder arrived. You can help us. Tell us how best to sneak in."

He stared at me for a long moment, then gave me a crooked smile. "There you are," he said softly. "There's the Margot I know. Always looking for a way to do the impossible."

For a moment, our eyes locked. My heart twisted.

But the last thing I wanted was to turn into a pathetic puddle for him like Josette had.

I slid my gaze away. "I'd do anything for my sister."

"Even though Lucie's not technically your sister."

I glared at him. "She's my sister in every way that matters."

"Fine." He sighed. "Let's just say I was feeling suicidal enough to go along with your plan. How would we even begin?"

I exhaled. I realized I'd been scared that even if we found him, he might refuse to help. He'd been pretty angry at me about that kiss. "I was supposed to meet Josette at La Sirène ten minutes ago. You know it?"

"Two innocent teenage girls, alone in that thieves' den? Like a couple of fat hens wandering into a pack of wolves. I'd insist on escorting you, but I have... an errand I need to finish first." He shifted the package under his arm. "Can you wait an hour?"

I'd shaken my head. "Josette's already waiting. But don't worry. We'll be fine." I'd tilted my head in a way I hoped showed sophistication and confidence. "We're not cloistered orphan girls anymore. Not after everything we've been through. I'm eighteen now."

"I see." He'd smirked at me from his own vast age of twenty-two. "Women of the world, eh?"

"Yeah," I'd told him with a cool nod. "We'll fit right in."

But now I wasn't so sure.

Josette and I had chosen this bar as our meeting point because we'd seen it across the street and liked the name. The Mermaid. That sounded appropriate for two girls who were on their own for the first time and wanted to feel brave, powerful and free. Two girls trying to pretend they weren't grieving the losses and anguish behind them... or terrified by the journey ahead.

But Roger wasn't wrong about this bar. La Sirène was a rough place, for fishermen who still spoke in the *langue d'oc* or at least had the drawl when speaking French, with leathery faces and squinty eyes beneath their flat caps. Even the younger men looked like that, with brutal faces and forearms thick from the effort of pulling in nets.

We were the only women here, of any age. And all those hard male eyes were still fixed on us—on Josette. I should have guessed that before we'd potentially meet up with Roger again, she'd change into her most clingy top, refresh her makeup, and carefully brush her red hair—her best feature. It certainly wasn't her brain, at least not when Roger was around.

Looking around, I realized a few men were staring at me too, even though I wasn't a beauty or even an aspiring starlet, as Josette was. With my bare face, casual striped top and wide slacks, my style could best be described as *practical*, or perhaps *impatient*. I'd used my red scarf as a headband to tuck back my wild dark hair rather than comb it out after my bath last night.

My cheeks went hot beneath the attention, and I slunk down a little in my chair, sipping the whisky I'd ordered in a show of bravado. Whisky, the drink for soldiers, for men who were strong and tough—or orphan girls who were trying to be.

Just the barest sip because it didn't taste nice. Not nice at all. And the licorice aroma of Josette's drink, on top of the stale smell of sweat and old fish around us, was enough to make my nose twitch and my belly heave in the hot, still air of the smoky, low-ceilinged bar.

Josette lounged back in her hard wooden chair, tossing her red hair, glancing around with a faint smile on her deep-red lips. She didn't feel threatened by all the male attention. She liked it. Glancing to the right and left, she took another gulp of her pastis. "How long did he say he'd take?"

Of course that was why she was happy to have so many male eyes fixed on her. For Roger's benefit. Why else?

"He should be here any minute."

"Good."

"Josette," I exhaled, praying for patience, then leaned forward heavily. "You promised you'd stop."

She froze, then looked up at me with an innocent smile. "Stop what?"

"Stop acting like such a ninny around Roger. You need to be strong. Rescuing Lucie is not going to be easy. Just getting back into occupied France might be difficult."

Josette scowled, leaning forward across the table. "If you want him for yourself, just say so."

My hand clenched over my whisky glass. I set it back carefully on the table. "You know I don't want Roger. I'm just trying to keep us in one piece long enough to save Lucie and get us on a ship to America."

But even as I spoke the words, they felt wrong in my mouth.

Tucked in my bag, next to Lucie's left-behind identity card, I still had my American passport, along with the identity card that my mother had suddenly produced at the American consulate yesterday. Both my identity card and the passport were in a name that was strange to me: Margaret Taylor.

My whole life, I'd grown up believing myself to be Margot Vashon, the orphaned older daughter of dairy farmers from Meaux. I'd only recently learned that St. Agnes's headmistress and a French doctor, Jean-Luc Ravanel, were my real parents.

Lucie didn't know we weren't actually related by blood. I had no idea how I'd tell her when I found her again.

If I found her again.

But at least my mother and the little Jewish orphans were safe now. Lucie, Josette and I would be in no greater danger in occupied France than anyone else.

Or were we? Josette had been a foundling, left at the orphanage as a newborn on Christmas Eve in 1922. None of us knew anything about her birth. For all I knew, her background could be as shocking as mine.

Even matronly headmistresses can have shady pasts.

It was astonishing now to think that, just a few months ago, I'd believed Helen Taylor was a boring, sternly respectable matron. On our journey to Marseille, I'd learned she was so much more. If I could just be as brave and daring as my mother had been in her youth, I'd find a way to somehow transfer my identity card and precious American passport to Lucie, to get her to safety in that peaceful country, while I remained in France to fight the Nazis.

Talk about a suicidal idea.

"Roger!" Josette's face lit up like a thousand suns as she leaped to her feet.

He came inside the bar, ducking to get past the low-slung door. He was wearing a dungaree work shirt and trousers, his leather travel bag on his shoulder. His eyes sought me out first, but when Josette offered her cheeks, he kissed them with a smile.

I didn't get up from the small table but took another furtive sip of whisky. His forehead furrowed, and he gave me a cool nod in greeting. I nodded back.

"I'm so glad Margot found you," Josette gushed, pulling out the empty chair she'd been saving for him. "We were both looking for ages."

"I'm glad too. My old army pal wasn't as thrilled to see me as I'd thought, not since he and his girl got engaged."

"Engaged." Josette sighed dreamily. I wanted to give her a good hard smack.

"Yeah. You'd be surprised how often it happens. Guy falls in love, he forgets his friends." Sitting down beside her, he looked at our glasses—Josette's nearly empty, mine nearly full. "Should I order a drink?"

I shook my head. "Let's go find food." I suddenly couldn't wait to get out of here. "Josette and I promised ourselves a nice steak dinner before we hit the road. We need to be north of Marseille by nightfall."

"Steak, huh? Guess what." His dark eyes glowed as he gave me a shy smile. "I just sold some radio parts I found in the back of that Nazi truck we stole. Capacitors." He beamed at us. "So for once, I have a little money in my pocket. I'll pay for your drinks and then—"

"No need for you to pay," I said quickly. "Monsieur Cleeton left us a bundle."

"He's rich, you know," Josette confided.

"He made our lives so much easier," I sighed, thinking of how kind Mr. Cleeton had been. So devoted to my mother and always looking out for us orphans, too. "He's just wonderful."

Roger stared at me in consternation.

"I just... can see why Helen fell for him," I said a little defensively. I knew it wasn't like me to gush, but I was grateful to the man. I knew he'd protect my mother in America and make sure she got the medical care she needed for tuberculosis. He'd helped us in our plot to get her on the ship to safety, too. "He's so strong. And his money will make such a difference."

"I see." Roger's earlier good mood had disappeared. Was he embarrassed by my sentimentality?

Brushing my fingertips over my eyes, I forced a smile. "Anyway. He'd be thrilled to know he's treating us to a big steak dinner to fortify us before our journey."

"Plus red wine," Josette suggested. "And *gâteau au chocolat.*"

"Yes. All of that." With a deep breath, I tossed some francs on the rough wooden table and rose to my feet. "Shall we go?"

Josette stood. "Maybe it won't be so hard to get back to Paris. Maybe we can sneak across the demarcation line before the Germans know what they're doing."

Remembering the difficulty we'd had crossing through Boulins last week, I was less sure. But I prayed she was right. "We have money now for fuel or train tickets, if we can find any. What do you say?"

Roger hadn't moved. An inscrutable emotion cast strange shadows over his face.

"It's very kind of Monsieur Cleeton to provide for us." He unfolded his lanky body and slowly rose from the table. After glancing around the slump-shouldered men drinking hard liquor across the smoky bar, he turned back to me with a smile that didn't meet his eyes. "You're right. With his money, traveling back to Paris should be easy."

Anger radiated from his tense shoulders. Shivering, I pretended not to notice as I turned away, heading for the door. But I knew why he resented me. I wished I'd never kissed him. Not just because it had been spiteful. Not just because it had been cruel.

But because now, for the rest of my life, I would forever be tortured by that sweet, brief memory of his lips on mine.

4

LUCIE

My sister wasn't coming for me.

No one was.

For the last two weeks, I'd waited patiently for word, a telegram sent from the American consulate in Marseille telling me my family was on the way—if not Sister Helen and Josette and the little girls, then at least Margot. My beloved older sister wouldn't forsake me. But there'd been only silence.

Had they even received the message? What could have happened?

What if my family had never made it to Marseille? What if they were injured, hurt, lost?

What if they were fine but they just didn't care? After all, they'd found me a place to stay. How were they to know I had run away in the night, trying to find them again?

I'd never told Herr Schröder the name of John Cleeton's villa. I'd wavered between longing for my family and fear of trusting a Nazi, even one as courteous and civilized as he appeared to be. But after that first day, he'd never asked me for information again. Either he'd discovered the villa on his own, or he'd lost interest in helping me further. But he *had* discovered

I understood German. A week after my arrival, when I was dusting his study before his men arrived, he'd casually asked a question in that language, and I'd answered without thinking. With an intake of breath, I'd stared at him in consternation.

He'd snorted out a laugh. "I thought as much. You speak some German, little *Fräulein?*"

"Just a little," I'd mumbled, then blushed. The truth was, even if I wasn't the most attentive pupil, I'd studied it for many years.

He set his jaw.

"Of course," he sighed. "*She* would teach you."

As he looked dreamily out the window, I'd suddenly felt bad for him. Just because he was a Nazi officer didn't necessarily mean he was evil. Lots of Germans were caught up in the war, whether they supported it or not. Like poor Fräulein Mueller, forced to return to her native Austria. Who knew what had become of her?

"Herr Schröder, you mustn't love Sister Helen," I blurted out.

He'd turned, his expression unreadable. "I mustn't?"

Embarrassed, I ducked my head. "I've seen men throw themselves at her. But she always turns them down. I just don't want you to be hurt."

His gray eyes had gentled. "Don't worry, little one. I won't be hurt." He'd given me a small smile. "I promise you."

"You expect we'll hear back soon?"

"Very soon."

But so far, there'd been no response to the telegram. Herr Schröder had assured me that communication lines between Paris and the American consulate in Marseille were still operational, as the Americans were neutral in the war. And apparently travel between occupied France and what remained of the French State, so difficult a few weeks before, was now safe and easy, with German troops bending over backward to make

French citizens comfortable. "Though it's still not safe and easy," he'd told me, "for a young girl traveling alone. So it's best you wait here."

Every day, I woke up with hope, and every night, when we had no word, I felt so abandoned and alone I thought my heart would break as I lay awake in an attic dormitory room, surrounded by nine empty beds.

What if something awful had happened to Sister Helen and Margot and the other girls? What if I never saw them again?

Choupette was my only comfort, sleeping at the foot of my bed, shadowing me constantly. And Berthe kept me close. She seemed glad to have my company, especially as her great-nephew Roger had been forced to flee when the Germans had unexpectedly requisitioned St. Agnes's.

She hadn't complained when Herr Schröder had informed her I'd be her new scullery maid, though I'd seen a flash of fear in her eyes. No doubt she was remembering all the previous cooking disasters that had caused her to banish me from the kitchen when I was younger.

But for the last two weeks, I'd tried my best to chop and peel vegetables without cutting my fingers. I'd barely gotten any blood at all on the carrots or onions or leeks yesterday.

Still, this morning, after I accidentally dropped the cutting board of raw pork onto the floor, Berthe irritably told me she didn't need any more help. She seemed cranky with Choupette, too, in spite of my dog doing her best to tidy up by gulping down the pork the instant it touched the floor. But then, she was probably stressed. Herr Schröder could be very particular, both about the cleanliness of the house and the perfection of his dinners. Poor Berthe was used to producing cheap, wholesome French meals in bulk for twenty orphans and six adults, not the more difficult German meals our new employer required for himself, and often his bodyguards and attachés.

So I left the kitchen as ordered and took Choupette out for

her morning walk. Wandering the streets of the new Paris—past the red German flags with their crooked black cross hanging over our government buildings, and all the depressed, bewildered French citizenry—was still painful. Everyone except the Germans seemed to be walking around with a dazed, broken heart.

As I returned from my walk, Choupette trotting beside me, I saw several soldiers at the front door, laughing over something on the step. Puzzled, I went towards them.

"No, but seriously, what should we do with it?" one of the soldiers was saying in German.

"I am serious. It would save us all a lot of trouble," the other said with a wink, adding in atrocious French, *"Dans la poubelle."*

In the garbage can? Had our snobbish rich neighbor left trash in our yard again? Though I couldn't imagine even Madame Hébert being bold enough to pick a fight with Herr Schröder, who seemed very important somehow to the German war effort, though as far as I could tell he mostly just spent hours in his study talking to his men and pushing paper around his desk, or driving back and forth to Nazi headquarters in his shiny black chauffeured sedan.

I came forward. "Did someone leave trash...?"

"Fräulein." Jumping in surprise, they turned to me respectfully. Every German soldier I met had treated me with utmost kindness, once it was known I was Herr Schröder's guest.

"It's nothing," another soldier said quickly in German.

"Nothing to bother you with, *Fräulein.*"

Choupette sniffed the air, then gave a whine, looking up at me. Now I knew something was wrong.

The first soldier cleared his throat. "Please thank Frau Cochet for her excellent dinner last night when you see her."

"Yes, of course I will, but..." Irritated that Séverine Hébert was still causing trouble even now, I peered around them.

At their feet, I saw first a tiny fist, stuck into the air, then I heard a soft wheeze of a snore like a sigh. With a harsh intake of breath, I realized it was a tiny sleeping baby, wrapped with a blanket inside a little basket.

I whirled on the soldiers. "You want to throw this baby in the trash?"

Shocked, the soldiers backed up a step.

"It was a joke." The soldier who'd suggested it had red circles on his cheeks.

"But whatever loose woman left this child at our doorstep clearly had no care for it, or she would have taken it to an orphanage," the other said, defending his comrade. Picking up the basket, he looked down scornfully at the baby, as if he were indeed looking at a pile of trash. "No one wants it."

I sucked in my breath. I thought of all the wonderful girls, my friends, who had been abandoned here anonymously, like Josette. Margot and I might have been left on the step like this, too, if Sister Helen hadn't found us after our mother had died.

"*It!*" I nearly shouted, ripping the basket out of his hands. "She's a baby, you imbecile!"

The soldiers looked astonished, as well they might, since I'd barely said a peep to anyone in all my time there, just a meek shadow scrubbing floors and peeling vegetables. But when I looked at that poor sweet baby they'd called *trash*, that they'd called "it", rage surged through me.

"*Fräulein*, please don't worry," he urged. "We'll arrange for the baby to go to the nearest orphanage."

"The nearest orphanage is right here," I snapped.

The baby woke at the noise and started to cry. I marched into St. Agnes's, baby crying, dog barking at my feet, the soldiers behind me, begging me not to bother Reichsbevollmächtigter Schröder over such a trivial matter.

But I could not let it go. How could anyone?

Without pause, I pushed open the door to Herr Schröder's

study. He, along with four other men, looked up from the documents spread across his desk.

"This place was an orphanage for three hundred years," I said in German, my voice shrill. "Some poor French lady left her baby here, and your men want to throw her in the trash. Is this how Germans show their famous love of family?"

I heard a low gasp, and everyone looked at Herr Schröder. For a moment, as he narrowed his eyes, straightening from the desk, enough reason and sense penetrated my brain to wonder if I'd gone too far. I'd yelled at Herr Schröder in his own study, in front of his men, and in very fluent German, too, since I'd been too mad to be self-conscious and hesitate. Still panting with the breathlessness of my fury, I lifted my chin, staring at the powerful Nazi officer.

Then the emotion was too much, and I burst into tears. My sobs were even louder than the baby's.

"Please, Herr Schröder. Please." My shoulders slumped. "We can't send this baby away. Everyone knows that the orphanages in Paris are overflowing, without enough food or supplies. Please. Won't you show mercy? Won't you let me take care of her?"

The cold-eyed man stared at me, considering. I held my breath, clutching the basket to my chest as Choupette nervously wrapped herself over my feet.

Then suddenly his hard features softened into a smile. "Your tender heart does you credit, Lucie. Yes. She may stay, if you are willing to be her caregiver."

Relief raced through me, so intense my knees almost gave way. Making demands of a powerful German officer in front of his men had not just been rude but very stupid, the sort of thing Margot might have done when she lost her temper.

"Thank you, Herr Schröder," I whispered, blinking back tears. "I am grateful for your kindness."

The middle-aged man tilted his head. "We Germans care about family. And so do I. More than you know."

"Yes, thank you—"

"What you are doing, taking care of her, is a woman's highest duty." He tilted his head, his smile turning lightly mocking. "And you can teach the baby German, since you speak it so well."

"Yes—yes I will," I stammered. "Thank you."

He waved me away, and I left holding the baby basket, sweating profusely, weeping. It was a miracle.

Maybe I'd been wrong not to trust Herr Schröder from the beginning. If all Germans could be so sensible and kind... maybe this war never would have started. I looked down at the baby. I could take care of this child, until I saw Margot again.

If I ever saw her again.

My heart twisted. Where was my sister? Was she hurt? Was she suffering?

Had she utterly forgotten me?

5

MARGOT

OCTOBER 1940

The fields should have been filled with vines groaning beneath the weight of lush grapes right before harvest. Instead, they were bare, the horizon wide beneath the warm blue sky. The vines themselves had been clumsily hacked down, nearly flattened, by men in a hurry, men who were not farmers, men didn't care about protecting future harvests—only defending borders.

On the southern edge of the field, Josette, Roger and I, dirty and worn, crouched together behind bushes in the dark, shady forest. We could see distant bumps of traffic, a slow march of ants, on the rural roads to the west and east. Nazi checkpoints straddled both.

"Well, *les filles*," Roger said dryly, leaning back on his haunches, "this might be as good as it gets."

Josette and I looked at him blankly, then at each other.

There was no cover to sneak under. The vineyards had been razed so thoroughly I wouldn't have been surprised to learn the Nazis had seeded it with salt to make sure nothing ever grew here again, not until the end of time—or at least the end of the thousand-year Reich they kept yammering about.

We were in the middle of France's heartland, right along the demarcation line that split between the French State, run by Vichy, and Nazi-occupied France to the north. The difference being that one pretended to be free, while the other didn't bother.

"Are you sure?" Josette asked, glancing nervously out at the empty fields. "Maybe if we went further east—"

Roger shook his head. "We've tried it. At least here, there's no river to swim. Nothing but the barest hint of barbed wire. We're far enough from those roads and checkpoints. If we stay low, and cross in the dark, maybe we won't be seen."

Josette studied him. I saw the exact moment her big eyes changed to limpid surrender.

"*D'accord*," she sighed, tucking her own good sense away in favor of her infatuated belief in him. "Whatever you think best."

Josette's love continually turned her to mush, and I'd sworn to myself I'd never let that happen to me. In the four months since that infernal kiss, I'd been as cold to Roger as I possibly could be, so he'd know I wasn't some silly girl chasing him. I wanted to earn back his respect. To return to being comrades in arms.

It wasn't easy.

"Margot?"

They were waiting, giving me the final word. And yet I hesitated.

My whole life, I'd yearned to be in charge, chafing against the ridiculous rules of the orphanage. No dessert. Say your prayers before bed. Wash your hands. But since we'd fled Paris back in June, ahead of the Nazi invasion, I'd learned how hard it was to actually decide things. How it meant, when things didn't go according to plan, it was your fault. Like when I'd left Lucie at the Lusignys' château in Boulins, thinking that would keep her safe. By the time I'd realized my mistake the next morning, it was too late, and I'd been trying to find her ever since. Yearning to tell her I was sorry.

Looking back at the flattened fields, a sullen brown beneath the bright blue sky, I stared hard at the distant Nazi checkpoints, the dots of cars crawling along the country roads. If I could see the cars, the German guards would be able to see us—wouldn't they?

It didn't inspire confidence. But we were running out of options. Running out of money and food and time.

We'd been so cocky when we'd left Marseille with our canvas bags, my mother's old service revolver and Mr. Cleeton's stack of francs. That first night, we'd recklessly toasted each other over a lavish steak dinner at a brasserie north of the city, feeling our rescue of Lucie was practically guaranteed. It was just a question of when and how.

But everything had gone wrong. We'd been delayed constantly. We'd nearly drowned in our attempt to swim across a border river, then were trapped by Josette's long-lasting illness in Châteauroux. I'd broken my ankle trying to run from a German checkpoint, and we'd been stuck in Limoges for nearly a month. I'd begged them to leave me, but they'd refused. Plus all those days we'd gotten lost or had to go in wide circles to avoid notice. The weeks Roger had been incarcerated in a small town by a mayor who'd threatened to give him to the authorities in Vichy, who would have handed him over to the Germans. Bribing that mayor had cost money and time. I was starting to hate my fellow countrymen almost as much as our conquerors.

We'd walked nearly twelve hundred kilometers since we'd left Marseille, tramping north to the demarcation line near Boulins, where Roger claimed he had a friend who could help us on the other side. But it was too difficult to cross the river there. So we'd walked almost as far east as Poitiers, looking for weaknesses, some unguarded place.

But weakness was not in the German vocabulary. All routes crossing into occupied France were now blocked by checkpoints, or swollen rivers, or thick barbed wire. After months of walking, we'd retraced our steps almost all the way back to Boulins.

"My old army buddy Bernard can help us get to Paris, if we can reach him," Roger insisted now. "I saw him when I first came south. He didn't wait around to become a prisoner of war, either. He's a wild man. He was planning to stay and sabotage the Germans. He'll help us. All we have to do is cross over."

"*All*," I muttered under my breath, staring at the field.

Though many French refugees were now being legally repatriated through checkpoints—the Nazis were eager for Parisians to return to their emptied city and staff factories for their war effort—the three of us could not go through legally. Every Frenchman Roger's age was either in a prisoner of war camp, working for the Germans, hiding or dead—none of which appealed to him. And Josette and I feared being dragged back to Otto Schröder as prisoners, ending all hope of Lucie's rescue if we so much as gave our names to a German soldier.

I wondered how much Schröder knew about Josette and me. If he discovered I was Helen Taylor's secret daughter, he'd no doubt devise some special torture just for me. But how could he know? Even Lucie had no idea.

His telegram had been waiting for us in Marseille, so he must have sent it right after he captured Lucie. It was only later he'd sent soldiers to attempt to kidnap my mother from Mr. Cleeton's villa.

At some point, Lucie must have told the Nazi officer both about John Cleeton and the Villa del Mar. How else could he have found us?

It scared me to think about the ways he might have made her talk.

I took a deep breath. "Let's take the risk and cross the field. We've been delayed for too long."

Roger's forehead smoothed over as he nodded. "We'll do it after dark."

We doubled back to the nearest town for supplies. Even though we were still technically in unoccupied France, and this time of year all the markets should have been filled with apples, pears, root vegetables and grapes from harvest, many of the farmers had little to sell. One of them confided in a whisper that he'd been forced to give most of his crops to the Germans for almost nothing. The pittance left to sustain the French populace had nearly doubled in price, and the cost was only increasing.

We managed to fill our bags with food and water, a few days' worth, enough to get us to Paris... we hoped. There was no telling what we'd find on the other side. The rumor was that Paris was running out of food, but of course it was impossible to know. Truth was the first casualty in war.

Once night fell, we tightened our full bags against our backs. We were lucky with the weather—the clouds were dark and low, threatening rain, blocking out the moonlight. We waited in the forest until the lights of the checkpoints seemed steady, without the blinking of passing cars or soldiers, in hopes that perhaps the watchmen would nod off.

Finally, we took a deep breath and headed out towards the flattened field, creeping invisibly beneath the low, thick clouds, afraid to breathe. I could feel Josette and Roger near me, moving like shadows. We crawled against the ground with agonizing slowness, one centimeter at a time.

We were almost there. I could see the thin string of metal over wooden posts in the distance. The barbed wire wasn't as thick or ferocious as we'd seen in other places along the border. Unguarded and unwatched, we planned to use shears to cut through the wire.

But when we were fifty meters from the fence, the clouds suddenly parted, flooding the field with moonlight. We gasped, huddling flat to the ground. But it was too late.

I heard shouting in German, then suddenly a floodlight moved across the fields, searching for us. A soldier's high-pitched voice ordered us to surrender, to come to the check-point immediately.

We looked at each other.

"Go back," I gasped hoarsely, and we all rose and started to run back from where we'd come.

I heard the sound of rifles firing, bullets landing all around us, just like when my mother and little Noémie had been strafed by German gunfire in June. We kept running until we reached the forest. Once safe, we stopped, doubling over to catch our breath.

"Warning shots," said Roger, panting, trying to give his usual careless smile.

Josette touched his backpack, wet from the water pouch that had exploded after being grazed by a bullet. "I'd hate to see when they're serious," she said ruefully.

"Any chance they'll come find us?"

"No, they won't risk looking in the dark, leaving the check-point unmanned. We didn't attack them. They won that round —there's no reason for them to be lured out here."

Once we'd caught our breath, we returned grimly to the town ten kilometers away and regrouped at an abandoned farm-house nearby. Over the summer, we'd learned to sleep anywhere, anytime, even on the grass or the pew of an empty church, or inside a medieval ruin, as we'd done once outside Avignon.

"I'm sorry." Roger wouldn't meet our eyes. He brushed his own lightly, his expression bleak. "I thought it would work."

"It's not your fault," Josette said consolingly, patting his shoulder.

He pulled away. "It was my plan," he said and looked at me.

I said nothing, turning away to sleep on the musty old hay. We all knew this was my fault, from start to finish. If I hadn't left Lucie behind in June, none of us would be trapped here now.

All of us tossed and turned. Finally, Roger rose to his feet in the darkness. "I'm going into town," he announced, his voice tight. "To find another way."

"Dawn's still hours off." Josette started to rise. "I'll come—"

"No." He looked at me, his expression haunted in the bit of moonlight peeking through the empty slats of the roof. "I put us at risk. I'll be the one to fix it."

I stared at his handsome, stricken face, my heart in my throat. I knew I should tell Roger our failure was my fault, only mine. But if I let myself be vulnerable, if I admitted it out loud, if I cried and told him I was sorry, I was afraid I'd fall apart.

I couldn't let Roger, or anyone, into my heart. Not now. I had to stay strong for Lucie, and for Josette and Roger, too. They expected me to be tough, a leader. If I collapsed into weakness and grief, we'd fail, and Lucie would be lost forever.

So I said nothing.

Instead, I reached into my bag and pulled out the revolver. Looking him straight in the eye, I handed it to him, handle-first. He waited.

I turned away silently.

Roger slowly exhaled, lingering a moment before he finally left. My heart ached, and in his departing footsteps, I heard the echo of all my unsaid words.

6

JOSETTE

The October dawn rose sad and gray, illuminating the thick mist frosting the plundered fields around the barn. Dead leaves whirled in a cold wind against the lowering sky.

I felt old and worn down, my muscles stiff and my joints aching as I got up from where I'd slept a few short hours, shivering against the ragged hay. Roger hadn't returned yet from town. Margot was sleeping in her clothes, curled around her dirty canvas bag like a mother protecting her baby. Though she'd given Roger the revolver, she'd insisted on keeping all Mr. Cleeton's money, as she had the entire journey.

We'd tried to reason with her, explaining it would be more sensible to split it between the three of us, in case her bag was lost or stolen. But we'd wasted our breath. The money was hers, and unless Roger or I wanted to physically fight her, so it would remain. What was left of it, anyway.

Silently, I changed my clothes, still shivering in the cold morning air. I put my feet into my cleanest socks, then my worn saddle shoes—which had cardboard covering the holes in the soles—before going out the gaping door of the barn. Using my last sliver of soap, I washed my face with the rainwater that had collected overnight in an ancient stone trough, now sitting crooked in the mud.

Carefully, I took out the ties I'd used to curl my hair as I'd slept. Fruitlessly, as it turned out. After so few hours, my hair just looked limp and frizzy, rather than curling as I wished. I looked down at the tangled ends and my heart sank. Hideous. I'd have to pull it back in a chignon again.

I twisted back my hair, pinning it with practiced fingers, hurrying because I didn't want Roger to find me in my beauty routine. I wanted him to think I just woke up naturally lovable. So every day I got an hour less sleep than anyone else.

I pulled out my compact, squinting at myself in the slowly brightening dawn as I powdered my face, then darkened my eyelashes and eyebrows with my last bit of cosmetics.

Margot thought I did it because I was vain. She was wrong. I did it to cover the deep, awful flaws that had existed in me from the day I was born. To hide the hideous monstrosity that had made even my own mother abandon me at birth. Whatever it was that had always made people think I was unlovable.

Before she left for America, Sister Helen had told me the shocking truth about my parents. It confirmed what I'd always feared: I was never meant to be born. So every day, when I put on my lipstick and tried to look my best, it was because I wanted someone to prove me wrong. And love me.

Not just someone. Roger.

"*Bonjour,*" he said behind me, amused.

I whirled around, snapping the compact shut behind me and dropping it—and my lipstick—into my bag. "*Bonjour.*"

He'd been so stressed and miserable last night. Now, he was relaxed, happy. "I've found a way to get us to Paris."

I sucked in my breath. "All the way to Paris?"

"All the way." His dark eyes glowed down at me, and my heart twisted. If only he would look at me again as he had that single day last summer, before he'd met Margot. If only he'd...

But even as I thought it, Roger was looking towards the barn. "Is she awake?"

We found her sitting up and pulling back the wild bird's nest she called her hair. Thick, dark and curly, it refused to be tamed. Just like her. My eyes slanted towards Roger as we approached. Even though I knew it would only hurt me.

"Oh," she said, yawning with a lazy smile. "You're back."

"I am," he said softly, looking down at her.

And the way he looked at her... I felt an ache in my throat. Why couldn't I stop myself from relearning painfully, again and again, what I already knew? Every time, hoping I'd be wrong. And every time, feeling my guts ripped out.

While I had some hideous flaw that made me unlovable, Margot had been loved from the day she was born. Loved by her sister. Loved by our headmistress, who'd turned out to be her mother. Loved by all the other girls in the orphanage, who'd instinctively looked to her as their leader and idol. And now, loved by Roger.

I closed my eyes. Would I ever be first in anyone's eyes? Or would I spend my whole life lonely and unwanted?

"Roger's found a way to save us," I murmured, turning to wipe my eyes. But it wasn't necessary to hide my tears. No one was looking at me.

"Did you now?" Margot asked him.

He smiled at her, all masculine confidence. "A merchant in town is taking wine and cheese into Paris. He says he can smuggle us in his truck, all the way to the city. We'll be at St. Agnes's by tonight."

"Tonight!" Her dark eyes lit up. Then she scowled. "Why should we trust a stranger?"

Roger shrugged. "I trust his greed. He's a businessman. I offered him a good price."

Her eyes narrowed. "What price?"

He took a deep breath. "Every sou."

"All of it?" she gasped. She clutched her bag and backed away. "No! How will we get out of France and get a ship to America if we spend all our money to get to Paris?"

"If we can't reach Lucie, there's no point in worrying about what comes after," Roger pointed out reasonably.

"But—without our money, we'll be vulnerable. Helpless." She twisted a long dark lock of hair anxiously around her finger. "I can't bear it, Roger. I can't."

He stared at her. "I didn't realize money was so important to you."

"It's important to everyone!" She twisted that poor lock of hair round and round her knuckle. If it wasn't all so serious, it would have been funny to see her so perturbed, just as our headmistress had once been, running an orphanage and caring for twenty girls with almost no money. Mother and daughter were so similar, it amazed me I hadn't seen it before.

But I hadn't, not until I'd stumbled over Margot's secret birth certificate back in June. It gave me some small satisfaction that I'd known before she did. Sometimes one had to take consolation in the little things.

As Margot and Roger argued in the half-ruined barn, I stood back silently. They were both such strong characters, their clashing was like steel against stone. No one asked my opinion, but for once, that was a relief. I had no idea what to do.

Finally, Roger said in exasperation, "What choice do we have? Every day, the demarcation line is fortified a little more. Soon, it will be winter. Do you want to still be stuck here, freezing to death, as our money slowly disappears? And have Lucie still be Schröder's prisoner?"

Her cheeks were pale. Her teeth chattered as she said, "N-No."

"Then"—he put his hands on her shoulders—"let's take a chance. Everything is a risk, you know that. But I'm running out of ideas. Aren't you?"

For a moment, Margot just looked at him, their eyes locking in the shadowy light of the barn as dust motes floated in shimmering beams of light from the broken-down roof. Then she pulled away.

"Fine." Her voice was short.

"Fine?"

"I said so, didn't I?"

And so, three hours later, we found ourselves in a small town of gray stone buildings spread out against the brilliant autumn landscape, the trees orange and yellow against the rolling green hills.

We met with a gray-haired, big-bellied man in the alleyway behind his shop, beside a truck his two men were filling with barrels and wax-wrapped wheels of cheese. He sold the best wine and cheese in all of the Auvergne, he bragged, because he convinced his neighbors to give up their wares for almost nothing, with threat of Nazi attention if they didn't. He made a tidy profit with every weekly trip to Paris, selling food on the black market amid the rising shortages and ration coupons.

Pulling his cap over his eyes with gleeful swagger, the merchant held out his hand to Roger. "As promised, *monsieur*?"

Roger counted out the money Margot had given him—every franc, including our coins.

"*Mais non.*" The man's lips twisted down with dismay. "I thought it would be far more. For the risk I am taking, I need greater recompense. What else can you offer?" His eyes lingered on our three bags, now sitting on the wet ground.

"Nothing," Roger said. "We have nothing more."

"There must be something." He picked up my bag. "Let me see—"

"Wait," I gasped, and the man's eyes glinted.

"Nothing, eh?"

"Just my documents," I said weakly.

The man put his finger alongside his nose. "We'll see, won't we?" A moment later, when he fished out the American visa Sister Helen had arranged for me, he grinned. "This is worth something."

"But—" At the man's imperious eyebrows, I relented. Glancing at Roger and Margot, I saw their resignation. What else could we do but agree?

But as I watched the precious visa disappear into the man's pocket, I suddenly saw the life swimming away that could have been mine—living near Hollywood. Trying to get discovered at Schwab's drugstore like Lana Turner. Perhaps becoming an actress on the silver screen. Being loved by all those audiences in the dark. All gone, all disappeared, like the ship that had taken Sister Helen, Estée, Rachel and Noémie off into the sunset glory of America.

Had I made a horrible mistake, staying here for Lucie? For Margot? For France?

For Roger.

"And this," the Frenchman exclaimed, finding the revolver in Roger's bag. "Useful in these difficult times."

I felt Roger tense beside me, but he said only, "I am pleased you find it so."

"I do. And what's this?" When he found Margot's American passport, he positively beamed, eyes twinkling. He made an expressive gesture, kissing his fingertips. "Do you know how much money this passport can be sold for? How many rich Jews have pretty daughters with dark hair?" I watched him take our identity cards, as well. He flashed a grin. "Huh. So what are you three playing at, sneaking back into occupied France? Very suspicious. You're lucky I'm an honest man, otherwise I'd be tempted to give you to the Germans."

We stared back stoically. He seemed almost disappointed we didn't react. He sighed.

"*Eh bien.*" Returning our bags, emptied of the revolver, the American passport and visa, our identity cards, and even our food and water, he pointed into the back of the truck. "Get in."

"How can you be sure soldiers won't search your truck, *monsieur?*" Margot demanded as we climbed inside, between the wine casks and boxes of cheese.

"I'm a businessman. They need what I offer. Trust me." He covered us with a blanket. "Now be silent."

The truck's back door slid closed, and a moment later, the engine started.

We were shaken by the road, huddling together, cradling our bags to our chests, praying, hoping. We could smell sour wine, the whiff of overaged cheese.

It seemed hours—but was probably only thirty minutes—before the truck stopped. We heard the engine turn off. The businessman and his driver got out, banging the doors behind them. We strained to hear quiet words in French and German. The back of the truck wrenched open.

I held my breath, praying that the German soldiers would give a cursory glance at the barrels and boxes, then close the door again.

Instead, the blanket was suddenly ripped off, leaving the three of us, aching from kneeling in that small space, blinking up blindly. Three silhouetted soldiers looked down at us.

"Just as you said." One of the Nazis turned to nod at the gray-haired man standing behind the truck. "*Danke.*"

"Just doing my part," he replied meekly. "If there's no trust, I'll be out of business."

The Nazi soldiers yanked us out, and we stumbled to the ground. Looking around, I saw we were back on the same river bridge in Boulins we'd crossed back in June. The Frenchman and the driver stood beside the checkpoint that marked entry into occupied France. They grinned at us, as if this was all a hilarious joke.

"*Espèce de cochon!*" Roger shouted. "You betrayed us!"

"I told you—I'm a businessman," he replied smugly.

Roger lunged at him but was held back by two German soldiers. Two others held Margot and me. The Frenchmen got back into the truck and continued north, waving back at us with a cheerful honk. A fifth soldier came out of the little booth and collected our bags.

"This one surely was a soldier," one of the helmet-headed Nazis said in German. He sneered at Roger. "Why aren't you imprisoned with your comrades?"

"Probably a deserter," another said in the same language.

"We're going to send you to Germany," one taunted.

"You'll work at our factories until you drop dead."

"It's what you deserve, for abandoning your duty."

"For thinking you could defy the German Reich."

They all laughed gleefully. The soldier checked Roger's pockets, then finished rifling through our bags.

"Aw, there's nothing." He set the bags down, disappointed. "Greedy Old Rocher. He could have left us *something*."

The soldier holding my wrists leered at me. "He left plenty. Look at this one. I like her red hair—it's like fire," he said, touching a tendril which had escaped my chignon. He licked his lips. "I'll enjoy searching her."

A snort from his friend. "You think this girl is one of the French thugs who've been causing trouble? Unlikely."

"A woman? Of course not." He raked me with his gaze, and my cheeks went hot. "But she might have contraband. It's possible."

"Be careful," warned another, holding Margot's wrists a little tighter as she struggled. "We're under orders to be polite until the French get used to us. Like training a horse, you must ease them into accepting who's master before you add the bridle and the bit."

The soldier winked at me. "She'll love it. You know how French girls are."

"We know how *you* are, Fritz," they replied, grinning.

He laughed. "I'd be a fool not to take what I can."

I glared at him, panting, my heart pounding.

"Oh ho—I think the girl understands you."

"Do you?" The young soldier drew closer, his breath hot. "Do you understand me, *Fräulein?*" Reaching around, he squeezed my backside with a rough hand. As I bit my lip to avoid crying out, he leaned forward, pressing his smooth cheek to mine. "You're going to love it, I promise," he whispered. "Both the bridle and the bit."

7

JOSETTE

"Get away from her!" Roger cried in French, struggling, but the two brawny Nazi soldiers had him firmly in hand.

"Ah, he doesn't like it."

"Let the cowardly deserter see that we Germans now own everything."

"Fritz," one of the others protested awkwardly, "you know it's against orders to—"

"The redhead is mine. You all can share the brunette."

As I looked at the soldier's laughing face, as he touched me in a way no man ever had—doing it simply because he could, because no one could stop him—fury whipped through me.

I slapped him hard across the face, yelling in German, "Let me go, you pig!"

The soldiers gaped at me, astonished. They'd thought of Roger as a threat but not me. All their rifles were still dangling on their backs.

"She hit me." Putting his hand on his cheek, the soldier looked astonished. Then his eyes narrowed. "I'm going to take you into the guardhouse," he panted, grabbing my wrists roughly, "and teach you some manners—"

His voice choked off as a loud explosion shook the bridge beneath our feet. The soldiers looked at each other, terrified. When the bridge didn't immediately collapse beneath us, they sucked in their breath.

"These French devils!"

A vehicle approached the southern edge of the bridge, then rolled forward and exploded into flame. The Germans gasped.

"Get them—"

"Watch the prisoners, Fritz."

"Wait—"

But the four others ran off, shouting, heading towards the southern riverbank.

Fritz, alone on the bridge, looked at the three of us. Nervously, he pointed his rifle in our direction.

"Nobody move," he said in German, and his voice hit a false note. He cleared his throat, looking at us angrily. "I'm a soldier of the German Reich, with all the power of that behind me. Don't even think of—"

Roger knocked the rifle aside, sending it spinning off into the river. Then, with two quick strides, he punched the young soldier in the face, knocking him to the ground. I exhaled, tearful with emotion as the man who'd assaulted me lay flat, blinking at the sky.

Roger turned to us. "Run!"

The three of us fled north across the bridge, snatching up our bags. Roger and Margot quickly raced ahead, both of them more athletic than I. But I tried to keep up, running until I had no breath left, afraid to look behind me. With every step, I braced to feel the sharp edge of a bullet pierce my back.

Racing into the streets of northern Boulins, I saw Margot disappear around a corner, Roger ahead of her. I pressed ahead, panting, my heart so squeezed I saw stars.

Then, suddenly, I went around another corner and crashed straight into Roger's arms.

"We're far enough for now. We can stop. Catch our breath."

We'd escaped. We were back in occupied France. But I had no energy to celebrate. I leaned over, wheezing, feeling like I was going to be violently sick in the little alley behind the *pâtisserie*, right in front of Roger and Margot.

"You're all right, Josette," Roger said, rubbing my back. "You're safe now. Safe."

He kept repeating the word until the stars left my vision. When I slowly lifted my head, he pulled away. My back felt cold without his hand.

"Everyone all right?" Margot asked, her eyes on me.

Swallowing, I nodded. "I don't know who bombed the bridge. Guardian angels must be looking out for us."

"*Angels*," Margot snorted. She'd never been very devout.

Roger looked at her. "How else would you explain it?"

"I don't know, but I can't picture St. Michael tossing grenades. Come on."

At the edge of the alley, we peeked in both directions down the slender street but saw only shopkeepers sweeping outside their steps, and townsfolk going about their daily lives. Boulins wasn't a mere village but a proper town of twenty thousand people, though the prosperity seemed to have faded since we'd last been through here, the night after Lucie first disappeared in June. Passing the town hall in the square, we saw even more of the pitiable messages looking for missing family members, posted in faded, ripped pages, one on top of another, a palimpsest of misery.

Walking swiftly, but not so swiftly as to draw attention, Roger led us down back alleys and streets, always looking ahead for any trouble. Finally, we arrived at an old derelict building on the northern edge of town. He knocked on the door. Waited.

No one answered.

He raked back his hair. "We'll just have to wait."

It was almost an hour before Roger rose to his feet with

relief, coming out of the bushes where we'd been hiding. "Bernard."

"*Salut*, old man. What are you doing here?" A sandy-haired young man, broad shouldered with scattered freckles across his crooked nose, beamed at Roger, then Margot and me as we rose uncertainly beside him. He took off his cap. "*Oh là. Salut, les filles.* Bernard Bartoli"—he gave a sweeping bow—"at your service."

"All right, enough of all that," Roger grumbled good-naturedly. He pointed at each of us in turn. "Margot Vashon. Josette Dubois. Now we're all introduced, what happened to your face?"

Bernard grinned, putting his cap back on his mop of sandy hair. "This?" He brushed at the bruised cut on his cheek. "A small disagreement with a Boche yesterday. I got my revenge, though. What are you doing in Boulins, Cochet? Thought you were heading for Marseille then de Gaulle."

"Er, not anymore." Roger glanced at Margot. "We need a lift to Paris."

"Oh, is that all. No problem. Easy."

The three of us blinked at each other. Easy? Was he joking?

"Well, that's good to hear." Roger cleared his throat. "I should probably warn you, the Germans might be after us. We had a little trouble on the bridge." He gave a sheepish smile. "We'd probably still be under arrest, except the soldiers were distracted by some explosions..."

"Ah, was that you?" Bernard flashed him a grin. "We saw someone getting the full treatment. If I'd known that was you, I would have set a couple extra sticks of dynamite, just to give time for your flat feet to get off the bridge." He inclined his head towards Margot and me with greater respect. "And to make it easier on you, too, of course, *mesdemoiselles*."

"You set those explosions?" Roger laughed, then clapped his

old buddy gleefully on the shoulder. "Of course it was you, you mad Corsican!"

"Not just me." Bernard Bartoli tried to look modest but failed. "A small group of us have been doing our best to make the Germans' lives miserable. It's lucky you caught me at the house today. Tomorrow, we're moving to the forest. None of those fat Germans will be energetic enough to fish us out, not in winter. We'll have free rein." He pulled a box of Gauloises from his pocket and lit one. "But why Paris? I'd say you're well out of that hornets' nest."

Taking an offered cigarette, Roger tilted his head towards Margot. "Her little sister is being held hostage by a German officer there."

Bernard snorted, offering the blue box towards me, then Margot. "It's not enough they hold the whole country hostage?" When we both shook our heads, he shrugged and lit a match. "Now they're picking fights with little girls?"

Roger lit his own cigarette and drew smoke deeply into his lungs. "Not just any officer. Otto Schröder."

His friend coughed, then gave a low whistle, blowing the cloud of smoke away with his hand. "Here I thought you were too lazy to make a proper enemy. *Otto Schröder?* What, was the Führer himself not available?"

"Um. Yeah. Well." Roger bit his lip. "I understand if you don't want to take the risk of driving us to Paris."

Bernard Bartoli stared at him for a moment.

"Are you kidding?" His friend's plain face turned almost handsome as he broke into a big, gleeful smile. "Sounds like the most fun I've had in ages. We'll leave at dark."

"Wait." Margot looked at the sandy-haired Corsican. "Could I ask a small favor?"

"Just say *thank you*," I whispered, yearning to give her a hard pinch. It wasn't enough that the man had already saved us on the bridge and was giving us a free ride to Paris, now she wanted more? Was nothing enough to satisfy her?

She had the grace to blush. "Thank you, of course, *monsieur*."

"Call me Bernard."

"Monsieur Bartoli, I am of course very grateful. But would it be possible to ask for something?"

"Margot," I said, "for heaven's sake—"

"Of course you can." He smiled. "A pretty girl can always ask a favor."

"Any girl, of any age, pretty or not," Roger hooted. "You've always had a gallant heart, Bartoli."

"*Scandale.* An outrageous lie." But his boyish grin belied the words. He tossed aside his cigarette butt. "What is it, Mademoiselle Margot?"

"I'd like to stop in La Ravelle, please, on the way to Paris."

"La Ravelle?" said Roger, frowning. "Why?"

"It's on the way," she rushed to say. "It won't take long. I just need to speak with someone."

"Who?" Roger looked puzzled. But looking at Margot's strained eyes, I already knew.

She wanted to find Dr. Ravanel. And tell him he was her father.

8

JOSETTE

We arrived in La Ravelle just an hour after we left Boulins, traveling on rutted dirt roads in the dark, without headlights, guided only by the moon. In Bernard's rusted old Peugeot, we felt every bump. The little car was tight, Margot and I crushed together in what could only generously be called a back seat fit for children. Even the two men in front had little space for their long legs.

But Bernard was crafty, it seemed, because he managed to get us to La Ravelle quickly and without the faintest notice. He dropped us at the little blue house we'd come to know back in June, while he went to go see someone he knew who might have fuel to sell.

Roger and I stood on either side of Margot as she knocked on the front door. I could see her shivering.

No one answered.

"What are we even doing here?" Roger said. "This man—he is a friend of yours?"

"We're friends of the family," she replied, not meeting his eyes.

"Hey. Hey there. You. Get away from the—" The

policeman came closer. His eyes widened when he saw us. "Oh. Mademoiselle Vashon. Mademoiselle Dubois." He nodded at me, then gave Roger a suspicious glare. "You are looking for the Ravanels?"

Margot bit her lip. "I'm so glad to see you, *monsieur l'agent.*"

"And how is your sister—and the little dog?" The man gave a beatific smile beneath the small streetlight on the slender cobblestoned lane. "We're all still in awe of that little girl. And grateful. Those villains will be locked up for a long time."

"That's... good to hear." Not answering his query about Lucie, she said, "Are the Ravanels away?"

"Moved to Paris."

She gaped at him. "But my—Dr. Ravanel said he'd never leave La Ravelle. Not when he was needed here."

"He's still needed, dreadfully. But no one blamed him for leaving. When the casualty lists came out, his son Daniel was on it."

"Oh no—Daniel." Margot looked horrified. Though she'd never met Dr. Ravanel's two oldest sons, which he'd had with his first wife before she'd died long ago, they were her half-brothers. "Injured? Missing? Surely not d—" She hesitated, unable to say the word.

"Sent to a work camp in Germany, *mademoiselle.*" His shoulders slumped. "We all are praying the war ends swiftly..." But then he looked even sadder because we all knew that the only way the war could end swiftly would be if the British surrendered and Germany completed its total conquest of Europe. He sighed. "Nothing to be done."

"What about their other son—Paul?"

He brightened a little. "That's it. Paul was seen in the capital. Some German soldiers came and told them about it. So up they went. Dr. Ravanel thought of going alone, but you know, his wife and daughter would never agree to be left behind."

"We know," I said dryly, remembering.

"Where are they staying in Paris?" Roger asked suddenly.

The policeman stared at him with a jaundiced eye, then said finally, "The American hospital in Neuilly needed doctors. I don't know more than that. And I think Madame Élisabeth's grandmother left her a small house in the city."

"Thank you, *monsieur*," I said when Margot didn't reply.

"Of course." The policeman looked at all of us, then added, "You know we have a curfew. The Germans." He looked grave. "I am off on patrol and didn't see anyone on this street." He lifted his eyebrows suggestively. "But if I come back in an hour..."

"We were never here," Roger assured him. He looked up. "Ah, in fact I see our ride."

"Good luck to you. And please do send our best to that sweet little girl."

"We'll tell her," I replied warmly.

Margot remained silent, blinking back tears.

The little Peugeot came rattling down the street, announcing its arrival by the noise of the engine. We helped Margot into the back. She did not resist. I could only imagine what it had cost her to steel herself to come here.

I knew I could never do it. Even though I'd learned a few months ago that both my parents were still alive. Or at least— my father was. I didn't know about my mother.

I looked out the window at the darkness of the countryside. I could hear Roger and Bernard chattering about the old days in the army, discussing wild plans to get revenge on the Germans, boasting about various things. I didn't listen. Like Margot, I was lost in my own thoughts.

Sister Helen had learned from a former housekeeper that my aristocratic father had seduced my mother, a young Polish maid. I'd been shocked. I knew the man's famous *hôtel partic-ulier* on the Île de la Cité. Everyone did. Walking along the

Seine, I'd often passed by that tall, thick stone wall. For all I knew, the man was there now, fat and happy, probably counting his piles of francs.

I wondered if my young mother had been seduced into the affair. Or if he'd forced her against her will.

You're going to love it, I promise. Both the bridle and the bit.

Feeling sick, I stared out the car window and tried to distract myself with other things.

Like Roger. I could see his silhouette in the front seat amid soft moonlight as we drove slowly over the dirt roads snaking through farmlands and forests. He'd changed my life that day last summer, just by making me feel *seen*. Making me feel *heard*. Making me feel, for just that one perfect day, like I was the most fascinating woman in the world.

I knew Margot thought I was a fool, caring for him so much. And maybe I was. Because after that perfect day, he'd met Margot, and it was all over. But after all these months traveling together, I felt chained to him more than ever—and desperate to return to how I'd felt that first day. When he'd smiled at me, his eyes sparkling. *You know you're pretty enough to be a movie star, Josette?*

Who had I been before I loved him?

Who would I be without that love?

I shivered, feeling alone and sad, though there were four of us packed into the tiny car, rattling over the narrow road. Closing my eyes, I leaned back in the warmth of the back seat and imagined what it would be like to be happy, a housewife in a comfortable little cottage, as Roger kissed me, our baby in my arms...

"Wake up, *ma petite*. Wake up." Bernard was gently shaking my shoulder.

I blinked. "Where are we?"

His plain face lit up with a broad smile. "Paris."

I saw the pink light of dawn over buildings on a street I

didn't recognize. But there was no doubting the Métro sign nearby.

"Where?"

"The eleventh. I didn't want to drive you all the way. One, I don't have fuel, and two, delivering you right up to Otto Schröder's doorstep is too much even for this mad Corsican."

"What? I thought you had no limits."

"I like my head on my neck." Bernard grinned, then stuck out his tongue. "I have a friend who'll help me find fuel for the way back. Might as well help myself to a few other things while I'm here."

"Perhaps a night at the Opéra?" Roger guessed.

He snorted. "A few old guns... armaments... one can always find such interesting things on the black market." He gave Roger a significant glance. "Don't forget."

"I won't." Roger looked thoughtful, and I wondered what they'd been talking about while I slept.

Margot, standing beside him in the street, hopped from one foot to the other, glancing at the Métro with obvious impatience.

"*Au revoir, mon ami.*"

"*Au revoir.*"

The two men shook hands, patting each other on the shoulders in a comradely gesture. Bernard shook hands with Margot, then me.

"Good luck," he told us. "*Bon courage, mes amis.* Whatever happens."

Then he returned to his little car and was gone.

9

MARGOT

The Corsican had barely left before I turned to Roger. "We'll take the Métro."

Frowning, he looked up and down the street. "Too dangerous."

We'd come so far, and now were so close, I could barely contain my longing to have my sister safely in my arms. She was all I could think about. "But it's faster—"

"If I'm seen, there will be trouble. I'm sorry, Margot. We must go slowly, stay in the alleys."

It was painful, but I tried not to complain. I knew we couldn't have made it to Paris without Roger. Still, it seemed hours before we finally made it all the way to the rue Commines on the eastern edge of the Marais.

I nearly cried when I saw the old arch stretching beneath ivy over the small cobblestoned alley. No cars or military trucks were visible. Everything was quiet in the cool early-morning air, the kind of air that smelled of apple cider, burning wood and rotting leaves, with just a soupçon of frost. I started to rush forward, but Roger grabbed my wrist.

"Wait! It's too dangerous in daylight. We should return after dark."

"*Wait?*" I stared at him. "Are you out of your mind?"

"It'll be dangerous after dark, too," Josette argued. "What about curfew?"

"We don't know what we're walking into—"

"I'm getting Lucie," I interrupted and, without waiting for his response, started walking down the rue des Orphelines.

They whispered harshly for me to come back, then when I didn't, they followed me, sneaking down the thin, shadowed street.

I gaped up at St. Agnes's, the only building facing the tiny alley. It looked utterly different, shining, almost new—if a three-hundred-year-old building could be new. The pink paint was gone and so was the wisteria. It was shiny now. With an evil new patina.

Josette's worried eyes met mine.

We didn't see any soldiers. She pointed, and I nodded. Silently, we crept through the back, past the unlocked gate, and snuck through the lush garden. Even here, much had been changed, the weeds cleared out, the overgrown foliage tamed. But the trees and roses still offered cover.

"What now?" Roger asked quietly.

"We go in," I said.

"We don't even know which room she's in!"

"We have to wait, Margot," Josette insisted quietly. "At least until we can get Lucie or Berthe alone."

"No—"

"You think it will help Lucie if we rush headlong into a house full of Nazi soldiers?"

I turned on her. "We don't know if there are any soldiers inside."

"You're right," she said pointedly. "We don't know."

Grinding my teeth, I glared at her, hating her for her good

sense, then nodded reluctantly. But as we sat waiting behind the rose bushes, I drummed my fingers anxiously against my skin. Every minute felt like an eternity.

As the morning deepened, I imagined I heard a baby crying. Then I heard the sound of German boots and the guttural language shouted as a few soldiers came out of the back door to smoke, and I was glad I'd allowed Josette and Roger to dissuade me from just walking in. We all held our breath as the young men stood outside in the garden, just a few meters from us, before they went back inside.

Later, officers arrived at the front door, their caps just visible above the stone wall, before they left with a middle-aged officer who limped down the front steps with his cane.

Otto Schröder. It had to be.

Still, we waited.

The sun was high above us in the sky, and my stomach was growling, when I finally saw a figure in the kitchen window. I gasped. Yes—there it was again—there could be no doubt. Lucie. My little sister was in the kitchen, pacing back and forth in front of the window, holding something I couldn't see. Was she worried? Was she afraid?

Her expression seemed pained, and she was talking to... I squinted. A petite figure with white hair pulled back in a bun. Berthe? It had to be. And with that, I could wait no longer.

I rose to my feet and recklessly left my hiding place behind the trees.

"Margot!"

"Come back!"

But I was beyond the point of being safe or sensible.

I grabbed a small stone from the ground and tossed it against the glass.

Lucie blinked, then looked out the window. Her eyes went wide as she saw me, and her jaw dropped. She turned hastily to Berthe, pushing the bundle into the other woman's arms.

I ducked behind a tree, just to be safe, shaking with emotion.

A moment later, Lucie herself came out the back door into the garden.

I peeked around the tree, frozen, holding my breath.

My beautiful sister.

She looked different somehow. Or was it just that, after all these months apart, I was seeing her with new eyes?

Her light blonde hair was pulled back into a severe chignon, a practical style she'd never worn before. She was wearing one of Sister Helen's old, matronly dresses, cinched to her slender waist with a belt, which should have made her look like a child playing dress-up, but it somehow didn't, not quite. Only her feet were the same, her white socks pushed into those leather shoes —scuffed now—that had been standard issue at St. Agnes's.

Her cheeks were rosy beneath the autumn sunshine. Looking right and left, she breathed uncertainly, "Margot?"

"Lucie." I stepped out from the tree.

We looked at each other for a moment, then burst into tears and fell into each other's arms.

I realized it wasn't until this exact moment, holding her, that I'd really believed I'd ever see her again. Before now, she'd been a will-o'-the-wisp, haunting my dreams, luring me forward into the mist before always disappearing. I'd feared my sister was dead, and that it was my fault. Now, holding her in my arms, feeling the beat of her heart and hearing her breath, for the first time since I'd left her behind, I felt like my own heart could beat again. Like I could breathe again. She was alive. And now so was I.

"Pull her back," Josette whispered, and when I didn't move from the embrace, Roger tugged us both gently behind the hedge of roses, so we couldn't be seen from inside the house.

Josette stared at me, and I realized I was weeping openly.

Tears slid off my chin, splattering noisily against the dead leaves shrouding the grass of the garden.

I couldn't let my sister go. Not now. Not ever.

"I'm sorry, Lucie," I choked out. "So sorry."

"You came back for me." Pulling back to look at me, she wiped her blue eyes. "It's been so long. I didn't think you were coming—"

"We've been trying to reach you since the first night we left you in Boulins." Ducking my head, I rubbed my eyes. "I knew within hours I'd made a horrible mistake leaving you with the Lusignys, but when we came back the next morning you were gone—"

"Remy attacked me—"

"I know."

"You came." My sister tried to smile through her tears as she looked from me to Josette and Roger. "I can't believe you're here."

As we all hugged each other, I couldn't tear my eyes from her. Lucie and I were so physically different. How had we never previously questioned the story that we were sisters?

She was still my sister, by love if not blood. And yet she'd changed somehow. I couldn't put my finger on it. Or maybe I was afraid to even imagine what had changed her. Loneliness? Suffering? Fear?

What had happened to her since she'd run away from that castle in Boulins?

"I'm so happy to see you all." Lucie's eyes were bright as she eagerly grabbed my hand—and Josette's. "Now come inside. I have something to show you."

"Are there Nazis inside?" Josette asked.

"What? No..." Lucie glanced uncertainly towards the slender cobblestoned street. "Well, not at the moment. Herr Schröder left with his men. I'm not sure when they'll be back."

"Schröder," I breathed, suddenly trembling. I turned to Lucie. "We need to get out of here. Now."

She frowned, her forehead furrowing. "Margot...?"

"Is my great-aunt in the kitchen?" Roger demanded. At her nod, he said grimly, "We're here to get you out."

Bemused, Lucie shook her head. "Berthe will never leave Paris. She's said so. Sister Helen left her St. Agnes's if she doesn't come back. And Berthe especially won't leave now, when—"

Roger exhaled, staring at the kitchen window. "I'll try to talk sense into her."

"We'll wait for you down the street," I said tersely. "The Nazis might return any moment."

My sister turned to me, her forehead furrowed. "But I can't—"

"Come on, Lucie," Josette coaxed. "We can talk later. After we're free."

"I can't leave." Lucie bit her lip. "Just come inside and you'll see—"

"No time." Why was she resisting? I tugged on her wrist, trying to pull her towards the back gate of the orphanage garden. "Whatever it is, just forget about it, leave everything behind—"

"Stop, Margot! I told you I can't!" Lucie yanked her hand away, standing her ground in the autumn colors of the garden in a way that made all three of us goggle in astonishment.

"Lucie," I gasped.

Taking a deep breath, she squared her shoulders and faced me. "I'm not leaving Paris," she said evenly. "Not without my babies."

10

———

LUCIE

Seeing Margot through the kitchen window, I'd thought I was dreaming.

Thérèse had been colicky and terribly unhappy all night, keeping poor Geneviève awake and leaving both babies wailing, so much so I'd been afraid that even Herr Schröder, who never complained about noise, might at last tell me that the babies were no longer welcome in his house.

When I'd first found a baby on the doorstep, after Herr Schröder had given me permission to keep her, I'd rushed back to the kitchen to tell Berthe everything. She'd stared at me in shock, then looked reluctantly at the baby in the basket.

Luminous tears had shone in the baby's big brown eyes, tracking down her woebegone face as she'd whimpered, sniffling up at us. She was tiny, just a few months old. Her little fists had waved towards us desperately.

Berthe had sighed, rubbing the baby's belly with her wrinkled hand. "Poor little thing," she'd said softly. "No country of her own, nor parents neither. You're right. She's ours now."

We'd looked inside the basket, but there had been no letter.

No clue as to the baby's identity or why her parents had surrendered her. They must not have realized that St. Agnes's was no longer a girls' orphanage.

So the two of us had named the baby Thérèse, after Berthe's favorite saint, and given her the traditional surname used for St. Agnes's foundling babies for hundreds of years: Dubois, after the small forest that once existed here.

I'd learned to take care of the baby. I'd risen three times a night to give her a bottle, changed her diapers, kept her close in her basket when I scrubbed the floors, sang to her and talked to her and kissed her cheeks, which grew plumper by the day. This Nazi house, unlike French homes, had plenty of food and money. Choupette's belly, too, grew fatter. I tried not to think about my hungry French neighbors and just be grateful, but it wasn't always easy. I might have been tempted to steal from our larder, to share food with neighbors, if Berthe hadn't threatened to whip my hide if I did anything so foolish.

"Steal from a Nazi, you'll put us all at risk." She'd nodded towards the baby, narrowing her wrinkled eyes. "Even her."

Baby Thérèse hadn't even been with us a month before, shockingly, another infant was left at our door, this one with a tear-stained note.

My baby's father was a soldier. He's dead now and cannot marry me. Please watch and keep her.

She was perhaps a month older than Thérèse, with blue eyes and golden curls. We named this baby Geneviève, after Berthe's second-favorite saint. The white-haired cook grumbled that she'd soon have to return to Mass at this rate, just to remember the names of her third and fourth favorite saints.

As the weeks passed, Berthe had helped me with the babies whenever she could, but she was terribly busy in the kitchen, plus supervising the newly hired French charwoman, a sullen woman by the name of Françoise. I'd nearly cried when Herr Schröder had told me he'd continue paying me wages, in spite of the fact that the majority of my time now went to baby care. I was grateful to Berthe, too, who never complained even once about no longer having my assistance in her kitchen.

We both managed together as best we could, Berthe juggling recipes for three meals a day, sometimes for up to ten Germans, sometimes just for Herr Schröder, who often spent his evenings locked up in his study alone. In September, he gave us each a little wristwatch to thank us, inexpensive but practical for me to keep the babies' schedules. It was pretty, too, with a gold-toned band and small, smooth face with Roman numerals.

I'd set up two ancient cribs next to my lonely bed in the attic, doing my best to keep the babies happy and well fed, so they would be less likely to cry and disturb the Germans in the house.

Last night it had been impossible. I'd spent hours walking Thérèse up and down the attic dormitory hallway, with her body nestled over my shoulder, as I walked back and forth, back and forth, and Berthe rocked Geneviève in the chair. This morning, we'd both been a little bleary-eyed over our late breakfast, eaten hours after the Germans had theirs. I'd had to manage only a few bites of toast and eggs with one hand while, between bites, I fed and burped each baby, then put the girls in their high chairs to give them a little oatmeal after their milk.

And then, while holding Thérèse over my shoulder, patting her back for a burp that just wouldn't come, I'd heard a *thunk* against the glass. I'd looked out the kitchen window and seen Margot, like a ghost, standing in the garden, staring up at me.

For a moment, I'd thought I was so tired that I was hallucinating—or maybe dreaming. But I'd blinked, and blinked again, and my sister had still been there, her chin stuck out desperately, her shoulders squared in that determined way she had. A shock had shuddered down my spine. Shaking, I'd handed the baby to Berthe. "Please, please take her—I have to go..."

"What in the world?" she'd said, her hands still covered with flour, as I'd thrust the baby into her arms. Without pausing to answer, I'd fled out the back door.

They'd come back for me.

I'd long since given up hope. We'd never heard any reply from the telegram. Herr Schröder had told me much later he'd discovered the name of their villa in Marseille and sent some of his men, but found it deserted. He'd told me he believed they'd all left Marseille via ship, for some foreign country.

Leave France! Sister Helen had said they were just going to Marseille.

I'd tried to tell myself they must have had no choice. The three littlest orphans were Jewish. It made sense she'd wanted to get them to safety.

But Margot? Josette? Just leaving me in France, without a word of farewell?

It was a stab in my heart. But I no longer had the luxury of crying out my grief, not even at night. Sleep had become too important to give up for feelings. Without sleep, I couldn't take care of the babies, and then where would we be?

In the garden, as I'd hugged my tough-as-nails sister, she'd wept openly, hugging me almost too tightly for me to breathe. And somewhere, deep inside me, a knot in my heart had loosened, and I'd wept, too.

Herr Schröder had been wrong. They hadn't left for a foreign country. My sister hadn't abandoned France—or me. She'd said last June that she would send for me when I could join her at her mysterious job in Marseille, and here she was. I should have trusted her.

Leave everything behind, Margot had just ordered me. For most my life, I'd followed my sister blindly. But...

Leave? I couldn't leave. Around me in the orphanage garden, the leaves had turned the color of rust, withered and desiccated in the first frost last week. The flower bushes had been deadheaded by Herr Schröder's new gardeners. Little Rachel Lévy, who'd always had a green thumb, would be astonished if she knew. Whatever country she was in now.

But there was no one to tend the babies. I certainly couldn't leave them to the mercies of German soldiers. The new charwoman Françoise despised children, and Berthe couldn't do it alone. I'd turned to Margot and Josette and Roger and said calmly, despite my panic:

"I'm not leaving Paris. Not without my babies."

Now, Margot and Josette and Roger stared at me in shock, as if they thought I'd lost my mind.

"Babies?" my sister said hoarsely.

Roger's gaze fell to my waist, invisible in my oversized dress. "What babies?"

I almost laughed at his suspicion that they could be mine by blood—I'd never even been kissed, and in my current life, it seemed unlikely I ever would be. "We've had two babies left here since June."

"Left?" Josette gasped. "You mean at the door?"

"But St. Agnes's isn't an orphanage anymore," Margot stammered.

"Who would be cruel enough to leave their baby with a Nazi?" Roger looked up with horror at the freshly painted house.

"Maybe they don't realize Sister Helen and the orphans are gone," I said. "Or maybe they believe a Nazi officer has more access to nutritious food." That was certainly true. "Who knows?"

They stared at me in consternation.

"Lucie..." Margot licked her lips, then tentatively placed her hand over mine. "I understand how you might care about two abandoned babies—you always worry about everyone who needs help—but you need to look after your own future now."

"Just come inside and meet them," I coaxed, then turned to Roger. "Berthe will be so glad to see you." Nearly two million of our young men, who'd originally waited in camps for Britain's quick and looming surrender, were now imprisoned indefinitely in German work camps, in unknown conditions. Because France never officially surrendered—we just "paused" the fighting—the legal protections of the Geneva Convention didn't apply, as Herr Schröder had explained to me for reasons I didn't quite understand. It still didn't seem fair. So I was relieved to see Roger. "She's been so worried since you left."

"Tante Berthe's the one who told me to leave Paris when the Germans came," Roger replied. He looked at the house. "Is she well?"

"Making schnitzel. She helps me with the babies."

"Lucie—we've come such a long way to save you," my sister whispered.

"Aren't you even glad to see us?" said Josette.

I bit my lip, an ache in my throat. "Of course I am, but—"

"So let's go!" Margot cried.

"Before it's too late!" Josette added.

I thought of the difficulty traveling when we'd fled Paris on the refugee road back in June. I couldn't imagine putting Thérèse and Geneviève through that. But I felt my sister's imploring eyes. Reluctantly, I said, "Could we bring the babies with us?"

The three of them looked at each other.

"Two crying babies across the border?" Josette said.

"They only cry sometimes," I said. *Like morning, noon and night*, I added silently. I tried to smile. "Come meet them. They're the sweetest little darlings. Would we take them with us, back to your job in Marseille? Would your employer mind having two extra babies stay? After you explain I'm your sister and the babies are under my care?"

"Uh..." Margot paced through the rose bushes, refusing to meet my gaze.

Josette glared at her. "Tell her," the redhead hissed.

"Tell me what?"

"Shut up, Josette," Margot snapped.

"What is it?" I looked between them. "What's the big secret?"

My sister clenched her teeth, then looked at me reluctantly. "All right, Lucie. We'll come in, just for a few minutes. And talk."

"*Go inside?* Are you out of your minds?" Roger demanded. "We're not going into Otto Schröder's house!"

"Lucie wants us to meet her babies," Margot told him tightly. "What else can we do?"

"We can bonk her on the head, that's what! I'll toss her over my shoulder, *et voilà*, we'll be out of this city before dark, heading for the coast!"

"You wouldn't..." Alarmed, I backed away.

Margot stepped between us in the afternoon shadows beneath the trees. "Of course not." She glared at him, then turned to me gently. "Don't worry, Lucie. We won't force you. We owe you that much. Where are the babies?"

"In the kitchen."

She glanced at Roger. "Stay here. If you see any Germans, throw a pebble at the window."

His eyes went wide. "Oh, I'm staying out here, all right. But if I see Germans, I'm not sticking around to throw any pebbles. This is pure lunacy."

"Do what you need to do, then," she said stiffly. Her eyes warmed as she turned to me. "Let's meet your children."

Then I saw the look that passed between my sister and Josette. Their plan was to come inside, pretend to consider my demand, then try to convince me to do things their way. They really thought I'd leave my babies behind.

But I wasn't the sweetly pliable girl they knew. Not anymore.

No one, not even my sister, could convince me to abandon my duty. My heart. My poor orphaned children.

11

LUCIE

Back in the kitchen, I found Thérèse banging her small table gleefully with a wooden spoon, as Geneviève, in her own worn high chair, attempted to stuff porridge in her mouth with her fat little hands, managing mostly to get it on her plump cheeks and golden curls.

Choupette, who'd waited anxiously by the door when I'd left her behind, greeted me with a bark, which changed to a trill of barking ecstasy when she saw Margot and Josette. She remembered them, even after all these months.

"Choupette!" Margot said happily, petting her.

"Aw, what a good girl. She's gotten fat and happy," Josette added, smiling.

"She's not the only one," I replied.

Baby Thérèse, chubby and thriving, held up her hands from the high chair when she saw me, dropping the wooden spoon she'd been playing with so it clattered on the tile floor. Smiling, I picked her up and held her close. I felt a rush of love at the feel of her sturdy little body in my arms, the smell of her lavender soap. She cuddled into me, then a moment later squirmed, reaching out towards her spoon.

"Margot! Josette!" Berthe gasped, coming in from the pantry as I returned both Thérèse and spoon to her high chair. The cook clapped her hands. Tears filled her rheumy eyes as she rushed to embrace them, kissing their cheeks. Then she drew away. "But you are both grown so thin!"

I frowned, realizing it was true. The months that had passed hadn't just changed me but them as well. Margot's dark eyes held a hardness that hadn't existed before. Josette's freckled face now had hollows beneath her cheekbones, and her shoulders looked weary beneath her worn sweater.

"What are you doing here?" Berthe demanded. "I thought you were in Marseille, or else gone to some foreign country!"

Margot shook her head. "Though Helen and the little girls did go to America."

I gaped with astonishment as she rapidly explained how the others had taken a ship from Marseille.

America! The thought of Sister Helen, Estée, Rachel and Noémie there shocked me. So far away from Europe's war, it might as well have been the moon.

"They're settled in California now with new families," my sister finished. "Well, except for Helen, who was going to Arizona. For her illness."

"Is she still sick with pneumonia?" I asked, concerned.

"Uh... something like that." My sister and Josette glanced at each other, and I had the feeling they weren't telling me something. A feeling I'd already had a few times.

"We *hope* they're in America," Josette added quietly. "There's no way to really know, is there?"

"Of course they are. They're safe and happy," Margot said fiercely, then turned back to me in the brightly gleaming kitchen. "John Cleeton is looking after Helen. They're in love..."

"What!" I gasped. Sister Helen had finally given her heart

to that kind, handsome cowboy? Was there no end to the surprises?

"But we're here to help you escape, Lucie. You too, Berthe. We'll take the babies to the best orphanage in the city before we go. But you must leave Paris with us. Now. Before that horrible man comes back."

I looked back at her, my brow furrowed. "Horrible man?"

"Schröder."

"He's evil," Josette added.

"He's not *really* evil. I mean, I was scared at first, but he's taken care of us all. He let me keep the babies. He's been..." I swallowed, cowering at the hard look in their eyes. "Kind," I finished weakly.

"Kind?" Margot repeated in disbelief.

"He's paid me a wage for their care," I said defensively. "Also, he tried to reunite me with you. The first day I came here, he sent a telegram to Sister Helen at the American consulate in Marseille. Later, he tracked down John Cleeton's villa—"

"He tracked it down? You didn't give him the name?" Margot gripped my shoulder. "I was afraid he'd tortured it out of you."

I blinked in surprise. "Nothing of the sort. All he did was ask. But I never told him because, well... he's a Nazi, and it didn't seem right to tell him anything about your whereabouts. Even if he's in love with Sister Helen."

The two of them looked at each other, then burst into laughter.

"Schröder's not in love with Helen," Margot said.

"He hates her," Josette added.

"But... that doesn't make sense." I frowned. "If he hated her, why would he stay here? He could be living at a luxury hotel or some mansion in Saint-Germain-des-Prés. And why would he be so kind to me?"

"Some nefarious plot," Margot said darkly. "Helen shot him in the leg. In Germany, years ago. And he wants revenge."

"Revenge?" I stared at her, my brow furrowed. I thought of his limp, his sharp-beaked cane. But... "Sister Helen, shoot someone?" I shook my head. "That's preposterous. It all must be some big misunderstanding."

"Lucie, why do you refuse to ever admit that some people are just bad?" Josette demanded. "The man was abusing his wife."

"He blames Helen for helping his wife and child escape Germany." Margot looked around the kitchen. "So when the Nazis reached Paris, he saw his chance. He took her house. And he took you hostage."

"*Hostage?*" I snorted a laugh, then sobered when I saw Margot was serious. I set my jaw. "You're out of your mind. He's been polite, and he's allowed me to raise my children when most men would have said no." My eyes lingered on the two babies, one happily babbling and the other still banging away with her wooden spoon.

"Just trust us. We have to leave. Berthe, talk some sense into her. Tell her you're coming with us."

"Oh, no. I'm not going anywhere," the elderly cook said, folding her arms over her shelflike chest. "Sister Helen left a notarized letter. If she never returns to Paris, this house is mine. I'm holding on to it as my investment for my old age. Especially now the new furniture is so nice."

"But, Berthe," Josette told her desperately, "you can't want to live here with a Boche—"

The older woman stared at her, wispy eyebrows arched. "You're telling me it's safer for me to hit the road at eighty, penniless in the middle of the war, rather than staying right here in this warm house I've lived in for the last fifty years?"

Josette gulped. "Uh..."

"Roger's in the back garden," my sister begged. "Go talk to him!"

"Roger!" With a gasp, Berthe glanced out the window. "No! There's a reason I told him to get out of Paris. No one cares about an old woman, but he'd get shipped off to a work camp for sure." She glared at us. "Why did you bring him back here?"

"To save you." Margot turned to me desperately. "If Berthe won't leave, maybe she can stay and watch the babies."

"What, watch them all by myself?" The elderly woman drew herself up indignantly. "Roger would never suggest anything so heartless. He's always had a tender heart for his great-aunt—and proper deference, too..."

"Don't worry," I said soothingly, patting her shoulder. "No one would expect you to do everything on your own. Your hands are already full. And you do such a wonderful job. Everyone loves your cooking. Herr Schröder couldn't compliment last night's *Schweinsbraten* enough."

"Thank you, *ma petite*." The elderly woman sniffed, mollified.

I didn't want to add that I'd sometimes heard her grumble under her breath, usually when she was irritable after a baby woke her or interrupted her cooking, that the government-run orphanages should be taking care of them. Berthe was a good woman, but if I found it difficult to take care of two babies at sixteen, how could Berthe do it at eighty, and all the cooking besides?

"We'll find a good orphanage," Margot suggested again.

I narrowed my eyes. "Everyone knows French orphanages are overwhelmed with too many children amid the food shortages. I'm not leaving my sweet babies to be ignored when they cry, or go hungry when there's not enough milk. There's plenty of milk here. Plenty of everything."

"Sure—because you're living with a Nazi!" Josette gripped my arm. "But you can't imagine it's safe!"

"Is Marseille really so much safer?" I turned to my sister, whom I trusted more than anyone. "Does your new employer have plenty of food and room? Will he allow us all to stay indefinitely? If you can promise that, along with an easy trip to Marseille, I'll pack up the babies right now."

Margot glanced at Josette, who bit her lip. Secrets.

"Babies would never make it, Lucie," Margot said awkwardly. "Travel right now is... difficult."

"Really difficult," said Josette.

"Herr Schröder says the Germans are bending over backward to make it easy."

Josette rolled her eyes. "Not for us. He would love to keep us and hurt us, for the sake of hurting Sister Helen."

"But you just said she was gone. Off to America. So even if he hates her, what would be the point now? We're just orphans. It's not like we're related to her by blood."

They looked at each other.

"Look, Lucie," said Margot gently, "if Berthe wants to stay here, there's nothing we can do. But you have to come."

"And the babies?"

"No."

I set my jaw, looking away. Then I took a breath.

"Or... you could stay in Paris." I looked at them hopefully in the sunlit kitchen. "Just until the end of the war. It might be soon. I bet Herr Schröder would give you jobs. You could earn money. Oh, do stay! I could use your help! And look how sweet they are." I beamed down at Thérèse's chubby cheeks, at Geneviève's gurgling laugh. I laughed too, seeing how the baby beamed at us, oatmeal smeared all over her face. "You could sleep in your old beds in the attic, just like the old days! And then, once the war is over, we could figure out what to do..."

"Lucie, it isn't like you to be so unreasonable..."

"It's exactly like her," muttered Josette.

"We've tarried here too long already." My sister grabbed my shoulders, her dark eyes intense. "We'll give you a few hours to settle your affairs. Then we'll be back to collect you after dark. You have to understand—"

"No." I shook her off. "*You* have to understand, Margot. Those babies need me. I won't abandon them. How could I, when not so long ago, it was us that had no home? I'd rather die than leave them."

Her eyes widened as she realized I meant what I said.

Over the noise of Geneviève's happy babbling, I heard a low patter against the window, like hard rain. Or maybe it was just the loud beat of my heart.

"If you won't stay"—I took a deep breath—"you'll have to go back to Marseille without me."

That wasn't what I wanted at all. I loved my sister—and Josette, too. And I needed help. I'd even have been happy to have Roger's help at this point.

"We're hoping to travel a little further away than Marseille..." Josette started.

My sister quelled her with a glance.

I frowned. "Where?"

"Lucie, please. Don't do this to me." My sister's face was agonized beneath her wild, dark curly hair. She had circles beneath her eyes, her skin pale. I wondered what she'd gone through in order to save me. How bad it had been for them.

"Margot, you know I love you." Tears welled in my eyes. "You too, Josette. I don't want to let you go." I wiped my eyes hard, trying to smile. "But we're grown now, all of us." I saw their lips twist incredulously at that, so I repeated firmly, "*All of us*. And we all must do what we have to do, what our hearts tell us is right—"

"Hello." The man's voice was low and polite behind us. "What's this?"

Whirling, I saw Herr Schröder in the doorway of the kitchen, smiling as he looked from Berthe to me to Margot and Josette. He looked courteous, but there was something still in his cold eyes. I tried to shake off the echo of Josette's words.

He's evil.

12

MARGOT

"Lucie. Frau Cochet." A dark-haired man with gray at his temples stood in the doorway of the kitchen. He was trim and fit in his uniform, his gray eyes clear and warm with his smile. But there was also something in the slippery shape of his mouth, in his taut posture, that reminded me of a cobra poised to strike. His gaze shifted to Josette and me as he added pleasantly in German, "And who's this?"

Had Roger warned us? Had we just not heard? I glanced nervously towards the kitchen window. I saw no sign of him in the garden. Had he fled?

For a moment, we were silent. My mind was scrambling as Josette's green eyes met mine. What name should I give—Margot Vashon or a fictitious one? How much did the man know?

If he'd somehow learned that Helen Taylor was my real mother, that my real name at birth had been Margaret Taylor, this was going to be a short conversation which would likely end with him yelling for bodyguards, throwing Lucie and Josette in prison, then finally dumping me in some wretched oubliette to die a horrible, lingering death.

"They're nobody," Lucie said in German, her cheeks pink. "Just some former orphans of St. Agnes's who were about to leave."

"Ah. I am Otto Schröder." He gave a short, clipped bow. "I have the honor of being Reichsbevollmächtigter of France and *Obergruppenführer* within the SS."

"Reichsbevollmächtigter Schröder," I greeted him politely.

"Herr Reichsbevollmächtigter," said Josette with a nod.

His smile broadened. "You are welcome to call me Herr Schröder, as Fräulein Lucie does. It is a pleasure to meet any friends of hers." He came forward. "And your names are?"

Though his voice was smooth, his gait was not. His limp was pronounced as he moved forward. I stared at his cane—it looked like a weapon, its glossy wood topped with the brass handle of an angry eagle. Physical weakness in a Nazi plenipotentiary? How the other German men must have taunted him, both behind his back and to his face. No wonder he hated my mother.

So what name should I give him?

I'd already hesitated too long before introducing myself. The curiosity in his eyes had changed to a deeper interest. He was intelligent and, from what my mother had told me, infinitely dangerous.

I'd split the difference, I decided, and replied in German, "I'm Margot Vashon. Lucie's sister."

Lucie's eyes popped. After all my warnings, had she expected me to use a fake name? It was too likely he'd discover the truth. A clumsy lie could be as revealing as a confession.

He gave her a hard stare.

"There was no need for such caution, Lucie," he chided. "Have I not yet earned your trust?" Her blush deepened, and she reached for the nearest high chair, juggling a baby as a convenient prop of distraction. He turned to me. "Your honesty does you credit, Fräulein Vashon. I didn't expect to meet any other former wards of St. Agnes's. Certainly not her sister! I'm very glad you're here." He held out his hand.

Reluctantly, I extended mine.

As we shook hands, his eyes narrowed. "You were traveling recently, were you not? In the south?"

"Why, yes," I said, smile frozen in place.

"I was not notified that you came back across the border."

So I'd been right. He'd been monitoring the demarcation line, looking for us. It was hard to remain casual, smiling. "That's not surprising. Travel is... difficult at the moment, is it not? It took some effort to reach Paris."

"Especially as our identity cards were stolen," Josette added, with real bitterness.

"Were they?" He stared at her, then released my hand. "How unfortunate." He gave a sudden smile. "But I can arrange new cards for you, as I did for your sister. I am glad you were able to reach Paris. The little *Fräulein* has been anxious to see you again."

"I missed her, too." For a moment, the bones in my hand seemed to ache. It was all I could do not to cradle my fingers, to check them for injury, for all he'd held my hand so gently.

He turned to Josette. "And your name, *Fräulein*?"

She followed my lead. "I'm very pleased to meet you. I'm Josette Dubois."

As they shook hands, the redhead's pretty face, carefully made up with lipstick and mascara as always, shone with pleasure, as if she really were delighted to make his acquaintance. *Hollywood missed out*, I thought.

"Dubois? Ah. The same surname as these sweet children." Pulling back, he motioned towards the babies. "You were a foundling?"

"Yes," she said, her smile stiffening a little.

"And now St. Agnes's has new orphans to care for." He tilted his head, looking at me from beneath half-lidded eyes. "A pity your headmistress is not here. I'd be glad to see her, too. Is she, perhaps, in Paris?"

I was not fooled by his casual tone. I saw the coldness beneath the surface of his smile. It made his handsome face look out of kilter, like two styles of architecture pressing against each other, or something false, like a modern façade newly built to hide a crumbling old building beneath.

"Unfortunately not." I shook my head regretfully. "She sailed to America, taking some orphans to new homes there."

Herr Schröder sucked in his breath. "America!"

Ha! So he hadn't known that, I thought smugly. He seemed grief-stricken at the thought. And no wonder. It meant my mother was out of his reach for good. He'd never be able to threaten her again.

His eyes returned to me. "But she didn't take you with her. Why?"

The remaining baby in the high chair—I couldn't remember her name—was fussing. Turning my face away, I picked her up. She calmed down in my arms, staring up at me, waving her pudgy, oatmeal-covered hand to grab some of my hair in her fist.

My eyes fell on Choupette, curled up in a pool of sunlight on the other side of the kitchen. She hadn't moved a muscle since the German had entered. And suddenly everything was clear.

Lucie was refusing to leave Paris. She wasn't going to change her mind. She'd decided the babies were her responsibility. So until we could find them new homes, that meant they were mine.

I had no choice but to stay.

I needed to give Otto Schröder a reason to trust us, to invite us to remain here, so I looked at him, blinking fast, and screwed up my face a little. "Sister Helen just left us. Josette and me. Can you believe it? She'd promised to get us visas to America, but then she got your telegram, and off she went without a word."

"Ah. So she did get it." His eyebrow lifted. "I wondered how she reacted."

I thought fast. "She said... she was scared of you and fleeing to where you couldn't threaten her."

"Ah." His lips curved up at the edges. Vanity.

Josette followed my lead. "She just abandoned us in Marseille. Without any money or help. She just got rid of us," she whispered. Her green eyes welled up with tears that were impossible not to believe. "Just as she'd done with Lucie. She left us because we were inconvenient. She didn't care if we lived or died."

That seemed pushing it a little too far. Would he buy it?

He reached into his pocket, then handed her a monogrammed linen handkerchief. "I am very sorry, *Fräulein*," he said quietly. "But I myself learned the hard way she is a woman without remorse. An unnatural creature."

"Thank you, Herr Schröder," she said, wiping her eyes. She made a show of blowing her nose. "We came to Paris because Sister Helen told us Lucie had returned to St. Agnes's."

"We were worried about her," I added, glancing at her.

"Of course you were. But she's been in safe hands." He relaxed a little, his cold gray eyes softening as he looked at my sister. "Lucie has become a valuable member of my household. She's a good-hearted young woman. She takes care of abandoned children. Her loyalty and self-sacrifice should make her an example to all womankind."

Said the man whose own wife fled with their child, I thought irritably. But I managed to say, "We were going to take Lucie back to Marseille, where I have a job." A job which had actually sailed west to America five months ago. "But perhaps you might have jobs for us here?"

He tilted his head, shifting his gaze back towards Josette,

with her curves and beautiful red hair, then to me once more. I held the golden-haired baby nestled against my shoulder, and did my best to look both pitiful and brave, which seemed to be what he valued most in a woman. I managed not to flinch as the baby's tight fists yanked on my hair, smearing it with oatmeal as she tried to shove strands of it in her mouth.

"It is disgraceful how Helen Taylor treated you." He watched me. "Did you hear the new rumor that she had a secret bastard child, years ago?"

"What?" This time I didn't have to pretend to be shocked. My heart was pounding. "Impossible."

"My source at the Paris embassy told me a rumor that Helen Taylor procured an American passport for her love child at the consulate in Marseille. Did you know anything about it?"

I shook my head, doing my best to look confused.

"Who would say such a thing?" Lucie gasped, her honest blue eyes shining with indignation. "It's slander."

Otto Schröder tilted his head, looking at me intently. "Usually my man at the embassy is reliable, but he couldn't get more information out of Marseille. No one would even confirm it. There was no paper trail. Helen Taylor must have people protecting her," he said darkly. He turned to Josette. "Have you heard of this... Margaret Taylor?"

"I might have seen a picture," she said innocently.

I tensed.

"What did she look like?" he demanded.

"Er... short hair. Light brown. Light blue eyes. And glasses," she improvised, describing the opposite of my long curly hair and dark brown eyes. "Very unpleasant-looking girl," she chirped, smiling at me. "Not pretty at all."

It was hard for me not to pinch her.

"How old?"

"It's hard to say." She pondered, then gave a decided nod. "Somewhere between ten and twenty?"

His eyebrows rose. He said slowly, "Ten... and twenty?"

She shrugged. "Girls' ages are so hard to gauge these days. Especially in pictures."

"So it's true? Sister Helen had a child?" Lucie said in shock. We'd left her in Boulins before my mother had told me the secret.

"I'm not surprised," Otto Schröder said coldly. "She is a woman without morals. It's a wonder that all of you in her care" —he looked around the orphanage kitchen—"are not completely wild. I give you full credit for that, Frau Cochet," he added with a bow.

"Thank you," she said, wheezing a little as she used a rolling pan to stretch out dough.

He turned back to me. "I would be glad to have you stay, *Fräulein*, if you wish. Both of you. Someone to help Lucie and Frau Cochet—"

"Finally," said Berthe, wiping her brow with the back of her sleeve. "Françoise is useless."

"You would have room and board and wages."

"How much does it pay?" I asked, as if I hadn't already decided to stay.

He told me the amount, adding, "In Reichsmarks."

With room and board, and the current exchange rate, the wages weren't bad. Plus, beggars couldn't be choosers. "Seems fair."

"Oh, Margot, really?" Lucie beamed at us, jiggling the baby on her hip. "You're going to stay?"

"I'll leave it to you, Frau Cochet, and you, Fräulein Lucie, to settle them in and assign them the tasks you feel need doing. Now, I must return to work." He paused at the hallway door. "But I am glad to help others victimized by that woman. Let America deal with her now. Europe is better off without her evil."

He left with a slight bow of his head. I stared after him in amazement. He wasn't pretending. He really thought that he was a good person and my mother was evil.

Josette dropped her smile and turned to me to hiss, "What did you just do to us?"

Without waiting for an answer, she ran to the window, peering out. I knew she was thinking about Roger. "Do you think he—"

"Hush." I glanced behind me significantly. For all I knew, Schröder or one of his men were listening behind the door. "Later."

Her eyes widened. She gave a single nod, her cheeks turning red.

"If you two aren't busy," Berthe said to Josette and me, "there are vegetables to chop."

"Let me get everything sorted upstairs first," Lucie said.

Berthe turned to her in dismay. "Oh. That's all right, Lucie. I'm sure the babies need your care—"

"We can all help you today, Berthe," my sister said happily.

She moved out into the hallway to the linen closet, where she grabbed blankets, sheets and pillows, then shoved them into Josette's arms. Her eyes looked tenderly from the baby on her hip to the baby still over my shoulder. "We'll get Geneviève cleaned up, too."

"Don't forget to clean her high chair," the cook called after us. "Don't expect me to do it, I'm up to my elbows in *Franzbrötchen!*"

We'd barely made it up the first flight of back stairs before Lucie turned to us with a laugh. "Berthe. So sweet and helpful." She hesitated. "And also..."

"So bossy," I said.

"You should talk," Josette muttered.

We continued up the next flight of stairs, dark and steep, built originally in the seventeenth century. I was used to it but still clutched the rail with one hand, holding baby Geneviève carefully. Behind us, I could hear Choupette's claws against the stairs. The animal was unwilling to let Lucie out of her sight. I was grateful she'd looked out for my sister.

We reached the attic's two large dormitory rooms, each filled with ten slender beds, with a shared bathroom in the hallway. Two old cribs had been tucked on each side of my sister's tiny bed, the only one currently in use.

"I'm so happy you're staying." She kissed the plump cheeks of the dark-haired baby in her arms. "Thérèse was the first. She arrived back in July, in a basket by the front door."

I looked down at my own baby. "And this one?"

"Geneviève was left in a cardboard box with a letter saying the baby's father was dead and couldn't marry the mother. Poor things." She kissed Thérèse's wispy head, and I knew she wasn't just talking about one abandoned baby but all of them that existed, plus the heartbroken mothers and dead fathers, and anyone who'd suffered grief and pain. That was how my sister thought about the world.

As I looked at the old dormitory, with its slanted ceiling and small beds lined up against the walls, nightstands slotted between them, my heart sank. Was I really back to this? Except now ruled over by a Nazi instead of a headmistress?

Just for a short while, I promised myself. I'd make my sister see reason. And I'd find someplace for the babies. I *would*. Hopefully in a day or two.

"Are you going to take your old bed?" she asked.

I sighed. "Sure."

"I'll take the one on the other side of yours," Josette said, dumping clean sheets and blankets and old flattened pillows on the two beds. "Estée doesn't need it now."

As she quickly made the beds with careful attention to the corners, as we'd been taught, Lucie rubbed Thérèse's back thoughtfully. "Can you believe what he said about Sister Helen? It couldn't really be true. A child out of wedlock?"

"We were surprised, too," said Josette dryly, looking at me. But she said nothing more, leaving it for me.

But how could I tell Lucie I wasn't really her sister, at least not by blood? That Violette Vashon, the woman we'd grown up believing to be our mother, had adopted me as a baby? That my birth name had been Margaret Taylor and that my real father was Jean-Luc Ravanel, the doctor who'd helped us when we'd fled Paris in June?

All those years together in the orphanage, Lucie and I had each felt lucky to have a sibling. The truth would leave her crushed, isolated, hurt.

And it could be dangerous information to share. I thought of the Nazi officer and the cold look in his eyes when he'd said, *Have you heard of this Margaret Taylor?*

Lucie would always be my little sister, the one I'd loved and protected since she was a tiny baby. And other than Josette and Roger, everyone who knew the truth about me was now in America. No chance of any of the little orphans accidentally letting anything slip.

I rolled my eyes, thinking of Josette's dig: *Very unpleasant-looking girl. Not pretty at all.* But as annoying as she could be, at least she knew how to keep a secret.

I wasn't so sure about Lucie. Because my sister believed the best of people, it wasn't natural for her to be guarded. She blushed when she told a lie, for heaven's sake.

I couldn't tell her the truth, I decided. Not until we were away from Otto Schröder. Not until we were safe.

Lucie bit her lip. "I feel bad." She ducked her head guiltily. "You're staying in Paris for me."

I shook my head. "It's fine." And I told myself it would be. I would *make* it be fine. Somehow.

I moved to the door and looked down the servants' stairwell, listening for the squeaky stair. I heard only silence.

I turned to Josette. "We're alone."

She exhaled. "What do you think happened to Roger? Was he seen?"

Bouncing Geneviève, who was starting to fuss, I shook my head. "He'd be in custody." I remembered hearing a slight *clink* against the kitchen window then. "I think he tried to warn us. He might still be outside."

"You think so?" Josette pressed her forehead against the dirty attic window, trying to peer down into the garden.

"He said he'd leave…" Even when I'd told him he could, I'd known he wouldn't.

"He's so heroic," Josette added dreamily.

I rolled my eyes.

She added, "I'll go look for him."

"No, wait," I said sharply. "Until we're sure we're not being watched. We don't want to lead the Germans right to him."

So we made the beds and washed the oatmeal off baby Geneviève, then trooped downstairs to help Berthe.

The afternoon passed in a surreal blur of cooking and cleaning. Except for the fresh paint and furniture, it was as if we'd never left the orphanage.

Well, except for the men we heard laughing and talking in guttural German in the front schoolroom, now Herr Schröder's study.

We made dinner for the Germans, and even Lucie managed to help without causing any kitchen injuries. As Berthe served it in the dining room, with its glossy new dining table, the rest of us did the washing-up, then we fed the babies and took them upstairs for their baths. Once Geneviève and Thérèse were in their cribs, we scrubbed the floor and washed our own dirty clothes.

Finally, an hour after dark, after we heard Herr Schröder go up to his large bedroom upstairs, I looked out the kitchen window.

"I'll go check the garden," I said.

"I'm coming with you," Josette said immediately, dropping the mop with a clatter in her eagerness.

"No," I said firmly. "You're useless when you're like this."

Josette glared at me. "He's my friend too—"

"Stay here, Josette," Lucie said. "Margot's right."

I looked at my little sister in surprise. It was unlike her to give a strong opinion. She'd done it only once before today, while we'd been traveling south to Marseille and she'd saved a little starving dog. Then today, she'd refused to leave her orphaned babies. And now this.

"All right," Josette said with ill grace. She looked at me pleadingly. "But tell him—"

"He already knows," I cut her off, then snuck outside.

The garden was deep in the shadows of night. There was a sliver of moonlight in the sky over Paris, and I saw the light in the window of the only neighboring house that overlooked our garden. The snooty Widow Hébert, who owned the elegant townhome facing the end street, had once made our lives difficult, hoping to buy our property. But there was no trace of her silhouette in the window, of the turban over her dyed black hair, her hard eyes or the jeweled walking stick that she could wield almost as viciously as her words.

I walked slowly through the garden, pretending to look for something in the bushes, on the off chance any Nazis looked outside and saw me.

"Here." Roger's voice was husky and low, causing a strange thrill through me. Because I'd found him? Because the risk was so high?

"We have to stay." I was careful not to face his direction, still staring down into the grass, as if I'd lost something small, perhaps a bit of jewelry. "You should go."

"Leave you?"

His voice sounded odd, reminding me of my own when I'd told Lucie I'd never leave without her.

"Go to England." My voice was soft as I moved slowly over the lawn beneath the slanted shadows cast by the weak moonlight. October had grown cold. The grass felt dry and dead against my fingertips. "You've done everything you promised. There's nothing to keep you from joining de Gaulle."

His voice was a low whisper. "You know that's not true."

The emotion in his voice made me suck in my breath. My heart lifted to my throat. I'd been pretending not to see what was right in front of me, telling myself he despised me after that kiss, telling myself I was now trying to earn only his respect. But he still loved me, and he still hoped. It filled me with shame.

"Roger..."

"I'm staying until I know you don't need me. I'll find a place in Paris. Take care of my great-aunt. Take care of... of all of you."

There was a rustle in the bushes, and I saw a shadow lift over the garden wall. My mouth was dry.

Why hadn't I insisted he leave Paris? He'd given up months of his life, taking endless risks to help me save my sister. Roger was in danger every minute he remained in the city. Now I'd been forced to see the truth of his feelings, why hadn't I spoken the magic words that would have set him free?

Why hadn't I told him, once and for all, that I'd never love him back?

13

MARGOT

A month later, it wasn't just St. Agnes's that had been transformed to fit Otto Schröder's taste; I feared we girls had as well. Each morning, I woke up praying I'd find a solution that would allow us all to flee the city. And each night, I fell into my same small bed in the attic dormitory, after another hard day's work as a Nazi's maid.

"I knew Schröder would kill us," I grumbled, my back aching as I mopped the kitchen's tile floor. "I just didn't know it would be slowly, rather than quickly."

"I don't know what you're complaining about." Josette wiped her sweaty forehead as she set down a glass of water on the table. "You're just scrubbing floors. And at least it's warm inside. I've been outside for the last two days washing the windows. My fingers are frozen." She peeled them apart underneath flimsy cloth gloves. "I think I'm getting chilblains."

"Stop volunteering to go outside in November," I pointed out, rolling my eyes.

Josette's red hair was tucked behind a kerchief, and though

her makeup had been applied, the effect was spoiled because her cold nose was almost as red as her lips. "I don't like being in this house."

I dunked my mop in the bucket of soapy water. "You never minded before."

"That was before. When it was our home. Now..." Josette's nose curled, as if from a bad smell, as she glanced towards the hallway. We could hear male voices conversing loudly in German in Herr Schröder's study. Her shoulders slumped, then her eyes went instinctively to the garden window as she whispered, "Plus, if he ever comes here, it'll be easier for him to talk to me if I'm outside."

Roger, always Roger. I resisted the urge to give a sharp reply.

It had been a month since he'd disappeared over the garden wall, and we'd had no word. Berthe thought he might have gone to stay at his stepfather's old flat in the Montmartre district, but she wasn't sure, as Roger had vowed never to return there, so maybe he was staying with a friend. We didn't have time to go looking for him. Though Herr Schröder had been courteous, paying what was actually a decent wage, I still saw him watching us sometimes. I had no idea how much he might be monitoring us. And the last thing I wanted to do was inadvertently lead him to Roger's hiding place.

Josette turned to me. "Have you heard anything?"

"No."

"Would you tell me if you had?"

I hesitated, which was all the answer she needed.

"Margot, I'm sick of your interference. I wish you'd stop hogging his attention. If you'd just set him free and give him a chance to really see me again..."

All my guilt and mixed feelings churned inside me. I'd never wanted to monopolize Roger's attention. Had I? No, of course I hadn't. I squeezed the dirty water out of the mop, then dunked it back into the soapy bucket. "I wish he would love you, Josette. I really do."

Gulping down more water from her glass, she glared at me, then wiped her mouth. "You're lying."

"Yes, I'm lying. I hate how you act around him."

She lifted her chin. "Because I act like a girl who's in love?"

"Like a girl who's a doormat." Which I never, ever wanted to be. "Any man who'd love *that* version of you wouldn't be worth having. You deserve better. So does he."

"He deserves *you*, you mean?" She stomped out of the house in her wellingtons. Through the window, I saw her go into the shed. She tromped out a moment later carrying some wicked-looking shears and a trowel. I feared some poor innocent bushes were about to be pruned to stumps.

"You should be nicer to her," said Lucie reproachfully behind me.

I jumped. My sister was swaying in the hallway, one fussy baby on her shoulder as she rocked the other back and forth in a baby carriage.

"I'm always nice," I snapped.

Lucie lifted an eyebrow, saying nothing.

"Well, I try to be," I said grumpily. "But people make it *so hard*."

After rinsing the mop, I wrung it out in the sink and poured out the dirty water from the bucket. I'd spent too long scrubbing the kitchen, putting off my next task, which was sweeping and waxing the hardwood floors in the parlor and dining room. I'd been hoping the Germans would leave for headquarters so I wouldn't have to be in their orbit, but no such luck. It could wait no longer, since Herr Schröder himself had complained to Berthe at breakfast that the study floors looked dirty.

I sighed, wiping my sweaty forehead with my shoulder. "Have you found any families?"

My sister's gaze slid away vaguely. "Families?"

"For the babies."

"Uh..."

"You told me last week you'd try." After replacing the mop and bucket in the broom closet, I pulled out a long brush and dustpan. "You said you'd find them within the month."

"No." Still swaying so little Geneviève's eyelids grew heavy, Lucie focused on me. "*You* said a month. I told you that it's impossible to find homes for them now. People are already going hungry with the Germans taking all the food. Who's going to want more mouths to feed?"

Now I was the one to feel annoyed. It was a truth I just didn't want to hear. "We need to get out of Paris. Before it's too late."

"If you want to go, then go." She looked at me, then sighed. "I'm sorry, Margot. For me, it's already too late."

Fear clenched my heart. No. We couldn't be stuck here permanently. I couldn't really actually be settling down to life as a maid, cleaning up for the man who'd tried to kill my mother and would almost certainly kill me too, if he knew the truth.

Just in the last month, as the autumn warmth of October plummeted into the frosts of November, change in the city had accelerated. Food shortages had increased—at least for the French—as the ration coupons weren't quite enough to stave off hunger, even when food could still be found on shelves. Now that the temperature was falling, the price of heating oil, and coal, and even wood, was rising to such an extortionate level, Parisians had started wearing gloves and hats indoors.

Not the Germans, though. Thanks to their bullying exchange rate, giving them twenty francs for one Reichsmark, not to mention their power to ignore the rules set for others and cut seamlessly through red tape, the lowliest German soldier was living more comfortably in Paris than all but the richest, most Nazi-sympathizing Frenchmen.

We'd been spared those problems because we lived with a

powerful Nazi officer, answerable only to Hitler himself. But if Herr Schröder decided to withdraw his protection, we'd starve.

Every day, I could feel the noose tightening around occupied France. Already, German soldiers were less patient than they had been, less polite. The only news now came from the radio, and the few remaining newspapers, all now overseen by Herr Schröder. He was responsible for swaying French hearts and minds to accept the yoke of the German Reich. Hitler apparently had an affection for France and wished to befriend us, rather than viciously crush us, as he'd done to poor Holland and Belgium, and others.

Each day, French radio announcers trumpeted the latest German victories, their brutal aerial bombing attacks all over England, which most recently had annihilated the town of Coventry.

But I also heard what the announcers didn't say. Compared to last June, no one was talking anymore about the war ending in weeks or days. No one was saying that Churchill and the British were, even now, anxious to discuss a surrender. And in the former schoolroom of this orphanage, I'd heard the Nazi officers quietly whisper that the British had somehow managed to bomb cities in the German homeland in retaliation.

The war wasn't ending. It was getting worse. Along with the food shortages, the cold and the mood of Paris's captors. And my sister's stubbornness.

"Lucie," I tried anyway, licking my lips. "We can find the babies good homes. I know we can—"

"But you've already been looking for weeks." She lifted her blonde eyebrows archly. "And what have you found?"

My shoulders slumped beneath her sharp, inquisitive gaze. "Nothing," I was forced to admit. "Everyone is scared they won't be able to feed their own families. No one can afford to worry about strangers."

"I told you," she said softly, nuzzling Geneviève close. She glanced at me. "I'm sorry, Margot. You can keep looking, if you want. But sometimes you have to face the truth of things, even though it's not what you wish it could be."

She kissed the now sleeping baby's forehead before wrapping her in a blanket and bundling her snugly against Thérèse, who was already tucked in the baby carriage. After putting on her coat, she pushed the carriage down the hallway, crooning to them as she headed out for their daily walk, Choupette trailing behind.

I stared after her with a lump in my throat as I heard the echo of Helen's voice. *I never found anyone who cared more.* I looked down at the broom and dustpan.

In Marseille, I'd been so sure I could handle this rescue mission better than my mother. Sure, she'd had that rough past, traveling the world as a nurse and more, through wars and pandemics. But she was fifty, and sick, and hunted. I'd honestly believed that with my youth plus a bit of bravery and luck, I could do better.

And this was what all my arrogance had come to: Josette weeding a Nazi's garden, Lucie trapped by a couple of abandoned French babies, and me scrubbing stairs and washing dishes for the Reich. And Roger hiding somewhere in Paris, instead of helping de Gaulle in England, as he'd once wanted.

Wearily, I started sweeping the hallway.

I hadn't even had a chance to go to my father, even though I knew where he was now, working as a doctor at the American Hospital in Neuilly, just outside Paris. I'd planned to briefly see him right as we all left Paris. That way, I'd decided, if he despised me after I told him I was his daughter, I could disappear and never look back.

But Lucie had defeated my plans in ways that German bullets and checkpoints hadn't. What if we were in Paris for the duration? Forever?

I dumped the dust in the bin in the kitchen. Any moment, I

expected Berthe to return from her daily trip to the shops, her arms full of groceries now only available mostly to Germans, like butter and white flour, cream and coffee. I rubbed my aching lower back.

After all my arrogance and hope, was this my fate? Working as a Nazi's charwoman for the rest of the war?

"*Fräulein.*" A German's head popped out of the door of the study, where none of us French were ever allowed to be without Nazi supervision. Herr Schröder kept the door locked at night, and only he had a key.

I blinked at him warily. "*Ja?*"

"Get a mop and come," the man said in German, pointing. He was one of Herr Schröder's men, stocky with wire-rimmed glasses beneath his officer's cap.

Bemused, I retrieved the mop and bucket from the closet and returned to the study.

"Clean it up, if you please," he said crisply, pointing at coffee spilled beside a broken china cup on the floor.

Head bowed, I got to work, intending to get out of there as soon as I could.

As I mopped, the attaché continued a conversation in German with Herr Schröder and a third officer, pointing at a mock-up of words and pictures pasted across a poster. "There's no reason to think it won't work here as well," he was saying. "French women are no different."

My gaze slid to the poster, spread across the oversized desk.

It was patriotic art. A young man stood on a hill in the background—healthy, cornfed and blond—looking triumphantly towards the viewer and holding a rifle pointed at the sky, as beatific children offered flowers at his feet. But in the foreground, as if making it all possible, was a young woman inside a small house, very lovely and glowing with health, also blonde. She was pregnant, standing beside a stove, one hand apparently stirring the pot as the other rocked a cradle. She looked almost saintly in her ecstasy.

"*Kinder, Küche, Kirche,*" the attaché said with a big beaming smile. He pointed to the poster, where French words on cards had been overlaid, in the same heavy Gothic lettering favored by the Germans, reading, *Les enfants, le cuisine, l'église.* Clunky, and anyway it should have been *la* cuisine, not *le*, but then Germans insisted on making everything masculine, even their propaganda that supposedly extolled the feminine.

A low snort escaped me. I didn't even realize it until three pairs of hard German eyes focused on me.

"You have something you wish to say, *Fräulein?*" Herr Schröder asked calmly.

"No, I'm sorry," I muttered, ducking my head. I could have kicked myself. For a month, I'd been so careful not to draw attention, to seem meek and placid and dull. And I'd just revealed my honest opinion of something in front of Herr Schröder and two German officers? Even Lucie's dog would've had more sense than to pee on the rug right in front of them.

"What does she know?" said the one with wire-rimmed glasses haughtily. "She's just a stupid young French maid."

"*Ja,*" I agreed, ducking my head. "Very stupid." I squeezed out the mop, desperate to get out of there. "I'll let it air dry, as you're so busy..."

"She's not stupid at all," said Herr Schröder. His gray eyes lingered on the hot flush of my cheeks, then he turned sharply to his assistant. "She's our target demographic, so her opinion on this matters more than yours."

"But, sir!" the young man sputtered.

Ignoring him, his superior turned to me. "Why did you laugh, *Fräulein?*"

"No reason. I was, er... thinking of something else."

I was afraid to meet his eyes. My feet shifted nervously beneath my borrowed, voluminous skirt—which the Germans preferred on women instead of the slim-cut cigarette pants I liked.

Herr Schröder came around his desk and put his hand briefly on my cheek, forcing me to meet his gaze.

"You won't get in trouble." His voice was gentle. "Just tell me."

I looked up, cheeks burning. "I..." I shook my head. "I'm not sure what you're trying to achieve, but no Parisienne would be swayed by *that*." I flicked my gaze towards the poster.

"No?"

I straightened, then said honestly, "It would only lead to mockery."

He paced, then stopped, tilting his head. "Your accent in German is excellent. Your teacher was from Austria?"

"Yes," I said, surprised. "How did you know?"

"Put that down. Come here."

Reluctantly, I obeyed. I went towards the large desk and stood by the attaché, who glowered at me, arms folded.

I ducked my head, looking more closely at the poster. Up close, it was even more hideous. "What are you trying to achieve with this?"

"That's classified," spat the attaché.

Herr Schröder gave a low, friendly laugh, chiding his fellow German. "Surely the war effort will not be overruled by pointing out a goal that should be obvious. In fact, it is our failure if it is not." He considered me. "In Germany, before the rise of the Führer, Germany was suffering. Corrupt. Bankrupt."

"Because of the Great War?" I knew the Germans had been humiliated by that loss twenty years before, a generation of young men decimated, forced by Britain and France to pay enormous reparations that left their economy in tatters.

He gave a thin smile. "That was part of it. But only part." He looked me straight in the eye. "It was our moral bankruptcy as a culture. Men being lazy, choosing not to marry or take responsibility. Women working to buy trifles, rather than starting families. All of them selfishly looking out only for their own pleasure. Modern vices were killing us."

I wondered how much of his opinion had been formed by his own poor abused wife choosing to leave him. But of course I didn't say so. Reckless I might be but not utterly idiotic. "What does that"—I pointed—"have to do with *this?*"

"We've recovered our souls in Germany by focusing on healthy values—family, hard work, home. That all starts with women."

"Women don't fight wars."

"You're wrong, *Fräulein*." His gray eyes seared into mine. "For the right woman, a man will do anything, battle anyone. Her morality and desire for a home are the beginning of any civilization. When good women hold fast to traditional values, a society will prosper. When they do not, it falls apart."

I stared at him. I didn't know what to think. Some of what he said seemed not entirely evil or wrong, but there was something I didn't like, though I couldn't quite put my finger on it. "What does that have to do with France?"

"The Führer, in his wisdom, has always admired your country. He doesn't want it destroyed, which is why we wish to enfold you in our tender embrace, rather than using some of the more... brutal methods we might use on other, less desirable nations."

My stomach churned. I wondered if he was thinking about Poland or perhaps the Netherlands. Maybe even Germany's own Jews, stateless with no nation of their own, fleeing from country to country looking for safe harbor. "How?"

He tilted his head. "It is a forced marriage between us, yes. But there can still be appreciation and respect. Even love." He tapped the poster. "It is my job to do here what I've already done in Germany. To drive out the more undesirable elements of your culture. And that starts by convincing the women of

France that their true place, their most noble mission, begins at home. Raising children, seeing to their family's moral and spiritual welfare, nurturing their homes and providing nourishment and happiness to the people they love most."

Again, it didn't sound all bad. So why was my spine tingling?

"But you don't like it," he said, watching me.

"It's not that I don't—"

"Of course." Cutting me off, he nodded towards the poster. "Tell me. What would you do differently?"

"Herr Reichsbevollmächtigter," a younger German officer sputtered, "I can't believe you're asking this chit of a girl—"

"Sit there," Herr Schröder told the two younger men, pointing at the chairs. "Don't say another word." His voice was calm and quiet, but they flinched and scurried to the chairs like schoolboys terrified of their tutor's leather strap. He continued pleasantly, "*Fräulein?*"

I was relieved he didn't send his men away. As rude and dismissive as the attaché was, I felt wary at the thought of being alone with Schröder.

I looked down at the poster, touching it softly with my fingers.

"Change the lettering," I said slowly. "The Gothic font just reminds us that we're conquered. If you want a Frenchwoman to listen..."

"Yes?"

"We want to be seduced." He lifted an eyebrow, and I caught my breath. "B-By the idea, I mean," I stammered, my cheeks hot. "Make us think it's our idea. Woo us with flattery. Assume we're intelligent. As smart as you, even."

"I see." He held my gaze a second too long, then glanced down at the poster. "What else?"

"This art." I ran my fingertips idly over the cherubic children offering flowers, the saintly pregnant madonna. "No

Parisienne aspires to be stuck in a hot kitchen, simultaneously stirring a pot and rocking a cradle. It means she lives in a tiny one-room apartment, and the steam is making her sticky, and she can't escape all the crying babies, both hers and the neighbors'. And for a woman to be immediately pregnant in such a situation, with a newborn, well..."

"Well?"

I shook my head. "I'd half expect that new baby to be left at St. Agnes's. Either her brute of a husband won't let her alone, or she's feeling trapped and overwhelmed. When I look at this woman's face"—my gaze swept scornfully over the beatific woman—"I assume she must either have drunk an entire bottle of wine, or perhaps have some kind of permanent brain injury, to look so happy in such a state."

His thin lips twisted. "Don't hold back, Fräulein Vashon."

I jumped a little, hearing him use my name.

"Anything else?"

I bit my lip, horrified I'd been so honest. Why hadn't I just said I liked the picture then fled? I shook my head.

"Very well." He waved his hand, returning to sit at his desk. "Thank you for your assessment. You may continue your work."

"Thank you, sir."

Quickly, I gathered up the broken pieces of china. As the three men spoke quietly, I backed up with the mop and bucket. But just as I was counting my good fortune to be escaping, his voice stopped me at the door.

"Fräulein Vashon."

Holding my breath, I looked back, my body cold with fear.

He smiled, tilting his head. "Leave your mop." He came towards me, his gray eyes glittering. "I have better use for you."

14

JOSETTE

DECEMBER 1940

I crept into the attic bathroom and pulled the overhead string. The bare bulb illuminated the mirror in an unflattering light.

My face looked back at me, bleary-eyed, my hair in ragged pin curls. I saw dark circles beneath my eyes and tried to smile, to see if that would make me prettier. It did not.

All night, unable to sleep, I'd tried to convince myself I wouldn't do this. But even then, I'd known I would. I had to. I couldn't help myself.

Today.

Yesterday morning, Berthe had come back from the shops humming happily to herself, her cheeks pink with excitement. Much later, after we'd finished serving dinner to Herr Schröder, alone in the dining room at his new table—big enough for eight —she'd waited for us to wash and dry the dishes, bathe the babies and tuck them into bed before she'd finally whispered her news.

She'd seen Roger. He'd been waiting for her, hiding in the

alley behind her favorite *boucherie*. He was now staying at his dead stepfather's abandoned flat, just as she'd first suspected. He'd told her to come see him if we needed anything.

I'd almost wept at the news. Roger was all right. He was found.

Glowing, Berthe had finally left for her own bedroom, downstairs off the kitchen. As we'd headed upstairs to bed, after evading Lucie's timid request to wake up with the babies in her place overnight, Margot had looked at me sourly.

"Don't even think of trying to go see him, Josette. That would be stupid even for you. You would put him at risk, as well as us."

"Don't be ridiculous," I'd snapped. "You think I don't know that?"

But even then, I'd known I'd do this. That I wouldn't be able to resist.

Every day since he'd disappeared, I'd wondered if he was dead or alive. If he'd been caught by the Germans. If he'd left Paris. If he ever thought of me.

Margot thought I was pathetic and hysterical. Even Lucie didn't understand why I loved him. Sometimes I didn't understand it myself.

We'd met two summers ago, when he'd come to stay with his great-aunt before being called up with the army. We'd spent time together, taking walks, washing dishes for Berthe, sitting in the sunset. But by then, though I didn't know it, it was already too late for me—he'd seen Margot. And in just that brief moment of meeting, before she disappeared for her summer job in Boulins, everything had changed.

Since then, I'd loved him patiently, as only women knew how to love—giving everything, holding nothing back. I'd convinced myself that if I loved him enough, faithfully enough, I could win him.

But it hadn't worked. Sometimes, since then, he'd flirted or winked at me, or made me feel special in a way that made my heart soar and gave me hope. Then the next day, he would ignore me, sighing over Margot.

I could never forget the image of her kissing him in Marseille. She didn't even want him. She'd done it just to hurt me. But I could still see the euphoria in his dark eyes when she'd put her hands on his broad shoulders and stood on her toes to press her lips to his...

Ugh. I pushed the memory away. I couldn't take it anymore, this slow drip-drip-drip of hope. Either way, it had to end. I had to know.

Was it Margot, or me?

I told myself I didn't already know the answer. But I felt a little sick as I looked at myself in the mirror.

I slowly swept the Bourjois face powder over my pale skin with my fingertips, to cover the freckles and blemishes, and added back a little bit of cream blush so I didn't look so pale. I lined kohl around my eyes—a deep brown, as black was too harsh for my coloring—and moistened Rimmel's cake mascara before applying it to my auburn lashes to make my eyes pop. My eye color was seafoam green, Roger had said once, like a mermaid's. I'd clung to that description, in spite of Margot uncharitably hooting at that story later and insisting my eyes were, in reality, a ho-hum hazel, "like slime splattered with mud."

My jaw tightened at the remembered hurt, but I kept working on my makeup, until the dark circles and imperfections were blended away. I did my hair next, turning my head upside down and fluffing out the curls, adding a mist of eau de toilette that smelled of tuberoses. It was Roger's favorite—he'd mentioned it once. When we'd been on the road to Marseille, I'd been careful not to break the bottle, not knowing how I could replace it or when. I had only a few drops left now and couldn't easily replace it. With Paris's rampant shortages, a new bottle of *eau de roses* would have cost me several months' salary, assuming it could even be found.

I looked at myself in the mirror, and the young woman who smiled back at me looked almost alive. Her eyes sparkled.

I put on my most flattering outfit—a green dress that made my breasts look even bigger and my waist smaller. With new fabric becoming so dear, I'd taken apart a jersey smock left behind by Fräulein Mueller and created a new dress in a style that flattered me. My sewing skills were the one thing I felt confident about.

I carefully pulled on my only precious pair of silk stockings, which I'd bought last year from my earnings washing dishes and peeling potatoes at a café, and saved for a special occasion. These same stockings would now have cost hundreds of francs. On top of those, I slipped on a pair of high-heeled shoes I'd found in the closet, left behind by one of our teachers in her haste to flee Paris with her Hungarian boyfriend. Lucie hadn't wanted them, and Margot's feet were too big.

One last touch. I carefully put on my deep ruby-red lipstick, then pressed my lips together.

"Please," the girl in the mirror whispered, eyes luminous with tears. "Let this be the day he chooses me."

Outside, the December air was frosty, and I could feel it beneath the thin wool of my coat. I wished I'd brought a hat, but that would have squashed my hair. The high heels clicked satisfyingly, but my toes hurt. Mademoiselle Aubert had smaller feet than I did, but all the pain would be worth it if Roger realized he cared.

Perhaps after all these weeks, he'd felt bereft without my devotion, support and caring?

Please.

In the pale dawn, I saw a light in the window of the rich widow's house at the end of our alley. Stepping out into the street, I wondered what Madame Hébert was doing awake so early. Counting her piles of money? Counting her blessings because Herr Schröder had requisitioned St. Agnes's rather than her much nicer, much bigger, much newer mansion? Or maybe she was coming up with some new way to taunt us. Though she couldn't do that now, not with Hitler's childhood buddy living here. A single small reprieve.

Or so I'd thought.

"You there. Girl."

I stumbled, nearly twisting my foot as the heel caught on a cobblestone. Looking behind me, I saw Madame Hébert coming out of her house. She was dressed theatrically as always, in purple silk with her jeweled walking stick, a bright woolen cape to keep out the cold, and a turquoise turban, decorated with a peacock feather, atop her head.

I forced my lips into a polite smile. "*Bonjour*, Madame Hébert."

"*Bonjour*," she sniffed dismissively, looking me over as she came down her steps. "You and those other girls seem to be living very well, I must say. You've actually taken in more babies? I cannot believe it!"

I stiffened. She was criticizing us for trying to survive? Criticizing Lucie for helping those poor orphaned children?

Suddenly, angry words spilled out of my mouth. "How dare you criticize us? He requisitioned our home! And I know you hate children, *madame*, but it still astonishes me that you'd apparently rather have an orphaned baby starve on the street than hear one cry next door. You rejoiced when the Nazis took over our city."

The woman almost stumbled back in surprise. "I never—"

"Don't deny it. I've heard you complain for years about our government. And now you criticize us for working for a German? Your theater's audience is full of them! I've always known you had no heart, but I am surprised to learn you're such a hypocrite!"

Her eyes widened, her face suddenly haggard and pale beneath her dramatic makeup. She said nothing. I felt a strange pang.

"Good day," I bit out, then turned away.

After all the years the rich widow had plagued us, trying to get Sister Helen to sell the orphanage so she could raze it for a garden, we orphans had dreamed of the moment Madame Hébert would get her comeuppance. But as I hurried away, I didn't feel vindicated or triumphant. I felt small, yelling at an old lady in the street. Sister Helen would have been ashamed of me.

Maybe our headmistress had been right, all the times she'd told us that being unkind never helped anyone—it only hurt.

Pulling the lapels of the gray wool closer to keep out the cold, I kept my head down past two German soldiers smoking and loitering on the corner. They stared at me in a way that made me feel vulnerable, calling out to me in atrocious accents, *Bonjour, mademoiselle, où allez-vous?*

I didn't look their way, just hurried down the steps to station Filles du Calvaire.

The Métro was crowded with tired Frenchmen, none of us meeting each other's eyes, vanquished anew every morning we woke up to find ourselves still in German territory, still German possessions.

I transferred at Strasbourg-Saint-Denis to arrive in Montparnasse. The neighborhood, once a vibrant, chaotic home for artists of every kind, seemed subdued, careworn, a pale imitation of its former self. Roger had told me bitterly of his life growing up here, hurt by his stepfather, neglected by his weak, ineffectual mother. Roger had been determined to escape. But here he was again.

I eventually found his five-story building, with its zinc roof, scattered with wrought-iron balconies. Going past the shuttered *boulangerie* on the ground floor, I spoke to the concierge for directions—an elderly widow—then went up four flights of stairs to the top floor. I smoothed my skirt nervously and knocked. I heard his footsteps, then the door creaked open.

"Josette." Roger's dark hair was uncombed, his clothing rumpled, his jaw unshaven. His eyes widened, then narrowed. "What are you doing here? Are you alone?"

"I wanted to—"

He peeked his head out, looked around, then without waiting for me to finish, he grabbed me by the wrist and yanked me inside.

I shivered inside his apartment. It was small and run-down, with paintings leaning against one wall, half covered by a tarp.

"Those belonged to your stepfather?"

He stiffened, glancing behind him at the paintings. "My mother left them to me."

"I'm surprised you kept them." I knew that his stepfather had beaten him whenever Roger did anything he didn't like, which had been almost daily until he'd run away at fifteen.

He gave a humorless smile. "I'm saving them in case I need something to burn for warmth."

"Smart." Shivering, I looked around. The only source of heat seemed to be the morning light from iced-over dormer windows. Dirty dishes filled the sink. Dirty wrinkled clothes lay on the chairs. Perhaps that was why he didn't invite me to sit.

His dark eyes looked me over, from my red lips to my carefully coiffed hair, my tidy gray wool coat, unbuttoned over the bosom, the dark silk stockings and black high heels. "You're dressed up."

I took a deep breath. "To see you."

"Why?" Hope lifted to his dark eyes. "Did Margot send you?"

Margot, always Margot. I tried not to feel my heart twist.

He was worried about her, even though she treated him so awfully. "No."

"Then why...?" His expression hardened. "You shouldn't have come here. The neighborhood's not safe."

I looked around, trying to pretend it was normal for me to be alone with a man in his apartment. "What do you mean? It's safe enough for you."

"That's different. I'm a man."

"Women live in the neighborhood, too, don't they?"

He shrugged. "Those who grew up here know how to protect themselves."

"And I don't?"

Roger gave a low laugh. "You? With your gentle upbringing and rose-colored glasses? You'd probably look around and think it's rather fine."

He wasn't wrong. Anyplace was better with Roger in it. Even Hades itself wouldn't seem all bad, if he could be there with me. "I came to talk."

His eyes turned wary. "About what?"

"About..." I swallowed. But I couldn't chicken out now. "About us. You and me."

Roger Cochet, the devil-may-care former soldier, who'd planned and executed our theft of a Nazi truck on the road to Marseille, who'd done so many other brave, reckless, foolhardy things, suddenly looked terrified.

"Josette..." He bit his lip; stopped. Took a breath. He looked out the tiny window that faced a brick wall. "This isn't... the right time. To talk."

"Of course it is." I grabbed his hands. "So much has gone wrong for us. But so much could go right, if we just let it. From the moment I met you, you changed my life. You've opened my world. All I want is to love you." I took a deep breath. "Won't you let me? Won't you tell me I have a chance to..."

My voice trailed off when I finally was brave enough to look at his face, pale and strange. He wouldn't meet my eyes.

"I'm sorry, Josette." His voice was low. "You are a good woman. You'd make any man a wonderful wife. But"—he lifted his darkly burning gaze—"you won't be mine."

Numbly, I released his hands. My heart was hammering in my throat. "You said I was pretty. You said I was special. You said—"

"Words," he said flatly. "Just words."

The rapid beat of my heart abruptly stopped. I whispered hoarsely, "You didn't mean it?"

"Oh, I meant it." His lips twisted bitterly. "But who cares? Yes, you're pretty. So what? It doesn't mean anything. I barely know you."

I flinched. "After all our months traveling together—"

"Then maybe it's that you don't know me." He ran a hand through his dark hair, giving me a smile that didn't meet his eyes. "You think I'm some great hero. I'm not. I guess a part of me liked the way you idolized me. But it's not fair to you." His dark gaze lifted to mine. "It's time you knew the truth about me. And who I am."

"I know who you are," I said miserably.

"I've done things. Awful things. I've lied. Stolen. Deserted the army."

"I know, and you had good reasons—"

"I'm a criminal. I've been working with—with someone since we arrived in Paris. Selling things on the black market."

"Striking a blow for France," I said, pretending I wasn't a little shocked. "Helping Frenchmen get food, clothing. There's nothing wrong with that."

"Always with your rosy glasses. *Non, ma petite*. I'm doing it for myself alone."

He moved to the front window and lifted a dirty curtain to glance out at the street. "I think back to when I wanted to help de Gaulle," he murmured, "and it seems like a dream." Then he dropped the curtain and faced me once more, his eyes cold. "I see now it's every man for himself. Why should I throw my life away for honor when I can get rich?"

"Rich?" Since when did he care about that?

"Rich," he repeated flatly. "When this war ends..." He looked around the cluttered, dirty, tiny apartment. "I will live in a big house and be respected, and I don't care which government happens to rule France. I'll be safe, powerful. And I'll have the wife I want." He met my gaze. "I'm sorry. It's not you."

"Margot," I said miserably. His face told me I was right. I shook my head. "You think she cares about wealth?"

"I know she does. She told me so." He shrugged. "She's a realist. She already knows I'm no hero. She'll accept the cost of the luxurious life I give her."

It took me every bit of good character I possessed to venture, "I think you're not giving her enough credit—"

"I shot a man a few weeks ago. I have no idea if he lived or died, and I don't even care."

Silence fell. Now I was truly shocked. "Why?"

"He was going to reveal me to the Germans. I'd just stolen his truck, and all his wine and cheese. I shot him with the same revolver he stole from us."

"The Frenchman," I said slowly. "Who betrayed us to the Germans when we tried to cross over."

"That's the one." Roger's eyes were cold. "The American passport and visa were gone, but I took everything else back, and more. I sold all his wine and cheese for a high price, and I used the profits to buy more. Revenge is going to buy me the life I want. The woman I love."

I stared at him, frozen. Clutching my hands, I whispered, "But if you'd just—"

"Are you really going to make me say it? I don't love you, Josette. I never will."

It felt like getting hit in the face. I stumbled back from his awful words. His handsome face looked almost ugly in the morning light.

"I'm not your prince, Josette. I never was. So stop loving me. And tell Margot..." He took a deep breath. "Don't tell her anything. I'll tell her myself." He gave a charming, crooked smile. "After I've built her a castle."

15

JOSETTE

The morning sky was in full bloom, soft blue with fluffy pink clouds, as I walked slowly back along the street. I could see my breath; the December air was biting cold as we approached the darkest day of the year. My body felt like ice, my skin clammy over my feverish heart, beneath the green dress I'd put on with such desperate, foolish hope. I wiped my eyes, smudging mascara on my fingertips like penitent ash.

Around me, shopkeepers were opening up, a milk truck rattled down the road to deliver bottles, and an elderly concierge swept the sidewalk in front of her apartment building. A few modest Christmas decorations were being hung over doorways or in windows. Paris was coming to life at the start of a new day.

I felt dead.

When I saw the entrance to the Métro, I suddenly couldn't bear to be buried in that hole in the ground. My knees felt weak. I wanted to collapse, and yet my nerves were zapping me with such restless energy, to do something, do it now—as if it were of any use, as if there were anything I could do.

I don't love you, Josette. I never will.

I'd walk. To put off the moment I'd reach home and the girls would ask where I'd been, why I was crying. I couldn't bear to face those questions. Waves of hatred pulsed through me, along with grief—for Margot, and Lucie too, for being loved and lovable. For myself—because I wasn't.

Wiping my eyes, I focused only on the hard pinch of my shoes against my toes. I walked north, all the way to the river, crossing the bridge to the Île de la Cité. As I continued numbly towards the Pont au Change, I saw a whitewashed brick wall out the corner of my eye, along the Seine, near the Marché aux Fleurs.

I stopped dead, then turned to look at it. Past the tips of the bare latticework of trees, I could see the top floor of a *hôtel particulier*, the old mansion that had belonged to the aristocratic Albret family since the days of Napoleon.

My father's house. I had been conceived here, when he'd seduced a young maid, a Jewish girl from Poland, only eighteen. Georges Albret had been a few years older, the cossetted heir. I'd never know if he'd seduced her or raped her, but he'd ruthlessly tossed her out when she became pregnant with his child.

As I looked up at the half-hidden mansion, my hands tightened at my sides. The upper windows were boarded up. The gate of the whitewashed wall was locked tight, with multiple padlocks. Of course, like other rich aristocrats, Georges Albret and his family had fled Paris at the first whiff of war, traveling to their lavish château in the south of France, or to Switzerland or the French West Indies. Money was magic, just like Roger said.

I'd always believed love was more powerful. But in a few weeks, I'd turn eighteen. And what did I know? I'd been born a mistake.

Blindly, I turned and stumbled for the bridge. On the other side of the Seine, I could see Madame Hébert's stately theater, with its blue roof and nineteenth-century columns. It was a beautiful sight, which just made me feel even uglier inside.

I walked slowly across the Pont au Change, with its busy traffic of vehicles and pedestrians traveling between the Île de la Cité and the right bank of the Seine. Once, this bridge had been filled with goldsmiths and money-changers. But now, the bridge felt like it was whispering of a different kind of change. To change my pain to something else. Anything.

On the island behind me, I could see the sprawling, stately Conciergerie, with its blue-roofed towers. Ahead of me, near the Théâtre Lutèce, I could see the sphinxes of the Fontaine du Palmier, supporting a slender column crowned with a golden statue of Victory to commemorate Napoleon's triumphs across Europe.

How far our country had fallen.

Edging away from the pedestrians hurrying across the bridge, I looked down at the dirty water of the Seine flowing by, far below. In spite of the flickering sparkles of sunlight, every wave concealed something beneath, as if to make a person believe the river hid jewels instead of pollution.

I leaned forward against the ledge, barely feeling the cold of the stone against my thin wool coat. I was mesmerized by the sinister rhythm of the waves.

It was said drowning wasn't the worst death. Just falling. One quick decision, and all would be over. I wouldn't trouble Roger anymore, or Madame Hébert, or Margot. I wouldn't be a burden, or have to keep trying and failing to prove I was worthy of being loved. Worthy of being born.

Growing up, I'd been just another orphan at St. Agnes's. Not clever like Margot. Not beloved like Lucie. My red hair had made me stand out, and later, my figure, which had brought attention from strangers ever since I was fourteen. But it wasn't the kind of attention I'd wanted. Even at that age, when much older men had whistled or talked to me in the street, or, once, pinched my backside, I'd known it wasn't love they were after.

Roger was different. The dream of him had sustained me

for an entire year of war and fear. Even on the darkest days, when we'd been driven out of Paris or slept on the dirt beside the road, I'd thought of him as someone devoutly religious might think of their patron saint. I'd felt protected, watched over, my soul safe, even when my body wasn't.

But that was over. I felt hollow inside, my blood replaced by acid.

He didn't want me, and he never had.

He didn't love me, and he never would.

I looked down into the cold, sparkling river. Behind me on the sidewalk, people hurried past in a crosscurrent of humanity, everyone with important places to be, families and jobs, with loved ones who depended on them. I took a deep breath. All my misery could soon be over.

But the water looked so dirty and cold. How would the policemen find me—if I was ever found—my beautiful silk stockings ripped, my green dress filthy with the dumped trash and oil of the city?

The color of slime, splattered with mud.

I took another breath, my hands shaking as I gripped the stone parapet. One moment, and I'd never have to feel like this again. I wouldn't feel anything at all.

My purse fell to the bridge behind me. I'd count to three, and then...

"Ugly water, isn't it? Not surprising, as it's the snaking heart of our city."

Blinking, I turned my head. A woman was standing behind me. With a jolt, I recognized her.

"M-Madame Hébert," I stammered, astonished. I looked around. Was I dreaming? Was I already dead? Why would our disagreeable neighbor be on the bridge talking to me? I blurted out, "I'm sorry I was so rude to you."

She snorted, then looked meaningfully at the river. "There's no need to be *that* sorry. What's your name, girl?"

"Josette," I said, wishing she would go away. Every second I stood here talking to her, I could feel my courage melting away. "Josette Dubois."

"So tell me, Josette Dubois." She leaned forward cozily. "Why are you thinking of jumping into the Seine?"

The long, stiff peacock feather attached to her turquoise turban fluttered and bobbed, almost like the bird itself, as her purple cape fluttered.

A strand of witchy black hair peeked out from her turban. Her makeup was severe, even startling—thick lines of black kohl over her eyes, thick black eyelashes beneath thick black brows, the bold line of her lips a red slash against ghostly-pale powdered skin.

An inkling of longing pierced through my despair. How wonderful it must be to wear such lovely, theatrical clothes. And even more wonderful not to care what anyone thought or need anyone's approval.

"Well?" Madame Hébert leaned on her walking stick, tilting her head as if I were the most interesting exhibit at the Vincennes Zoo, or the loveliest pink macaron on display beneath the glass at Ladurée.

"No reason," I mumbled. "I just..."

Suddenly, I thought: why not tell her? Séverine Hébert was nothing to me. I'd despised her for years, just as she'd despised us. What would it matter?

"It's a man," I whispered. My eyes stung. "He doesn't love me. No one does."

I waited for her to say some platitude that we'd both know was a lie but she'd say for politeness's sake, before she quickly backed away and left me to my jumping. Or perhaps she'd tell me the same thing Sister Helen (gently) and especially Margot (not so gently) had been telling me for ages: that I was stupid for making such a fool of myself over a man.

Instead, Madame Hébert said, "*Donc*, you're lucky."

I'd turned to stare longingly at the river again. But at her words, I blinked. Sure I'd heard wrong, I looked back at her. "Excuse me, *madame*?"

The sexagenarian gave a cool smile, her eyes glinting as brightly as the jewels on her fingers in the rich, golden light of morning.

"Love is a wonderful thing... for a man. How happy it makes him, all the cookery and lovemaking and praise! How wonderful to have a permanent employee to whom he never has to pay wages, who will worship him with her body and with her labor and with her devotion until he dies, who will put up with anything—his rudeness, his neglect, his drunkenness, his affairs!"

I frowned. Her husband had died before I was born, but when Madame Hébert had sent *gendarmes* to search our garden for venomous snakes imported from the Orient, I'd heard Berthe mutter unkind things about him to Yvonne, the house-keeper. Much older than his wife, he'd apparently perished of a heart attack in the arms of two showgirls young enough to be great-granddaughters. *But with such a hard wife,* Yvonne had added, *who could blame the man for wanting to escape her?*

For all Séverine Hébert's airs and graces, everyone knew she'd grown up barefoot, tending goats in the Provinces before she'd come to Paris to act on stage. Barely twenty, she'd married the owner of the Théâtre Lutèce. No children had come from their marriage. *Because she hates children,* Berthe had sniffed.

Looking at Madame Hébert now, the woman who'd been such a thorn in the sides of all St. Agnes orphans, my eyes fell on her gray roots below the black hair peeking out from the silk turban. And I suddenly felt sorry for her, maybe because no one else did.

For just a moment, imagining another woman's misery made me forget my own.

As people hurried past us on the bridge, their eyes lingering on my red hair and the widow's jewels, Madame Hébert looked out at the sunlight sparkling over the Seine's dirty water. Her vibrant red lips twisted down bitterly.

"A man's wife must strive to keep him happy at every moment, providing him service and pleasure without ever showing a need of her own. She must watch her figure and carefully clean up his messes, all while proclaiming to adore even his smelly breath and stinking feet. You should be grateful you were spurned, Josette Dubois. You won't have to try to bear his child, over and over, and have him scream at you when your body fails. You won't be abandoned for a girl half your age and forced to listen to children playing and laughing next door, while every moment it reminds you of your own loneliness and failure." She gave me a thin smile. "That's what you've escaped by him not loving you."

I stared at her, my eyes wide. I'd never heard such a speech in my life.

She took a deep breath, seeming to gather herself. "You've learned your lesson while still young and strong enough to make your own path. You are the most fortunate of women."

Some Nazi soldiers passed us by on the bridge, nudging each other in the ribs as they said rude things in German about both of us, in different ways. Looking up, I could see the monument of the Place du Châtelet above clawlike branches of bare trees, like bony hands trying helplessly to grasp the blue sky.

"B-But," I stuttered, since she seemed to be waiting for a reply, "a woman who's not loved... is no one. Nothing. I tried to give him my life. He didn't want it."

She lifted a dark penciled-in eyebrow. "No one deserves your life more than you. No one can take better care of you... than you."

"I don't understand."

Madame Hébert suddenly smiled, and it was strangely

kind. "No. Now you're thinking of what you've lost. Take a while and think of what you've gained."

Kindness? From the Widow Hébert?

"But, *madame*, I don't understand. Why are you being so kind? You hate us. You've set the police on us. You wanted to drive us all out so that you could raze our house and turn it into a garden... didn't you?"

She shrugged, a grand gesture. She seemed to make no small ones. "Children are noisy when I want to sleep. It is painful to hear. *Painful*," she repeated flatly. I thought of how she'd never had children of her own, and felt unwilling sympathy. She lifted her chin. "And you must admit your orphanage was a disgrace. The weeds! That awful pink paint! I think I would have preferred a bawdy house in my backyard."

"Uh..."

"Of course I wanted you out. It was annoying that your headmistress was able to keep the property as an orphanage, though I'd offered twice as much money. That's not how the world should work. But later... after you were gone, I had second thoughts. Just as I did with the Germans." She glared at a Nazi truck passing us on the bridge. "I hated the French government—for their snobbery, for the way they talked down their long noses at me. *Find some man to run your theater*, they told me. As if I were helpless! I thought the Germans might be an improvement." Her eyes narrowed beneath the black kohl. "I was wrong."

She spoke the last words in a voice that rang across the bridge, clear as a bell, with a slight accent that betrayed her country roots. I gaped, giving quick looks from side to side. I could hardly believe her boldness, saying such things with German soldiers strolling all over the sidewalk, German trucks crossing both directions along the bridge. The hideous Nazi flag was visible even now, flung smugly across the Conciergerie.

"You say this aloud?" I whispered. "Without fear?" Where

did bravery end and stupidity begin? Glancing one last time at the Seine, I added with a humorless laugh, "There are many ways to end a life."

Her expression changed, and she drew closer.

"Listen close, girl. I stood on this same bridge once, long ago. I almost..." Her eyes grazed the river. "I was only forty then, but I thought my life was over." She glared at me fiercely. "I'll tell you what saved me. And it's the only thing that will save you. Want the secret?"

"Yes," I breathed through numb lips.

She looked down at me. "It's you. You're the secret. You want to be important, protected? Decide you're important. Protect yourself. Don't wait for someone to love you. You want to be loved? Love yourself. Then see what happens." She grinned. "And what fun you can have."

At my stunned expression, she gave a short, satisfied nod. "Now, I must go." With a swirl of her bright wool cape, she started to turn towards the Place du Châtelet on the other side of the bridge. "I'm late for rehearsal—"

Desperately, I grabbed her wrist. She stared at me, her expression miffed as she glared at my hand. Abashed, I released her. But I couldn't let her leave, not yet.

"But, Madame Hébert," I said quietly, "how would I know how to love myself, when no one else has?"

Her eyes flickered. "Your mother, surely—" Then she caught herself. "You're an orphan." She tilted her head, suddenly considering me. "Come with me."

"Where?"

"My theater."

"The Théâtre Lutèce?" My eyebrows rose. For all my dreams of becoming an actress, I'd never been there because tickets were so expensive. "I couldn't."

"Why?" Her lips curved as she gave one last long look at the Seine, tumbling in its dirty, shiny depths beneath the Pont au

Change. She lifted a penciled eyebrow. "Do you have somewhere else to be?"

With that, she swept away, crossing the bridge without a backward glance, clomping her jeweled walking stick as she went.

I looked back one last time at the frigid, polluted river, so far below the bridge, and exhaled, suddenly in a cold sweat. What madness had possessed me to think of such a drastic measure, even for a moment? Why had I placed more importance on Roger's judgment than my own?

The theater. A place of magic. Blood, like longing, rushed into my heart, making it pump again. I turned with an intake of breath and a hoarse cry.

"Madame Hébert! Wait!"

16

LUCIE

I was woken by Thérèse's cries before dawn. Geneviève promptly woke up too and began to howl. The December night was so cold that the windows were frozen on the inside, just as they had when we were little, before Mr. Cleeton generously paid for water radiators to be installed throughout the house. But now it was too dark and frozen for them to keep up.

I'd barely gotten Geneviève back to sleep a few hours before. Miserable with a cold, she'd been unable to eat much from her bottle, with her nose stuffed up, and she'd started crying just past midnight, hungry and pitiful. Her cries awakened Thérèse, so I'd fed both babies, burped them, wiped Geneviève's nose, changed their diapers, swaddled them and cuddled them each back to sleep, in the same old wooden rocking chair that had calmed St. Agnes orphans since the time when France had been ruled by an emperor. Returning them to their cribs, I'd held my breath, then silently backed away and climbed into my own small bed nearby.

Just this once, I'd intended to leave Berthe on her own to prepare and serve Herr Schröder's breakfast. I'd prayed we'd sleep until at least the sun was all the way in the sky.

But no.

"Oh, can't you keep them quiet?" Margot moaned and rolled over, covering her head with a pillow in the gray light of early dawn to block out the babies' crying.

I looked around the attic. Josette's bed was empty. Had she gone out, as she had all day yesterday? Had the baby been startled by the slam of a door?

I felt tired. So tired. Margot was too busy to help, doing some kind of office work now for Herr Schröder. When I'd asked her about it, she'd given only vague answers.

Josette was busy, too, with housework and yardwork. She'd seemed sad and distant lately, lost in her own thoughts. And where had she been yesterday? Where was she now?

I was still the only one doing the night shift with the babies, as well as the one in charge of both of them all day long. They rarely napped at the same time, so I felt like I hadn't slept in days. I'd asked Margot again last night if she could be in charge of them for a few hours, to give me a chance to sleep one night through. She'd looked at me incredulously.

"But, Lucie, you'll wake up anyway if you hear them crying. So there's no sense me waking with them. Then we'd *both* be tired."

And as I'd looked at her then, I'd felt something new in my heart. Something...

No. I couldn't be angry. I wouldn't let myself be angry at the people I loved. I would just try harder. And maybe if I asked very nicely, Margot and Josette would help me some other night.

"I'm just so tired," I whispered aloud.

Choupette, curled up on a patchwork rug beside my bed, looked up at me with a sympathetic wag of her tail.

"We're all tired," Margot groaned.

Wearily, I picked up Geneviève and placed her against my

shoulder, patting her back until her sobs subsided to a low sniffle of tears. In the other crib, Thérèse continued to wail.

"Could you pick her up?" I asked, forcing a smile. "I don't want them to disturb Herr Schröder. If he gets too annoyed, he might not let the babies stay. Remember how cranky Madame Hébert always got when we made noise early in the morning?"

"Let the old bat just try and send the *flics* now." Sitting up, she glanced over towards Josette's empty bed, then frowned. "Is she downstairs?"

"I don't know. I haven't seen her." I walked over to Thérèse's crib, with Geneviève against my shoulder, then rubbed the other baby's back with my free hand, trying to calm her wails. "Perhaps outside?"

Margot snorted. "What, a gardening emergency?" She rose, pulling on an old-but-warm robe over her flannel nightgown. With a sigh, she picked up Thérèse. "Now, no more tears," she crooned. "You're a good girl."

Both babies clung to us, their cries falling away but tears still hovering over their lashes, and Geneviève's nose running down to her mouth in the bargain.

"Poor little mites," I whispered, looking between them. "It's hard to be a baby."

"It's hard to be grown-up, too," Margot said, running her hand impatiently through her dark tangled hair.

We changed the babies on one of the empty beds, the one that used to belong to Rachel before she'd left for America.

"How do you think they're all doing—Estée, Rachel and Noémie and all the rest? And Sister Helen?" I said wistfully.

"I'm sure they're fine," my sister replied. "But... we won't know until the end of the war, will we?"

We looked at the empty beds. The babies fell quiet, and for a moment, in the rising pink dawn, I could almost hear the chatter of all the orphans, the warmth, the love that had made us a family. All those girls remained here still, like ghosts of a remembered life—before the Nazis changed everything.

A cupboard door banged in the kitchen downstairs, and the ghosts fled. The dormitory room turned quiet and empty again, dust motes floating lazily in soft beams of morning light pouring through the dormer windows.

"Come on," Margot said. "Let's see if Berthe has breakfast going."

"And coffee," I said, yawning. I thought I could smell it.

Tossing on some clothes, not bothering to brush our hair, we carried the babies down the back stairs, careful not to be seen by Herr Schröder, who sometimes woke early to work. Josette would be horrified, I thought. She never left the attic bedroom without being impeccably groomed and dressed. I had no idea why. I would certainly never sacrifice my sleep just to look a little prettier. I yawned again.

"Good morning," Berthe said when we reached the sunny kitchen. She was dressed in an apron over her stocky figure, her white hair pulled back in a bun.

She came over to chuck under the babies' chins. "How are you, *mes petites*? Did I hear you crying? *Oh là là.*" She clucked her tongue sympathetically. "I have warm milk ready, the bottles boiled."

"You're an angel, Berthe." I looked at the baby in my arms. "Geneviève didn't sleep much last night."

"For shame," she told the baby chidingly but smiled, because even with her cold, Geneviève really was very cute. She had big blue eyes and soft yellow curls like a porcelain doll. After chucking her under the chin again, Berthe went to the stove to pour me a steaming coffee with milk and sugar.

I took a gulp, then sighed in pleasure. Maybe I would survive this morning after all. "I can help serve breakfast—"

"Herr Schröder was in a hurry. Just eggs and bacon and black coffee, then he was off in that big shiny car."

"He's polishing his propaganda campaign at headquarters." Still juggling baby Thérèse on her hip, Margot took a piece of toast, hot from the toaster, and nearly dropped it. Holding it with two fingers, she blew on it gingerly. "He wanted his mockups printed in full color before they were sent by special messenger to Hitler. For review."

Berthe and I turned to her in shock.

"What?" she said defensively.

"Directly to Hitler?" I said faintly.

She shrugged. "They're childhood friends. Don't look at me that way, Lucie. I was only helping out."

"I thought you were sweeping the floor," Berthe said.

"I was." Munching on the dry toast, she didn't meet our eyes. "He's asked for my opinion on some projects." She finished the toast in just a few bites, then turned to pour herself coffee. Margot had recently started taking her coffee black, saying she had no time to make it creamy or sweet. Now, she hooted, "You should have heard their original ideas. *Ridicule.*"

Berthe and I looked at each other.

"Herr Schröder wanted your... opinion," the elderly cook said faintly. "Since when would a Nazi officer ask a French girl's opinion about anything that wasn't..." She scowled. "Is he trying to seduce you?"

"No," Margot said, shocked. "Of course not."

"There's no *of course* about it." Berthe wielded her wooden spoon vengefully as she scooped eggs and bread, then placed the plates heavily on the nearby table.

"Berthe, he's old enough to be my father!"

"It's surprising how often men don't care about that."

"Really! He doesn't think of me that way at all!"

Berthe squinted at her, then relaxed. "All right, then."

Keeping the babies juggled in our laps, with their bottles of warm milk, my sister and I sat at the dinged-up table in the warm kitchen, taking little bites of our own eggs, bacon and tartines with raspberry jam. I felt guilty, eating such wonderful things, but it did make me feel a little less tired.

Berthe pulled her coat from the hall closet, then left the kitchen for the shops with a stack of Herr Schröder's money and all the ration cards anyone could want. I had many things to do but still lingered over breakfast.

Margot must have felt bad about not helping me last night because she lingered, too.

"Lucie..." She bit her lip. "I've been meaning to talk to you."

"About what?" I busied myself with Geneviève, just in case Margot was going to launch into her usual speech about abandoning the babies at the nearest overcrowded orphanage so we could leave Paris.

"About..." She hesitated. "We missed you on the trip to Marseille, you know. It was... It was a hard journey. Some... odd things happened."

I looked up. Was she criticizing me for not being there to help? Was she saying I'd taken the easy way out, getting mauled by Isabelle Lusigny's brother, then kidnapped and dragged to Paris by Nazis? Stung, I said, "I would have helped you all get to Marseille if I could. I wanted to."

"I know. That's not what I'm saying. I..."

She lifted her gaze to mine, and I saw something in her face that scared me.

All my earlier fears returned, vulture-like, to dig their claws into my soul. "What is it?"

Thérèse started to fuss, and Margot placed her in a high chair, giving her a hard, stale biscuit to gnaw on, to soothe her gums. Then she sipped her third cup of coffee and rubbed her shoulder. I waited.

Choupette started whining by the back door. Geneviève began to moan in harmony, and it was extra pitiful because of her runny nose and sniffle. Still, Margot didn't continue.

I looked at my little wristwatch. "Well?"

"Never mind," she said weakly. "It's nothing."

Nothing's wrong, I told myself and tried to believe it.

"All right," I said, even though it wasn't. "It's time for our walk." With a shy smile, I added, "You could come with us?"

Shaking her head, she clawed back her wild hair. "I... I need to go to Neuilly today." She sighed. "I keep putting it off."

My brow furrowed in confusion. Neuilly was a suburb on the edge of Paris. What business could Margot have there? "Why?"

She suddenly wouldn't meet my eyes. "We stopped by La Ravelle on the way to Paris—did I tell you? The Ravanels aren't there anymore. And Daniel's imprisoned in Germany."

I sucked in my breath. "Oh no!" I felt sad for them but grateful that at least they knew their son was alive. If only this war would end! "And Paul?"

My sister shook her head. "Still missing. There was a rumor he was seen in Paris. So Dr. Ravanel went to work at the American Hospital in Neuilly." She looked at me. "I need to go talk to him, Lucie, because... because..."

"We should all go," I said warmly. "Oh, I do hope they've found Paul. They were so very kind to us, weren't they? Like family."

Again, Margot's dark eyes shifted away. Her hand was shaking. "Lucie." She paused, then cleared her throat. Her voice was hoarse. "That's what I'm trying to..."

"What's this? You two still lazing about?" Berthe appeared in the kitchen doorway. "I forgot my hat and gloves."

"No one cares about that anymore."

"The Germans have taken quite enough." She sniffed. "They can't take my sense of propriety." She frowned. "Is Josette still not awake?"

"Uh." We looked at each other.

"She surely can't still be sleeping. It's almost eleven—"

But as she spoke, we heard a noise through the back garden door. Suddenly, Josette herself was there, looking at us breathlessly.

"Oh good. I didn't miss anything. Did Herr Schröder ask where I was?"

Berthe shook her head. "But where were you?"

Margot demanded, "Yes, where?"

"Why do you ask?" Josette said demurely. She looked uncommonly pretty. Her red hair was perfect, but it was more than that. Her hazel-green eyes sparkled, her cheeks rosy. And she was smiling in a way she hadn't in... well. I couldn't even remember.

Berthe immediately set down her hat and gloves and pulled a plate of fruit and bacon from the icebox. "I made this for your breakfast, *ma petite*."

"For me?" Josette hung up her coat and took the plate. "Oh, thank you." Sitting at the table, she tucked eagerly into the food. "It's been *such* a morning. I'm positively starving!"

"Well?" Margot glared at her. "What's your explanation?"

Delicately, she nibbled a piece of bacon. "Do you need one?"

"We were worried!"

Josette's ruby lips curved. "Were you really?"

"Of course we were!"

"We were," I said sincerely.

Her green eyes softened. "I'm sure *you* were, Lucie. Oh, thank you." She took the glass of orange juice Berthe had set before her. After a long gulp, she wiped her mouth. "Well. Yesterday, I went to see Roger."

"Roger!" Margot gasped.

"Josette, you promised you wouldn't!"

She shrugged, looking between us with amusement. "Oh, come on. You knew I'd do it."

Fury flew into my sister's eyes, quickly veiled. I was astonished. Why was Margot so angry? Of course she'd be worried about Roger being discovered by the Germans. But the anger seemed like something more.

It was impossible that Margot could be jealous—she'd barely noticed Roger last summer. But these days, she seemed to get irritated at Josette all the time, for the littlest imagined slights.

Margot leaned back stiffly in her chair. "How is he?"

"Fine." She glanced at Margot from beneath her darkened eyelashes. "Earning money. On the black market."

"The black market?" Berthe gasped. "What's he been doing?"

Josette shrugged. "Ask him."

"Doesn't he know it's dangerous?" Margot demanded.

"He doesn't care."

Josette's voice was flat. I didn't know what to make of that. Usually she couldn't shut up about him.

"But what did he say?" I asked, picking up our empty plates and going to wash them in the sink with the other breakfast dishes. "Was he at least happy to see you?"

Her smile was long gone. "No."

My heart hurt for her. I sometimes dreamed of meeting a man I could adore, in a grand, mystical, magical love. But the idea scared me, too. Everyone knew love was uncontrollable. An accident. There was no way to predict how it would change your life—whether it would be like winning millions of francs in the National Lottery or getting hit by a train.

For now, I was happy to stick with raising my babies and keeping Berthe and my sisters as my only companions.

I ventured slowly, "Does Roger know how much you love him?"

"Men can be so stubborn. They don't always know what's good for them." Berthe sighed, looking pointedly from Josette to

Margot. "I would give thanks to *le bon Dieu* if my great-nephew would finally be sensible and settle down with either of you."

Margot's face looked as if she'd sucked on a lemon. She started playing patty-cake with Thérèse in her high chair.

Josette gave a low laugh. After finishing off her orange juice, she handed me the glass for the sink's soapy water. "He told me yesterday he'll never love me. Never ever."

Margot looked up from her game. We all looked at each other in confusion.

"You seem to be taking it rather well," Margot said.

Josette started to speak, then stopped herself. Finally, she said quietly, "On the way home yesterday, I ran into Madame Hébert. She was going to her theater and invited me along. It turns out... there's a job for me there."

"As an actress?" Now I was the one to clap my hands. "I knew your dream could come true, Josette! I—"

"Not an actress." But she was smiling again. "Better."

"Better how?" Margot asked, frowning. For a year, we'd heard only two subjects from Josette: Roger and her dream of being a famous actress.

"You should have seen it." Josette turned away dreamily. "Such a ragtag group. Carpenters, set designers, lighting crew. Madame Hébert introduced me, and they said they were looking for an assistant seamstress, and so... I went back this morning and started stitching." She turned to us. "But it means I can't work for Herr Schröder anymore. Do you think he'll mind terribly? If I pay for my room and board?"

Berthe, Margot and I looked at each other blankly.

"I'm sure you can work something out," I said, though I wasn't sure at all. I think he liked having us around all day, as if we were his daughters and the babies his granddaughters. He seemed lonely at times. Plus, who would do all Josette's work? I prayed no one would expect it to be me.

Josette's red hair flew as she whirled in my direction. "Lucie, you'll talk to him, won't you? He likes you best."

"I'm not sure about that," I said doubtfully. "Margot should talk to him. He's been asking her advice about his work."

She turned to my sister, wide-eyed. "Advice?"

"Oh, stop," she said crossly. "He's asked my opinion about a few things, that's all, then asked me to type and translate and do a little secretarial work..."

"Secretarial work," Josette snorted.

We all knew how much Margot despised it. But she only shrugged.

"It's better than scrubbing the bathroom." She rose back to her feet. "Do you hear someone at the door?"

I thought she was trying to change the subject, but then the doorbell rang. There really was someone at the front door. The four of us looked at each other.

"Herr Schröder?" Margot guessed.

"Why would he ring?" With Geneviève hiccupping in my arms, I headed for the hallway. "Berthe, watch Thérèse!"

"Sure, I have nothing better to do," she sighed, "except go buy groceries and scrub down the counter and table, then start chopping the potatoes for dumplings and marinating the beef roast, and then..."

Her grumbling faded as I hurried down the hallway, followed by Margot, Josette and my sweet loyal pup, her claws clicking on the wood herringbone floor.

As we passed Herr Schröder's locked study, I glanced through the peephole of the front door, then frowned.

"Who is it?" Josette asked.

Shaking my head slightly, I opened the door.

A haggard-looking woman in an inadequate coat stood on the front steps with a small sulky child.

"This is St. Agnes's, is it not?" she said, peering at the baby in my arms.

"Yes, *madame*," I said in bewilderment. "Can I help you?"

"Ah, good. This is for you."

She tried to push the child forward. The little girl, who looked no older than five, clung to her.

"You're abandoning her?" Josette said behind me, a little accusingly, circles of red high in her cheeks. She always took it so personally.

The woman shrugged. "I'm sorry. I'm just her neighbor. I tried, but I can't take care of her anymore. I have three of my own." She turned to shout at three little boys who were scuffling in the cobblestoned alley behind her. "Stop it, Simon. Let your brother go!" She turned back, huffing with a flare of nostril. "I can't do it all."

"Don't leave me, Madame Giroux," the little girl whimpered. "I'll be good. I promise."

"Her mother died six months ago; her father's off in the war," the woman continued, absent-mindedly trying to peel the girl's fingers from her waist. "We heard he's in Germany, but it's so hard to know if he will... Anyway, I was friends with her mother and promised to... but that was when we never thought... Well." She cleared her throat. "Her name's Fauve. Fauve Paquet."

"You know, *madame*, we're not really an orphanage anymore," Margot said. "This house has been commandeered by a Nazi officer."

Madame Giroux paused, then drew back to reconsider the three-story house, the fresh paint, the tidy garden. Even the cup still in Josette's hand, with the creamy, fragrant coffee. I could almost see the wheels turning as she considered the potential Nazi threat and benefit against the inconvenience and uncertainty of changing her plans. She decided with a nod. "So she'll be well fed."

"*Non, madame*, that is impossible," Margot said indignantly. "We cannot accept more children."

"I already tried three orphanages, but they refused to so much as open the door. If you will not take her, I'm afraid I must..." Madame Giroux's eyes fell on Geneviève, wriggling in my arms, and she said accusingly, "But you cannot tell me that baby is your own."

"No," I replied. "But we had to take her. She was left at the door."

"Just so. Consider this a child left at your door."

The woman turned to the little girl. "You'll be better off here, Fauve." Kneeling, she briskly straightened the little girl's dress, which she wore over a Peter Pan-collared shirt. The dress was wrinkled but clean, though her patent-leather shoes were scuffed and dirty.

When she rose, she pointed to a tiny, forlorn suitcase and told us, "That's her things."

Another child to care for, on top of our two babies? A grief-stricken, abandoned, traumatized child who clearly didn't want to be here? My heart sank. I'd barely slept the last week. How could I manage to take care of another child?

Margot's hands were clenched at her sides. "*Non, madame,* absolutely not..."

The little girl flinched. I looked down at her. There were agonized tears in her big brown eyes. My heart broke to see an abandoned child forced to endure the tug-of-war—or rather push-of-war—between two women who didn't want her.

I threw myself between them. "We'll take her," I said firmly.

"Lucie..." My sister looked as if she'd like to strangle me. The older woman exhaled in relief.

"Good— Stop, Fauve!" the woman snapped at the crying girl, now clinging to her skirt. "It's just until your papa gets back. You'll be happy here. You'll see. All those trees to climb. And look—a dog. Haven't you always wanted a dog?"

The girl didn't even look at Choupette, who sat at my feet.

There was a loud smack against the cobblestones, then a howl coming from the smallest of the roughhousing boys.

The neighbor yanked the little girl's fingers off her skirt with an apologetic smile at us. "I must go." She patted the girl's head. "You'll be fine." After glancing around, she leaned forward to whisper to us, "And don't worry. There's no official record she's Jewish."

Our eyes widened as we looked at each other.

"Jewish?" I echoed.

"Her mother's mother. From the Ukraine. Her heritage was never officially recorded, and her surname doesn't prove anything, so..." She shrugged, trying to act nonchalant, but I could hear the slight tremor in her voice, see the sweat prickling her temples. She was desperate. She wouldn't risk sending Fauve into the lion's den if she wasn't. I'd seen it in her eyes. Her alternative was to abandon a five-year-old girl to starve on the street.

"We can't," Margot pleaded.

"We can," I told her firmly.

Madame Giroux drew back, tilting her head to look up at St. Agnes's. "The most famous girls' orphanage in Paris. My promise to your *maman* is kept." Exhaling, she looked down at the little girl. "You'll do well here, until your papa gets back."

But the little girl was weeping. "No, Madame Giroux, please, *please.*"

"*Au revoir.*" The woman bent to give her one quick kiss on the cheek. Then she turned away.

Still clinging to her as the woman strode down the steps, the girl tripped, falling to the hard stones, her knee bloodied as she wailed frantically, "*Non... non... madame...* Papa. Maman." She wiped her eyes as she wailed helplessly to the blue sky, "Maaaa-maaaaan..."

My heart broke for her. I gave the baby to Josette, then

kneeled in the front grass and cuddled her into my arms, rocking her back and forth.

"It's going to be all right, Fauve. Don't worry." I looked down at her, wiping her tears away as I gave my warmest, most reassuring smile. "This is a happy place. See? Look." I pointed up at the house. "I grew up here, too."

With a sniff, Fauve looked up. Tears tracked down her cheeks, but she wiped her eyes and looked at me with something between trepidation and hope.

"Now." I hugged her. "Are you hungry? Would you like a sandwich? Our cook, Berthe, makes the best *croque monsieur* in all of France." My smile widened to a conspiratorial grin. "Though when I was little, she made us awful, wholesome porridges and stews. Luckily for you, nowadays it's mostly schnitzel and spätzle. Which sounds very exotic, but it's actually just veal cutlets. And noodles. Lots of butter, too."

"Butter?" Tentatively, she returned my smile, though her eyes were still swimming with tears. She was trying to be brave.

I would try to be brave, too.

I stood up and reached out my hand to help her up. Her hand trembled in mine. Poor little thing.

"Just promise you won't feed your sandwich to Choupette beneath the table," I said with a wink, nodding towards my dog, who lifted her head on hearing her name. "She's the sweetest little thing. Go ahead. You can pet her."

Nervously, Fauve reached out and touched her curly, bronze fur. The dog tilted her head, lolling her tongue happily. With greater confidence, Fauve petted her again, her small shoulders relaxing.

Margot and Josette glanced at her, then each other, with troubled eyes. My sister shook her head, and I saw, with a sinking heart, that I would be raising one more child all on my own.

I could do this. I could do this.

I took a deep breath.

"Let's go clean up that knee." I made my voice cheerful.

As we went inside, Choupette trotting happily beside her, I squeezed the little girl's shoulder. "See?" I gave her a warm, comforting smile. "Everyone loves you already. Everything's going to be fine."

But inside, I felt suddenly afraid it wouldn't be fine at all.

17

LUCIE

"You can't say a word, Lucie," my sister warned hours later.

"You're the one who insisted she stay here," Josette said, unusually pale. "So protect her."

I looked between them indignantly. "What do you take me for? Of course I'm not going to tell him!"

"You're the worst liar in the world," Josette said.

"Your cheeks always turn red."

"No, they don't," I protested and felt my cheeks get hot. Which made me even madder, which made my cheeks go even hotter.

Josette snorted, then glanced at Margot. "Let me do the talking."

I set my jaw mutinously. It was obvious even to me that the little girl's heritage had to remain secret or she'd be in a world of trouble. The Nazis' treatment of Jews, already a scandal in Germany and Poland, was starting to turn similarly ugly in France. That was why Sister Helen had felt she had no choice but to take our orphanage's three little Jewish girls all the way to America. If I could have sent Fauve to America, I would have.

But she was stuck in Paris, either with us or alone on the street. Which meant I'd have to lie.

"Lucie, stay here," Margot said.

"Wait," I said with more confidence than I felt. "I can do it."

Margot's dark eyes looked huge in the dim hallway light. "Lucie…"

"No. Josette was right. If I ask, Herr Schröder might say yes. He did before. I can do it," I repeated when they looked at each other uncertainly.

And so it was that, ten minutes later, I did all the talking when the three of us went to Herr Schröder in the parlor, explaining that an "orphaned French child" had been left at the door. Clasping my hands in front of my heart, I pleaded for her to be allowed to remain. My heart was pounding, but I dug my fingernails into my palm so the pain would distract me. And like a miracle, it worked. My voice was calm. My cheeks did not betray me in that telltale burn.

"A little French orphan?" Herr Schröder just smiled, despite my nerves. "Of course she may stay."

I looked back at Josette and Margot in relief. How lucky that he seemed in a relaxed, expansive mood. Berthe had served him *Sauerbraten* and *Kartoffelklöße* for dinner, and he sat in front of the fire in the front parlor, reading a German newspaper in his new leather chair. Even Josette's nervous request a moment later to start working outside the home was well received.

"You'd be working for Madame Hébert? At the Théâtre Lutèce?" Herr Schröder took a sip of his bourbon, relaxing after a hard afternoon at the Nazi headquarters in the former Hôtel Majestic. Or had it been hard? I couldn't imagine enjoying such a day, but based on his mood, he must have. He continued, "She's well known to be a sensible woman, one of the few in this neighborhood to actively welcome the Reich. Her theater seems wholesome enough. I know several officers who attended the last performance and found it pleasing." He stroked his chin, considering Josette. "What exactly would you do there?"

"I'd be assistant seamstress, if you please, Herr Schröder," she replied. "I'll help make and repair costumes. But I don't wish to cause you any trouble. I'm happy to pay for room and board, or I could even—"

"Not necessary." He lifted his hand, indicating the comfortable front parlor, once cluttered with orphans, now sparely decorated with expensive new furniture. "This place was your home before it was mine. As I said, you're my guest. Working for wages has always been your choice."

"Thank you, Herr Schröder. That is most generous."

"Although in return"—his cold eyes rested on her—"you will let me know, won't you, if you hear any treasonous words backstage? Actors, along with artists and singers, do not always act in their own best interests. They can easily... lose their heads."

"Of course, Herr Schröder."

Her gaze fell to the floor. Though she appeared calm, I noticed her hands were shaking as she tucked them behind her.

"Lucie, my dear, you and Berthe are at liberty to hire any additional help you'll need, for the house or grounds." The fireplace crackled as he sat up straight in his easy chair and lowered the newspaper into his lap. "Or even childcare, as long as you vet the woman properly." His lips curved in a smile. "I'm not a slave driver."

"You're very kind," I murmured. "But perhaps my sister—"

"Fräulein Margot," he interrupted, "will be working exclusively as my secretary and translator from now on."

I looked at my sister. She seemed struck dumb.

He frowned, his smile turning strained.

"Thank you, Herr Schröder," she said softly. "I'm not worthy of such an honor."

"Nonsense." Relaxing, he waved his hand. "Your typing and shorthand are exemplary. Say what one will about Helen

Taylor, she taught you well in secretarial skills. German, too. Your translation is very good. But it's more than that. You have an eye... an ear... for our target demographic. It was agreed at the highest level that we are on the right track. France is ours. We intend to keep it that way." He nodded towards the parlor wall. "What do you think?"

Turning, I stared blankly at a new painting that had replaced the spot where the old handstitched sampler had once hung.

"Is that a Renoir?" Josette asked.

"Yes." He beamed at her. "Appropriated by the Reich from Jews who'd greedily stolen such important French patrimony. The Führer himself arranged for it to be presented to me today as a gift. He has every confidence that, thanks to my efforts, there will never be any significant French resistance from the populace." His smile widened, showing the glint of his white teeth. "And if there is, I will kill it." His cold gray eyes warmed as he turned to Margot. "I appreciate your assistance with the psychology of *la Parisienne.*"

"Oh." Margot's cheeks were red. She was not such a good actress as Josette, who discreetly elbowed her in the ribs. With a jump, she said weakly, "I hardly did anything."

"To the contrary." He gave a brisk nod. "You'll receive an increase in wages, commensurate with your skills. I'll expect you full-time, starting tomorrow after breakfast." He chuckled. "And tell that battle-axe in the kitchen it will all be quite proper." He carefully folded the newspaper and placed it on the side table. "*In loco parentis,* as they say. I will treat you like a father would."

Margot seemed to flinch at the word *father.* "Please, Herr Schröder," she blurted out, "I just remembered. Would it be possible if I started later tomorrow? I have an errand in the morning."

"An errand?"

"Shouldn't take long."

He waited.

She sighed, then explained with obvious reluctance, "I need to go to the doctor."

"Are you ill?"

Biting her lip, she confessed with obvious embarrassment, "It's, er, a woman's issue..."

"Say no more." Alarmed, he waved away the topic before she could say another word. "Will noon give you enough time?"

"Yes," she said sweetly. "Thank you, Herr Schröder."

The three of us left the parlor, walking slowly back to the kitchen. I looked at Margot anxiously.

"Have you been ill?" That would explain why she hadn't wanted to stay up with the babies last night. How could I not have noticed she was ailing? What kind of sister was I, selfishly worrying about my own exhaustion?

"Not exactly." She grinned. "Though I am planning to go see a doctor."

I stared at her.

"You're going to see Dr. Ravanel," I said accusingly. I shook my head. "Why didn't you just say so? Why all that business about *women's issues?*"

"So he wouldn't ask questions." My sister quirked an eyebrow. "Anyway. It's good practice. I might have to be his secretary, but Herr Schröder doesn't have to know everything, does he?" She grabbed my arm. "Good job keeping Fauve's secret."

"Yeah," Josette echoed, tilting her head to look at me from beneath her darkened lashes. "I didn't know you had it in you."

"Um. Thanks." I wasn't sure it was praise. And I still wasn't sure how I'd managed not to blush at the lie of omission, except I'd had no choice but to protect Fauve.

In the kitchen, Berthe was showing the little girl how to roll pastry dough to sit overnight in the icebox for tomorrow's breakfast. Fauve was standing on a step to reach the counter, the older woman's wrinkled hands over her own as they used the rolling pin on the flaky, buttery dough. "This will make a fine streusel."

"What's a streusel?" the girl asked.

"It's like a tart. With raspberries. Herr Schröder likes it, and so will you." Berthe turned to us, her eyes sharp. "Well?"

I looked at Fauve and smiled. "She can stay."

The white-haired cook exhaled. "Good." Her fingers were covered in sticky dough as she cocked her chin towards the high chairs, where Thérèse and Geneviève had each fallen fast asleep, one's chubby little body slumped forward holding a spoon, the other's pudgy cheek squished against the table. "They're ready for bed."

"Oh, gracious." I hurried forward and gently eased Thérèse's favorite wooden spoon from her grip. She loved to bang it in rhythm against any surface, laughing at the sound. I gently picked her up but couldn't figure out how to maneuver the second baby out of the high chair with only one free hand. I glanced behind me. "Josette?"

"Sure." She picked up Geneviève and cradled her against her shoulder, then beamed at us. "I can't wait to spend my days at the theater."

"Lucky you," Margot said a little sourly.

The redhead's smile lifted to a grin. "Cheer up. You always swore you'd never be a secretary, but it might not be so bad. Like you said. Better than scrubbing toilets." Her expression changed. "So you're going to see Dr. Ravanel tomorrow?"

"So?" Margot said quickly, with a sideways glance at me.

"I'm happy for you, that's all." As Josette cuddled the yawning baby against her chest, she glanced at me, too. "It's about time."

There seemed some kind of tension between them I didn't understand.

"Time for what?" I asked, bewildered, looking between them. "Is there something you know about Dr. Ravanel that I don't?"

"The thing is, Lucie..." Margot's voice trailed off. Licking her lips, she said weakly, "Christmas is in a week, and I'm hoping he'll invite us for dinner."

"Oh, is that all." I felt relieved. I'd really started to wonder if it was something awful—like Dr. Ravanel had heard bad news about one of his sons, or even about Sister Helen, Estée, Rachel or Noémie. Though how he would hear anything about them in America, I was unsure. Communication lines were tightly controlled by the Germans.

Berthe gave a *tsk*. "Such manners." She placed rolled circles of dough in the icebox, telling Fauve, "Now go wash your hands." As the little girl obeyed, she told us reprovingly, "You don't visit people in hopes they'll invite you to Christmas dinner. We taught you better than that."

"I know." Now Margot was the one with red cheeks. "That's not the only reason."

"What else?"

"I... I owe Dr. Ravanel a lot. I..." Margot looked at her shoes.

"We all do," I said, a little bewildered. Dr. Ravanel, his wife Élisabeth and their teenage daughter Suzanne had taken such wonderful care of us when we'd gone to them in desperation last June, when Sister Helen and little Noémie were injured. I didn't understand why Margot was acting strange about it.

Josette stared at my sister, waiting, then she sighed, rolling her eyes. "Come on, Lucie. Let's get these babies into the bath."

"Thanks for the help," I told her. "You can come help too, Fauve," I called to the little girl across the kitchen. She shyly came towards us, sucking on one of her fingertips.

"You want me to help with the babies? Me?"

I nodded, smiling. "Yes. Then you'll take a bath yourself. Where's her suitcase, Berthe?"

"I took it up."

I turned back to the little girl. "There are seventeen free beds in the attic. You can pick the one you want."

Her brown eyes were big. "I get to choose?"

"All up to you," I confirmed, hugging her. "Think of us as your new big sisters. Do you have any other sisters, Fauve?"

She shook her head sadly. I saw the exact moment her thoughts went from her lack of siblings to her mother who'd died and the father who'd disappeared. "No." Tears welled in her eyes. "I just have—"

"You have all of us now," I promised gently, stroking her hair. "Berthe, Margot, Josette, the babies and me."

"And Choupette."

"*Bien sûr.*" I smiled down at my curly-haired pup, who was leaning against her, instinctively offering comfort as only dogs knew how to do. "Until your papa comes home. For however long it takes."

She swallowed hard. "Really?"

"Really." I squeezed her in another hug, until Thérèse, nestled in my other arm, gave an indignant squeak. But Fauve still sucked her fingertips nervously, glancing back at Berthe, as if she wasn't sure she wanted to leave her or the warmth of the kitchen.

In Josette's arms, Geneviève gave a tentative whimper.

"I'm heading up," Josette said and carried the baby up the back stairs.

"Be right there." I turned to Fauve. I didn't want to drag her up to her bath. She needed to want to go. I had a sudden memory of Estée, our resident bookworm before she'd left for America. "After your bath, I can read you a story before bed. We have just a few books left, but they're really good ones..."

"A story!" Her eyes lit up. She put her little hand in mine, and my heart twisted.

But as I turned to go, Margot blurted out, "Lucie."

Frowning, I turned back. "What?"

"The thing is, you should know..."

"Yes?"

Thérèse started crying now, rubbing her eyes. Fauve, her earlier reluctance gone, was now tugging eagerly on my hand. And I was already looking ahead to the moment that all three children could be tucked soundly into their beds so I could take a quick bath, too, wash away all the sweat and exhaustion of the last few days, and then try to sleep. I realized I'd never gotten around to eating my own dinner, and though my stomach was growling, I already felt too tired to do anything about it. "What is it?"

The light in Margot's eyes faded.

"Here." She reached for Thérèse. "Let me help."

"Both you and Josette helping tonight," I said, smiling through my yawn. "Thanks, Margot."

I hoped it was just the start. Maybe, now they were both doing other jobs that didn't involve cooking or cleaning, they'd have more energy to help me with this most critical task: loving and raising these orphaned children.

As we went slowly up the steep back stairs, my hand in Fauve's, I mused out loud, "Do you ever wish our mother had left a how-to manual? Or Sister Helen, even? It would be so nice if I could know when I'm doing it right. And wrong."

Margot didn't answer. I looked at her back as she climbed the stairs ahead of me with the baby, and wondered if she was thinking I was in over my head. If she was still upset I'd ruined their plans to escape Nazi-occupied Paris. If she thought I was a fool for giving up my life for these children.

But when we reached the top floor and Fauve raced into the first dormitory room hollering with delight, Margot drew her arm around me.

"I love you, *ma sœur*. You know that, don't you?"

A rush of tears filled my eyes. I hugged her back fiercely. "I know." I wiped my eyes. "I'm sorry you had to give up your plans for America. But maybe someday…"

Margot drew back, her forehead creased. Then, looking at the baby in my arms, she exhaled, briefly closing her eyes.

"No. We'll never make it to America." She looked at Fauve. "There are too many of us now." The five-year-old was rushing around the room, loudly exclaiming over this bed, or that one, as if the tiny single beds, each with a lumpy pillow and scratchy woolen blanket and small worn nightstand, were luxurious enough to rival the many-mattressed splendor of *La Princesse au petit pois*. "We're in Paris. Until the war ends."

I hung my head guiltily.

She patted my shoulder. "It's all right. You could never have left the children behind. Knowing you as I do, I should have realized that the first day. And I know I haven't helped as much as I should. You're wearing yourself out, and that's not right."

The thought of getting more help with the children brought tears to my eyes. "Thank you, Margot…"

"Plus, I have an idea."

"What?"

With a wink, she placed her finger along the bridge of her nose. "I'll tell you if it works out."

Nearby, in the large bathroom that separated the two dormitory rooms, I could hear the bathwater running and Josette singing as a baby babbled in reply. With such good sisters, I knew we could get through this war—together.

I would do better, I vowed silently. Try harder. I would not fail them.

18

MARGOT

I looked out the attic's dormer window in dismay at the soft morning sun lighting up the frosty blue December sky. Part of me had been hoping for a sudden violent snowstorm that would prevent me from finally facing my father.

I'd planned to look my best that morning, but unfortunately Josette had already disappeared at the crack of dawn for her new job, wearing my mother's nice wool coat. So I had to make do with my old hand-me-down, which I'd worn since I was fourteen. Made of blue, bulky boiled wool and missing a button, it was warm but ugly, which meant there was no point in trying to wear a fancy dress underneath. So I'd put on my preferred striped shirt and close-fitting pants, and I'd found some sturdy little boots to wear, as my old clunky shoes that I'd used to cross France, Roger's cast-offs, had finally fallen apart. These boots had once belonged to Fräulein Mueller, and I was lucky her feet were as big as mine. I looked at myself in the mirror. As was typical, my hair wouldn't behave, falling over my shoulders in tangled dark curls.

I set down the brush. No point trying. Anyway, Dr. Ravanel had already seen me in an even worse state, covered in sweat and travel dust in La Ravelle back in June. And besides—my lips twisted—he was to blame for my hair, wasn't he? My half-sister's looked exactly the same.

In spite of my words last night, I hadn't helped Lucie with the children at all this morning, or Berthe with the cooking. It had taken all my strength just to get dressed, my heart pounding like a drum.

Downstairs, I found my sister in the kitchen, still wearing her robe, juggling two babies and Fauve in the bargain. I watched her gulp down a cup of coffee without her usual milk or sugar. I'd heard her up late, getting up with each of them when they couldn't sleep. She was now standing near the kitchen table, trying to teach Fauve how to write the first letter of her name.

"You and Berthe are going to hire someone to help soon, aren't you?" I asked.

Lucie gave me a smile that didn't reach her weary eyes. "Berthe had second thoughts about firing Françoise. Apparently, the woman's only son died in the trenches of the last war."

I sighed. Berthe's own son had died in 1916. Even the doughty cook couldn't be reliably hard-hearted these days, not when a sad story so closely matched her own. "But Françoise doesn't do anything. She comes just to pilfer the butter."

"Well, maybe she'll work harder now." But even my sister sounded more resigned than hopeful.

Changing the subject, she tried to smile, though her eyes were tired. "Tell Dr. Ravanel hello for us."

I nodded and, after a single bracing gulp of black coffee, I left. Butterflies tumbled through my belly as I hurried from St. Agnes's and went down the steps to République station. They only worsened as I climbed on the number three train to Neuilly.

This would be the first time I'd seen Dr. Ravanel since Helen told me he was my father.

What would he say when I told him I was his secret daughter? Would he despise me? Blame Helen for not telling him sooner? Would he understand that she'd done it in a misguided effort to protect him?

Because it had been misguided, in my opinion. He deserved to know. And that was why I had to tell him. For his sake.

I took a deep breath. First, I'd tell Dr. Ravanel.

Then Lucie.

Coming up from the Pont de Levallois-Bécon, I wiped my eyes. I realized I was shaking. I guess I could understand why Helen had been scared to tell him. Because I was scared to tell Lucie we weren't actually related by blood, no matter how Josette pushed me or rolled her eyes about it.

It made sense to be cautious—I couldn't risk Herr Schröder finding out I was his enemy's natural daughter. But also, I was still scared of how Lucie would feel. How it might change our relationship.

She was already having a difficult time. Technically, there were three children to care for, and even without Françoise, there were four women to do it, counting Berthe. So why did it seem so much harder than I remembered, back when St. Agnes's had held twenty orphans?

Because Helen had been in charge, I realized. Back when I'd known her only as a stern headmistress, not as my mother, I'd taken her for granted, pushing against her rules. It was only now she was gone forever I realized what she'd given us. And what it must have cost her.

Plus, Josette was selfishly busy doing other things.

I walked along the cold, sunny street until I reached the American Hospital, which was bustling and crowded. I heard people speaking American English and wondered why they'd stayed in France during war, when their own country across the ocean was safe and peaceful. Why my mother and father, who'd met in the Great War and traveled for years afterward, had chosen to help during epidemics and smaller wars. What would inspire anyone to put their lives at risk when they didn't have to, when no one they loved was in the crossfire?

"*Bonjour*. May I help you, *mademoiselle*?" a hospital receptionist asked in French.

"Yes, please," I replied in English. "I'd like to speak with Dr. Ravanel."

She looked me over. "You are a patient?"

"A family friend."

She pointed. "Wait there."

Twenty minutes later, he came out into the waiting area—his eyes dark like mine, salt-and-pepper hair, broad shoulders in his white doctor's coat. He looked tired, but his expression lit up when he saw me.

My father.

"Margot! What a surprise. I thought you were headed for Marseille."

"Change of plans," I said thickly, emotion filling me as I looked at him. "Josette, Lucie and I returned to Paris."

"And..." He looked around the waiting room.

"Helen did leave. She took the little girls to America."

"Oh. Oh. That's good. Did she ever find out...?" He hesitated, as if unsure how much I knew. "Her lungs—"

I put his mind at ease. "Not cancer. Tuberculosis."

He closed his eyes, whispering a prayer to *le bon Dieu*. Tuberculosis was serious but not the lung cancer Helen had feared.

I added, "She's going to recuperate at a sanitarium in America."

Dr. Ravanel's dark eyebrows lifted in worry. "All by herself, with those children—"

"No." I wanted to put him at ease in this, too. "Not alone. There's an American who gave his money to the orphanage for years. He was in love with her for a long time, hopelessly. It was only after we left you"—I paused—"and she saw him again in Marseille, that things changed for them. She was able to finally care for him."

I saw a flash of pain in his eyes, and then relief, then finally joy, a clear sense of the rightness of things. He wiped one of his eyes as if bothered by a speck of dust, then wrapped his arms around his white coat. "I am glad to hear it. She deserves every happiness." He cleared his throat. "So, what are you doing back in Paris?"

"After we left you in La Ravelle, Lucie got lost..." As I explained, his eyes grew round. The truth was, I hardly knew what I was saying. All I could think was that I was talking to my father. I had a father. He was right here. I could reach out and grab his arm, if I wanted.

"So you, Lucie, Josette and your old cook are raising three children in the old orphanage, which has been requisitioned by Otto Schröder?" he said faintly.

Put like that, it did seem like insanity. "Um, yes?"

"And when you go back there this morning, you'll work as his secretary? For a Nazi plenipotentiary who can do whatever he wants and reports directly to Hitler?"

I blinked. I realized that, lately, I'd forgotten to think of him as the fearsome Reichsbevollmächtigter Schröder, Hitler's right hand. Instead, I'd started to see him as just plain old Herr Schröder, who liked schnitzel and read his German-language newspaper with his slippers by the fire. But of course he was a dangerous man. How could I ever let myself forget that, even for a single moment?

"Uh. Yes."

"It's not safe. Helen would do something drastic to get you out of there, if she knew."

"You're right." I lifted my chin. "But she's not here. And what she doesn't know won't hurt her."

Dr. Ravanel snorted, then sighed. "But it might hurt you."

He raked his hand through his dark hair. "I wish I could tell you to leave that house and come stay with us instead..."

"Yes?" I said eagerly. That had been exactly the idea I'd had —that all of us, Berthe and orphans included, could leave St. Agnes's and go live with the Ravanels instead. But my hopes were immediately dashed.

"But our house here is tiny," he said sadly. "Just two rooms, really, with a garden. If I invited six more people to stay with us—"

"Seven."

He flinched, then gave a rueful smile. "My wife would probably make room by telling me to find a new place to live."

"Of course. I understand." Disappointment went through me, though of course he was right. It was unreasonable to ask that seven extra people cram into their two rooms. Then came the small thought: Would Dr. Ravanel's wife, who was a kind, motherly person, feel more obliged to make room if she knew I was her husband's child?

It was a new thought. How would Élisabeth and young Suzanne feel when they knew the secret? Would they feel betrayed, though I'd been conceived before Dr. Ravanel's marriage? I'd been so worried about Lucie, I hadn't considered the others who'd be affected by my news.

So I stalled, changing the subject. "I heard about Daniel. I'm so sorry."

"Thank you." He bowed his head. "We just have to hope the war ends soon, so he can come home."

"And Paul? Is there any news?"

He got a strange look in his eyes, then said sharply, "Why do you ask?"

Why did he look so guarded? I stammered awkwardly, "W-When I stopped in La Ravelle looking for you, the policeman told me there'd been a rumor of him in Paris."

Dr. Ravanel looked towards the window. "You know Paul

was working as an attaché at the highest levels. He disappeared during the Armistice, then a few months ago was caught outside Paris." He looked at me. "The rumor is he killed a German guard to escape."

My mouth fell open as I shivered between relief that his son was safe and fear that he wouldn't be for long. "Killed a guard...?"

"Now the Nazis will never stop looking for him. We learned of his escape when they came to search our house in La Ravelle. They've searched our house here twice, as well. But Paul is too smart to hide anywhere so obvious." Pride filled his voice. He leaned forward. "But I need to know if they're close to finding him." He tilted his head. "Maybe you could help."

I goggled at him. "Me?"

"Helen would skin me alive if she knew I was asking," he muttered, clawing back his hair. "But I'm afraid for my son. And you're living in the man's house, working as his secretary. You could be so useful to us." He looked at me pleadingly. "Is my son in danger or safe? Are the Germans close to tracking him down?"

Shocked, I stared at him. "How would I find out?"

"Carefully, discreetly," he said desperately. "Without Schröder even realizing you were asking..."

A shiver went down my back. Excitement? Fear? What he was asking was dangerous. It would mean espionage, just as the Nazis were starting to twist their iron grip around the helpless French populace.

But I hated the Germans. I loved my father. And Paul Ravanel, whom I'd never met, was my older half-brother.

Though how would I manage? Subtlety had never been my strongest suit. The truth was, I was as bad at lying as my sister, though in a different way. And for different reasons. Lucie always strove to be virtuous because she had an angelic soul. I had a difficult time lying because I tended to blurt out every irritating truth, whatever the consequences.

I'd only kept one secret in my life, and it was because I was scared. Scared Lucie would be broken-hearted when she learned we weren't really sisters. Scared that Dr. Ravanel would reject me as his daughter. Scared I'd lose the only family I had left. Even Roger didn't know. Roger had seen me at my worst, and yet I was afraid to tell him about my father. Why?

"I'm sorry." Dr. Ravanel's dark eyes faded. "I have no right to ask. Forget I said anything."

I bit my lip uncertainly, my hands tightening. "I'd like to try..."

"No." He forced a smile. "Forget it. I mean it. Now, what were we talking about?"

Nervously, I tried to formulate the right words to gently lead the subject to Helen and long ago. *If you want good news about a child being found... do you remember your favorite nurse you traveled with all those years ago? I'm the product of your one-night affair.*

"Dr. Ravanel." A nurse suddenly appeared at the waiting-room door. He held up his finger for her to wait, pulled a note-book from his white coat pocket, scribbled in swift strokes, then handed the page to me. "Our address in Belleville, in case you need anything. Or did you need something now?" He looked at me searchingly. "Did you seek me out today for some special reason, Margot? Or just to tell us you're all in Paris?"

I stared at him for a heart-stopping minute, trying to find the words. Then I heard my own voice mumble, "Just... just to tell you."

"Well, I'm glad to know." He sighed again. "Glad but also not glad. You would all have been safer in Marseille." He glanced back at the nurse, who was now waving frantically. "I must get back to my patients. But it's good to see you, Margot. Give our love to your sister and Josette."

Numbly, I watched him go. *Stop him. Tell him.* But how could I blurt it out? Yell across the waiting room filled with people who were watching, listening? *Dr. Ravanel, I'm your illegitimate daughter. Isn't that a laugh?*

"Oh. Margot. One last thing." My father turned at the door and beamed back at me. "You're all invited for Christmas. You'll come, won't you?"

19

MARGOT

I couldn't be late. I'd promised Otto Schröder I'd be back by noon, and as my father had reminded me, he wasn't a man to be rude to.

But I was so distracted, I somehow got off at the wrong Métro stop and had to double back. I arrived home with no time to find something more secretarial to wear. I was hungry, cranky and mad at myself. Luckily, I found that Berthe had just made a pot of coffee. Good old Berthe.

"Thank you," I breathed.

"Not for you." She slapped my hand aside. "It's for Herr Schröder and his men." She set the carafe on a tray beside four china cups, a small container of cream and a bowl of small lumps of white sugar. "Take that to the study."

So far the morning wasn't going at all like I'd hoped, and I had no one to blame but myself. I should have kept my mouth shut when I'd wandered into Herr Schröder's study and seen that silly propaganda poster. And I should have told my father everything that morning. But as usual, I'd blabbed my mouth off when I should have remained silent, and vice versa. When would I learn?

I found Herr Schröder and two of his intelligence attachés standing around his large desk, arguing over the newest iteration of his campaign, which included scripts for French radio dramas of women bravely lifting their husbands' spirits with well-kept homes and well-kept children, as well as article ideas for Paris newspapers that would laud French housewives who gloried in their domestic sphere, as apparently German matrons did.

Several young officers, all with the skull insignia on their uniforms, were leaving the study as I approached, bidding farewell with that wretched "Heil Hitler" salute which always seemed to me like a ritualized group seizure. Impressively, I managed to refrain from telling them so.

One of the young officers, a pale, chubby man with hard eyes beneath wire-rimmed glasses, stared at me insolently as he passed. Lowering my gaze, I felt my cheeks burn. I was relieved when they left the house.

"*Endlich*," Herr Schröder said when he saw me standing in the study doorway. He beckoned me impatiently inside, pointing at a script on his desk. "Read that."

I placed the coffee tray on a side table. Herr Schröder waited as I read the pages. I read quickly, barely squelching a laugh.

"You find it amusing?" Herr Schröder purred.

Looking up, I felt a twist of fear. "No, I..."

But he was smiling. "It's quite all right. I hired you for your honesty. Pleasant lies are useless to me."

I bit my lip. "Well," I said slowly, looking back at the pages, "in the script, the happy Parisienne is baking a pie for her husband and children."

"So?"

"Where is she to have gotten the ingredients for her pie? Are you encouraging grocery purchases on the black market?"

"Of course not—that is illegal."

As our eyes met, his lips curved. We both knew that he himself made use of black marketeers, without apology. I smiled a little, then fiddled nervously with the script.

"Also, how is it possible her husband is even home, providing funds to pay for these magical pie ingredients? Unless he's old enough to be her grandfather, he's likely in Germany, not sending money home, and certainly not sitting beside the fire with his pipe, discussing how comfortable Paris has become thanks to German values and efficiency." I clutched the offending pages. "I'm sure there are many women who wish desperately they could bake a pie for their husbands but cannot. Why remind them? Why taunt them?"

"I see your point."

I knew I should keep quiet, and yet I couldn't. "How can you push women to raise large families and not work outside the home when, without their men, there's no way to get pregnant and no way to support a baby even if they did? And besides, if they stay home, who will keep Paris bakeries and factories and buses running, when the only French males remaining in the city are children, or else so elderly they can barely lift a *boule* in *pétanque*?"

I panted, caught in the certainty and justice of my opinion.

"Elderly? You mean fifty?" Herr Schröder said with amusement.

It occurred to me that he himself was probably somewhere around that age. My cheeks went red. "Um..."

He handed me a different paper. "What about this, *Fräulein?*"

Nervously, I scanned a list of proposed newspaper articles. A glowing story about a woman single-handedly raising her seventeen (!) children. Ideas for co-opting all the "unused space" in our cathedrals to worship the Führer in place of the Almighty. Instructions for how to denounce neighbors who spoke badly of Germany.

He waited. "Well?"

Shut up! I yelled at myself. *For once in your life!*

I shook my head, handing back the paper. "I'm just a girl—I don't know anything. But these, uh, articles seem fine. Definitely."

Herr Schröder looked at me from beneath heavily lidded eyes. I could tell he knew I was holding back, maybe because I was biting my lip hard enough to draw blood.

He crumpled the paper in his hands and tossed it in the trash bin. "Thank you, *Fräulein*." He turned and saw the coffee tray for the first time. "Ah. For that as well."

"Berthe made it. I was kept late at the doctor's." A sudden thought occurred to me. Dangerous, but when had I ever let that stop me?

As I poured him a cup of coffee, I said, "Herr Schröder, I wonder..."

"What is it? Ah, no." He held up his hand as I motioned towards the cream and sugar. "Growing up, cream and sugar were often unavailable. So I learned to take it black."

I handed him the cup in the saucer. I knew it wasn't safe to reveal my connection to the Ravanels. So I tried to think of some sideways approach. "Your attachés seem very devoted to you..."

He took a sip and sighed in pleasure, then grimaced. "Yes, I suppose. For all their foolish ideas. Becker is the one who wrote the script."

"But still. They are devoted." I carefully organized the coffee tray. "Any leader needs such men to support him and carry out his orders. Even de Gaulle, I suppose..."

"De Gaulle." His face wrinkled in disgust. "The man was nothing, just the most minor French official until he fled. His only skill, if you can call it that, is ingratiating himself to Churchill."

"Did many of his men escape, too?" I held my breath as I adjusted the lid of the silver carafe, not daring to look up.

"A few." He took another reckless gulp of hot coffee. "And some military men have gone to support him. Muselier. Larminat. Nobodies. The rest of the French government surrendered. Anyone who tried to defy us is in prison or dead."

"All of them?" I asked innocently.

His eyes darkened to slate, the angry color of clouds before a storm. "There was one young attaché. We caught him outside Paris in September, but he killed a guard to escape. Monstrous. I feel badly for that dead soldier's family." He ground his teeth into a smile. "But don't worry. We'll find this Ravanel. We're watching all the ports, north and south. He'll never have a chance to join de Gaulle."

"Ah. Good." I kept my placid smile, though my back was slick with sweat. Herr Schröder must never learn Paul Ravanel and I had the same father. Just as he could never learn Helen Taylor was my mother.

Fear tightened its icy claws around my throat. Every moment I shared with such an enemy, every word I spoke, was a threat to me. Herr Schröder was older, cleverer and far more dangerous. If I had any sense, I would run as far away from him as I could.

But we couldn't leave St. Agnes's now, not with three orphans in Lucie's care. And I couldn't leave Lucie in his clutches, alone. There was no hope of escape. Nowhere to hide.

Unless... unless Herr Schröder himself chose to leave St. Agnes's.

"Delicious." He sipped from the delicate china. He had an artist's hands, I noticed—long, expressive fingers. "Berthe is a treasure."

I looked at him boldly. "Is that why you're staying here, sir? And not billeted with the other officers? Because of Berthe?"

He shrugged. "Among other reasons."

My heart was pounding. If I could convince him to leave, we could all be safe. Or at least safer. "Wouldn't you be more comfortable at the Hôtel Raphael, getting room service in luxury in the heart of Paris? Rather than being stuck out in the Marais, with babies crying and Choupette barking, climbing through our maze of rooms and rickety stairs." I carefully didn't look at his cane. "All the lovely new paint and furniture doesn't change how inconvenient this place must be for you."

"I suppose it is." Still holding the coffee in one hand, he walked a few unsteady steps across the study to sit down at the large leather chair beside the fireplace. He stared out the front window. "I'm here for revenge."

I was surprised at his honesty. "On Helen Taylor?"

He gave a crooked grin, his gray eyes crinkling under his peaked cap. "Though it sounds ridiculous to say it aloud. Revenge on a woman who will never know about it, now she's fled across the ocean."

"For that?" I let my gaze fall on his stiff leg.

His cheeks reddened a little. "It's strange to talk of it. My men pretend my limp does not exist." He looked back at the window, then sighed. "It's not just my leg. She stole my family."

"Your wife? But Helen said you—" I stopped myself.

His eyes sharpened. "She claimed I beat Flora, didn't she?" His jaw tightened. "My wife lied. She wanted to return to her lover in Scotland. So she brought an assassin into our home."

Assassin. The room went silent with the weight of the word. It was startling to hear him refer to my mother that way. The stern, bland, prim headmistress I'd known most my life—an assassin?

"Flora didn't like my long hours away, working all day, then attending political meetings at night. But the Führer and I, we'd been friends since we were boys in Vienna. We were both rejected by the Academy of Fine Arts." His lips quirked. "We decided to be artists anyway, and for many years we both starved. I finally left for an advertising job in Munich. He followed when he came into some money. We both were angry at how the political system failed ordinary Germans. We were arrested for our attempt to reorder things in 1923."

I'd read about the Beer Hall Putsch, when the newly created Nazi party had first attempted a coup d'état against the German government. "That must have been interesting."

He snorted, looking at me sideways. "My wife had just asked for a divorce. I'd refused. I'd made a vow to love her for the rest of my life. I was perhaps a little out of my mind." He looked towards the crackling fire. "But why was I working day and night, if not for my family? To provide them with a better life? To give my country a better future?"

"I'm sure you did your best."

He shook his head. "Things were bad in Germany then. Austria, too. Our people struggled with poverty and shame while corrupt leaders prospered. What kind of man could see this and do nothing?"

I thought of what Josette had told us about Madame Hébert, and how she'd hated the French government before realizing the Nazis were even worse. "Lots of them."

Herr Schröder snorted, then leaned back in his leather chair and took a sip of coffee. "Flora yearned to return to Scotland, her own home country. When I wouldn't let her go, she did the unthinkable." He took a breath, closing his eyes. "She told me our four-year-old daughter wasn't even mine."

My eyes went wide. I'd never heard that part. I sank down in a nearby chair. "What did you do?"

"I was upset. I slapped her—I admit it. But"—he looked up, his gray eyes glittering—"after the coup in Munich failed, I was sent to prison with the Führer and others. When we were released from prison early, I came home just in time to see Flora leaving our home with our child. When I tried to prevent them going, her friend shot me. For loving my wife and child and trying to keep our family together, I was shot, humiliated, crippled. And I never saw my daughter again."

"Never?"

He shook his head, grief lining his handsome face. "And I still don't know if she was mine or if that was another of Flora's lies. Now I'll never know. My daughter no doubt grew up believing I abandoned her. That I was some kind of monster."

Sunlight fell through the window, tracing a pattern on the herringbone floor. It was the same story I'd heard from Helen but slanted in a totally different way. I wondered how much was true.

His hands tightened. "I heard Flora lived in sin with her lover for years. She finally married him after Scottish law allowed her to divorce me for cruelty and my so-called criminal convictions. My adulterous, lying wife stole my peace, my happiness and my child—and was rewarded." His Adam's apple moved as he swallowed, whispering, "But even now, I cannot blame her entirely. No." He looked up at me. "I blame her cold-hearted friend who made it all possible, with her viciousness and modern thinking on divorce. Who came into my home with a gun."

"I'm sorry," I said and meant it. However much of his story was true, it was clear he believed he was the injured victim, not a villain. I felt bad for him, as well as the wife. And my mother, who'd simply gone to Germany to help an old friend escape an abusive marriage. Three different stories. Where was the truth?

Assassin. I remembered the obsequiousness of the man at the American consulate in Marseille last June when he'd learned my mother's name. It had seemed strange even then.

What exactly had she been up to, after she'd abandoned me as a newborn with farmers in Meaux?

"So this is my revenge, inadequate as it is." Herr Schröder gave me a calm smile, indicating the large study. "Helen Taylor took my family, my home." He looked at me. "So I'm taking hers."

I stared sharply at the word *family*. But his expression was bland. I exhaled, relaxing back in my own chair—as much as I could, since it was new, in Art Deco style, and made of hard wood—and returned his smile.

"A strange sort of revenge," I observed, "taking care of us all, allowing the orphanage's mission to continue."

He shook his head. "I'm sure she told you I was a monster. But I'm not. And I'm proving her wrong every day." He picked up his coffee cup, then made a face and set it back down. It was empty. "Even if she's no longer in Paris, the world can see it. So can I."

I rose to my feet and refilled his cup.

He touched my hand. "Thank you."

"It's nothing." I returned the carafe to the tray. That at least explained his courteous behavior. He didn't want to see himself as evil but as a good, decent man who'd been hard done by. He was a romantic.

As much as any hideous Nazi could ever be romantic, that is—laced with an edge of cruelty.

"But that's in the past. Let's talk about the present." He tilted his head. "I ran the largest advertising agency in Munich. For the last decade, wherever we ran a government propaganda campaign across Bavaria, we saw marriage rates increase by an average rate of three points, and the childbirth rate by five."

My jaw dropped. "Advertising can actually change people's behavior?"

"The right words change everything." He grinned, quirking a dark eyebrow. "I'd love to take all the credit, but it's also Germany's new prosperity, new purpose," he said softly. He looked away. "I promote family because I believe in it. Love is the only route to happiness."

I stared in shock at the incongruity of a middle-aged

German officer in full uniform speaking earnestly about love and family. Could he not hear how ludicrous he sounded?

But there was something deeply emotional about it, too. Something that made me sad.

"So, *Fräulein*, I appreciate your help." Leaning on his cane, he rose stiffly to his feet. "Not just for dictation and typing and shorthand." He looked at me. "I need you to translate the French woman for us."

"B-But I'm very ordinary, nothing special..."

"You speak German, you understand the French, and you're not afraid to challenge me when you think I'm getting it wrong. That already makes you rare." He gave a brief smile. "You will accompany me to the Hôtel Majestic and take notes."

The Hôtel Majestic was Nazi headquarters. A cold trickle went down my back. "Are you sure?"

"But not dressed like that." He looked over my slightly tattered striped shirt, my cigarette pants, my serviceable little boots. "I'll have my secretary at headquarters order you something more appropriate to wear. Unless you'd prefer to select it yourself? I can get you carte blanche at the Galeries Lafayette, or perhaps Schiaparelli..."

This was bad. He said he wanted my help. So why did I feel like he was buying me wholesale, down to the clothes on my back?

And the worst of it was what he'd told me about his wife. From the limited things I knew about men, they rarely showed vulnerability or weakness. In spite of Roger believing himself to be madly in love with me, he'd told me almost nothing about his past. Learning secrets was a double-edged sword. It could bring two people closer—or make the one who felt suddenly vulnerable seek to punish and silence the one who knew too much...

I bit my lip, suddenly wishing I was scrubbing toilets after all.

"You're very kind," I managed. "I'm not convinced I'll be useful to you..."

He gave a thin smile. "You will. Trust me."

"If you think so, Herr Schröder."

"I do," he said firmly. He limped back to sit across from me at the desk, stroked his cheek, then pushed a paper and pen towards me. "And when we're alone, you may call me Otto."

Fear fluttered inside my belly. Increasing our familiarity was the last thing I wanted to do, but what choice did I have? "All right. Otto."

"Thank you, Margot." He smiled, then pointed at the paper. "Jot this down. It should be every Frenchwoman's right to have the home and family she wants, without any economic forces preventing her..."

I scribbled the shorthand symbols rapidly. But I was barely paying attention.

I'm sure she told you I was a monster. But I'm not.

No. I wouldn't feel sorry for him. *Wouldn't.* He might be playacting as our father, but I knew he wasn't.

Besides, I already had one. And if I hadn't been so cautious and scared, Dr. Ravanel might already have embraced me as his daughter.

Or he could have rejected me utterly.

As Otto kept talking, I kept mechanically taking notes, trying to convince myself to be brave, dreaming about what could happen on Christmas Day. When I told Dr. Ravanel what I'd learned about his son.

And this time, nothing, absolutely nothing, would stop me from also telling him about his daughter.

20

JOSETTE

Joy lifted my heart as I clutched at my coat against the cold wind, hurrying down the street towards the theater. Each morning, I could hardly wait to leave the Nazis and noise behind, along with the dreary gray winter, and return to a beautiful world of warmth and color and belonging. It felt like coming home.

No. It felt like a glorious dream.

The Théâtre Lutèce, called after the Roman name for Paris, had eight hundred cushioned seats, including the elegant stacked balconies, beneath the mural on the ceiling, bright like the sky, with specks of gold leaf for stars. The theater, the smallest of the trio built by Baron Haussmann on the Place du Châtelet the previous century, overlooked the Fontaine de la Victoire on one side and the river on the other. Across the Seine, you could almost see the ruins of the Arènes de Lutèce, the old gladiator arenas where once men had fought to the death, Christians were eaten by lions and other thrillingly awful things.

The Théâtre Lutèce was just as exhilarating, only without quite so much death. All the danger was pretend, on stage.

Or so I'd thought.

That first morning, Madame Hébert had barely walked me in before she was enveloped by admiring employees, who'd been rehearsing something on stage. She seemed an utterly different person than the crotchety neighbor who'd been the bane of all orphans at St. Agnes's.

She'd smiled at the cast and crew, gorgeously outré in her glamorous cape and turban with the peacock feather, her jewels and dazzling walking stick, and her dyed black hair and red lipstick against powdered skin. And in that moment, all I could think about was that if Séverine was playing a role, it was one I now dreamed of playing, too: a woman who lived on her own terms, with her own people, who clearly respected and adored her.

My closest comparison was Sister Helen, who'd been respected and perhaps even loved, but also dowdy and stern, always scrambling to come up with enough money and time to raise twenty orphans with few benefactors and no government support.

Nor could I look to memories of my own mother to mentor me. From what little I knew, her family, once refugees from the Great War, had left her in Paris when they'd returned to Poland. They'd believed that Rivka, with her live-in position as a maid for the aristocratic Albret family, was secure, with opportunities for advancement.

It hadn't worked out that way.

"And who's this?" a plump middle-aged woman had asked at the theater, looking at me behind Madame Hébert.

"Josette Dubois," the widow had replied. "Find her something to do."

A pretty blonde girl had looked me over from the stage with some apprehension. "Are you an actress?"

I'd taken a deep breath, knowing this was my big chance. The desire to be loved by audiences had filled my brain ever since Roger first casually suggested it last year. I yearned to be someone who mattered, someone who was wanted and loved. It was how Sister Helen had nearly convinced me to move to America, by promising I could live near Hollywood.

But looking at the beautiful actresses on stage—who were far more beautiful than I could ever be, even with all the makeup in the world—my throat had closed.

You know you're pretty enough to be a movie star, Roger had said admiringly when we met. But those long-cherished compliments were overshadowed by his harsh words earlier that day: *I don't love you. I never will.*

Suddenly, the thought of trying to be an actress, trying and failing, or trying and briefly succeeding before failing, trying and never feeling good enough—had sent a wave of despair through me. I couldn't stomach more rejection, more failure, more heartbreak. I'd looked at the circle of faces around me in the theater, six actors and perhaps another ten who were in the crew, all older than me, then glanced at Madame Hébert. She'd given me a tranquil smile and waited.

"I can sew," I'd blurted out.

The actresses had seemed relieved. But I'd been shocked. Where had that come from?

It was true that for years I'd made my own clothes on St. Agnes's old sewing machine, and clothes for the other orphans too, before the machine had been sold. It was satisfying to be able to duplicate any outfit I wanted from a magazine, with or without a pattern. But I'd never thought of it as a potential career.

A woman about ten years older had stepped forward, her expression skeptical. "Look here, *mon amie*, I know every teenager is enamored of the theater, but it requires more skill than just being able to sew a few stitches when there's a hole in your sock..."

"I made this." I'd indicated my green jersey dress, which

clung to my curves, cut on the bias. "I recycled fabric from an oversized smock, took it all apart and created a pattern to duplicate a dress I saw Arletty wear in *Plaisir de France*."

They had all looked at me differently then, as if seeing me for the first time. The woman who'd spoken had come closer and looked at the seam in the dress's shoulder. "You did this? From a smock?"

"In just two hours, start to finish." I'd tried to keep my voice modest. Failed.

The woman had clapped her hands. "Séverine, it's a Christmas miracle—you are an angel."

Madame Hébert had folded her arms and lifted a penciled eyebrow as if she'd known all along this would happen. "I know," she'd said smugly.

"And just in time, too. I've been so worried about this next play..." The woman had turned to me with a smile. "I'm Judith." She'd thrown her arms around me in an extravagant, almost theatrical embrace. "Josette Dubois, welcome to the Théâtre Lutèce."

I'd been working there almost a week now, and I loved it, going to this beautiful building to work with new friends. I didn't have to pretend to be glamorous or try to make anyone think I was beautiful or even convince them to like me. Instead, I got to create clothes with my own hands. And in every costume, I didn't just create a new person—I created a new world.

Sewing came easier than love. My stitches never unraveled, or betrayed me, or told me I was no good. Or if they did fall apart, they could easily be replaced. After all, it was only thread.

At breakfast this morning, Christmas Eve day, Berthe and the girls had sung to me over homemade vanilla cake. Then I'd unwrapped the gift of a small gold-toned wristwatch left by Herr Schröder, to match Lucie's, which left me at a loss because

I hated to owe him anything. It was bad enough he expected me to spy on my fellow crewmates; I didn't want to feel like he owned me. Berthe had given me homemade lavender soap, Fauve a drawing of a flower. Then I'd gasped at the present from Lucie and Margot: new stockings.

"Count it as your Christmas gift as well," Margot said a little sourly, and I wondered how Lucie had talked her into it.

On top of my joyful anticipation of going to the theater, it all made me feel so warm inside, I hadn't even minded walking forty minutes after I discovered the Métro wasn't working again.

Finally, I was eighteen like Margot, giving her one less thing to lord over me. The previous headmistress had chosen my arrival day at St. Agnes's as my birthdate because no one knew exactly. But legally, I was eighteen.

The same age my mother had been when she'd had me.

The thought made me stop dead on the sidewalk, causing people to nearly run into me. After walking around me, two soldiers leered back, their eyes roaming my face and figure. But for once, I didn't care.

For the first time, I really thought about my young mother. How she must have felt to be alone, Jewish, penniless and pregnant in Paris in 1922, when the world was even less forgiving of such things.

Growing up, I'd always been focused on my own hurt, feeling like there was something profoundly wrong with me, that I'd been abandoned as a newborn, left at the door of St. Agnes's like trash. But now, a new thought pierced my heart: Rivka had been my age. Would I have done any better in her place? Pregnant with no money, no husband, and no job?

She'd been terrified to face her family back in Poland with a nameless baby. We'd learned that much from the housekeeper who'd supported her until my birth, then given her her train fare home. My mother had known her baby had no good future, either in Poland or in France, as the illegitimate child of a penniless maid.

Tell the girl her mother loved her, the housekeeper had gasped on her deathbed to Sister Helen. *She gave her away as an act of love.*

For all these months, I hadn't let myself think about it; couldn't let myself believe it. But now, at eighteen, I had new compassion for the mother who'd abandoned me. Maybe she hadn't hated me. Was it possible there was nothing inherently wrong with me? That she'd just been alone and scared and done the best she could?

She'd left me at St. Agnes's, where I'd learned and grown. It had made me who I was today.

An assistant costumer for the Théâtre Lutèce.

My shoulders squared proudly. As I walked the rest of the way to the theater, I gave a silent prayer for my poor mother, wherever she was. I hoped she was safe in Poland. Or better yet, that she was safe in a country that didn't persecute Jews. Wherever that place might be.

"Josette! Happy birthday!"

I nearly cried when I arrived at the theater to discover another impromptu party, this one arranged by Judith, the head costumer. There wasn't any vanilla cake, as butter, sugar, flour and vanilla were impossible to come by, but the cast and crew had made little cards for me on the backs of used programs, and Judith brought me an orange, hard to find and precious.

"You, my darling," she told me, smiling brightly as she patted my cheek, "are the best thing to happen to this theater in years. The best thing to happen to *me*."

We spent the day sewing together. I was in awe of her costume design, her knowledge of history, her attention to detail. Backstage could be cold, as Madame Hébert saved the radiators for paying customers, so I kept my coat on and borrowed a pair of Judith's gloves, which had their fingertips cut off. But my heart was warm. We got on very well.

The hours flew by, and when most everyone left early, as it was Christmas Eve, I didn't want to go. Even as night approached, I remained, stitching by the small light, my back aching, my eyes growing strained.

"Enough," Judith said kindly, rising to her feet. "It's Christmas Eve. Go home."

"But it's not curfew yet. I could—"

"Go." Her voice was firm. "Have a merry Christmas, already."

"Thanks, Judith." I stood and stretched, then straightened. "And happy Hanukkah. Doesn't that start today?"

She looked astonished I'd wish her a happy holiday in her own faith. Then she smiled. "Thanks, kid. Now get out of here."

After giving back the borrowed gloves, I left, traipsing through the auditorium, which was empty and dark. But I'd barely made it to the door before I realized that I'd never thanked her for my lovely birthday party. Ashamed, I turned back.

But the costume room was now empty. Every room backstage seemed dark, almost haunted. Though I'd seen Judith just moments before, and Madame Hébert and a few of the crew some ten minutes ago, they'd all just disappeared. I shivered.

Then I heard a muffled noise.

Frowning, I followed the sound and found a door that was always locked. I'd never paid much attention, vaguely assuming it was a closet or perhaps a second electrical panel, keeping our rickety electricity going with prayers and glue. But this time the door was open.

Peering inside, I saw steps leading into the bowels of a dark basement, then, further down, shadowy old props and painted canvas backdrops that seemed decades old, maybe even before the turn of the century. I was just turning to leave when I heard low, muffled voices. Was Judith down there with the others, perhaps sorting through old props for the next show?

I looked down the stairs doubtfully. It looked cold and dark, almost... menacing. I didn't want to go there. Then I heard her voice and sighed. I couldn't leave without telling Judith how much her thoughtfulness had meant to me.

But still, my knees shook a little as I went down the rickety steps.

The voices were coming from behind one of the backdrops. But where exactly?

Creeping carefully through the darkness, over the cracked floor, I found an almost invisible door, nearly closed, with pale light shining through the crack. I pushed it open.

Four people were hovering over a desk beneath the dim light of a single swaying bulb. Madame Hébert, Judith and two older members of the crew whose names I couldn't remember. They looked at me with an intake of breath, horrified.

"Judith, there you—" I frowned, drawing closer. "What is that?"

"Nothing." They all instinctively stepped in front of whatever was on the desk to hide it.

"Get out of here, girl," snapped Madame Hébert.

"Please, go home," said Judith.

"What are you looking at?"

Coming closer, I saw a small, heavy-looking mechanical contraption, matte black metal, with a mechanical crank, with circles and wheels. Mesmerized, I reached out a hand, then froze, remembering La Belle aux Bois Dormant pricking her finger on that spinning wheel and falling asleep for a hundred years.

Hesitating, I looked up. "It looks like... some kind of torture device."

"Nothing of the sort," the middle-aged man harrumphed. "It's just—"

"Albert," the older woman warned.

"It's an old printing press," Madame Hébert told me flatly.

There was a gasp around the desk.

"Someone left the door unlocked." She lifted her eyebrow at Judith, who blushed. "And the girl caught us. There's no point in lying." She turned to me. "Twenty years ago, the theater used the press to make programs. Now... we're using it for something else."

I gaped at the four of them. At their secrecy, waiting for everyone else to leave on Christmas Eve. Then I saw the page still tucked inside the plate, with a black-and-white photo. "Is that...?"

Judith stepped in front of it and put her hand on my shoulder. "You don't want to know more, Josette," she said quietly. "Leave now, and for the sake of *le bon Dieu*, forget you saw anything."

But it was too late. I looked up at her.

"You're forging identity cards," I breathed aloud.

Judith looked at Madame Hébert, who gave a grim smile.

"More than that, my girl. We're helping Jews get out of Paris. They need travel documents to get past the demarcation line and, if they're lucky, to Marseille."

I thought suddenly of my poor mother—perhaps trapped in Poland, perhaps dead, murdered by Germans—and stared at them, my heart pounding. "I want to help."

"*Non,* Josette," Judith said, scandalized. "It's too dangerous. Séverine, tell her!"

"You'd risk your life," the widow said frankly.

I drew myself up. "I'm not afraid of the Germans." In that moment, I almost believed it.

Madame Hébert considered me, raising one painted eyebrow. "What use could you be to us?"

"You're just a kid," the elderly woman who cleaned the floors interrupted, staring at me sourly.

I thought fast.

"You need official Nazi signatures, don't you?"

They looked at each other.

"We're getting by," the middle-aged man said.

I thought of what I'd seen in the study. "I could get you Herr Schröder's rubber stamp."

A gasp. "Otto Schröder?"

"His signature is uncontestable," I pointed out. "Think of what you could do with it!"

"Oh heavens," Judith breathed. She looked at the other two, then they all looked at their employer.

Madame Hébert tossed back her turbaned head and lifted her arm in a dramatic movement, looking every bit the chorus ingénue she'd once been on stage.

"On your head be it, Josette Dubois," she intoned. Her shoulders relaxed as her red lips lifted in a wicked grin. "Welcome to the *real* Théâtre Lutèce."

21

LUCIE

Christmas morning dawned clear and bright. I was woken, as always, by a baby. It was better than any alarm clock.

I sat up in bed bleary-eyed. Last night, after we'd served Herr Schröder his Christmas Eve dinner, and opened a few small gifts to each other, we'd all dutifully attended Midnight Mass. Margot, Josette and Berthe had gone to see other French faces, rather than for the sake of any great religious devotion. But looking around the cathedral, my soul had felt comforted and strengthened. As I'd sat in the crowded pews and listened—in between calming the children when they fussed—to the pure voices of the boys' choir praising the birth of the Christ child, I'd looked up at the soaring stained glass and thought, *What more can I do? How can I make it magical for them?*

Then I'd gasped.

Now, as I rose from bed at dawn, my gaze fell on the small, fresh Christmas tree I'd set up long after midnight, decorating it stealthily with the orphanage's old electric lights after everyone was asleep.

"Oh, can't they sleep late for once?" Margot moaned,

covering her head with a pillow. Then she pulled it away, staring, astonished, at the little tree. "Where did that come from?"

"A tree!" Little Fauve bounded out of bed, her eyes dazzled. She looked at us in wonder. "Who brought it? Was it Père Noël?"

"*Père Noël*," Margot snorted, then caught my glare. Clearing her throat, she told the girl. "Who else?"

"Yes, who?" echoed Josette, smiling as she sat up in bed.

Both of them turned to me, their eyes glowing, and in that moment, all my exhaustion was worth it. As long as I didn't think about *how* I'd obtained that tree.

I moved to the crib, lifted out a whimpering Thérèse and nestled her close. She was wet—no wonder. As I changed her diaper, the dirty cloth reminded me about all the laundry piling up, too. She continued to fuss. Probably hungry, poor thing. Geneviève, I was grateful to see, was somehow sleeping through it all.

Fauve looked out the dormer window. "Oh." She turned back, crestfallen. "No snow."

"That's good, *ma petite*," Margot said, yawning and stretching her arms as she stood up, her wrists poking out from the too-short sleeves of her flannel nightgown. "We need to travel across the city this afternoon for our dinner at the Ravanels'. Snow would slow us down."

At the little girl's furrowed brow, she reached out and hugged her skinny body close. "Don't worry. They specifically said to bring you."

"They did?" Fauve's timid face lit up. "They asked for me?"

"Of course," Josette said, smiling, though I saw dark circles under her eyes. "The Ravanels are our friends, which means they're your friends, too. Anyone would love you, Fauve."

The little girl's face looked so happy, it was enough to break a person's heart.

As Thérèse's fussing became a loud whine, I turned away. "I'll go feed her downstairs. You'll watch Geneviève?"

I didn't wait for an answer.

Downstairs, the house was still quiet. Even Berthe was sleeping. I made the baby her bottle, then fed her in the dark kitchen, relishing the quiet. After she'd greedily sucked down her milk, I put her against my shoulder to burp her, pacing up and down the hall, all the way to the lavish, expensively decorated tree in the parlor, which Herr Schröder had paid handsomely to have delivered, with all the sparkling new ornaments and lights. Children weren't allowed in the parlor. Fauve had been so disappointed. Then I'd had the idea to give the girls a tree just for them. For us.

I jumped a little when I heard the muffled sound of the doorbell from the front of the house. Frowning, I turned around in the hallway, shadowed by the lights of the tree in the parlor. Who would come calling at this hour? On this day?

It rang again. Herr Schröder was likely still sleeping upstairs in his bedroom, once our music room, and Berthe still hadn't stirred yet. There was no one but me to answer.

Still holding the baby, I gingerly opened the door a crack. "Yes?"

A young German soldier stood awkwardly on the steps. "*Bonjour, mademoiselle,*" he began. "*Je suis... uh... J'ai...*"

He spoke French like he had a mouthful of marbles, but I gave him credit for trying. "Can I help you?" I said in German.

Relief flooded his handsome face. He was blond, perhaps only a few years older than I was, broad-shouldered, with kind eyes. "Good morning—that is to say, merry Christmas, *Fräulein.*" His gaze shifted. "And you too, Baby."

"Merry Christmas," I responded, smiling.

He cleared his throat. "I've come to spend Christmas with my uncle." He shifted awkwardly. "I'm early."

"Come in." Now that I thought of it, perhaps Herr Schröder had mentioned something.

I held open the door, and he entered, taking off his cap.

"He's still sleeping. Shall I wake him?"

"No." His expression turned alarmed. "Don't disturb him."

Paris was generally a post prized by German soldiers, but from his tight jaw and darting gaze, I got the impression the young man wasn't happy to be here—not in this city and not in this house. "All right."

He took off his overcoat, clutching it and his officer's cap with the tips of his fingers. "Where shall I put these?"

I held out my free hand. "I can take them—"

"Oh no, *Fräulein*." He seemed scandalized. "I wouldn't expect you to do it for me." His gaze rested on the baby in my arms. "You have your hands full."

Surprised at his courtesy, I pointed at the corner. "Over there, then."

He hung up his overcoat and cap a little haphazardly on the coat rack, treating the Nazi cap as something he couldn't wait to be rid of rather than reverently, like the other officers did. "Is there somewhere I can wait?" He gave me a crooked smile. "Perhaps a little coffee?"

"I can make you some..."

"Just point me in the right direction, *Fräulein*, and I'll make it myself." He added with grim amusement, "I'm good for that much, at least."

"Follow me," I said, a little bewildered. Make his own coffee? Though the other German officers had been polite, they'd all still expected us girls to take care of them. Herr Schröder certainly didn't do his own washing-up or clean his own clothes, but then, at least he paid us.

I led the young man to the kitchen and pointed out the coffee pot, the cream, the sugar. His eyes lit up, and he smacked his lips. "Now that's a Christmas gift."

"The cream and sugar?"

"Not much of those in Austria at the moment." He gave me a slight bow. "Thank you, *Fräulein*. I'll be fine here until my uncle is awake."

But I saw a shadow pass over his face. Did he have some reason to dread seeing his uncle? Were they not a close family? I said tentatively, "Will you be staying for long?"

"I'm not sure." His gaze shifted as he fiddled with the coffee pot. "My uncle sent for me because... I said some unwise things. About the Reich."

My jaw dropped. I'd never heard any German hint at anything the Nazis might be wrong about. "Whatever did you say?"

"Things I would be foolish to repeat." He looked back at me with a sheepish smile, then sobered. "My uncle needs me to be rehabilitated. So he yanked me out of my regiment to work as his attaché. To make sure I won't cause any more trouble or shame."

For a moment, we looked at each other in the shadowy kitchen. Then he held out his hand. "I'm Klaus Schröder."

"L-Lucie Vashon," I stuttered.

We shook hands, and for a moment, I held my breath. His palm felt rough and warm against mine. It was strangely intimate.

Then my cheeks went hot as I recollected that I was standing in a dark kitchen with a stranger, wearing only my ratty flannel nightgown, holding a baby. I pulled away quickly. "If you'll excuse me."

Gallantly, he bowed again, this time with a polite, impersonal smile, our earlier sense of intimacy vanished. "Merry Christmas, *Fräulein*."

"Merry Christmas," I managed—and fled.

22

JOSETTE

After we'd served Herr Schröder and his new guest Christmas lunch, the rest of us tumbled joyfully out of the house to head to the Ravanels': babies, Fauve, Berthe, Josette, Lucie and even Choupette in a jaunty red bow, laughing and carrying home-made gifts and the remains of Herr Schröder's Christmas Eve dinner as a gift.

I was glad to leave the house. I couldn't look Herr Schröder in the face. I was scared if I did, he'd see plainly what I'd promised to do: steal the rubber stamp so we could forge his signature. It was dangerous, but it felt like the least I could do, hiding in the shadows, hiding my own Jewish heritage.

Margot paused to look back at the old orphanage from the end of the cobblestoned alley. "I'm so happy to be away."

"You and me both," I said devoutly.

"I feel bad for him," Lucie said.

We turned to gape at her.

"Don't be ridiculous," I said.

"Why would you?" said Margot.

"Not Herr Schröder. His nephew." She suddenly wouldn't

meet our eyes. "I talked to him when I let him in the house this morning. He seemed rather nice."

"*Nice?*" Margot said in disbelief. She and I looked at each other.

"I... I think he's different from the other Germans. And he's afraid of Herr Schröder, even though they're family. They were so silent over lunch. Then, afterward, did you hear it? The yelling? The threats?"

"We all heard it," Margot muttered.

Muffled through the study door, Herr Schröder had angrily shouted at his nephew, telling him that he was going to stop his defiance and behave as a proper member of their family. A moment later, I'd heard a hard sound like a slap. But so what? "The boy's a Nazi, Lucie. I guess he can handle himself. And his uncle."

She looked at me. "You're very cold."

I shrugged. "I have bigger things to worry about." That seemed like the understatement of the year. Sometime over the next week, I'd have to sneak into the study, steal the rubber stamp, and then, without it being missed, return it later that night. The thought was exhilarating. Terrifying.

Margot patted her hair, twisted into a *couronne* of dark braids crowning her head. "I'm glad the two of them have each other for company. While we escape to Christmas dinner with the Martins."

"The *Martins*," I snorted.

She returned my grin. She'd warned us repeatedly to keep the name of the Ravanels a secret, and instead she'd made up a fictitious family we were supposedly visiting today called the Martins.

"There are so many Martins in Paris, he'll never figure it out," she'd told us.

I supposed it made sense. It would have been dangerous for Herr Schröder to realize Jean-Luc Ravanel was her father, which would easily have led him to discover Helen Taylor was her mother. But I still thought it feeble she hadn't told Lucie yet. Lucie could keep a secret.

Probably.

"Come on, girls." Lucie quickened her pace, then started laughing as she had to untangle herself and Fauve from Choupette's leash, while the curly-haired dog darted about, sniffing everything. Ahead of us, Berthe pushed the stroller with the two babies, walking fast to show how tough she was, even at eighty. But occasionally, when she thought no one was looking, she leaned against the stroller while she took a breath. She'd seemed unexpectedly excited to go to the Ravanels. My steps slowed as I suddenly wondered if she'd invited Roger.

Catching my gaze, Berthe straightened. "Come on, *les filles*! No lagging!"

Sunlight filtered through the lacework of bare trees, and with us all bundled up in layers, the babies in extra blankets, no one complained about the December cold. We made a game with Fauve, telling her how the white smoke of our breath was from a fire-breathing dragon, as we hopped over the cobblestones.

It took our group nearly an hour to walk to Belleville, the working-class neighborhood on the edge of Paris where the famous singer Édith Piaf was born. But encumbered as we were with the stroller and a dog, we had no choice but to walk to the Ravanels', and had to stop twice for directions. The address wasn't far from the sprawling Père Lachaise Cemetery. We trooped cheerfully—until we saw it.

Pasted up on a stone wall was a large poster with stark black words, posted three times side by side. It announced the execution of a Frenchman, Jacques Bonsergent, by the Germans.

"But what has he done?" Lucie gasped, looking back at us.

"Nothing." Margot and I looked at each other. "Nothing at all."

Someone had slashed through the cold signature at the bottom, *Der Militärbefehlshaber in Frankreich*, with a blood-red pen. Candles had been left on the sidewalk beneath the posters, flames flickering in silent protest. Beside the candles, there were sprigs of honeysuckle—hard to come by in December. I stared at the slightly wilted blooms against the concrete.

"How can the Germans be so cruel?" Lucie whispered.

"The poor man did nothing." Berthe shook her head in disbelief. "I heard at the *pâtisserie* he was just a bystander. He witnessed someone else speaking rudely to a German soldier." She turned to us, her wrinkled face pale with horror. "And for that he's killed by firing squad?"

"I made a mistake," Lucie said suddenly, her face white as a ghost as she looked between me and Margot. "I should have made you two leave Paris. That first day."

Now? She was realizing this *now?* Fury bubbled up inside me. "A little late to—"

"We couldn't leave you," Margot cut me off. "And you couldn't leave them." Her eyes rested on Fauve, Berthe and the baby carriage ahead. She squared her shoulders. "I'm glad you made us stay. So we can fight to get the Germans out."

I looked at her, and some of the tension in my body eased. "You're right," I said quietly. "Whatever it takes."

For a moment, Margot and I looked at each other in surprise. It was strange to agree. But we did on this. Though I was actually doing something to fight the Germans. And she wasn't.

How I wished I could have said that aloud!

"But how can we fight?" Lucie blurted out. "We're not soldiers. What can we do?"

"What's wrong, Lucie?" Fauve, who could only read her name and a few simple words, tugged on her coat, staring at the wall of posters. "Why are you all so upset?"

"It's nothing, my darling. Nothing for you to worry about."

But after Lucie had wrapped her arm around the little girl and we started walking again, she looked back at the posters with troubled eyes.

For the rest of our walk, I saw Paris in a different light. Much had changed just in the months since we'd arrived. Lucie had described the German soldiers last summer as being courteous to the point of obsequiousness. But now, if we walked past soldiers, their eyes moved boldly over our bodies. The young Germans walked not just with pride but swagger. They punished anyone who defied or disrespected them—or even witnessed it, like that poor man, Bonsergent.

Some of our glumness melted away when we reached the Ravanels' house. The little stone cottage, small and careworn, was surrounded by a stone wall on both sides of the house, with a garden—a rarity in Paris. St. Agnes's was an anomaly, as it had been built on farmlands belonging to a convent, and later, the city had grown up around it. But in Belleville, it was even more unusual.

"Are you sure it's the right address?" Lucie asked, looking up.

"Are we here?" asked Berthe, huffing from our walk, her cheeks red. She gripped the handle of the baby carriage, where Thérèse and Geneviève slept peacefully.

"I guess we can't stand here all day wondering." Margot trooped up to the door and rang the bell.

A moment later, the door wrenched open, and a petite blonde woman appeared. She gasped with joy and clapped her hands. "Girls!"

"Madame R—uh, Martin!" Margot, Lucie and I flung ourselves into her arms.

She fell back, laughing. "*Martin?*"

I glanced at Fauve. "We'll explain later."

"Jean-Luc, Suzanne, hurry—they're here!"

We were welcomed joyfully into the Ravanels' tiny,

crowded cottage. We hadn't seen them since June, when we'd stayed briefly at their home in La Ravelle. They'd taken such good care of us then, when we'd been so desperate and afraid. Now, we were hugged, our simple gifts of Berthe's homemade jellies and Fauve's drawing of our dog exclaimed over.

"Just like Choupette!" Suzanne praised the girl, then turned to hug the dog as the animal licked the girl's face. She crooned, "Look at you! So chubby and clean!"

Even Berthe and Fauve, who hung back shyly at first, were hugged and welcomed warmly, and the babies were instantly in the arms of Élisabeth and her fifteen-year-old daughter. In the months since we'd seen them, Suzanne had grown and now looked startlingly similar to Margot. I wondered how no one else saw it.

"We also brought this." Blushing, Margot held out the basket of food. "I hope you don't mind. It was left over from last night. There's roast goose, some buttered dumplings and frosted fruit stollen. We didn't want it to go to waste, though of course if it interferes with what you've already done..."

"Hooray!" crowed Suzanne. "So much better than chicken soup and plain bread!"

I looked at Margot's face as the teenager hugged her. She looked as if she were about to cry. Suzanne was her sister, though the girl didn't know it. Then Margot turned to Dr. Ravanel, smiling on the other side of the small parlor, and I realized the reason she'd taken such care with her hair. She'd chickened out when she visited him in Neuilly, but now she was *finally* going to tell the man he was her father.

I was suddenly envious of Margot. To have a father so steady and kind. Who I was sure would embrace her with open arms.

Forcing a smile, I turned to Madame Ravanel, who'd already taken the basket of food. "Can I help?"

"Oh, yes." The sweet, motherly woman, who was at least a

decade younger than her husband, beamed at me. "This is going to be so delicious—"

"That food." Dr. Ravanel's voice was unusually sharp. "It was from the Christmas dinner of Otto Schröder?"

We looked at each other. "Why, yes."

"Throw it away," he said harshly.

The smile slid off his wife's face. "Jean-Luc...?"

"I made it," Berthe said, looking a little hurt. "There's nothing wrong with it."

"I'm sure it would be delicious, *madame*," he replied politely. He shook his head. "Unfortunately, we cannot eat it."

His wife pleaded, "But..."

"*Non*, Élisabeth. The Germans have taken my sons, my country, my pride and my peace. I will not allow my family to now eat from his plate like beggars. I will not do anything that compels us to be *grateful* to them. *Non!*"

She looked at her husband for a long moment, then, with a sigh, she handed Margot the basket. "Thank you. You're very kind to think of us," she said quietly, "but we prefer our soup."

Berthe, Margot, Lucie and I looked at each other. And I knew what they were thinking about because I was, too: that poor French engineer who'd been murdered.

"You're right," Margot said slowly. She looked down at the basket. "Where is your rubbish bin?"

Relief flashed in Dr. Ravanel's dark eyes. He pointed across the small parlor to the tiny kitchen area.

She crossed it in just a few steps and was about to dump it in the trash can, when Madame Ravanel stopped her.

"*Non*, Jean-Luc. Not everyone can afford such pride." She turned to Margot. "Leave it on the counter. I will get it to those who might otherwise starve." Her eyes filled with tears. "They will be glad of a delicious home-cooked Christmas dinner, no matter its provenance."

Dr. Ravanel's jaw tightened as he considered his wife, then

he reluctantly nodded. Margot deposited the dinner as bid, then brushed her hands together.

"I've always loved your soup," she told Madame Ravanel, smiling. "I'd be grateful to have it for Christmas."

That worthy lady embraced her, then as the rest of us murmured agreements, she hugged us all again, saying over and over what good girls we were, and how she was so proud of us, and Dr. Ravanel was shaking Berthe's hand and telling her how grateful he was that she wasn't taking it personally. She was replying stoutly that it was fine—he was right, and she'd overcooked the goose anyway. Only Fauve and Choupette seemed bewildered, the little girl tugging on Lucie's dress and asking why they were giving their Christmas dinner away, as the little dog stared mournfully at the counter.

In spite of having plainer food, and less of it, we were a happy party, in their warm, tiny home, decked with candles and homespun Christmas decorations. Though there wasn't much actual chicken in the soup, there was plenty of broth and carrots and leeks, along with homemade brown bread, and some wrinkled apples. Once the Ravanels confirmed that the jellies had been canned by Berthe before the invasion, Dr. Ravanel allowed that to be added as well. We happily ate it all.

Throughout the meal, I noticed Margot kept glancing at Dr. Ravanel. It seemed clear she was hoping to find a moment to speak with him private. I prayed she'd find it. The situation had gone on quite enough.

Then came the coup de grâce: Madame Ravanel went to the small icebox and came out a moment later with a little cake shaped like a Yuletide log.

"A *bûche de Noël*," Dr. Ravanel gasped. His eyes were full of tears as he looked at his wife. "Élisabeth, how...?"

"I know it's your favorite," she said, smiling as she set it on the small table. Her eyes glowed in her round, pretty face. "I cut back on little things, saving for months to get the cocoa and sugar and butter for your Christmas, my darling."

"My sweet girl." He rose to his feet and threw his arms around her. She leaned against his chest, eyes closed. When he finally pulled away, he kissed her tenderly on the lips. "You're the best wife in the world."

She looked at him, smiling through the tears sparkling in her blue eyes. "You're the best husband."

"Come." He waved us forward. "We'll all share."

"Oh, we shouldn't..." I looked longingly at the frosted chocolate cake. It was very small, barely big enough for two.

"I insist." He started cutting it into thin slices. But just as we'd clustered around the small table, standing since there weren't enough chairs for us all to sit, there was a knock at the door.

"Is this a private party?" Roger's dark head peeked around the door. "Or can anyone drop in?"

"Roger!" cried Berthe.

He was greeted with hugs from his great-aunt and Lucie. I didn't move, though my heart was pounding. And I wasn't the only one holding back. Margot was staring at him, her arms wrapped tightly around her chest. As if she, too, was afraid of what might happen next.

23

MARGOT

As Berthe rushed forward to embrace her great-nephew, all my good feelings from a moment earlier fled. Everything I'd tried to forget since the night Roger had disappeared from the garden of St. Agnes's rushed back, swirling around me.

After a brief, awkward greeting—holding out my hand when he leaned in to kiss my cheek—I managed to avoid Roger for the next hour, standing by the Ravanels' tiny, sparsely decorated Christmas tree with Fauve and watching him sideways from beneath my lashes. He was currently holding a glass of red wine in one hand and a thin slice of chocolate cake in the other, talking with Élisabeth Ravanel and his great-aunt.

I'd suspected Berthe might invite him. I just hadn't expected him to show up.

Since that October night, I'd tried hard to put him from my mind. Now, I wondered how I'd managed to even try. Had Roger's shoulders always been so broad, his arms so powerful, his jawline sharp? Or was it just that I'd missed his strength, his presence, even if I couldn't admit it?

Every time his dark gaze rested on me, I felt it. Felt his eyes on my skin, my body, my heart.

No, I thought, clenching my hands. *No*. If I gave him the slightest encouragement, he'd come talk to me and ruin everything. He wasn't why I was here, so I could fall apart for him like Josette had. I didn't care for him, not in that way. I *didn't*.

I was here to tell my father what I'd learned about Paul. And then I'd tell him the rest.

Turning from Roger, I went to Dr. Ravanel and said quietly, "Could I talk to you for a moment?"

He set down his small glass of red wine. The bottle Roger had brought had been shared between all the adults, even Suzanne. The Ravanels had been thrilled to accept the precious wine after learning—with a wink and a nod—that it had come from defying and confounding the Germans in the black market rather than groveling to them. Dr. Ravanel had poured himself a nice big glass, patted Roger on the back, and proclaimed him a gentleman and a patriot.

"Sure," he said now.

I glanced around us, then whispered, "In private?"

He frowned, looking around the small parlor. I could see why he'd said there was no room for all of us to stay here. This cottage was so tiny, just half the size of one of our attic dormitory rooms. "Outside?"

I nodded, and he called to his wife, "Margot's coming to help me chop wood for the fire."

"All right, darling."

Outside, in the small patch of earth surrounded by chipped stone walls, were bare fruit trees, overgrown bushes and desiccated weeds that had never been cut back after the autumn. His gaze followed mine, and he sighed. "Élisabeth's grandmother would turn over in her grave. But I'm at the hospital all the time, and Élisabeth... well, it's all she can do to keep us fed. This place has no electricity. Or hot water."

"It's very... traditional," I ventured.

"That's one way to say it." He gave a wry smile. "Grand-mère Gerard disliked being indoors. Her flowers were her love." He glanced from the small woodpile, a raggedy axe still stuck in the stump, to the dilapidated greenhouse, filled with honeysuckle, by the back stone wall. "Élisabeth hates it here. She misses our home in La Ravelle, our friends."

"So why stay?"

"For my son," he said, then bit his lip, as if he'd said too much.

I sucked in my breath.

"I have news," I whispered, glancing to the right and left as if the trees might be listening. "About Paul."

"What?" He stared at me. "But I told you—"

"I wanted to help. How could I not?" When he continued to frown, I added, bragging a little, "It wasn't even hard."

He clawed back his dark hair. "And?"

"And the Germans don't know where he is."

"How can you be sure?"

"Herr Schröder hates him for killing that guard—"

"He had no choice," Dr. Ravanel interrupted.

"I know," I said quietly. "They'll never stop hunting him now. But... they don't know where he is. At least, not yet."

"Are you sure?"

"Schröder said they're searching all ports, north and south. If they knew where he was, they wouldn't have to."

He stared at me, then a smile lit up his face, his dark eyes beaming with joy.

"Thank you, darling girl!" He hugged me, but so fast and quick I could barely appreciate it before it ended. He frowned, looking down at me. "He didn't suspect anything?"

I shook my head. My heart hurt, wishing for another hug. But just having him look at me so admiringly was its own reward.

"Thank you, Margot." He wiped his eyes. "I'll never forget how you took such a risk for our family." He took a deep breath. "And don't worry—I'll never ask you to do it again."

He turned and picked up an axe. I watched as he swung the blade, chunking it heavily into the wood.

"You didn't force me," I said slowly. "It was my choice."

He glanced at me, lifting an eyebrow. "Helen would still have my hide."

As he continued to split the logs, I stared at him in surprise. Dr. Ravanel still thought of me as a child. But I was grown and no longer needed or wanted others to protect me. I wanted to be the one to protect others now.

Leaning back against the handle of the axe, he gave me a crooked smile and wiped his forehead with a sigh. "It's a shame, though. Schröder has his fingers in all sorts of pies, military, political. We could have used you."

My eyebrows lifted. "*We?*"

His cheeks turned red above the unshaven scruff on his chin. And I had a sudden flicker of memory. When he'd asked me to find out about Paul, he'd said, *You could be so useful to us.* At the time, I'd thought he meant useful to the Ravanel family. But now...

"Who's *we?*" I repeated.

He got a strange look on his face, then shook his head, turning back to chopping with a vengeance. "Better you don't know."

I watched him intently in the private, shadowy garden. "Did you see the Bonsergent posters today? How the Nazis shamefully murdered that poor man?"

He nodded. He was biting down on his lip.

"Someone scratched out the name of the German commander on the posters," I said slowly. "And placed flowers and candles beneath. An act of defiance to show everyone in Paris they don't need to be afraid. It was very brave."

"Uh," he managed, as if something were choking him. And then I was sure.

"You're working with someone," I said accusingly. "Against the Germans."

Dr. Ravanel froze, then straightened. He looked me straight in the eye. "Leave it alone, Margot."

"But I hate them, too! I could help!"

"You're just a kid." Setting his jaw, he went back to chopping wood again.

"What is it you do?"

"Argh." He glared at me in exasperation. "Nothing. I hear things as a doctor. I pass on those things to him. Nothing more."

"*Him?*"

"Drop it!"

A man had just been executed by firing squad for standing in the wrong spot on the street. And yet I heard myself say, "I could be useful to the Resistance. You said so yourself."

"I can't do it, kid."

"First off, I'm not a kid, not anymore. And second, Helen would understand," I argued. "She told me about the two of you..."

His expression changed. "What did she say?"

My throat closed. She'd told me everything, how they'd worked together fearlessly during the last war, doctor and nurse, how they'd then traveled to dangerous places to heal the sick and injured. I took a deep breath. "She said... you were brave, and honorable, and taught her how to fight."

"I did at that," he said, rubbing his chin ruefully. "First time she ever held a revolver was with me. Good thing, too. Helen told me what happened in Germany, how she had to shoot Schröder in the leg just to help his poor battered wife escape."

That was what happened, I told myself firmly. Not Otto Schröder's version. And yet...

"So I know how dangerous he is," Dr. Ravanel continued,

giving the wood another vengeful chop. "She would hate it if she knew you and the girls were living with him." His forehead furrowed as he looked at the tiny cottage. "Maybe we could make room here after all..."

Once, I'd dreamed of him saying this. But not anymore. Not since I'd seen the actual size of the cottage. It was impossible. Plus, a strange hope had started flickering inside me. The stirring of possibility, of a new purpose...

"It's just as you said. You don't have enough room for the seven of us, not even on your floor. And I have no desire to try to camp through winter in your garden with an elderly woman and three orphaned children. But thank you."

"Then..." He licked his lips. "You could go to La Ravelle. I'll find you a ride."

I tried to picture taking everyone to La Ravelle, many kilometers to the south. We'd still be in occupied France. Berthe would never come with us. And we'd be in a small town where we knew almost no one, with no Nazi officer to helpfully supply food, heat, and clothing for the babies.

And no powerful official to supply me information I could give Dr. Ravanel's mysterious contact. Information that could potentially help us get rid of the Germans, once and for all.

I said in a small voice, "What if I want to stay at St. Agnes's? And help you?"

He paused mid-swing, staring at me. "But I just said—"

"Remember how we fought off those men in La Ravelle? And saved Choupette?"

"You and Lucie and Josette, scaring away men twice your size?" Dr. Ravanel leaned against the axe handle, his gaze admiring. "How could I forget?"

I lifted my chin. "I'll give you information, and you can either use it or not. But I'm helping you. I'm as French as you are."

It was truer than he knew.

"Helen wouldn't—"

"She's not here," I interrupted. "And we both know she would fight."

"It's dangerous," he said bluntly. "If you're caught, you could be imprisoned. You could be killed."

"I know." I fixed my gaze on his. "But would Helen do any less? Would you?"

He stared at me, and I saw the exact moment he recognized me as an adult, capable of making such a weighty decision, of choosing to risk my own neck for a cause I believed in.

He said slowly, "You really think you could do it?"

A thrill went through my heart. He was going to let me help!

"Herr Schröder has no idea we're connected," I said. "I didn't want him to be curious about you. So I told him we were spending Christmas with a made-up family called the Martins."

"Ah, so that's what all that was about?" His eyes twinkled. "Smart."

As I basked in his praise, he slowly nodded. "We'll come up with a way for you to sneak any interesting information to me without his suspicion."

"At the hospital," I suggested. "Or in a park, where no one would see us together." If I was going to be a spy, I needed to act like one, and assume I was being watched and followed at all times. I'd act like I imagined my mother would.

He seemed to have the same thought. "I guess I underestimated you. Helen raised you. But I never expected you to be just like her."

It was my opening. I took a deep breath. "In more ways than you know—"

"She'd be scared for you. But also proud. I'm glad she's out of this war." He glanced back towards the cottage. "I just wish Élisabeth and Suzanne were, too." Turning sharply, he warned, "My family can't know anything about this."

"You haven't told them?"

He shook his head. "It would be too dangerous. My most important job is to protect my family."

I thought of his wife's ferocity, his daughter's vivacity. "I think you're underestimating them, too."

"Keep them out of it," he said flatly, cutting off any further discussion. Then he gave me a crooked half-smile. "Now, I guess I'd better finish chopping this wood before my wife wonders what's taking so long."

Staring at him as he swung the axe heavily into the split log again, I realized I was at a crossroads.

I could tell Dr. Ravanel he was my father.

I could help him save France.

But not both.

He already felt guilty at the thought of involving me in something dangerous. If he knew I was his daughter, he'd see me as too precious to risk—that his job was to protect me.

And I'd also lose this chance to know him and be his ally in something so important. Something that gave me purpose and pride instead of just feeling helpless—and bitterly ashamed of working for a Nazi, trying to entice the hearts and souls of my fellow Parisiennes. I thought of Herr Schröder, who'd told me to call him Otto when we were alone. *The right words change everything.*

"All right, Dr. Ravanel." As he lifted chopped wood into his arms, I forced my lips into a smile. "I'll keep our secret."

24

MARGOT

Once back inside the cottage, I looked around at all the people we loved in the warm, colorful room, drinking the last of the wine Roger had brought, eating the last crumbs of the *bûche de Noël*.

"Took you long enough," Élisabeth Ravanel teased her husband. "Did you hike out into the forest for that wood?"

"I wanted to get it just right." His voice was tender. As he stacked the wood beside the fireplace, I listened to the slightly off-key rendition of "Un Flambeau, Jeannette, Isabelle" sung by Lucie and Suzanne, who were holding the two babies, along with Fauve and Berthe. Beside them, Choupette was snoring on the rug near the fire.

"Margot." Roger's husky voice sounded right beside me. "I'm glad to finally see you."

I turned and caught my breath. His eyes were dark, fathomless. Unwillingly, my gaze lowered to his sensual mouth; the five o'clock shadow along his rugged jawline. I could almost feel the heat from his skin, the scent of him like woodsy soap. Something about him was pulling me in.

I had to resist. It wasn't just my heart that now depended on it or even my life. But all of France.

"Hi, Roger," I said, ducking his gaze. "Merry Christmas."

He stepped into my view. "Is it?" His eyes burned through me. "You haven't said a word to me all night."

Our eyes locked, held. Just for that moment.

With an intake of breath, I turned away.

"I'm afraid it's getting late. We must be going," I called to the girls. "We have a long walk ahead. We should go."

Madame Ravanel seemed bewildered. "Must you? So soon?"

I glanced at the window, where the late afternoon light was starting to fade in the early way of December. "Thank you. It's been lovely, but it'll be dark soon, and the little ones need their rest."

Not just the little ones. Berthe's hand seemed to shake as she reached for her coat. I said gently, "We could find you a taxi, Berthe, if you're tired."

She looked at me indignantly. "I'm sorry. Do you take me for someone old?"

It took me a few moments to wheedle the white-haired cook out of her displeasure. But her hands still shook as she lifted the plump, sleepy infants into the baby carriage. I wondered what her pride cost her.

As Lucie covered Thérèse and Geneviève with blankets and Josette got Fauve into her oversized hand-me-down coat, which had once been owned by an orphan now fostering to the south, I couldn't resist one last glance behind us across the room. Roger's dark eyes were stricken, his handsome face vulnerable.

He turned to speak quietly to his great-aunt. Then he hugged her. "*Joyeux Noël*, Tante Berthe."

Her wrinkled eyes sparkled as she reached up to pat his cheek. "Merry Christmas to you, *mon petit*."

Yes. It was better this way. Keep my distance from Roger. Feel nothing.

I could barely manage to deal with keeping the secret from my father.

"Goodbye." I shook hands with Dr. Ravanel. "I know where to find you when..."

"When," he agreed, glancing back at his wife and daughter.

But I was happy with my choice. Better to be able to act boldly, and at my father's side, than tell him the truth that would have stuck me in a cage marked "for protecting."

We left the Ravanels' tiny cottage with a whirl of farewells, holiday wishes and good hopes. We prayed 1941 would be the year the war ended. Then, after a few last hugs, we departed to start the long walk back to the Marais.

We'd barely gone down the street before I heard Roger's voice behind me. "Wait!"

I tensed. When I ignored him, Josette flashed me a hard glance.

"He doesn't deserve how you treat him," she muttered.

She was right; I knew she was right. But I didn't know how to be kind without losing myself as she had. Guilt made me sharp. "What do you care? He doesn't want *you*."

I expected Josette to lash out in return. I wanted it, to give relief to my feelings.

She just flashed me another glance—softer this time. "Don't toy with him, Margot," she murmured. "You're better than that. Aren't you?" She turned away and hurried forward. "Lucie, let me help—"

Looking up, I saw my sister pulling Fauve with one hand as the little girl yawned and rubbed her eyes, whining she didn't want Christmas to be over; with the other, Lucie was trying to comfort Thérèse in the baby carriage, as she had just woken up after being moved and didn't like it, and Geneviève was whimpering and sniffling with little hiccups. My sister clearly needed help. She'd told me so repeatedly over the last few weeks, and I knew she wasn't sleeping much.

I'd hinted I'd soon be able to help more because I'd planned to ask Dr. Ravanel if we could live with him. But for various reasons, both selfish and otherwise, we couldn't.

Reluctantly, I glanced back at Roger, still following us. With a sigh, I stopped to wait.

This neighborhood was quiet, the shops and cafés closed for Christmas Day. Parisians walked by, heads bowed, presents tucked under their arms. They seemed unwilling to linger even long enough to wish a passer-by holiday greetings, perhaps because the sky was starting to threaten cold rain. Or perhaps because, at any moment, German soldiers could appear.

Roger's dark eyes looked haunted as he approached. He smiled, looking at me as if I were some kind of precious treasure, which made me feel worse still. I didn't want to hurt him—why was he forcing me to?

"Sorry to make you wait for me," he said lightly. "But I can't allow my great-aunt to walk all the way back to St. Agnes's unescorted. There might be trouble."

"If anyone could bring trouble, it's you," I replied crisply. "If the Germans see a young man on the street, they'll want to see your identity papers."

"Let them."

Which meant he either had false documents, a powerful protector or was just being stupidly reckless. I sighed. "I worry about you."

"Do you?" As we walked down the street, trailing behind the others, his eyes grew hopeful again. "Margot, you must know I'd do anything for—"

"You told me once you wanted to join de Gaulle. Why are you still in Paris? Are you really working in the black market?"

"As I told my aunt"—his voice was sharp—"I'm helping in

my own way. Finding food and supplies in the country and bringing them to Paris for those in need."

"Those who can afford it, you mean. And no doubt lining your own pockets."

"Why shouldn't I? Isn't that what you want?"

Above us, the clouds had darkened, like a portent. My steps slowed on the dirty street. "What do you mean?"

His dark eyes turned accusing. "You told me it takes money to be safe. You said you'd never marry a man who's poor and helpless."

"I never said that." Had I said that? It didn't sound like me. My mind was spinning. "When did I say that?"

"I'm trying to build our future. So we—we can be together. And the only way to be safe is to be rich and connected. I'm doing this for you."

He tried to take my hand as we walked. I ripped it away.

"Roger..." I didn't want to hurt him, but how many times had I tried to avoid the issue? "I've come to accept now that the rest of us have to stay in Paris. Probably until the war ends. But you're free. Don't stay for me."

I walked a little faster. He had to increase his pace.

"If you're worried about Josette's feelings, don't be," he said, giving me sideways glances. "I talked to her. Let her down as easy as I could."

"I know." I stared ahead at the ragtag group of Josette, Berthe, my sister and the babies, now turning the corner ahead of us in the twilight. "You told her you could never love her."

"She told you?" He stopped, surprised. Then he rushed to catch up with me again. "I'm glad." He rubbed the back of his head sheepishly, looking towards Josette's curvaceous figure and bright red hair at the end of the street, then at me. "Because... now there's nothing to keep us apart."

Josette must have had her heart ripped out, I thought suddenly. When she'd first told us, I'd been distracted, and feeling sorry for Josette was never my first instinct. But now, against my will, I felt bad for her. Licking my lips, which still tasted a bit of wine at the corners, I turned to him impatiently.

"Look, Roger, I'm glad you're doing well. We were all worried when we didn't hear from you for weeks. And if staying in Paris and making a fortune selling bacon and butter to restaurants that serve Nazis is what you really want to do, I'm happy for you." My tone was acid. "But don't kid yourself you're doing it for me."

"Of course I am. Margot, you're all that matters." He put his hand on his heart, over his shiny new black wool coat. "I knew from the moment we met that you were the one. That you—"

"Stop," I said, annoyed. "Just stop. You're being stupid."

He sucked in his breath, his face as hurt as a boy's. "What?"

"Your foolish romantic fantasy. It's as ridiculous as Josette's. You don't love me."

"How can you say that?"

"You have a dream of me, nothing more." We passed the stark trio of beige posters with their ugly black lettering announcing Bonsergent's execution. The candles and flowers weren't there anymore, no doubt cleaned up by the Germans.

The light was fading fast now. Curfew would be coming soon, and Berthe and the orphans needed to get home to safety. We all did.

Though who was I kidding? St. Agnes's was no longer safe. As long as Otto Schröder was there, as long as the Germans controlled us all, nowhere in France would be truly safe.

"We need to hurry." I looked at Roger. "You shouldn't be out after dark. If the soldiers see you, they'll assume you're up to no good."

"I'm not worried."

"How?" I demanded. "Who would protect you?"

He shrugged. "I'm useful to the Germans now. I have a few regular customers who would wish to keep their source of good wine and cheese. They won't send me to a work camp. Or shoot me on the street."

I gestured back at the posters with my thumb. "Perhaps he thought that, too."

We walked in uncomfortable silence until we finally reached the rue Commines. The street was empty, as if everyone was hiding in their own homes on this cold Christmas night. The rest of our group had already disappeared down the ivy-covered arch over the tiny alley of the rue des Orphelines.

Twilight was deepening. The rain had held off, the clouds clearing as we approached the orphanage, so I could now see red skies over the buildings. From Widow Hébert's five-story townhouse, warmly glowing lights looked down on us. "Good-night, Roger..."

His hand shot out and wrapped gently around my wrist, stopping me in my tracks. His skin was warm and rough against mine.

"Margot," he said in a low voice, lifting glittering dark eyes, "I know you're afraid. You'd never want to give your heart to anyone. But you can." He took both my hands and whispered, "Your heart is safe with me."

Beneath the latticework of dark bare trees, stretching up into the fading light, Roger pulled me into his arms.

"Roger," I whispered, my heart pounding. "Please..."

"My darling," he said huskily and lowered his head to kiss me.

His lips were soft and warm, and the sensation of his mouth on mine caused a hot sizzle through my veins, across my body, making me ache. I felt dizzy. I felt lost.

"I love you, Margot," he breathed as he finally pulled away. He pressed his rough cheek to mine. "I'll love you forever."

My eyes were still closed. I was afraid to open them. I felt like the whole world was spinning around me, like I was standing at a precipice, on the very edge, and if I let go, I'd fall, and I wouldn't stop falling until I collapsed, crushing into a pile of jagged bones.

"Marry me," he whispered. "Say you will. I can take you away from all this. Soon."

With an intake of breath, I blinked at him in the twilight. "Take me away?"

He smiled, tucking back a dark curly tendril of my hair. "I'm making a deal that should be enough to support us. I can get us a house. You won't have to work. You can stay home." He cupped my cheek. "Bring Lucie, if you want. The orphans too. I don't care. Whatever you want. As long as you're mine."

I thought of Josette, who'd been so eager to toss her dreams away for love of him. I thought of my adoptive mother Violette, who'd become a prostitute after her husband had died, leaving her destitute with two children. Even Isabelle Lusigny, whose own husband must once have promised to take care of her forever, leaving her utterly dependent on him, had been forced to become his servant when the money was gone.

I can take you away from all this.

A wife was legally the property of her husband—she couldn't vote or have her own bank account, she could only work with her husband's permission. That was his "protection." If he became a drunk, or beat her, or beat their children, or ran away with his mistress, it was still difficult to get a divorce. A wife was chained in marriage forever, especially after children were born. I'd seen lots of children left at St. Agnes's, children abandoned as babies, children abandoned at ten or twelve, whose fathers must once have promised their mothers exactly what Roger was promising me.

I can take you away from all this.

I couldn't let myself have feelings. Not because I was afraid, I told myself. Because I was realistic.

I pulled away, my eyes narrowed. "So we'll all live jolly lives, will we, as you support us by selling sugar to the Nazis?"

He stared at me, then his forehead lowered like a storm cloud. "Are you really judging me for that?" He pointed towards the alley. "You're working for a Nazi! Living in his house!"

"What about your dream of joining de Gaulle?"

"*That's* the fantasy. The Germans have annihilated Europe in *months*. No one can stop them." He set his jaw. "I'm not going to let them ruin my life." He looked at me pleadingly. "Or yours."

The Germans have taken my sons, my country, my pride and my peace... I will not do anything that compels us to be grateful to them. Non!

I looked at Roger. "So you're going to be a lapdog? Surrender your honor for a comfortable family life?" I glared at him. "How long would it take before you started blaming a wife for that? Despising her?"

"As you're despising me now?" His eyebrows lifted. "Typing up letters for Hitler's buddy doesn't exactly make you Joan of Arc."

I'd hurt him. His formerly breathless tone was turning defensive, sour. I yearned to tell him my secret plans with Dr. Ravanel, but I couldn't. So I said something else that was true—that had to be true.

"I'm sorry, Roger." I looked him straight in the eye on that lonely street. "I don't love you. I never will."

His eyes gleamed in the fading purple light. The hard contours of his handsome face were deep in shadow. "But the way you just kissed me—"

I shrugged. "It was just a kiss."

As if I'd kissed dozens of men, when in fact he'd been my first and only. As if his kiss hadn't made me feel anything at all. As if my heart were actually the stone I wanted it to be, instead of pounding so desperately.

Roger blinked. He paced two steps, as if he wanted to leave

and wanted to stay all at once. Then he whirled on me, his expression anguished.

"So this is how it felt," he whispered. "To her. When I told her—" He took a deep breath, closing his eyes. When he opened them, it was as if a mask had fallen over his face, no longer showing his feelings. He was all casual charm, flashing his usual crooked smile. "Don't worry about it. I'll go. You'll never see me again."

Never? Fear plucked at my insides. But wasn't this what I'd wanted? To send him away? I swallowed. "Please don't think—"

"I don't think anything. I have to go. A shipment's coming on tonight's train. So many Nazis to satisfy, so many others to pay off." His dark eyes glittered. "I'll be rich anyway. Then you'll see."

"Please, don't—"

"Merry Christmas, Mademoiselle Vashon." He touched his cap. "I wish you good luck," he added softly. Then he turned and was gone, enveloped into the deepening shadows.

I stared after him and touched my lips, which still tingled from his kiss.

"Margot."

Turning, I saw Josette standing near the ivy-covered edge of the alley. I wondered how long she'd been standing there. Her face was impassive. I waited for her to scream at me—or insult me.

Instead, she said quietly, "Herr Schröder sent me to find you. He needs to dictate a letter tonight. And Lucie wants our help putting the kids to bed."

"*D'accord.*"

Ducking my head, I followed her. Our footsteps echoed in the silence of the dark cobblestoned alley. There would be frost again tonight. I could see our mingled breath, like white smoke against the lights of St. Agnes's, only half dimmed by blackout blinds.

Outside the door, I turned to her in a rush.

"I'm sorry, Josette," I choked out. "You have to know I never—"

She stepped back coldly. "Herr Schröder is waiting. Don't make him upset."

Without another word, she went into the house, its silhouette dark against the bruise-purple sky. And I knew nothing would be forgiven—or forgotten.

25

LUCIE

The children were finally sleeping. The attic was quiet. A Christmas miracle.

A silent night at last, after a lovely party, followed by a rather less lovely long walk home in the cold twilight, which involved all three children wailing and sniffling, and even Berthe making irritated remarks about Josette and me going too fast, her gait slowing to a shuffle as she clutched the handle of the baby carriage like a walker.

But it had been worth it.

Berthe had retreated to her private bedroom near the kitchen as soon as we'd returned, while I'd taken the babies and Fauve upstairs for baths, then I'd rocked Geneviève and Thérèse to sleep, telling Fauve a bedtime story as Josette took a long hot bath. After the children were tucked in, I'd snuck off to have a bath of my own, my first in days, though sadly there was little hot water left. I feared Margot, who was bathing now, after typing up an urgent letter for Herr Schröder, might be enduring water as icy as a Swiss mountain glacier.

But now, the attic dormitory was warm and dark, lit softly

by the old electric lights on the little tree I'd set up the night before.

The two slumbering infants were peaceful in their cribs, their eyelashes fluttering, their mouths pursing as they suckled in their sleep. My heart turned over as I glanced at them. There was nothing sweeter than a sleeping baby.

Fauve, too, was asleep in the bed she'd chosen, across from mine. Our feet pointed at each other when we slept. Darling little girl. I vowed to keep her safe until her father's return.

All three children, asleep at once. I breathed a silent prayer of thanks. And prayed we'd all sleep through the night. Please, let it be five hours at least. Or six—how luxurious six would be.

I went to the window and peeked past the blackout curtain, then boldly pushed it aside, practically daring British planes to bomb us. But I wanted to see the stars. And surely no one would be coming to bomb us on Christmas night?

I took a deep breath. With Margot and Josette both so busy, and even Berthe becoming less reliable, I hadn't just felt exhausted lately—I felt scared. What if I couldn't give the babies the care they deserved? What if I failed them?

Though in a few months I'd be seventeen, sometimes I felt so small and uncertain. How I wished I had someone braver and stronger to lean on. Closing my eyes, I whispered silently, *Please help me stay strong. Help me.*

Unwillingly, I thought suddenly of Klaus Schröder's handsome face, his kind blue eyes. He was a Nazi, I reminded myself. Just as Josette and Margot had pointed out. But my heart still hurt for him, this young man I didn't even know, as I recalled how I'd heard Herr Schröder shout at him behind the closed door of the study.

But, Uncle, I'd heard Klaus say desperately, *you have to see that what we're doing is wrong. Children are starving. Innocent people are being jailed, killed, sent away in cattle cars. In Poland, in the Low Countries, in France—*

A sound like a slap, then Herr Schröder's panting fury. *Not another word, Klaus! My brother did not raise you to be a traitor to your country. Is it your mother who taught you to be disloyal? Perhaps I should send the Gestapo to question her—*

A gasp. *No!*

Don't make me hurt you. Or your mother. You're the future of the party, Klaus. Of our family. Act like it.

Opening my eyes, I looked out at the cold stars over Paris, lit by the softening glow of the moon. Maybe all of us, in some way, were trapped into a life we'd never imagined, while dreaming helplessly of so much more.

A shadow moved in the alley below. I saw the figure of a man, his shoulders slumped, a forgotten cigarette in his hand, burning down to ash. He looked up at the moon, and the opalescent glow caressed his pale, anguished face.

Klaus Schröder.

"The Christmas tree looks beautiful, Lucie," Josette said behind me.

I dropped the curtain guiltily and whirled to face her.

She smiled. "How did you manage to find it?"

She spoke softly, so as not to wake the three sleeping children. My cheeks were hot, but she didn't seem to notice. I forced a sheepish smile. "I'll tell if you promise not to scold me."

Margot came in from her bath, wearing her robe and old flannel nightgown. She rubbed her wet hair, then wrapped it in a towel. "Why would we scold you?"

"Because..." I bit my lip, then whispered, "it's not really a tree. I cut off the biggest branch of the old pine tree in the garden. Oh, I know it was wrong of me, but..."

"I think it's good," said Josette with a soft laugh. "Take everything from the Germans you can."

Margot seemed unusually quiet. She looked at Josette almost imploringly.

The redhead turned away from her coldly, smiling only at

me. My heart hurt at the thought of them fighting, today of all days. I pleaded, "It's been a good Christmas, hasn't it?"

"Oh, I almost forgot." Margot returned to the door and retrieved a wrapped gift. "Herr Schröder just asked me to give this to you."

"For me?" I looked at the large gift—in shiny silver paper with a big red bow—then frowned, looking at her and Josette. "Did he give you gifts, too?"

Josette shrugged. "We're newcomers."

"Anyway," Margot said darkly, "we don't need gifts from him."

On the rug near the radiator, my dog yawned, stretching out her four limbs in ecstasy at the comfort and warmth. Her belly had become downright rotund since we'd been living in Paris. But then, Herr Schröder liked dogs and always told Berthe to make sure Choupette got plenty of scraps and juicy bones.

But as I thought of how Dr. Ravanel had refused to eat Herr Schröder's Christmas leftovers, my smile faded. He was a Nazi. A powerful leader of the same awful people who'd murdered that poor Jacques Bonsergent. And he himself was bullying his own nephew into being part of their ruthless regime.

"Is it wrong of me to open this?" I asked slowly. "Wrong to let Herr Schröder support us? The babies, Choupette, me?"

They looked at each other, then Margot sighed, sitting beneath the lights of the makeshift tree. "With things as they are... I don't know." Her eyes fell on the sleeping children. "It's hard when others are depending on you. And your life is no longer your own."

"You might as well open it," said Josette, more practically.

My sister held out her hand, and I came to sit next to her on the rug. Clutching the big wrapped gift against my chest, I put my head on Margot's shoulder like I'd done when we were little. A moment later, Josette sat on my other side, all three of us in our old orphanage nightgowns and woolen socks.

For a while, we just sat together in the quiet of the attic, looking at the tiny, flickering electric lights on the wilting pine branch. Any moment now, I expected one light would burn out, and then they'd all go dark.

Outside, the world seemed calm and bright, just like in the Christmas carol. The darkness of our alley, with only the windows of the Widow Hébert's house on the corner visible from here, made it almost possible to pretend we were someplace far away.

When the attic had been filled with orphans, sometimes one of the teachers would read us bedtime stories, and afterward, as we all grew drowsy in the darkness, we'd whispered stories to each other, pretending we were sailing the sea like Babar, or maybe in the African jungle with Tintin, or perhaps caught up in Dorothy's Kansas tornado. The rue des Orphelines was so private, so dark, surrounded as we were by our private garden, we could imagine ourselves anywhere.

But it had always been others who'd yearned for escape, not me. All I'd ever wanted was to be with the people I loved, my family and friends, and keep them safe and warm and well fed, with no one arguing or squabbling. That was enough of a dream for me.

"Do you remember how the orphans used to pretend?" I asked. "That we could leave all the porridge, homework and chores, and travel far away?"

Margot smiled. "The Australian Outback."

"London," Josette said. "Never-Never Land."

I took a deep breath. "We can still do it. Whatever is going on in the world, we can make it however we want. As long as we take care of each other."

"Sweet Lucie." Margot squeezed my shoulder, then looked at the present. "Open it."

With a deep breath, I pulled off the wrapping paper.

I nearly cried when I saw what was inside: new winter

coats, for all three children. Mittens and hats, too. And a hand-written note in German:

For my favorite Little Mother. Your children are fortunate in you.

I bit my lip, uncertain how to react. Herr Schröder had somehow known that a gift for them would be far more mean-ingful than anything he could give me. But I felt an underlying fear I couldn't shake away. *Don't make me hurt you.*

"It's very kind," I said slowly. "The children need coats."

"They need coats because their parents abandoned them," Josette pointed out. "Because of the war the Germans started."

"And we can't afford to buy them coats, even with our wages, because there's nothing to buy, or else it costs ten times the price. They've taken everything for their war. Fabric, food, even this house," Margot said.

"The Germans take everything," Josette sniffed, "and then expect praise if they give a tiny bit back."

I couldn't think of what to say. It seemed churlish to criti-cize someone who'd just given me something my children desperately needed. And yet I couldn't stop hearing that slap. Or forget the lurid posters about the murdered man.

I scratched behind Choupette's ears.

As the sparse lights twinkled on the tree, the only sounds were the children's soft breathing and Choupette's happy snore.

Suddenly, Margot looked at the redhead sitting beside me on the floor.

"Josette," she said humbly, "will you forgive me?"

I'd never heard Margot sound so sorry for anything. I looked between them. "Forgive what?"

Josette looked towards the shadowy corner where Fauve was sleeping. "It's not your fault." She sounded as if she were trying to convince herself. She said more firmly, "It's not your fault."

"Do you mean it?" my sister asked, as if trying not to cry.

She reached for Josette's hand, and a moment later, the two of them were hugging each other. I didn't know what they'd been fighting about; I could only be glad that the fight had ended, so astonishingly, in Margot's total capitulation and Josette's absolute forgiveness. A Christmas miracle for sure. Openly crying myself, I hugged them both.

Quietly, of course. Even in the throes of emotion we did everything as quietly as we could. We weren't silly young girls anymore.

But as I wiped tears from my eyes, I suddenly wished, like Fauve, that Christmas would never end.

"Look," Margot breathed, staring at the little bit of window not covered by the curtain. "Snow."

Rising to our feet, we lifted the curtain and looked out the window at white flakes falling softly outside. I looked down, but Klaus was gone now.

"So much has changed." Josette smiled. "Remember last Christmas, when the house was so full, and we were moaning about our classes? And everyone called it a joke of a war— without fighting?"

"The Germans seemed so far away," I sighed.

"I wonder what the world will look like in a year," my sister said.

Silence fell amid the flickering lights. Outside, in the dappled moonlight that slid between the low clouds, Paris was frosty and white.

"Just a few months ago, I dreamed of getting you both safely to America." Margot looked wistfully between us. "I would have liked you to be safe, Lucie. Even you, Josette."

"Thanks," the redhead said with a crooked grin, without

acrimony. She looked thoughtfully out the window. "But maybe there are more important things than being safe."

"Maybe so," said Margot, her expression pensive.

"Maybe by next year," I said, my heart full of longing, "the war will be over."

Somehow, I prayed, *let this killing stop. Let the Nazis return to Germany, so everyone can be safe again. Let there be food and coats for all.* I thought of Klaus. *Let families heal and everyone be allowed to follow his conscience. Let the world become peaceful again.*

Please, I prayed silently, looking out at the snowy Christmas night. *Please let everything change for us in the New Year.* And as I looked between Josette and Margot, now smiling at each other, in that moment, anything seemed possible.

PART TWO

26

MARGOT

I could feel hard eyes on our chauffeured black sedan as we traveled through Paris to Nazi headquarters at the Hôtel Majestic. Angry, resentful glances seemed to follow the car wherever we went. Hatred for Otto, yes.

But even more hatred for me.

It had been almost twenty months since I'd started my unlikely career in espionage, passing along secrets to my father, who gave them to his contact, a man I knew only as Le Lérot. Twenty months of spending time with the powerful Nazi nearly three times my age.

It was still strange for me to call him Otto in private. I'd had no choice but to comply, but the intimacy of it made me nervous. Back in 1940, I'd pictured him as a father figure. But I was coming to worry that he didn't see himself that way.

As if I didn't have enough to worry about.

"No traffic today, sir," the chauffeur said. Once, Jean Pagnier had been part-time mechanic at St. Agnes's, keeping our rickety truck in order. He had cynical lips, wrinkled from a lifetime of smoking Gauloises. He didn't smoke them in front of his boss, but his uniform always reeked of tobacco.

"Good." As Otto sat beside me, focusing on what he was scratching in his little leather-bound black notebook with his black ink pen, I shivered in spite of the summer sun, looking out the window.

Sitting beside the chauffeur in the front, Otto's nephew Klaus smiled as he looked at his wristwatch, then back at us. His smile didn't meet his eyes. "We'll be early."

Paris had changed since the Christmas Klaus Schröder had arrived. Back then, we'd thought we knew hardship, with food shortages, ration coupons and the fear that Germany's lightning brutality would conquer the rest of the world as quickly as it had smashed up France. But looking back, my naïve optimism of those days seemed painful.

The Soviet Union was no longer Germany's ally but its deadliest enemy, since Hitler had invaded Russia last summer. Six months later, Hitler also declared war on America, after the Japanese destruction of Pearl Harbor. He seemed eager to fight every country at once.

Since then, the Germans were slowly realizing world conquest wouldn't be as easy as they'd thought and were grimly settling in for a slow, grinding fight beside their remaining allies, Italy and Japan. The Nazis' earlier arrogance had evaporated as they were challenged on all sides, by England, by America and, most of all, by the Soviet Union on that vicious eastern front.

Needing to squeeze every bit of manpower and war matériel out of its conquered lands, Germany pressed France even harder than before. And France had complied. The Pétain government in Vichy, with no more young soldiers to add to the work camps, had rounded up hundreds of thousands of its own civilians and sent them as forced labor to Germany.

Those who remained suffered, too. The Nazis in Paris no longer pretended to be remotely kind or obliging. Many more people had died since poor Jacques Bonsergent. France's Jews were now forced to wear gold stars on their clothing. Some had already been sent to mysterious camps in the east. And there were whispers that something more awful for Paris's Jews might be coming soon.

Most French people were thinner, with rations now barely above starvation levels. They wore the same clothes they'd had before the war, now threadbare, with holes in their shoes. There was no new leather, silk or wool for the French. There was no butter or wine. It all went to Germany.

Sitting in the back seat of the chauffeured sedan, I stared down past my black silk stockings to my glossy new black leather pumps. My skirt suit was elegant, made to order by a Parisian designer. As was my chic little hat. For breakfast that morning, we'd had a traditional German breakfast of ham, eggs and fried potatoes smothered in cheese, along with white-flour baguettes and raspberry jam.

No wonder my fellow French hated me on sight.

"Are you making any changes, Uncle?" Klaus asked politely, looking at the little book Otto was writing in.

He didn't look up. "Perhaps."

"I'm sure whatever you do will be right." The younger Schröder never showed emotion. It was odd. He fetched coffee or anything his uncle needed, and accompanied us when we went to Nazi headquarters several times a week, but the rest of the time, Klaus hung about the house, taking time to talk to Lucie in the hallways. I was grateful for that. Even if the man seemed like an automaton, without feelings, he often wordlessly helped my sister if she needed something from upstairs, like a blanket or a clean diaper.

Which reminded me: I had to find a way to help Lucie more. Impossibly, we'd had three more orphans arrive since 1940 and now had six young children living with us in the attic, all needing love and care. Fauve, still the oldest, also needed schooling. It was a lot of responsibility. As everyone else in the household remained pleasantly well fed, I'd seen my little sister's face grow pinched with worry and exhaustion.

But Otto wanted me at his side nearly all the time, from the moment I woke up until the end of the evening, when he'd insist I accompany him to cocktails and after-dinner drinks with other officers at Maxim's or Le Boeuf sur le Toit. What could I do?

All my energy was spent memorizing secret notes so I could write them down later and give them to my father, who would pass them on to the unknown Resistance leader. The leader's codename, Le Lérot, came from the dormouse with the black patch of fur over his eyes, like a bandit, who always remained dormant and hidden until the right time to strike.

Finding a way to pass on those notes to Dr. Ravanel without being caught was growing increasingly difficult. As I was well aware, Otto was no fool.

To French eyes, I was Otto's collaborator, a secretary to a Nazi—or perhaps even his doxy. I'd heard all the whispers. They'd made my cheeks flame.

C'est une honte, one elderly woman had hissed at me when I'd dared to walk down the rue Commines, on my way to sneak notes to Jean-Luc. Another time someone had spat at me. *Espèce de catin*.

I rolled down the window in the back seat, desperate to feel a breeze against my hot cheeks in the stifling summer air. I'd heard of other Nazi cars being assaulted by rotting fruit. But fruit was so dear now, even in summer, that no one would be stupid enough to throw it at me surely?

It was grim humor, but Paris had changed. And so had Otto.

The sedan paused at a streetlight, and I glanced at the propaganda flattened against the soot-stained building's walls. Gone were the happy posters encouraging women to devote themselves to being good wives and mothers. I almost missed those days.

Now, the posters were angry. Ugly. The latest one threatened that any French citizen who defied the laws of the Reich would risk not just his own life but that of his entire family. The posters last week had demanded that French citizens report and denounce any neighbors who complained about German treatment.

Otto no longer asked for my help understanding the psychology of Frenchwomen. He just used me for dictation, typing and shorthand. And occasionally for docile companionship, to stand by his side and smile at events. Every day brought me new agony, endured in secret. And every day he seemed increasingly tense, worrying about political rivals such as Goebbels and Abetz, who'd long been jealous of his influence with Hitler.

Soldiers under his report had already caught and passed on for execution several accused "traitors," Resistance fighters. The forests were now filled with young men who'd fled orders to present themselves as slave labor for Germany. Only women and old men and children were left in the cities, and most of them had gaunt cheeks and hungry eyes.

As I stepped out of the chauffeured black sedan outside the Hôtel Majestic, Otto waited for me, extending his hand. As he helped me out, his hand lingered on mine. I pretended not to notice.

But I could feel the hard eyes of my fellow Parisians on the sidewalk, judging my neatly gleaming leather pumps, my black peplum skirt suit and new silk stockings with black seams running down the back of my calves and thighs.

They didn't know I was as patriotic as they, that I'd been risking everything, enduring everything, secretly spying on my boss.

No one knew but Dr. Ravanel. Not Josette—not even Lucie. We'd be arrested, probably killed, if anyone knew. And our families might be, too: Lucie, Josette, Berthe, Dr. Ravanel, even the orphans. Otto was not a forgiving man.

"Do you have the notes?" he asked as we walked.

I shivered again and quickly turned to look through his briefcase. I smiled—wearing the red lipstick he preferred, as he said it looked professional and pleasing in a secretary—then nodded. "We're ready."

Klaus following us, we walked side by side into the Majestic.

Built at the turn of the century as a grand hotel, it had been converted into government offices shortly before the onset of war. The Nazis had been pleased to requisition the whole building for their military headquarters. It was filled with men in uniform, most of them middle-aged or older, some dour and suspicious, others with honest faces and big smiles. In the furniture, in the architecture, you could almost imagine the days when this had been a luxury hotel, filled with laughter and music. It was said George Gershwin had written *An American in Paris* here. We sometimes also visited a different headquarters on the Avenue Foch where, just months before, I'd overheard a discussion of what they called the Jewish question. They were looking for a solution about how to get rid of an entire race.

It had all gone into my secret reports. Every hint of a murder, every obscene violation, every strategic war plan. Though I hadn't heard many of those, as they weren't in Otto's purview. His mission was to break France's will and bring the populace to heel. But what I did hear was bad enough. Each new horror that I couldn't bear, that would have ripped me apart if I let myself think about it, I put in my secret reports. Then tried to forget.

We headed upstairs and walked into one of the upper conference rooms. Otto's men were discussing plans for nipping rising French resistance in the bud, "killing it in the cradle," as they put it. As the meeting went on, I served coffee from the pot on the roller cart provided by the middle-aged Nazi secretary, who glared at me, then shut the door as ordered.

"Why do you trust her?" I'd heard one of the bolder officers ask Otto last spring, staring at me from the other side of the room. "Why do you prefer her to your German secretary?"

"Maybe because I like the look of her," came the reply. "Or maybe because she knows where her bread is buttered, and we have a common enemy." He'd looked at me with narrowed eyes, and I'd realized he was thinking of Helen. If he only knew the truth! "Also," he'd added in a low voice, "she is French, which means she cannot betray me."

Which didn't make sense then but did later once I became aware of the political struggles between Nazi leadership, all of them jockeying for position. Otto wasn't worried about me because he saw me as entirely his creature, instead of someone likely to undermine him to one of the other powerful factions led by Abetz or Goebbels.

Today, as I wrote down notes in shorthand on my steno pad, I kept my face impassive and tried to memorize important details. There was to be a renewed focus on demonizing the Soviets as savages, as the German army was approaching a place called Stalingrad, and Hitler was determined to take the city, to humiliate the Soviet leader with the decimation of his name-sake. Though Otto had sent his old friend letters, arguing against it, hoping to convince Hitler to make a separate peace with the Soviets.

"We can't continue to fight on every front. We will still win," he'd told me a few days before, "but it takes too long. It hurts too many. Plus, the Red Army is made of blood, and Stalin doesn't care how much he spills of it."

Which had made me think that Hitler and Stalin were made for each other, but that was another thing I didn't say. I'd just put it in my mind to include in my later report for Le Lérot.

"And now," a colonel said in the conference room, tenting his hands as he looked narrowly down the long table, "we should discuss the black market. It's spiraling out of control."

"These black marketeers," another officer sputtered. "Can you believe they've been caught charging Germans more than French? The arrogance of them."

My hand stilled, the pen hovering over my pad. *Black market.* I thought unwillingly of Roger, his dark eyes, the frosty twilight when he'd kissed me that Christmas a year and a half ago. I hadn't seen him since—we'd had nothing but a message, relayed through Berthe, that we were to contact him if we needed anything. But he must have said more to her than that. Because when she'd told us, her wrinkled eyes had looked at me with pity.

Since then, I'd tried not to think about Roger because when I did, I felt a sense of loss so wide I could hardly bear it.

If I could, I would have put that into my secret reports, too. Just so I could write it down and forget him, along with all the rest I couldn't bear to remember.

"What do you have against the black marketeers? Don't you enjoy the steaks and oysters and oranges?" another Nazi officer jibed. "Where do you think our favorite restaurants get their ingredients? What about costumes for the theaters and sable stoles for our mistresses?"

The man's eyes seemed to linger on me.

Otto's jaw tightened. "We need to remind the French they belong to us, that their lives and fortunes exist only because we allow it so, and ensure they are reporting all activities against the Reich..."

"Yes," another complained, "but that is small compared to the threat of rebellion. Have you heard of this leader, this...? What is he called? The furry creature with the black mask across his eyes? The bandit?"

I suddenly couldn't breathe. Had I made a sound? I prayed I hadn't.

Otto glanced at me, then gave the men at the table a cold smile. "Le Lérot."

"The Dormouse." Another man snorted. "What a stupid name. Hibernates, then attacks a garden."

"Whatever his name, he's troubled us for far too long and grows bolder by the day."

Another officer demanded, "How dare he think he can hide in the shadows and defy us? Half a dozen sabotage efforts have already been linked to him."

"More than that."

"What can we do?"

"Find him," Otto said. "Find anyone who might *be* him. And make an example of every such man, one by one. Until none are left."

They continued for a while in this vein, each threat making my blood turn cold.

Then Standartenführer Becker, the ambitious officer in wire-rimmed glasses I'd never liked, said suddenly, "We just learned of a possible link to Le Lérot. I believe we should share this and could set a trap for him, as soon as tonight."

"Tonight?" Otto stroked his chin thoughtfully. "Interesting. Perhaps I will take care of this myself."

"Not pass on the information to the Gestapo?" Heinrich Becker said in surprise. There'd been a rumor, as yet unproven, that the man was secretly giving information to Otto's rivals there.

His eyes narrowed, even as he said with a smile, "It will be faster." As the younger man started to answer, he cut him off with, "Let's discuss this in private. Later."

"*Jawohl, Herr Reichsbevollmächtigter.*"

After a heated discussion with his officers, Otto finally turned to me. "Fräulein Vashon"—he always addressed me formally in public—"please read back your notes from the beginning."

I kept my voice cool as I read back from my shorthand in German, finishing, "... and anyone convicted of activities betraying the Reich will be questioned, then executed by firing squad, perhaps joined in death by his family and friends, and even his entire village."

"There are neighborhoods in Paris," another officer added viciously, "I'd be pleased to clean out. Let's get rid of these vermin."

"Yes." Otto's smile spread to a grin. "Starting tonight."

27

MARGOT

As we left headquarters, Otto seemed relaxed, whistling a little tune. He'd spoken with Heinrich Becker for a short time in private, perhaps just ten minutes, but I desperately wished I could have heard their discussion. All I really knew was that some kind of trap was happening tonight. I was vibrating with fear for the unknown Le Lérot and for anyone who might get caught up in the Nazi grip.

But as we walked to the sedan waiting on the Avenue Kléber, Otto chatted with Klaus about various Paris happenings that had nothing to do with the war at all.

"*La Femme de Machiavelli*, opening night," the older Schröder said with satisfaction, referring to the popular new play. "Sold-out show. From what I've heard from Josette, we're in for a treat."

In the last year, Otto had taken an almost proprietary interest in the Théâtre Lutèce. He liked the Widow Hébert, who was always a good friend to the Nazis. It was why Otto had given Josette her requested late-night curfew pass, a precious, rare gift that allowed her to travel in Paris after 9 p.m., unchallenged, on nights she had extra sequins to sew on or some other ridiculous task. Whoever heard of a sewing emergency? But Josette had nearly wept when he'd agreed to it, and Otto had basked in the glory of her sniveling gratitude.

"You have something to wear?" Otto asked his nephew now, not bothering to look at the chauffeur holding open the passenger door.

Klaus's bland face creased. "Uh... my dress uniform?"

"Very correct," Otto said, leaning back into the leather back seat. I climbed in beside him stiffly, holding papers in my arms. I was barely listening to their discussion, trying to commit to memory the more shocking things I'd heard today. Le Lérot was in danger. Not just him but any man who could potentially be him. It was clear the Nazis were willing to murder any number of innocent people to achieve their aims. But every time I thought I'd learned the furthest reach of their brutality, they came up with something new to shock me.

"Of course it is always good to be in uniform, to remind these stiff-necked Parisians to bow to our control," Otto continued amiably as the sedan moved from the curb, merging into the traffic. He tilted his head. "But sometimes it is also correct to show our softer sides. We are powerful enough that we do not need to wear our uniforms by rote." Turning, he gave me a smile. "I was considered quite the dandy before the war, in Munich."

"I'm sure," I said, returning his smile with effort.

That morning, when Otto had invited his nephew to attend the play's premiere instead of me, I'd been overwhelmed with relief. He usually expected me to accompany him to evening events, often buying me a new gown for the occasion at one of the department stores, or even Jacques Fath or Nina Ricci, where we were fawned over by desperate French salesgirls who needed a commission to feed their families. Sometimes my eyes would meet theirs—a shared moment of shame before we'd both look away. Afterward, when I was dressed in stylish new outfits or, even worse, couture, I blushed on the street as I passed my fellow citizens in their twice-turned clothes, the soles of their shoes worn through from walking, their hems ragged from bicycle riding since most private cars were disallowed.

"But, Uncle, I don't have anything but my uniforms. Dress and daily." Klaus looked down at himself, stone-faced as always. "I don't own a tuxedo."

Otto smiled good-naturedly at his nephew, who preferred the simple comforts of a *Soldatenkaffee* to French cuisine. "Well, I suppose it's fine. You young, you look good in everything. Don't you think so?"

He'd turned to direct that last comment to me. Absent-mindedly, I shrugged. "I don't think age matters."

His smile increased, making his cragged face eerily handsome as his gray eyes glowed down at me. "Exactly."

Later that afternoon, in the study at St. Agnes's, he dictated a letter to Hitler, seeking once again to persuade the German leader of strategic reasons not to attack Stalingrad and to make a separate peace. It was the third such letter he'd sent. My hand was shaking as I transcribed the words, then typed it out.

"Breathe nothing of this," he said to me as he signed the letter and folded it into an envelope, sealing it with wax. I nodded with big eyes. He smiled. "I know I can trust you, Margot."

I watched as Otto put a copy of the letter in a diplomatic packet, which was picked up by a courier a few moments later. Afterward, he called his nephew in from down the hall, where he'd been entertaining Lucie and the children.

"Come now, Klaus. Let's start the night off right." He poured them both a glass of schnapps, then looked at me questioningly.

I shook my head.

"Ah, women and their delicate constitutions. What will you do tonight all alone, Margot? Will you miss me?" Otto asked teasingly, but I saw how his gray eyes watched me.

"Of course." I forced a smile. "But I'll be well rested for work first thing tomorrow."

"No." He waved a careless hand. "We may be out late. You may sleep in."

"You're too kind," I said with real appreciation.

"You deserve it."

Our eyes locked, and I felt my cheeks burn—with guilt? With something else? He was looking at me so strangely.

I left the two men in Otto's study, speaking about family members back in Germany and Austria—Klaus's mother, his sister and his young nephews, barely older than babies, were apparently doing well. Klaus, visibly relieved, whispered, "Thank you, Uncle."

Otto saluted him with his glass. "To family. And duty."

His nephew clinked his glass, but there were tears in his eyes.

After finishing their schnapps, the two men set out on their planned dinner excursion to the gilded delights of Chez Georges, where they'd no doubt enjoy lobster pâté and steaks at the "German discount."

I hurried upstairs, intending to change my clothes into something invisible. Otto and Klaus would be at the theater for hours. Josette, too. I rarely had such a good chance to sneak away without anyone's notice, and I intended to take advantage of it. I heard Lucie feeding six noisy children their dinner in the kitchen. I paused, then shook my head. No time to help her unfortunately. I went silently up the back stairs. I'd make it up to her. I would. Later.

But when I reached the attic, my mouth fell open.

"What are you doing here?" I blurted out.

"I live here," Josette replied tartly, peeking her head back out from an open closet.

"But... it's right before the premiere. You're always so busy then. Sometimes we barely see you for days."

"I... needed something."

"What?"

"Don't worry about it." She stuffed something in the pocket of her dress, then turned to face me, her face unreadable.

Josette was now nineteen and a half, while I'd just turned twenty. She'd once been a clotheshorse, but even though I'd been forced into glamour these days, she oddly never seemed jealous.

Instead of the saddle shoes and bobby socks she'd brandished as a would-be Hollywood ingénue, she now wore plain, simple dresses, remade from old fabric, in deep blue, that fit her curves without drawing undue attention to them. Her low-heeled shoes were sensible and carefully polished to disguise the leather's wear. Even her red hair, her greatest vanity, no longer fell in carefully coiffed waves over her shoulders. She wore it in a tight chignon, swiftly constructed to get out of the way. She wore lipstick and some powder and mascara, but nothing more.

And somehow, she'd never looked better. Or more confident.

It was annoying. I didn't know why she would be so self-important over her job at a theater, even if she'd recently become head seamstress. "So you're heading back now?"

"Yes, must hurry. I need to check every hem before opening night and make a few changes, as our lead actress often gains weight right before the first show. She eats when she's nervous." She rolled her eyes. "You'd think I'd learn, but every time she swears it will never happen again, and every time I believe her."

"How is it going, your first play as head seamstress?"

"Costumer," she corrected. Then her smile faded. "It's been... fine."

We looked at each other grimly. The Théâtre Lutèce's former head seamstress, who for over a year had been Josette's champion, had disappeared in March. She was Jewish. No one knew where she'd gone.

The lives of France's Jews had grown increasingly worse. At first, it was just the foreign-born refugees who were arrested. Then French Jews, too, had been forced to register, demonized with propaganda, and in March, their deportations had begun. The Germans claimed they were "resettling" Jewish people into a new homeland of their own, somewhere to the east. But where exactly?

The Germans had ordered all Jews over the age of six to wear a yellow star on their clothing. I passed them sometimes on the street, women and children holding each other close, hollows beneath their cheekbones, scared to lift their eyes. And I felt shame when I thought of how I must have appeared to them: a well-fed, prosperous, disgusting German collaborator!

I swallowed hard. "Did you ever find out what happened to Judith?"

"No," she said tightly.

"Did she escape? Is she safe?"

"*I don't know.*" Josette sounded almost angry, as if she resented me bringing up the reason for her career promotion. She always refused to talk in much detail about the Jewish plight. It seemed a little unfeeling and strange, for anyone who had a heart.

She turned away, her hands placed oddly over her pocket. "I have to go. Are you coming tonight?"

"No," I said in real relief. "Otto's taking Klaus."

She stared at me. "I still can't believe you call that man by his first name."

My cheeks burned. "He asked me to, in private."

"But you're not with him now." The redhead paused at the door, then looked back. "Don't forget which side you're on, Margot."

She was gone before I could formulate a retort. There was nothing I could say, anyway. I couldn't tell my sisters what I was doing. Not without putting them at risk and exposing my father's involvement. Not that Dr. Ravanel knew he was my father, of course.

Lies upon lies.

But it stung to think that Josette, and perhaps even Lucie and Berthe for all I knew, might think I could really be on Otto's side—ever. It was true I pitied him sometimes. But not nearly as much as I feared him. He treated me carefully, like an asset. But I'd seen his ruthlessness. If that viciousness should ever be turned on me—if he ever learned how I'd betrayed him...

Shaking the thought from my mind, I went to the wardrobe and pulled on the dowdiest clothes I could find—trousers and an oversized shirt which Helen had left behind as too plain, its fabric too worn for even Josette to try to refashion into something better. In the bathroom, I wiped the makeup off my face. Wearing these clothes, with my dark, wild hair tucked beneath an old cap left behind by the gardener, I could almost pass for a young boy from a distance. A plain, boring boy of about twelve, no threat to anyone.

Holding my breath, I snuck down the back stairs and out of the house through the garden to the secondhand bicycle we all shared. I walked it down the rue des Orphelines, unable to relax until I was on the Boulevard Saint-Martin.

It took almost an hour for me to bicycle to Neuilly and find Dr. Ravanel at the hospital. Once, it had been known as the American Hospital, but now the Americans were our supposed enemies, the hospital was run under the supervision of the French Red Cross.

It was busy, crowded with people in the waiting area, some moaning with their ailments, treated by overworked staff.

When Dr. Ravanel saw me, his eyes widened. "Nurse, I need to see that patient immediately," he said.

Once we were in a private examination room, he turned eagerly. "You have something?"

I swiftly told him about Stalingrad and everything else I could remember. "Le Lérot must be warned—whatever he's doing tonight, he might be walking into a trap. And anyone who's close to him, or might be mistaken for him, must be careful. The Germans are planning to cast a wide net."

"Thank you. I'll tell him." He embraced me.

Feeling my father's arms around me, I briefly closed my eyes. When would I be able to tell him the truth about me?

When would this war be over?

Some of my anguish must have appeared on my face because when Dr. Ravanel pulled away, he frowned. "How are you, Margot? Are you in any danger?"

I shook my head. "Otto—Herr Schröder," I corrected myself, "he trusts me."

In the small, private examination room, he stared at me with narrowed eyes, then shook his head. "I don't like it."

"Because I used his first name? You must take nothing from it."

"Because he trusts you so much. A man like that—sooner or later he'll feel vulnerable, and he won't like it, and he'll turn on you."

It was a thought I'd had myself, once or twice. I thought of Otto's ex-wife and how Helen had been forced to use a revolver to get her away. And though he said he didn't have anything directly to do with deporting Jews, he'd created the propaganda that pretended to justify their treatment—and his men had executed many others branded "traitors."

And those were only the things that he'd spoken about in front of me. Who knew how much worse it might be?

Women and their delicate constitutions.

"Don't worry," I told my father now. "I'm keeping an eye on him."

"That's something else I'm afraid of."

My eyebrows lifted in disbelief. "Are you afraid I'll start to care for him?"

Dr. Ravanel looked at me sadly. "Sometimes we become what we pretend to be."

"I feel sorry for him, that's all. Pity isn't the same as love."

"Isn't it?"

"No," I replied, shocked. "There's no love without respect." My voice trembled as I thought how lucky I was to have Dr. Ravanel as a father, someone I both loved and respected.

He frowned at me, looking at me more closely. "You're wise for a twenty-one-year-old."

"Twenty."

"What?"

"I just turned twenty."

"But Helen told me you were born in 1921." He looked at me sharply. "Why would she lie?"

"O-Oh," I stammered, my cheeks turning hot. "She, um, must have made a mistake. Confused me with one of the other orphans."

He stared at me in a way that was almost frightening in its intensity. "Tell me about your parents."

"My parents?"

"She told me she found you and your sister in 1924. When you were three."

"When were you talking about me?"

"When I was replacing bandages after her bullet wound. Back in La Ravelle. I was... curious about you."

Suddenly shivering, I looked away. "Why would you be curious about me? I'm no one."

"I'd just seen a resemblance, and I thought... Then she told me when you were born, and I knew I was imagining things." His dark eyes looked like fire as he reached out to grip my shoulder, looking down at me. "Was I imagining it, Margot? Was I?"

My mouth was dry, my heart pounding. I knew I had to lie to him. I'd judged Helen for keeping me a secret. But now I better understood her reasons.

If I told him the truth, everything would change, in ways I couldn't control. He might tell me I couldn't bring him secrets anymore. He might be ashamed of me and tell me to stay away from his family. Or he might embrace me as the daughter he'd never known. I didn't know what would happen. And that was terrifying.

My lips parted.

"Margot." His voice was quietly pleading. "Tell me the truth."

Just those four simple words, and the lie I'd been formulating disappeared into thin air. Everything came into sharp focus. *Tell me the truth.* How angry had I been at Helen for keeping the fact that she was my mother a secret for all my life? How hurt?

My body was trembling. I lifted my gaze. Jean-Luc Ravanel's dark eyes were just like mine. His dark, wavy hair, though shorter, was exactly like mine. I'd wondered how it was possible he'd seen Helen Taylor after all those years, when she'd resurfaced, and never once wondered if I could be his. Now I understood. Because Helen—the upright, prim, honorable Helen Taylor—had looked into his face and lied.

But I couldn't.

"You're not... wrong," I whispered, looking away. "But I didn't know. Not until after we left La Ravelle. I always thought

Lucie was my sister. I thought the woman who died in the Place Pigalle was my mother."

"But she wasn't, was she?" His voice was calm, low.

I shook my head.

"Who?" he said.

"Helen."

His hand gripped my shoulder almost painfully. "And your father?"

My eyes swam with tears. I couldn't answer.

"Margot." His voice caught. "Please tell me."

With an intake of breath, I looked up. "It's you."

2 8

JOSETTE

"There." I drew back, looking at the blonde critically before I brushed a red tendril of hair off my sweaty forehead and exhaled in relief. "It works."

The young actress playing the ingénue, only a few years older than me, looked at herself in the mirror, then sighed in pleasure. "It's perfect. How did you find it?"

"I made it," I replied tartly, but I was smiling. It was a sleekly ingenious hat, if I did say so myself, made of velvet loosely in the fifteenth-century Italian style. I'd modified it to also clamp down on the tips of the girl's unfortunate ears, which stuck out so badly that if she'd had an engine, you could probably have climbed on her back and flown her over La Manche. The period-appropriate hairstyle, of loose frizzy curls around the temples and cheekbones, wasn't nearly enough to do the job.

But my hat was.

As I watched the actors take their places behind the curtain —including the lead brunette playing the fictional version of Marietta Corsini, the eponymous wife of Machiavelli, now in an appropriately fitting bodice over her plumper waist—I felt my heart quicken. This always happened on opening night. I could hear the chamber orchestra warming up in the pit; the heady buzz of the audience. We had a sold-out house.

Of course we did. Germans would be interested in Machiavelli's sly use of power—and the fictional romantic shenanigans of his wife.

At least, I assumed they were fictional. Otherwise, she was quite a lady, manipulating her husband so deviously, juggling multiple lovers, all while also running a household and raising seven children.

Glancing back at the red velvet hat, I felt a wave of pride. Judith had taught me so much. She would have been proud of me.

I hoped she'd made it to Switzerland. It had probably been a mistake, choosing Switzerland, when we'd only had one forged Swiss visa to copy and had to do it by hand. But as we'd teased her through tearful laughter, she'd always had a *tendre* for cuckoo clocks and cheese. But even reaching for that perfect safety was a gamble. Swiss visas were rare. If any German official went looking, it wouldn't be hard to trace it back to us.

Especially since I kept stealing Herr Schröder's official rubber stamp for the identity cards, travel passes and exit visas. I'd found a way to pick the lock of his study with a pin and sneak in. I'd brought it back and forth many times now. I'd fled to the attic when they'd returned early today—where Margot had nearly caught me.

I was starting to take ridiculous risks. But hopefully today would be the last time I'd have to steal it. Madame Hébert had told me she'd finally found a trustworthy forger with both the materials and the skill to create a perfect facsimile of the signature into a new rubber stamp. I'd nearly cried with relief. Breaking into the study felt increasingly dangerous.

The widow had asked many times if I wanted out. But I couldn't stop. Not because I was brave but because I was such a coward. While French Jews were being persecuted, I remained safe. Because no one knew.

Closing my eyes, I said a little prayer for Judith and another for Fauve, who Herr Schröder must never know had a Jewish mother. For good measure, I even tossed in one for Sister Helen and all the girls who'd gone to America two years ago—who we hadn't heard from since.

"Josette!" An anxious hiss.

I opened my eyes. The middle-aged man playing Machiavelli had a panicked look in his eyes as he held out his elbow, where the seam had loosened, revealing his skin in the tight sleeve. "I was just pulling on a thread... I swear... then it all just..."

Before the words had finished leaving his mouth, I'd already yanked a needle from the pincushion I kept tied to my wrist with a silk ribbon. In less than a minute, I'd loosely stitched the seam together and cut the end of the thread with my teeth, finishing just a minute before he had to go out on stage.

I was the head costumer now. It was my only purpose.

Not just what happened onstage. What happened here at night, in secret, when the Germans couldn't see.

Glancing out at the house from the wings, I saw smiling German officers sitting next to well-dressed, well-fed French citizens. Otto Schröder was likely out there, too, though I couldn't see him. While most of Paris was suffering, there were a few that were doing well, very well indeed, in the new regime. Generally, they were the same few who'd prospered in the old regime, too. Who somehow managed to thrive in every regime.

Someone had to protect the ones who could not.

As the play progressed, actors rushed off stage between their scenes, some needing quick hems, the plump lead actress complaining that the seams of her costume were still too tight, complaining about my stitches, as if she hadn't stuffed herself with an entire basket of chocolate creams right before the curtain rose. The chocolates, nearly impossible to find now, had been a gift from an infatuated Nazi colonel, who almost certainly had a wife back in Germany. I said nothing, just calmly kept replenishing pins and thread in the pincushion attached to my wrist. A trick I'd learned from Judith.

To my relief, other than a few minor rips and tears, opening night went without a hitch. It was always a little nerve-racking, especially after we'd done a play last year in which, during the kissing scene, the buttons from the hero's uniform had caught on some netting in the heroine's bodice and ripped it, revealing the entirety of her breasts on stage. It had caused a sensation, and after that, we'd sold out the entire season. But though the men in the audience kept hoping, the mistake never happened again. Judith had made sure of it.

I missed her. Every day. And idolized her. And felt wretched.

No one knew I was half Jewish by blood. I felt guilty with every breath I took, and it had only grown worse as the Nazis clamped down. I didn't have to wear a gold star on my clothing, leaving me vulnerable to abuse from strangers. I was allowed to have a job. I was accepted as a citizen, as French Jews no longer were—even if their ancestors had lived in France peacefully since before Napoleon.

I was lucky that no one knew. But I was also ashamed.

The only way I could bear my shame was by helping others.

"Fräulein Dubois."

I jumped. "Herr Schröder."

It was startling to see him backstage. The play had ended. In full dress uniform, he loped forward using his cane, his nephew behind him. I was glad he hadn't brought Margot for once. It was disgraceful how much time they spent together.

He beamed at me. "A triumph. You should be congratulated."

"Thank you." Then I added wisely a moment later, "It is in

great thanks to you, for allowing me to have the after-curfew pass. Otherwise, the actors might all be wearing flour sacks."

"It's nothing, nothing at all," he tutted, but he seemed delighted with the praise. "I've always been a lover of the arts." He turned when he saw the widow backstage. "Ah—Frau Hébert."

"*Monsieur.*" Madame Hébert gave a slight nod. She was wearing a dress even more dramatic than usual, a kaftan in murderous red, her neck dripping with jewels, though the jewels were all paste—she'd told me the real ones had been sold long ago. All she had left of her husband's coal fortune was this theater. Even her luxurious five-story townhouse on the rue Commines had been mortgaged to pay for repairs to the theater's foundation and roof, and to reupholster all the seats in 1939.

She held out her hand grandly. Her black hair, now with a streak of white at the roots, gave her a stark appearance, along with her bejeweled walking cane.

Herr Schröder took her hand in his, bowing his head over it like an eighteenth-century chevalier. "I am glad theater in Paris is in your trustworthy hands."

"*Merci.*" She pulled back her hand and drew herself up with an imperial smile.

"You've always been a good friend to Germany. I won't forget." He glanced, smiling, from her jeweled walking stick to his own cane, made of glossy wood with the sharp brass head of an eagle as the handle. "If there's anything you need…"

"You've done it already, sending Josette to us. I am truly grateful, *monsieur*. Any success of the Théâtre Lutèce is thanks to you," she said, laying it on thick, just as I'd done.

I had learned from her to play nice.

He beamed. "Thank you, thank you." He glanced at his steel wristwatch. "Ah, we must be off."

"You have an appointment? At this late hour?"

"The Reich stops for no one, not even on nights like this."
He gave a significant glance at his nephew, clicked his heels
with a little bow and left.

I stared after the two men, wondering what on earth could
send him out so late. Usually Herr Schröder was a man of bour-
geois habits—early to bed, early to rise. I hoped it didn't involve
Margot. If it did, I'd give her a good shake and threaten to tell
Lucie—or worse, Berthe.

Though it almost made me laugh to think of 8 p.m. as late.
Curtain times in France were now astonishingly early, to give
the audience time to get home before the citywide curfew. Even
Berthe could easily have attended without a single yawn.

The theater was only briefly busy after the end of the
performance, as others came backstage to congratulate us, and
German officers brought competing roses for the actresses, who
seemed to enjoy watching their rivalry.

But they all left soon, even those few who had passes to
break curfew. Paris went completely dark at night, to protect
against any potential attack from Allied planes. The Renault
plant, now building vehicles for the German army, had been
bombed into oblivion in March. It was still strange to me how,
every night, the city of light disappeared completely into
darkness.

The audience and cast and crew made haste, tumbling out
noisily from backstage in search of late dinners, wine and
private nooks. Just before nine, the theater was very quiet. Ten
minutes later, Séverine Hébert looked at me.

"Get the light."

I followed her and the two others in on the secret—Albert, a
middle-aged carpenter, and Clothilde, the woman who cleaned
the theater at night—to the nondescript door. Madame Hébert
took the key ring out of its usual hiding place and unlocked it,
then led us down the rickety stairs, all of us carrying flashlights.

This building was new—only seventy-five years old, built

under Baron Haussmann—but it had been built over a far older stone foundation. "Take care not to wander off," she'd warned me. "This basement is a rabbit warren. My late husband took advantage of it, by building a secret staircase to a hidden passage he created behind the walls of the changing room upstairs. He enjoyed spying on the chorus girls." She'd added with sardonic amusement, "It was the only time he took exercise."

The basement smelled of mildew, and contained the dribs and drabs of old things piled in boxes no one bothered with, left to molder away.

Once we were inside the secret room, tucked behind the old scenic backdrops, Madame Hébert pulled the string of the single light bulb that hung from the ceiling above the table and printing press—barely enough to chase the shadows away—then locked the door behind us so we could get to work.

"How many today?" I asked.

"Five. Do you have the stamp?"

I nodded. The precious official stamp was too risky to leave in the theater, on the chance it would be missed by Herr Schröder. "How long will the forger need it tonight?"

Her lips pinched. "He's been delayed. He'll do it during the performance tomorrow."

"Tomorrow," I said in dismay.

"Can't be helped," she said briskly. She looked at her list. "A widowed mother, two children. A young man. A grandfather."

We gathered around the little table. I squinted at the names on her list. For a year and a half, we'd forged identity papers. For Jews. For teenaged boys trying to escape being sent to forced work camps in Germany. For anyone considered "undesirable."

I'd become proficient at adding names in exactly the right script and ink. Madame Hébert looked at my work carefully under the glow of a flashlight. With steady writing, the right kind of paper and the officious stamp, sealed together in the press, *voilà*—widowed mother Miryam Cohen became Manon Chamier, and her young children were given names to match. "You've become good at this."

"Thank you," I said, with a lump in my throat. Madame Hébert almost never gave praise.

These fake papers would help save these five people from imprisonment—or worse—by getting them to a neutral country like Portugal and Sweden, or colonial outposts that offered refuge, like Algeria, or Martinique in the Caribbean.

Madame Hébert pulled up a chair and worked beside the three of us, as diligently and soberly as a newly hired clerk at his first job.

"There, that's good," she said finally. "We should lock up before the morning crew arrives. Now go get some rest."

I stretched my aching body before I rose to help tidy up. We didn't know how she got the names, or how she passed on the identity cards and travel papers to people in need. Clothilde, the elderly charwoman, had a theory she was working with Le Lérot, though none of us were sure. The Resistance leader had become so well known that everything that happened in the Marais, good or bad, was now credited to this legendary figure. No one knew anything about him—or her, though Albert, the craggy-faced carpenter, had scoffed when I'd suggested it might be a woman.

"Women can be strong and clever, can't they?" I'd looked to Madame Hébert for confirmation, but she'd only shrugged.

"The strongest and cleverest avoid notice when they choose," she'd said.

Albert and Clothilde, who had no after-curfew passes, settled in to their sofas backstage, to try to get some rest until they could safely leave in the early morning. But I followed Madame Hébert out.

As she locked up the Théâtre Lutèce behind us, I took a

deep breath of the cool summer air. The stars were bright over Paris.

The older woman, who'd somehow finagled her own pass from somewhere she wouldn't admit to, looked at me from the door. "Thank you for this, my dear. I rely on you."

"Will Le Lérot be pleased?" I asked coyly.

She gave a wistful smile. "These particular passes are not for him but for friends of friends I will be helping directly. But Le Lérot is an amazing young man."

So it's a man, I thought. "You've met him?"

"Yes. Someday soon you will, too."

"Soon?" I held my breath.

She smiled. "He knows your name. Perhaps he will reach out to you."

The Métro was closed after curfew, and bicycling would have drawn too much attention, so we always walked back to the Marais together.

But not tonight. She looked at me outside the theater. "I must get these passes to them immediately—there's no time to waste. You'll be all right walking on your own?"

"Of course," I said. But I felt a nervous flutter at the thought of walking home without her. At night, the empty streets of Paris felt dark and dangerous. I realized I'd come to depend on sharing her courage on the walk. No ruffian or Nazi would risk her wrath.

She paused, her heavily made-up face strangely young in the moonlight, like a girl playing dress-up in her grandmother's lavish silks and jewels. "Good night, my dear. Stay safe."

"You too." I'd walked home many times before. I could do it alone, I told myself. I had my after-curfew pass. I had nothing to worry about.

But I'd barely gone two streets over when two German soldiers accosted me.

"What could you be doing out past curfew, all alone..." But

their sly, suggestive looks disappeared when they saw Otto Schröder's name on my pass.

"We will escort you the rest of the way, *mademoiselle*," one told me in halting French.

"It's really not necessary—"

"We cannot risk you being injured by some evil Frenchman on your route. Like Le Lérot. We'll walk along the Seine, for the moonlight."

And so they walked me back to the Marais, very politely. I listened to them speaking German, which they did freely, in the apparent belief I would not understand. I kept my face blank so I didn't give myself away.

"So there was no one there?"

"No one."

"Someone must have warned him."

"Oh ho. I wouldn't want to be him, having to explain to the Führer there must be a mole in his department—"

"Shhh," one hissed, looking at me.

But I didn't react. Across the river, in the moonlight, I'd spotted the mansion belonging to my father. For two years, since before the invasion, it had been boarded up, abandoned, but now, there were bright lights in the windows. I imagined I heard music, laughter, floating across the water. Dancing until dawn? With all that forbidden light?

"Is something wrong, *mademoiselle*?" one of them asked in halting French.

"N-No, nothing," I replied and kept walking. But my eyes were wide.

The sky had turned from slate to light gray when they left me at the door of St. Agnes's with a bow.

"Give our compliments to the *Reichsbevollmächtigter*," one said to me, again in that awkward French.

"Our commiserations, more like," the other jeered in German under his breath. He was elbowed by his comrade.

"Bonsoir, mademoiselle." He touched his cap, and they both fled.

What were they talking about? Why would Herr Schröder be upset? He'd seemed in excellent spirits at the theater, and before, when they'd come home from headquarters and nearly caught me relocking his study door.

St. Agnes's front door would be locked now, too. I went into the garden to knock on Berthe's window. She opened the back door for me, scowling, her white hair a mess, her robe wrinkled.

"What time is it?" she demanded, and when I told her, she looked straggle-eyed at the sky, then sighed. "I might as well start making the *Nußschnecken.*"

"I'm sorry, Berthe. I'll make it up to you."

"You keep promising to get me theater tickets."

"I will," I said brightly. "Just tell me the night."

She looked at me hopefully. "Tomorrow night would be..."

But I was already tiptoeing up the stairs, yawning and exhausted. I prayed I could sneak into the attic room without waking up the children—or Lucie's dog. I just needed a few hours of sleep.

But when I reached the attic room, I found only the six little orphans, sleeping alone, guarded by Choupette, who was snoring on a rug.

Where were Lucie and Margot?

I heard noises in the adjacent dorm room. No one ever went in there. Had Lucie and Margot gone to sleep in the empty room for some reason?

I went in and turned on the light.

Lucie leaped up from the nearest bed, her cheeks red, her eyes wild. "Josette," she cried, "where have you been?"

"Where have I been? At the theater!" I looked from her to the slender bed she'd been sitting on in the dark. And not alone. "What's going on?"

Klaus, Otto's nephew, rose in his turn, his uniform wrinkled, his expression equally guilty. "We were only—"

"Yes, I can see what you were only," I ground out. At least they were both fully dressed. "How could you? She's only—" Then I remembered that Lucie, whom I thought of as still a child, was in fact eighteen. Older than I'd been when I'd fallen for Roger—a crush I'd embarrassingly thought would last forever. Setting my jaw, I shook my head. "You both should be ashamed of yourselves."

"M-My intentions are honorable," Klaus stuttered. He turned. "Lucie, you must know—"

I whirled on her. "What were you thinking?"

Lucie looked about to cry. "We... we were just..." She wiped her eyes. "I've been so worried. We've been waiting for you and Margot all night."

"Margot's missing?" I gasped. That had never happened before.

"I hoped she was with you." Lucie looked past me, out into the empty hallway, her pretty face anguished. "Where has she been all night?"

29

LUCIE

We had six orphaned children now. *Six.*

It had been over a year since Herr Schröder had caught Françoise, our previous charwoman, stealing food from his kitchen. He'd had her whipped and sent to prison, a shocking turn of events, and Berthe had hired a stolid middle-aged widow to replace her. Marceline did the cleaning and occasionally helped with the cooking, for complicated recipes or days Berthe was feeling poorly.

"Do you want help with the children?" the cook had asked me then.

I'd shaken my head. It had seemed feeble that I couldn't manage three children on my own. Many mothers had three children, didn't they? I should be able to handle it. Though I often felt so tired I could have fallen asleep standing up.

Margot and Josette were always too busy to help, Berthe had enough responsibility already, and I hated the idea of having some stranger in charge of my children. "I'll be fine," I'd told her. "Children grow up so fast."

But just as Fauve, Thérèse and Geneviève had all started sleeping through the night, new surprises had come our way.

Now, looking back to when I'd only had three, I sometimes mused about how easy it had been back then and wondered what I'd been complaining about.

In the last year and a half, three newborns had been left at our door, one of them a boy, even. The first boy to be welcomed to St. Agnes's since it had been built for lost and abandoned female orphans back in the seventeenth century—other than Berthe's own son, of course, whom she'd raised here as a single mother before he'd died in the first war.

But people apparently believed the children would receive better care at a Nazi officer's home than at overwhelmed French orphanages struggling amid the shortages.

Jeanne had been left at our door first, red-faced and squalling, in February 1941. There'd been no note, but Berthe had named her after Joan of Arc, and I'd imagined a story for her. Her father had been a soldier who'd meant to marry her mother, but died too soon. I pictured the young mother weeping as she'd kissed the baby on the forehead one last time.

The second abandoned baby had been left outside the garden in August 1941. Berthe had named her Bernadette, after a recently canonized saint. She was perhaps a few months old then, but soon became fat and mischievous, with a jolly laugh.

The last baby to arrive had been Louis, this past January, the only one who'd been left with a note. He and Bernadette were likely the products of forbidden affairs between French women and German soldiers—or else the women had been forced. I didn't like to think about that. They'd all been given the surname of Dubois, per St. Agnes's tradition.

Jeanne and Bernadette were now toddlers, who ran around the hallways, chortling, after Thérèse and Geneviève. They were often underfoot in the kitchen, the bane of Berthe's patience, trying to taste things, or stepping on Choupette's tail. Bernadette in particular brought gleeful chaos, following the other three girls and leaving messes in her wake.

As for Louis, after an early bout of croup, he'd turned into the sweetest, most peaceful baby in the world. He watched the older girls with tranquil brown eyes and only cried when he was hungry, or needed to be changed, or perhaps if Thérèse was being naughty and had pulled his pacifier out of his mouth. He was six months old, and still needed to be carried and held. He seemed as peaceful and wise as the saint he'd been named after.

They were my responsibility, solely, all at once: Fauve, Thérèse, Geneviève, Jeanne, Bernadette and Louis.

Fauve was the one I worried most about. Her Jewish heritage was a secret so dangerous that even Josette, Margot and I never spoke of it aloud. We vowed that no one must know— ever.

After the laws decreeing Jews had to wear gold stars on their clothing were passed, I became so scared for the little girl that I wished desperately that I could get her out of the country. If only there was some safe way—and someone trustworthy to take her. I'd hinted that much aloud, but neither Josette nor Margot were interested. For two people who'd once been so desperate to leave Paris, they now seemed utterly determined to stay. I didn't understand it.

But Fauve must have sensed my worry. She had a good heart and tried to help with the babies, but she was a child, not yet seven, and shouldn't be forced to be a caretaker. So I tried not to let her. But sometimes I had to—and then felt so guilty.

Everything had changed on a sunny afternoon this past March.

I hadn't slept in days because of Louis's croup, and the world seemed like it had been gray and colorless for months. Josette had an afternoon off from her job at the theater and told me to take Louis for a walk, to get some fresh air and sun on my skin. She and Berthe promised to watch the other five children.

By this point, I wasn't sure who was crying harder, me or the baby, so I agreed. Five minutes later, I found myself dressed, with Louis wrapped in the baby carriage, as Josette and Berthe gently pushed me out into the sunshine.

Louis stopped crying, and so did I. As I looked up into the blue sky, I saw birds and heard them singing. It was spring at last. If one didn't look too closely, it was simply Paris as always —the smoke-stained, cream buildings, the Tour Eiffel. But instead of the French tricolor flag, blood-red Swastika-adorned standards were everywhere—and German soldiers with their jackboots and rifles.

There was more dust and dirt, and uncollected trash being picked over by hungry Parisians. Restaurants and families that tried to get by without the black market, or couldn't afford it, went hungry with meager rations. For a few months, I'd snuck small bags of food from the kitchen, and left them outside the doors of hungry families. Until Berthe caught me and warned I was putting my own children at risk. "I'm sorry for those going hungry, but look what happened to Françoise. Who will take care of the children if you're in prison?"

So I'd stopped. I could barely remember the days when I'd thought Otto Schröder to be polite or kind. He now frightened me desperately. How I wished now that I'd taken my babies and fled Paris, that first day when Margot, Josette and Roger had appeared!

Though Fauve, Jeanne, Bernadette and Louis would then all have suffered and perhaps starved. My heart hurt when I tried to think of an escape for them—for any of us. At least at St. Agnes's, we had shelter and food and no one dared hurt us. We had new clothing for the children, some from Herr Schröder, some anonymously provided through Berthe—gifts I knew must come from Roger. But every day still hurt more and more.

Over the past year, I'd seen dirty, hungry-looking children running wild in the streets, and seen German soldiers scream at them. Once I'd seen a soldier punch an old man in the face. I'd longed to go fight, to defend him. Once, I would have, no matter the cost. But at that moment, I'd had five children and Choupette with me, so I'd been forced to turn away from the old Frenchman's bloody face as he'd fallen to the ground at the feet of the mocking soldiers. I'd had to protect my own. It had been bitter. I'd felt ashamed.

When I'd told Margot about it later, after she'd gotten home from Nazi headquarters, where she often went now, she'd been oddly unsympathetic. She'd told me shortly I had to choose my battles, and then she'd gone into Herr Schröder's study and closed the door.

But while I took that springtime walk with baby Louis, I saw a hungry little girl, her cheeks hollow and dirty, with a gold star on her ragged jacket, and forgot all the rules Berthe had impressed on me. I reached into my pocket and pulled out the paper-wrapped sandwich I'd brought for my own lunch.

"Here," I whispered, smiling as I handed it to her.

She sucked in her breath, her dark eyes huge, her expression uncertain, then grabbed it in a rush. The paper fell to the sidewalk as she backed away, gobbling it down.

Then I was startled by a shout.

"You. You there."

Three young German soldiers standing at the corner were staring at me. One boldly came forward, his rifle hanging over his shoulder. He said in good French, "What are you doing? Giving food to..." His lip twisted in disgust.

I straightened. "To a hungry child, *monsieur*."

Another soldier's eyes narrowed at my tone. "Is that so?" He looked down at the carriage. "Where do you think you're going?"

"I'm taking my baby on a walk, *monsieur*." My heart was pounding. Usually, when I left St. Agnes's, I traveled with a crowd of children, my dog and sometimes even Berthe, when her sciatica wasn't acting up. Now I was alone.

"Pretty little thing, aren't you?" he murmured, touching my cheek. "Let me see your papers."

"Of course." But when I felt in my pocket, I realized in the tumult of leaving the house, I'd left my identity card behind. "I'm sorry." My cheeks flooded with heat. "I seem to have forgotten them."

"Oh ho." His eyes widened, and he flashed a shark-like smile. "Did you now?"

"If you'll just come with me, you'll see, I live at St. Agnes's, where Otto Schröder is our—"

"She doesn't have papers, fellas," he told the other two in German. The three soldiers clustered around me, leering.

"You have a baby."

"No wedding ring."

"Some men get all the fun."

"Hey, we're lonely, too."

"There's a place around the corner. You could show us your papers there." His heavily lidded eyes flickered as he looked me over insolently in my oversized jacket and old, worn dress. "I bet we can find them under all that fabric."

"Yes, I bet we can."

"No—no please." I desperately tried to push the hands off me. "I have a baby—"

He shrugged. "Leave it behind."

"Leave the baby!" I looked wildly around the street, hoping for someone to save me. But my fellow countrymen looked away, some of their expressions filled with rage, others with shame and pity. But no one intervened, just as I hadn't that time I saw the man punched. "I can't just leave him on the street!"

"If you care about him, you'll come around to the alley and do what we want, and be quick about it."

"Just two minutes should do it," said one, looking me over.

Another one, with fleshy cheeks and pale blue eyes, leered at my breasts beneath my oversized jacket, smacking his lips. "Thirty seconds for me."

The others snorted, teasing him in ribald words, while he laughed and spoke proudly of being an example of German efficiency.

These young men laughing and joking as if using a baby as hostage was all in good fun... It turned my stomach.

"No," I cried, looking around. "Please. Just take me back home. I work for the *Reichsmo... Reichsbevoll...*" I could never manage all the consonants of his most important title. I tried to remember the other one, his military one. "The *Obergrup-grupen...*" Nope. I took a deep breath. "Herr Otto Schröder. He—"

"I'm sick of you French girls acting like such prudes when clearly you're not." He looked from baby Louis to my leather shoes, which were new, Christmas gifts from Herr Schröder a few months before. "Acting like prostitutes, expecting payment," he complained. "How can an honest German soldier compete with rich officers?"

"I've had it." One gripped my arm painfully. "Come now. Or the baby carriage might accidentally roll into the street. How would you like that?"

I sucked in my breath, looking towards the busy Boulevard Beaumarchais, with its gleaming black sedans for Germans and dilapidated bicycles for everyone else. Then I looked down at my sweetly sleeping baby.

"What's this?" a low voice said behind me in German.

I turned, gasping when I saw him. The tall, handsome officer who'd been so kind to me for the past year. The young German who'd tried to speak out against the Nazis, only to be blackmailed into compliance by his uncle's threats—Klaus Schröder.

The soldiers bowed their heads, looking nervous at being spoken to by an officer.

"It's nothing, sir," one soldier muttered. "Just dealing with this French girl who has no papers."

"Yes. Dealing with her." The other soldiers nodded eagerly.

Klaus looked at me. For a long time now, I'd thought how handsome he was—his blond hair, stocky build and calm, friendly blue eyes.

Calm and friendly for me. But very cold indeed as he looked at the soldiers.

"I know this lady. She is under the protection of Reichs-bevollmächtigter Schröder—you know the name?"

They paled a little. "I'm sorry, *Herr Leutnant.*"

"We were just trying to follow orders, sir. She has no papers—can't be too careful."

"Thank you for your vigilance." His voice was like ice. "I will escort the young lady and her baby back to her home."

"But, sir—" the first soldier protested, angry at losing his prey.

"Yes?" Klaus tilted his head coolly and waited, in the exact way I'd seen his uncle do.

The other soldiers fell back, and the first soldier realized he no longer had strength in numbers. His shoulders sank. "Nothing, *Herr Leutnant.* Thank you, sir."

Klaus turned to me, his jaw hard. But his voice was gentle as he motioned with his hand, not touching me. "Come with me, please, Mademoiselle Vashon."

He'd spoken to me in French. His accent had much improved since he'd arrived that long-ago Christmas.

I started walking, pushing the baby carriage. "Thank you, Klaus."

Beside me, he said quietly, "I am glad I was here."

"Me, too." My cheeks colored a little as I glanced at him out the corner of my eye. Then the baby carriage bounced over a curb, and Louis started crying. I tried to comfort him with my hand on his belly as we walked, but his crying worsened, so I stopped and picked him up in my arms. He wouldn't be consoled, though.

People gawked at us openly—a Nazi officer, a French girl and a wailing baby. Klaus didn't seem to notice.

"Poor lad. He's the one who was just left here, wasn't he?"

"Two months ago."

He held out his hands. "My sister has two of her own. May I try?"

I hesitated, then nodded.

He pressed the baby against his shoulder and rubbed his back with a large hand, humming some German lullaby in his low, deep voice. Then he started to walk. I followed, pushing the empty carriage.

For a moment, the baby continued to wail. Then, slowly, his sobs subsided, soothed by the weight of the hand, the rhythm of the steps, the reverberations of the low voice. Louis gave a little hiccup, then looked sleepy. The tears on his cheek dried; his eyes grew drowsy, then closed altogether.

"How on earth...?" I breathed.

Klaus gave me a shy smile. "Nice to see I haven't lost my touch."

Seeing a powerful, handsome young man holding a sleeping baby so gently and tenderly against his shoulder made my heart pound strangely in my chest. I bit my lip. "Do you want to put him back in the carriage?"

He glanced down at the baby's cheek resting against his shoulder. "He's not asleep just yet, I don't think. Poor little thing. How could anyone just abandon a baby?"

"There was a note," I said quietly. "It said, 'A German did this to me; let the Germans take care of it.'"

"Oh." His face flooded with confusion and shame before he looked away. I felt bad for him.

"Thank you for your help. Not just with the baby. But... with those men." I glanced behind me with an involuntarily shiver.

"They wouldn't have hurt you." But he sounded more hopeful than certain.

I looked at him. "Don't you think so?"

Klaus glanced at me swiftly, then his jaw hardened. "I should have gotten their names. I should still. I can go back—"

"To accuse them of what? Asking for my papers?"

He exhaled. "I never thought my countrymen could..."

But he stopped, as if he'd already said too much, betrayed too much.

My eyes met his.

"I know," I said softly. "I heard what your uncle said to you, when you first arrived. I know about your mother. I know everything."

He sucked in his breath. The look he gave me was electric, vibrating my bones, my blood, my heart. It made the world spin.

With an intake of breath, I turned away.

We walked in silence down the rue Froissart, then turned down the little half-hidden arch that led to the cobblestoned alley of the rue des Orphelines.

"I've seen you so busy, Mademoiselle Vashon. Your orphans remind me"—his voice was stilted—"of my nephews back home. My sister and mother are both widows now. And all my friends are risking their lives on the front, even those who secretly hate what our country is doing. If we speak out, our families will be ruined, our lives threatened. Nothing is as it should be. Nothing at all." He grew quiet, then looked at me beneath the blue sky. "Except you."

"Me?" I searched his gaze. "I don't understand."

His lips curved. "I've seen how hard you work to take care of everyone you love. I admire it very much. And I yearned to have you know that I'm not like my uncle, that I..." He caught himself. "If there's anything I can ever do to help you with the children, anything at all, *mademoiselle*, I am always at your service."

"But," I said, bewildered, "you're a German officer. Why would you help me with my children?"

"When I'm near you, I forget the grief and loss and suffering and fear. When I'm near you, the world is good again."

Our eyes locked, held. I suddenly wanted to cry, and laugh, and sing, all at once. I realized it was spring in Paris, and I was nearly eighteen.

I ducked my head shyly, then glanced at him out the corner of my eye, smiling as I hadn't smiled since the Germans invaded France. "Call me Lucie."

He touched my hand, and my life suddenly exploded into color.

Oh, I thought. This was what I'd heard about.

Our eyes met again, and I suddenly couldn't breathe. *Oh.*

And in that moment, my whole world changed.

30

LUCIE

Now, as Josette stared at us accusingly in the attic, after she'd just caught us kissing, I shook with panic and guilt.

"Klaus was waiting with me, Josette. He was trying to comfort me. You both were missing! I didn't know what to do!"

He pulled me into his arms. "Shh," he whispered, stroking my hair. "It's going to be all right. You'll see."

I closed my eyes and pressed my cheek against his chest. Through his uniform, I could hear the beat of his heart.

He'd never meant for this to happen. For us to fall in love. Neither had I.

Since the day he'd saved me a few months ago, we'd grown closer. He'd helped me with the babies, telling me in passing about his childhood in a village near Salzburg, how he'd tended flowers and chickens in his mother's garden. His father had been killed in the last war, and after his much older sister had married, it had been just the two of them, mother and son. Klaus had planned to become a farmer but had been conscripted. Since then, he'd felt trapped in the Nazi party, as trapped as I felt in Paris.

He was happiest when he was helping me with the children, when he could get away from his uncle. Those were my happiest moments, too.

I'd been so lonely. I saw that now. Even when Margot and Josette were around, they were preoccupied with their own concerns, which they refused to share with me, and had no room in their hearts to ask about mine. To them, it seemed I was still just silly Lucie, a little girl with a dog, playing with her dolls or nagging them for attention.

But Klaus saw me differently. He saw me as a woman—and not just that. He saw me as a strong, caring woman trying to make the world a better place, who deserved his help and admiration.

All the children, from Louis to Fauve, had come to adore him. He read them stories, and we'd all gather round to listen. He had a knack for making even the crankiest baby fall asleep, held against his shoulder, listening to the low thrum of his deep voice.

It was easy to spend stolen moments together, since we lived in the same house—he was in the remodeled bedroom downstairs, down the hall from his uncle's. Two weeks ago, he'd held my hand for the first time. It had felt so daring, so wonderful, I'd held my breath.

So tonight, when he'd come home late after the play, and his uncle had stalked upstairs in a foul mood, he'd found me pacing the attic. With the children sleeping, and only Choupette to offer comfort, I'd gone to the next room to pour out my fears to Klaus. It was nearly midnight then, and though Josette sometimes stayed out as late as eleven, Margot was always home before curfew. Where were they? Were they injured? Hurt?

Had German soldiers accosted them, as they'd once tried to accost me?

"Shh," he'd said, holding me in his strong arms. "Everything is going to be all right."

I'd closed my eyes and almost believed him. I could trust

him. It was as if he were part of me. He would protect me. I would protect him.

When I'd collapsed into tears, sinking down on the bed, he'd gently put his arm around me. "Don't worry. They're probably just running late. Josette has the pass... and my uncle would forgive Margot anything." He'd brushed back my blonde hair from my face, looking earnestly into my eyes. "Everything will be all right, *Liebchen*. You'll see."

Liebchen. Darling. Beloved.

His gaze had fallen to my lips—then he'd sucked in his breath and pulled away. "I'm sorry. I shouldn't..."

A romance was as forbidden for him as it was for me. Fraternization between German soldiers and French girls was technically not allowed, and he could be punished if it was found out. I'd overheard Herr Schröder planning for him to marry a girl from a grand Nazi family.

With the right alliance, who knows? You could be the next chancellor of England after Churchill is forced to lick our boots.

But, Uncle, I don't want—

Quiet, boy! You'll do as you're told.

Another danger. Another secret. I'd often thought I could not endure more.

But as Klaus had started to rise from the small bed in the empty attic dormitory room, I'd clung to him and whispered, "Please don't leave me."

"Oh, Lucie. Oh, my darling." He'd cupped my cheeks and lowered his head, giving me plenty of time to pull away. But I hadn't.

His lips had pressed against mine, and based on how he'd trembled, I'd known it was his first kiss, too.

And *that* was when Josette had turned on the light.

She was still staring at me with incredulous eyes—judging me, judging Klaus—and I felt a sudden flare of anger.

"What about you, Josette?" I demanded. "What have you been doing all night?"

"I told you." Her gaze shifted away. "At the theater. It was opening night."

"But the play ended at eight—didn't it?"

"Y-Yes," she stuttered. She'd always been the best actress of us all, but this time, her cheeks turned as red as her hair. She was hiding something.

I narrowed my eyes. "What's the real story?"

She looked at Klaus, then shook her head.

"Fine," I sighed. "Don't tell me. You never tell me anything. Just like Margot."

She put her hands on her hips. "Don't try to make this about me. Or Margot. It's about you, and what you were up here doing in a dark bedroom with..." She eyed Klaus.

"I told you. I was worried." I tossed my head defiantly. "I kissed him, all right? I kissed him! So what?"

Josette blinked, her mouth agape.

Klaus turned to me tenderly. "You kissed me?" he asked, smiling.

"Well, didn't I?"

"I thought I kissed you." His blue eyes were glowing with happiness. Holding my hand, he turned back to Josette. "As I said, my intentions with your sister are entirely honorable."

She looked sour. "She's not my sister."

"Ah, then it is Margot who...?"

Josette ducked her head, refusing to answer him. It seemed strange. Not to mention rude.

"Yes, Margot is my sister," I replied for her.

She set her jaw; she still wouldn't look at us. "Margot is missing, you say?"

"Yes."

"We need to find her before Herr Schröder asks for her this

morning... unless"—she paused—"it's possible she's with him in the study already?"

I shook my head.

"My uncle took to his bed in a foul temper," Klaus said. "He led a raid personally last night, hoping to find Le Lérot. But his prey eluded him. He felt rather foolish, I think. He doesn't usually lead these kinds of raids. It's left him vulnerable."

I looked at him. "Vulnerable? To whom?"

"To everyone, *Liebchen*. Politics."

Josette turned to the window, where the dawn was growing brighter. "Berthe is probably awake by now. I'll check and see if she knows anything about Margot—"

She fled down the stairs.

Klaus looked at me. "She doesn't approve of me." He tilted his head, then added softly, "I don't either. Not for you. I'm not safe for you."

"I'm not safe for you, either," I said.

In the silence of the room, we looked at each other. Then he pulled me back in his arms and lowered his lips towards mine—

We were interrupted by sounds coming from the next room: Louis's polite babbling; Bernadette's soft cry. I heard Geneviève's sweet voice calling for me, as little Noémie had before she'd left for America, "Wucie, Wucie."

Klaus and I looked at each other with regret, then we both smiled.

"Shall we get them?" he said.

"You're not too tired to help?" I said.

"Dead tired." He took my hand. "But I'll rest when you do."

Somehow, in that moment, as he looked at me, with the way my heart was glowing, I didn't feel tired at all.

31

MARGOT

I twisted and turned on the lumpy blankets spread over the hard-packed earthen floor. The tiny larder, barely bigger than a small wardrobe off the kitchen of their Belleville cottage, was used to store potatoes and apples, or at least it had been when they'd had extra food to store. Without a stone foundation, it was a full step below the rest of the house, and cooler. But tonight, the Ravanels had fashioned it as a place for me to sleep after I'd missed curfew.

The main room, which comprised the kitchen and parlor, was already packed full, with Suzanne sleeping on the sofa next to the small round dining table. Past the larder door, in the single small bedroom facing the garden, I could hear Dr. Ravanel and his wife whispering, now they obviously thought we were asleep.

"Why didn't you tell me?" Élisabeth Ravanel's soft voice betrayed her tears.

"I didn't know," he repeated stolidly.

"You said she refused your marriage proposal in Greece. Why would she do that, if she was pregnant with your child?"

"She didn't know. By the time she came to France to tell me, it was too late."

"How did you never imagine Margot could be your child? Not even when they both were at our house?"

"She said Margot was an orphan and lied about her age. I had no reason to even consider it."

"Margot looks so much like Suzanne..." A pause. Then she tremulously asked, "Would you still have married me if you'd known? If Helen had arrived one day earlier?"

For a moment, he didn't answer.

She choked out a sob.

"Yes, yes, my darling," his deep voice rushed to say. "Of course I would. It's you I love, Élisabeth. My love affair with Helen Taylor, it was one night long ago, long in the past."

More sobs, more whispered words. Finally, bravely, his wife sighed, "I'm sorry." She gave a sodden laugh. "I'm being silly. It happened before we even met. When you were a widower on the other side of the world." Another breath. "But I always wondered, if I hadn't been nanny to Daniel and Paul, if you still would have married me. If you... if you settled for me," she choked out.

"Don't be silly. I love you," he sighed, and I could imagine him hugging her.

"I love you so much," she said. "I can't live without you."

Silence, then he said: "Do you have it in you to accept the girl? As my daughter?"

Another pause; another sigh. "Of course. I love Margot. I'll love her even more knowing she's yours."

Élisabeth Ravanel was a kind-hearted woman, but I couldn't help but think even she might have found it difficult to be so generous if Helen were still in Paris, rather than far away in America.

Their whispers faded then, but still sleep wouldn't come. So

I opened my eyes and stared into the dark, replaying every moment that had led us to this.

I'd barely told my father I was his daughter at the hospital before we were interrupted by a nurse needing his assistance with a bleeding patient. Dr. Ravanel turned to me, his eyes wild. "I have an hour left in my shift. Can you wait?"

Of course I waited. I'd been dreaming of this moment for two years, caught between hope and fear.

Dr. Ravanel always took the Métro to work, a journey which, on a good day, took him nearly an hour each way. But I had my bicycle, so after he was done, we walked together through Paris, all the way to Belleville. It took more than two hours.

At first, as we walked down the avenue de Neuilly, we glanced at each other shyly, neither of us quite knowing what to say or how to behave.

"I wish she'd told me," he said. "I wish..." He sighed. "I don't know."

"She arrived just in time to see you outside the church in La Ravelle with Élisabeth in a white dress, with your two little boys. Helen didn't want to cause problems in your new marriage. Your family."

My father looked at me. "You call her Helen?"

My cheeks grew warm. "It's habit."

He looked down the street as we continued to walk, my hands guiding the bicycle on the sidewalk beside me. His face turned wistful, and he glanced at me with a self-conscious smile.

"Growing up, we all think love will be a fairy tale. But it's not so simple."

For some reason, Roger popped into my mind. The intense

kiss we'd shared that dark Christmas night. The look on his face when I'd pulled away. *I don't love you. I never will.*

I stared at my own footsteps as I walked, watching the movement of the sun's shadow against the pale sidewalk, then my father's broad stride. My legs looked almost as broad as his, given my oversized trousers—part of my disguise. The whirl of the bicycle's spokes moved the shadow like a hypnotist's rotating disk machine, leaving me dizzy.

"Everything would be different now, if Helen hadn't changed her mind about marrying me..." He looked away with a sigh. "And yet I can't regret it. Because her choice gave me Suzanne. And Élisabeth."

"Yes," I murmured, trying not to feel jealous of the childhood my half-sister had enjoyed.

"Sometimes, I did wonder where Helen might be in the world." We walked past a café full of German soldiers and smiling, hungry-eyed French girls. "I was shocked when she showed up at our house in La Ravelle."

"She didn't want to see you," I said slowly. "Even when she was bleeding, after she'd been shot by that plane, she argued against it. I think she was trying to protect you still."

Dr. Ravanel gave a brisk nod. "That sounds like her." His lips curved. "But what happened between the time she saw me getting married to Élisabeth and when she became headmistress of the orphanage? There are a few missing years there."

"I think she unraveled after she had to give me up. She's hinted at doing some dangerous things. In 1924, she shot Otto Schröder in Germany—"

"She told me." Reminded of the subject, he scowled. "You know, Margot, it's really not safe for you to live—"

"Then," I pushed forward quickly, "she did something in South America. I'm not sure exactly, but whatever it was, the American government owed her a big favor. The man at the Marseille consulate seemed a little scared of her."

"*Scared.*" He snorted in disbelief, then sobered at my expression. "What could she have done?"

I shook my head. "She wouldn't tell me, but whatever it was, she was rewarded with American visas for Noémie, Rachel, Estée and Josette."

His eyes widened. "Well, how do you like that?" He grinned. "When I first knew Léna"—that was his old nickname for my mother, I'd learned—"I had to show her how to load a gun, how to aim, how to throw a punch."

"Like you've showed us over the last year?"

He smiled briefly. "She was a quicker study, but then, we were constantly in danger on the battlefields. She worked harder than anyone I'd ever seen. Cared more."

I smiled ruefully. "That's her, all right."

"But it's dangerous to have you continue living at St. Agnes's with that man." To my chagrin, he'd returned to the subject. "Does Schröder still walk with a limp?"

"Yes."

"And here I've had you spying on him." His jaw was tight. "When you're Helen's daughter. His enemy's daughter." He looked at me shyly. "And mine."

"I wanted to do it, D-Dr. Ravanel." *Papa.* I wished I could call him that. But my mouth couldn't form the sounds. My cheeks burned hot just at the thought of doing something so bold. Suzanne could call him that. I could not.

As we walked down the Boulevard Haussmann, past the leafy green trees and the elegant nineteenth-century buildings with their blue-gray roofs, the sun was lowering to the west. I knew I should say *au revoir* and bicycle home. Curfew wasn't too far away.

He gave a sudden frown. "Does Schröder know? About me?"

I shook my head. "Only as Paul Ravanel's father. He doesn't suspect you of anything. And as far as he knows, Helen Taylor's mysterious illegitimate daughter went to America with her. He knows me only as the orphan, Margot Vashon."

His shoulders tightened a little at the word *illegitimate*. But he said only, "Are you sure?"

"If he knew, he would treat me differently." With a crooked grin, I added, "Throw me in prison, or torture me, or something."

"It's not a laughing matter. We shouldn't underestimate Schröder." His eyes narrowed. "I want you to leave his house. Bicycle home, pack a bag. Tell the others I'm taking you all to La Ravelle."

"You're overreacting," I said, tossing my head. I was punished for my bravado when my cap nearly fell off and tendrils of wild hair went every which way. Tucking it back firmly, I looked at my father. "We've stayed with him for nearly two years without him finding out. I'm not worried."

"You should be. His trap for Le Lérot will fail tonight, thanks to your warning. And then Schröder will suspect there's a mole. He'll start looking at everyone more closely. Including you."

"How—" I wondered when Dr. Ravanel had found time to warn Le Lérot. At the hospital? Or perhaps he'd snuck out amid his shift? Or used the phone?

It didn't matter. I knew he wouldn't explain. Anyway, I had a sinking feeling he was right. I'd already worried I was becoming too important to Otto Schröder. A man like that would want to control me, to protect himself.

"How what?" he said.

"You don't need to be more worried, you know, just because I'm your daughter."

"Of course I do." Slanted light caught at the raised pink scar on his cheekbone as he glanced at me. I wondered how he'd gotten that scar. "But I'd be worried now no matter what. You've provided actionable intelligence that will cause his personally led mission to fail tonight. He will start looking at everyone close to him. And it's like you said. If he learns you're Helen's daughter, he'll kill you. Probably torture you first, to find out what you know about Le Lérot. Or maybe just for fun. It's nothing to joke about."

I tried to imagine Otto hurting me. Would he? My greatest fear over the last few months had been that he liked me too much. I'd seen his gaze linger on my lips, a wistful expression in his gray eyes.

But I also knew he was dangerous. I'd known it from the moment we'd received that telegram in Marseille two years ago, demanding that Helen exchange her life for Lucie's with such icy, malevolent courtesy. Or even what he'd said at Nazi head-quarters a few hours before.

We need to remind the French they belong to us, that their lives and fortunes exist only because we allow it so...

I'd convinced myself that because Otto hadn't yet discovered my true link to Helen, he never would. But I'd been whistling past the graveyard. I suddenly saw how vulnerable we were. Not just me, but Lucie, Josette, the children. Even Berthe.

"You're right," I breathed.

Relief flashed over Dr. Ravanel's face. "Good. No one will look for you at our old house, I don't think." He pondered a moment, then added, "And we'll figure out a backup location, in case we're followed."

"La Ravelle..." I pondered. It could work. We'd still be in occupied France but further from official eyes, off in the country. "How will we get food, supplies?"

"We have friends there still. They will help you."

"There's no way we can sneak ten people out of Paris, though. The babies. Berthe." Assuming the elderly cook even agreed to come, given how adamant she'd been about remaining. "I don't see the Nazis giving us all travel papers, do you?"

He said briskly, "Le Lérot has a source for forged documents. You have the pictures?"

I nodded reluctantly. Months ago, he'd asked me for small photos of everyone in our household, in case we ever needed to create fake documents to escape. I'd thought it was just an insurance policy. I hadn't thought it would actually happen.

"We can't wait long," my father said. "Every hour you remain is a risk. I can get travel documents made as soon as possible. I think by tomorrow night."

I bit my lip. "What if we sent all the others to La Ravelle but I stayed in Paris? I still want to help France." *And spend time with you,* I didn't say aloud. "I don't mind risking a little more, not when it's so important to..."

Dr. Ravanel was already shaking his head. "How would you explain their departure to Schröder? What would you say when he asked where they were? And how they'd obtained travel visas without him knowing?"

"I'd figure something out," I said with bravado. "I want to stay and fight. With you."

"That's over," he said firmly. "Go home. Get everyone packed tonight. Come to my house tomorrow afternoon, whenever you can all get away without suspicion."

I glanced at a passing shopkeeper closing up his windows. In the distance, I heard forlorn accordion music, an accompaniment to the sad squeak of my bicycle wheels as they turned in the twilight. My hand hurt from steering it as I walked.

I stared down at the sidewalk. "But then I won't see you again..."

He looked at me fiercely. "We will see each other. Someday." He added, "You'll need to be with your sister to protect her, and all the children, and Berthe. Even in La Ravelle, they'll need someone with your strength and sense to look out for them."

I knew he was right. But I was so tired of worrying about

other people. When could I be selfish? When could I do what I wanted to do for myself?

"Please," I whimpered and shook my head, tears in my eyes. "I'm not ready. I've waited my whole life for a father."

Dr. Ravanel's expression crumpled, but then he reached out and briefly touched my shoulder. "So let me be a father to you now. Let me keep you safe."

I took comfort in the warmth of his hand on my shoulder, though it only lasted a moment.

He pulled away and took a deep breath.

"I need to ask you a favor. If I leave my wife and Suzanne with you, will you look out for them?"

"Of course." I tried not to worry about how *twelve* people would fit into the small house in La Ravelle, or how Élisabeth Ravanel would feel about being separated from her husband. It was his problem to convince her, not mine. And it warmed my heart that he thought me capable of being their protector.

He stroked his chin, which at this late hour was bristly with gray-and-black shadow, and seemed like he was thinking the same thing as he said, "It will be tight to fit everyone in the old truck."

"The same truck that was stolen by those criminals in La Ravelle?"

"The very one." He flashed me a grin. "I was allowed to keep it for medical emergencies. Plus it's so rusty and temperamental, the Nazis didn't want it." He blinked. "Élisabeth will be so happy once I tell her you are my daughter." He pushed back his salt-and-pepper hair with a rueful smile. "Eventually."

"You're going to tell her? About me?"

"I always tell my wife everything. Well. Almost." He glanced at the lowering sun. "Here—if you take that corner, you can take the Boulevard du Temple straight home—"

"I need more time," I begged. "Just give me a few more

hours to talk to you. Please. The next time I see you, we won't be able to talk like this."

Dr. Ravanel fell silent. I heard the noise of a honking car, someone shouting in the distance. Soldiers across the street laughing, speaking loudly in German.

"You're as stubborn as your brother Paul," he sighed at last in capitulation. "Come for dinner. But with curfew, you'll have to stay the night," he warned.

Happiness rushed through me. "I can stay?"

"Will you be missed?"

I shook my head. "Herr Schröder won't look for me until after breakfast. Anyway, if he does, my sisters will cover for me." I realized I'd referred to Josette aloud as my sister—that would have made her choke on her milk. But Otto had never offered me an after-curfew pass, and I'd never asked for one. But I couldn't regret that, not when it meant I could spend the night at the Ravanels' now.

My father looked at me shyly. "I wouldn't mind having time to talk to you, too."

As we walked towards Belleville, I still tried to think of some way I could stay. I'd help settle Lucie and Josette and the rest in La Ravelle, but then return to Paris. My father might let me stay with him, once his wife and younger daughter were safe. Especially if he had no choice.

I smiled, imagining the two of us living in that Belleville cottage, working side by side to save France. Maybe I'd finally meet Le Lérot...

My smile fell. It would be impossible to leave everyone else I loved in La Ravelle, if I was worried about them going hungry without me.

Roger, I thought again. Of course. The black market big shot, floating through the criminal underworld. He could feed everyone, if he wanted to. I'd ask him for help. *Convince* him. After all, he'd loved me once, hadn't he? My shoulders relaxed.

But first I'd have to convince Josette and Lucie to leave Paris, and I feared that might be just as big a task as Dr. Ravanel convincing his wife and Suzanne...

When we reached his tiny cottage with its walled garden, my father looked nervous. "Élisabeth has probably been worried, wondering why I'm so late."

"Do you want me to wait in the garden while you talk to her?"

He looked at me, then gave my shoulder a quick squeeze. "No. Come inside." He smiled, his dark eyes glowing, wrinkles at the sides. "We're family now. All of us."

His wife was in the kitchen, boiling something on the rickety old stove. "Jean-Luc! You're so late, I was starting to—"

She seemed startled when I appeared unannounced behind him, to join their family for dinner. But she quickly recovered and insisted on giving me a big bowl of her homemade chicken soup. It was only afterward I realized that she'd given me her portion. She hid that from her husband, too, no doubt knowing he would object and give up his soup instead.

She seemed oddly stone-faced when her husband told her and Suzanne the truth over dinner, but Suzanne gasped aloud and leaped up to embrace me. "I've always wanted a sister!"

The three of us spoke together till almost midnight, about everything and nothing. Only Madame Ravanel had held herself apart, her expression numb as she watched us, like a spectator, scrubbing the same spot in the kitchen with a washrag over and over.

Afterward, wearing pajamas borrowed from my half-sister, I went to rest on the makeshift blankets in the larder. It was only after all the lights were out and enough time passed that I might be asleep that I heard the married couple's whispers begin...

. . .

I rearranged the blankets over the hard earthen floor once more and told myself I needed to sleep, to think of anything else. I wondered how Roger would react when I asked for his help. I pictured his handsome face. The pain I'd seen in his eyes. I hadn't seen him since I'd spurned his love. All this time, I'd tried not to think of him, but now... I was suddenly glad to have an excuse to see him again. Though I was also nervous. I'd heard whispers of rumors that Roger was more than a black marketeer; that he was also a criminal, a thug collaborating with the Nazis —but surely that couldn't be true? Any more than the rumor that I was Schröder's doxy?

The larder had no windows, so the night was absolute. But I must have slept, because suddenly, through my half-open door, the darkness had turned gray. I could hear the muffled plaintive singing of morning birds.

I put on my oversized trousers, shirt and cap, then folded the blankets and borrowed pajamas into a tidy pile.

To my surprise, I found my father sitting alone in the tiny kitchen, with only the sunrise for light. I set down the blankets, saying shyly, "*Bonjour.*"

"I wanted to see you before you left, Margot." He held out something that glinted in the light. "This is for you."

It was a slender golden ring with a small, dully gleaming red stone.

"It was hers," he said. "The ring I gave her."

32

MARGOT

I stared at my father in the soft, pink light of dawn. We kept our voices quiet, since Suzanne was still sleeping nearby.

He held up the ring. "I bought it in Athens. Before I proposed to your mother. She gave it back to me the next morning."

"And you kept it all this time?"

His cheeks colored a little, and he looked away. I had the sudden thought that it might be one other thing he hadn't told his wife about.

I looked down at it. "It's a ruby?"

"A garnet."

"Are you sure you want to give it away?"

"It belongs with you," he said simply, leaning forward over the small table. "I haven't had a chance to be a father to you. But I want that to change. Someday, once this war is over, once you're all safe, I hope you'll give me that chance."

My heart overflowed. "I want that too."

I didn't tell him that with any luck, it would only be a few days, not months or years, before we had that time together. How would he react when I returned to Paris? Would it prove to him that he could rely on me—that he didn't need to protect me?

I slid the ring on my finger. It fit perfectly, gleaming warmly in the pale light. The ring he'd given my mother. How different my life—all our lives—would have been if she'd never given it back!

"I'd better go," I said thickly and turned away, my muscles still aching from the rough night on the floor. From all the tension. From overwhelming emotion.

"Wait," he said and hugged me. When he pulled away, he said unsteadily, "Return here as soon as you can, without raising Schröder's suspicions."

I nodded. "Right after dinner. He usually goes to bed early." Perhaps, by some miracle, I'd be able to get away from Otto sometime during the day, long enough to contact Roger. Otherwise I'd send Berthe with an urgent message. "And you might need time to convince Élisabeth and Suzanne."

He glanced over at the small sofa where his daughter slept, snoring lightly.

"I might at that," he sighed, then looked towards the back bedroom where his wife still slept. His jaw clenched. "But if you get a chance, come earlier. I think Schröder is more dangerous than you realize. I don't want any of you in his house a minute longer than you need to be. If he finds out who you really are..."

He didn't have to finish.

I shivered. "I'll hurry," I promised. "Dr. Ravanel—" I gave him a tremulous smile. "I'm not sure what to call you now."

His eyes were gentle. Hopeful. "Papa?"

My heart ached, unable to contain that much joy. And this time I had no problem saying the word. "Papa."

We hugged one last time, and when I pulled away, my eyes were swimming with tears—as were his.

I hopped on my bicycle as the sky lightened to a brilliant

pinkish-gold over the scattered clouds, then gave him one last wave and started on my way. The truth was I could have floated home in happiness.

I had a father I could look up to for support and advice, after two years of feeling like I had to be strong for everyone else.

I put away my bike, then snuck through the garden and into the back door of St. Agnes's, just as the grandfather clock was sonorously chiming seven o'clock from the parlor. I crept inside the kitchen, holding my breath, praying I hadn't been noticed, that everyone was still asleep.

Instead, I found four people—my sister, Josette, Berthe and, astonishingly, even Klaus—standing around the table. They whirled on me accusingly.

"Where have you been?" Lucie cried, and she threw her arms around me.

For a moment, I just stood shocked in my sister's embrace, then Fauve ran into the kitchen, Choupette barking at her feet, and tugged on Lucie's sleeve. "Come quickly! The baby's crying. Bernadette woke him up because she wanted to play, and the others are fighting..."

Turning from the counter where she'd been making coffee, Berthe looked between us. No one moved.

"I'll handle it," she said heavily, making it clear that we really owed her for this. The steep back stairs were becoming more difficult for her. "Just take the coffee tray into Herr Schröder."

"Thank you, Berthe," Lucie said gratefully.

"I want all the details later," the elderly woman said and left with Fauve.

My sister turned on me. "Well? Where were you all night?"

How could we talk about this in front of the enemy? I glanced at Klaus pointedly. "Good morning, Klaus. Is your uncle awake?"

The young man shook his head. "I don't think so. He had a hard night."

"Oh?" I said innocently. "Why?"

He looked at Lucie. "His plan to capture Le Lérot did not work. The man never showed. Someone must have warned him."

I tried to keep my face blank. "Well, let's try and make him feel better today. Please take the coffee tray into the study so it's ready for him when he does wake. I'll follow in a few minutes. And please don't say anything about me being out this morning. There's a perfectly innocent explanation."

He lifted an eyebrow, waiting. Then, at Lucie's slight gesture, he sighed, gathered up the tray with the coffee and left the kitchen.

My sister turned on me. "You don't need to worry about Klaus," she said, hands on hips. "He already knows you were out all night heaven knows where. He was waiting with me while I was sick with worry."

"I found the two of them together in the middle of the night," Josette murmured. "Kissing in the attic."

"What?" I whirled back on Lucie. "Are you out of your mind? He's a Nazi!"

Her cheeks turned pink, then her chin rose. "He's not! Not really," she added mildly, "And it's really none of your business."

"None of my—" It wasn't just her defiance that shocked me but the way she was so calm about it. Glaring at her, I hissed, "I spent the night at the Ravanels'. Dr. Ravanel thinks we're in danger. He wants us to pack up and leave Paris tonight. Before Herr Schröder digs any deeper into my past."

"*Your* past?" Lucie asked, her expression bewildered. "Why just yours? What could he learn?" She snorted. "That our father was a dairy farmer from Meaux? That our mother took us to Paris after he died? That we're orphans?"

Josette and I looked at each other.

"Pack them all up," I told Lucie. "Even the babies."

"All of them?" she gasped. "But how—"

"Please, Lucie," I begged. "Just get ready to go."

"Where would we even go?"

"The country." I didn't want to say La Ravelle, in case she blurted it out in front of Klaus or his uncle. I tried to smile. "Fresh air, farmland, good for children." In actuality, we'd be living on a street in the middle of a small town. "Don't you want all that wholesome living for the orphans?"

"Well, I suppose." She frowned. "But... leave Paris? Now, when..." She blushed.

"Don't even *think* of saying you don't want to leave Klaus Schröder." Honestly, I'd thought Josette's old infatuation for Roger was unbearable—now my baby sister was consorting with a Nazi? What on earth was wrong with her? "How long has this been going on?"

Lucie stood alone in the kitchen, her angelic hair and pale eyelashes lit by the golden morning light pouring in from the garden window.

"Klaus is always there for me. He's helped me, all summer. When the two of you"—she looked between us—"were too *busy*. You helping Herr Schröder threaten the French," she accused me. She turned to Josette. "And you, sewing sparkles on costumes."

Josette and I blinked. It wasn't like Lucie to go on the attack. We looked at each other. Josette's cheeks were as red as her hair. My cheeks felt hot, too. I could understand why Lucie would resent *her*, neglecting the orphans to waste her devotion on those silly plays. But it hurt to think my sister actually believed I was helping Herr Schröder work against my own people.

How I wished I could tell her I'd been secretly helping Le Lérot—how quickly her criticism would have changed to pride!

Later, I promised myself. Once she was safely in La Ravelle.

"Why did you stay all night at the Ravanels'?" Lucie asked.

I couldn't tell her about my father being involved with Le Lérot. And this seemed like the wrong time to explain that he was my father. Biting my lip, I hedged, "Dr. Ravanel needed my help with something, and then it was curfew, so I stayed."

"Help? With what? You don't know anything medical," Josette scoffed. "The times he's offered to teach us first aid, you always begged off."

"He needed to talk about his... daughter."

Josette's eyes widened. She knew which daughter I was talking about. But Lucie still looked confused.

"Is Suzanne all right?"

"Fine." I pulled off my cap, letting my hair tumble over my shoulders. "I'd better go change. Herr Schröder can't see me like this." I looked down at my wrinkled, dusty, shapeless shirt and trousers. "But while I'm with him, start packing up the children. Convince Berthe to pack, too."

"I still don't understand why... or how," Lucie said. "Won't it be even more dangerous to leave? How will we get papers? How will we get food or shelter?"

"I'll explain everything," I said hurriedly. "I promise."

"But—"

"Think of Fauve," I said ruthlessly. "Don't you want to see her safe?"

That did it. Lucie's face went pale and she bit her lip. "Yes..."

Relieved, I turned. "Josette?"

Unexpectedly, she tossed her head. "You can all leave Paris if you want. I'm staying."

I scowled. "Don't be stupid, Josette. Doing costumes for some stupid play—"

"It's not stupid!"

"—isn't worth your life. Just do what I'm telling you for once. We'll leave after Herr Schröder heads for bed. The only reason we're delaying even that long is because Dr. Ravanel needs time for Le Lérot to get us travel passes."

"Le Lérot?" Lucie gasped. "Why would he do that for us?"

A strange look passed over Josette's face. She started to say something, then stopped. What now? What on earth could she be fretting about that was more important than all our lives at risk?

Irritated, I told her, "You can set up the play for tonight, say goodbye, then come straight home. We might need your after-curfew pass with us."

"I can't leave Paris," she said stubbornly. "I'm needed here."

"*We* need you," I retorted. I needed her to keep an eye on everyone in La Ravelle, so I could quickly return to Paris to help my father. "Honestly, Josette. The Widow Hébert can find a new seamstress. You act like what you do is so important. Can't you think about someone else for once?"

"But, Margot, you don't understand..."

"What?"

"Forget it," Josette said, turning her head away.

More of her dramatics. But it seemed a little strange. I wondered if there was something she wasn't telling me, something that wasn't just stitches and sparkles.

My sister had been turning her head back and forth between us like a spectator at a tennis match, a blank look on her face.

"Don't breathe a word of this to Klaus. Now go," I told her roughly before hurrying off to change.

On my way upstairs, I found Berthe limping down, holding baby Louis, followed by a passel of children like the Pied Piper. It seemed too good a chance to miss, as it was unlikely I'd be able to sneak out unnoticed today. I swiftly explained that we were planning to leave tonight and asked if she could get a message to Roger.

"Sure," she said grumpily. "I'll just hop the Métro to his

new place, shall I, with all the children hanging over me and breakfast still needing to be cooked?"

"New place? I thought he was in Montparnasse?"

"He moved," she said in a tone that didn't invite questions.

I sighed, then continued upstairs. I hadn't even dared to suggest she leave Paris with us. I'd just have to hope that Lucie had better luck talking things over.

I put on a chic peplum skirt suit, lined silk stockings and pumps. My dark hair was too wild to contend with, so I pulled it into a chignon, brushed my teeth, then smoothed on some red lipstick. I looked at myself in the mirror and waited until my heart stopped pounding so I could force my lips into a natural smile. Then I went downstairs to the study.

"You're late," Otto greeted me sourly.

I glanced at his nephew, who gave me a slight shake of his head.

"I'm sorry." I gave my employer my best smile, as if I didn't notice his simmering fury that infected the room like a bad smell. "You're getting started early this morning. How was the play?"

He ground his teeth and ignored my question. "The raid on Le Lérot was a bust. The man never showed. Someone has been spying on me. Sharing my secrets. And I'll soon know who."

He gave me a long, searching stare.

"I can't imagine anyone would dare betray you, Herr Schröder," I said, ducking my head. "I'm sorry Le Lérot wasn't there, but perhaps his plans just changed last night. Or perhaps Standartenführer Becker had incorrect information."

"That could be, Uncle," Klaus said.

"Did either of you"—he sipped his coffee, then set the china cup carefully down on his large desk—"tell anyone?"

"Of course not," Klaus said.

He turned to me with a lift of his dark eyebrow. Trembling inside, I wordlessly shook my head.

"I'll find out." He set his jaw and looked away. "I promise you."

Any hope of getting away to see Roger was soon dashed. After last night's failure, Otto was determined to work all the harder on his next project. We went with Klaus to headquarters, where one of his rivals, followed by attachés, stopped him in the hallway.

"I heard about your failure last night. I suppose you're not really cut out for leading raids, Herr Schröder," he said under the pretense of sympathy, though there was a gleeful glint in his eye.

He wasn't the only one who was clearly glad to see him cut down to size. Several other officers clustered around us, offering their smug sympathy.

"Le Lérot will soon be dead. As will anyone who antagonizes me." Otto's jaw was so tight, I wondered if he'd break the bone, or if a couple of molars might fall out. He clutched his eagle-headed cane, and as he walked, his limp seemed more pronounced than ever before.

It was past five by the time we left for St. Agnes's. He'd left Klaus behind at headquarters without explaining why. The uncertainty made me sick to my stomach. I didn't trust either of them.

Otto and I were silent in the back seat of the sedan as the chauffeur drove us home. He'd received some kind of typed message, which he was looking at, careful not to let me see it.

Tension thrummed through me. Was he looking at me strangely, or was that my imagination? Did he know?

My heart pounded. I had the strangest feeling he knew everything, but I told myself I had to be mistaken. If he'd known, he would have immediately arrested me. Right?

"I'll go check on your dinner," I said once we reached St. Agnes's.

"Do that," he purred.

I fled to the kitchen, where I hurried to find Berthe putting schnitzel and spätzle on a tray.

"I can take them in," I said gently, hoping her mood had improved.

She blinked at me, then slowly nodded. "Thank you."

I looked at her pleadingly. "Did Lucie talk to you about leaving Paris?"

"Yes," she sighed.

"And?"

"And... I think you and Dr. Ravanel are right. It's getting too dangerous. For Fauve. For all of us."

I exhaled in relief. Thank heaven for my sister. "So you'll come?"

The white-haired cook looked down at her hands. "I've had enough of cooking for a Nazi. No house is worth that, not anymore." She squared her shoulders. "But I don't care to live in the country, either. I was born in Paris, and I'll die here. I'm going to live with Roger."

"With Roger?" I faltered. "But... you've heard the rumors. Of the life he lives..."

"I don't believe them, and neither should you." Her rheumy eyes met mine. "My great-nephew has money and connections, perhaps enough to get Fauve to Switzerland." Her eyes softened. "For one child, he'll find a way. I know he will, if I ask."

I took a breath. "You're taking Fauve with you?"

I yearned for Fauve to be free and safe in Switzerland—but now how would I convince Lucie to leave? And she had to leave. Aside from the danger, my stomach churned when I thought of my baby sister kissing a Nazi. I had to get her away.

"Perhaps he could hire a *passeur* to escort her," she said hesitantly. She brushed at her eyes. "Though it hurts to think of sending her away. She's become like... the grandchild I might have had, if my son hadn't died."

I knew the two were close, but I'd never realized how much

she loved Fauve until now. The elderly cook rarely spoke of the son she'd raised when she'd arrived at St. Agnes's, pregnant and unwed, at the end of the last century. After he'd died, she'd been left with no family. Except us, and Roger, of course. And now Fauve.

"Did you tell Lucie your plans?"

"I haven't had the heart. She loves the child almost as much as I do."

"Let me do it." I told myself that if I didn't explain everything, it would only be for my sister's own good. Once she and the babies were settled comfortably in La Ravelle, and her mad attraction for Klaus had passed, she would thank me. "When you're both safe, send a message through Dr. Ravanel."

"You do the same," she said soberly. She handed me a small paper. "Here's Roger's new address."

Taking it, I hid a smile, thinking of how surprised she'd be when I returned to Paris to live with my father. How soon could it be? A week? A few days? I was glad to have Roger's address. I might need it.

The cook looked around the kitchen sadly. "I've lived here for half a century." She shook herself. "Once we've kicked the Germans out, I'll be back."

"I'd expect nothing less," I said. "When will you go?"

"Right now, since you're taking him his dinner. I already packed Fauve's things."

"Be careful." I hugged her. "We love you, Berthe. And Fauve, too. But remember, leave Lucie to me."

"Och. I'm happy to have you tell her. It will break her heart to let the child go." Her wrinkled cheeks turned pink as she gently pushed the tray into my arms. "Don't let his dinner be late. He'll be suspicious, and anyway I have too much pride to let it get cold. Go on with you. Hurry now."

I wiped my eyes and took the tray, then served Otto his

dinner at the large glossy table in the dining room that had once served twenty-six women and girls.

He seemed oddly subdued, taking notes in his notebook, sipping a fine French wine.

"Will you need me for anything else tonight, sir?" I murmured, already backing away.

"No, thank you, Margot." He cut into his schnitzel. "I'm going to the play."

"What play?"

"*La Femme de Machiavelli.*"

"But you just saw it last night." I tried to smile. "It must be some play."

"Hardly." He chewed the breaded veal; swallowed. "It's a silly story about Machiavelli's wife, the mother of seven children, pretending she was a secret genius, the manipulator behind his power, so superior in her intelligence that she knew how to hide herself. A woman! I don't know whether it's supposed to be a tragedy or a comedy." He tilted his head, looking at me sideways. "But tonight there will be a show of a different kind. I'm going to make an arrest."

"Who?" I tried to hide my sudden shiver.

His cool gray gaze rested on me. "We've discovered the identity of Le Lérot."

"Yes?" I gripped the edge of the table.

"It is"—he cut another piece of meat free with the sharp knife before placing the morsel daintily in his mouth— "Séverine Hébert."

"Madame Hébert!" I gasped. Could it really be? "No!"

"It is so." He looked mournful as he placed his napkin in his lap. "She played us false, in spite of all her fine words. But we discovered some Jews trying to escape France and make their way to Switzerland. The six-year-old child gave the wrong name at the border, so we knew the documents had to be forgeries. After... questioning the mother, we traced the source back to the Théâtre Lutèce." He looked up at me. "It's her."

I stared at him in shock, my jaw agape. Then I gasped. "But Josette—"

"Yes," he said mildly. "The girl might have been helping her. We will find out." He continued to slice his meat with the gleaming knife. "You must be brave, my dear. There is some chance your friend might be a traitor."

My heart was pounding in my throat.

I'm needed here, she'd said. *You don't understand.*

All this time I'd thought Josette was selfishly indulging her vanity, caring only about sewing sequins onto costumes. What if I'd misjudged her? What if, like me, she'd been toiling in secret, taking risks to work against the Nazis?

I should have trusted her.

"Margot?" I looked up. "Have you seen my stamp? The one with my signature? I had it locked in my desk." His voice was mild, but he seemed to be watching me. "I can't seem to find it."

I frowned. "Your stamp? No. Isn't it in the bottom drawer?" Who cared about his stupid stamp at a time like this? I glanced back at the door longingly. "I can go look, if you like..."

"Ah, no. Don't worry about it." He waved his hand airily. "I'm sure it will turn up."

"Oh. All right. Well." I started backing away. "I, uh, promised Lucie I'd help her take the orphans on a walk after dinner."

"Go ahead, then. But don't try to warn Josette. Concern for a friend is admirable, but in times like this we must focus on the greater good. If she is an enemy to the Reich"—he sawed at his meat once more with his vicious little knife, chewed, swallowed —"she will be punished."

"Y-Yes," I stammered.

He stared at me as if waiting for me to sprain my arm flashing a robust *Sieg Heil*. It might have helped. But I couldn't do it. No one had ever claimed I was wise. In fact, Josette routinely told me I was an idiot.

Josette.

I turned on my heel. "Good evening, Herr Schröder."

"One last thing."

I paused at his silky voice. My palms were sweaty as I turned back. "*Ja?*"

He looked up from the long, glossy dining table. His gray eyes seemed to glitter in the shadowy light. "We make a good team, don't we?"

"Yes."

Our eyes locked, and suddenly, time stood still.

"We could be more." He set down his napkin and rose to his feet—adjusting his uniform coat as always—then limped towards me, cane in hand. He stopped, towering over me. "I'd like you to be more."

Then he reached out with his free hand and cupped my cheek. His touch felt like a chill against my skin, and I froze in revulsion and fear.

He smiled self-consciously. "I know I don't cut the heroic figure I did in my youth. But my heart is still the same heart."

I didn't know what to say. My own heart was pounding like a desperate rabbit's would, caught in the grip of a snake. I was trapped.

I couldn't show it. Couldn't.

I forced myself to smile. To lean in to his touch.

He moved his hand to stroke back tendrils of dark hair that had escaped from my chignon. "After I capture Le Lérot today," he murmured, "the Führer will be reminded of my abilities and wisdom. He will listen to my advice about Stalingrad before it's too late. Germany will make peace with Russia. Then we can turn all our attention to Britain and America." He smiled, his gray eyes warm, like sun breaking through rain clouds. "I'll be freed from this exile and will be allowed to return to Germany as my reward. So will you."

"Me?"

"There's something about you... From the moment we met, I felt drawn to you. As if we knew each other in another life."

Was he about to make the connection? See that the reason I seemed so familiar was that I resembled my mother?

I shivered. "Oh..."

"I thought I'd always be alone. But I dreamed of finding a wife of beauty, loyalty and virtue. I dreamed of you." His hand lingered on my shoulder. "Once I'm back in Hitler's favor, I'll be able to give you everything you deserve. Home. Children. Jewels. Furs. You'll rule over the height of German society. I'll take care of you. And everyone you love."

Otto looked at me. "I ask only one thing in return. Love me, Margot," he whispered. His voice caught. "Just love me."

And then he pulled me tight against his body and lowered his lips to mine.

33

LUCIE

As we walked along the rue Froissart, the late-afternoon sun was warm on my face. Four children happily skipped around me as I pushed Louis in the baby carriage. Five children under four, with only me to keep track of them, excepting the occasional assistance of Choupette. Berthe had asked Fauve to stay behind, to help her with something. Thérèse, who at three was the oldest, was jumping ahead of us on the sidewalk following hopscotch lines drawn only in her mind.

And I felt desperately unhappy.

The street was quiet, without much traffic, as we returned from the park. We moved slowly, causing other people to stare, some with encouraging smiles, some with flat eyes. And through it all, I couldn't stop hearing the echo of Margot's voice demanding that we must all leave Paris. Telling me I'd never see Klaus again.

Think of Fauve. Don't you want to see her safe?

Baby Louis was awake and cooing. He laughed as I looked down at him. His eyes were sparkling, his cheeks chubby and rosy in the golden warmth of summer.

Choupette trotted beside us, sniffing at every bush and tree and dark-painted postal box in the city. She'd finally learned to ride herd, just as I'd once promised the Lusignys she would. Though it wasn't sheep she was protecting now but little girls, keeping them close and making sure no one wandered far.

I took a deep breath, blinking fast as I looked up at the vibrant blue sky.

How could I abandon Klaus to face the Nazis alone? I didn't want to leave him. I felt like my life had just truly begun.

Because Klaus had kissed me last night.

He'd kissed me.

I couldn't stop replaying the moment in my mind. The heat of his lips on mine. His arms around me. The electricity through my veins, making my body curl around his. My first kiss.

Both Josette and Margot had treated him shamefully, refusing to see how different he was from the other Germans. They didn't know.

But I did.

For an hour, I'd struggled with what to do. At least in Paris, we lived under Herr Schröder's protection. No one looked at us too closely. We had food. Shelter. Safety. There was nowhere safer for Fauve to be—as long as he never found out her secret.

But what if he did? What if one day the babies were wrenched from my arms and I was thrown into prison for defying the laws against hiding Jews—and Fauve taken to some wretched camp, then those hot, overpacked trains traveling to some mysterious place in the east?

And how long would it be before the Nazis found something wrong with all my babies? Perhaps they'd say one had a disability, or another had been born to a communist, or another had gypsy blood?

But what if leaving was even more dangerous than staying?

I hadn't known what to do. So... I'd followed my heart. To Klaus.

Before he'd left for headquarters with Margot and Herr Schröder, Klaus had come to the attic to say farewell as I got the children ready for the day. And even with her warning pounding in my ears, I'd blurted out, "Margot says we must all leave Paris."

"Leave!" He'd looked startled. "Why?"

I'd shaken my head. "I'm not sure. She just says it's not safe anymore."

Klaus had pulled me into his arms and, for a long moment, he'd held me close, stroking my back, vowing in a whisper, "I'll always keep you safe. I promise. Whatever happens."

He'd sounded almost like he was trying to convince himself of that, even more than me.

Troubled, I'd looked up at him. "Is something going to happen? What aren't you telling me?"

His worried blue eyes slid away from mine. "I just know I can't bear to lose you, Lucie. Not now. Not ever."

"Me either," I'd whispered, pressing my cheek against the buttons of his uniform.

The orphans had interrupted us then, tumbling around us and yanking on our clothes. He'd kissed me briefly, then turned to the children clamoring for his attention—even Fauve, who'd rushed in as soon as she heard his voice. She loved Klaus more than she loved anyone, except Berthe.

After he left for headquarters, I'd felt newly calm. I'd told myself Margot must be overreacting. After all, she hadn't given any real reason why Dr. Ravanel was suddenly so worried about our safety. It didn't make sense we'd be in more danger now than we had been yesterday or anytime in the last year. Besides, Josette had said she wasn't going, either. Why should I uproot my children and leave in a blind panic just on my sister's say-so? Until Margot explained, I'd decided I wasn't going anywhere, and neither were the children.

I'd immediately felt better. And after lunch, once I'd tucked in the children for their nap, after my own sleepless night worrying about Margot, I'd slept soundly for several hours.

But now, as I walked with the children, all my worries found me again. They were churning around us, like miasmas in the air. I trusted Margot. I trusted Dr. Ravanel. And I loved Klaus. It wasn't safe here. It wasn't safe there.

I couldn't stay.

I couldn't go.

With a deep breath I looked from baby Louis to the four toddlers, savoring the feeling of the sun on my face. I bent down to thank Geneviève for her gift of an old dandelion she'd found on a crack in the sidewalk, then rose—and froze in shock.

My sister was pelting towards us, her dark eyes wild, clutching her bag and mine.

"Lucie—turn around. We can never go back to St. Agnes's."

"What? What are you talking about?"

"Herr Schröder. He just—proposed to me."

"Did he?" I gave an incredulous laugh. "No, you must have misunderstood. He's two—nearly three times your age!"

"It's no mistake. He proposed." Her cheeks were bright red, and she seemed to gulp for air. "He even... kissed me."

"Kissed you!" I was well and truly shocked. Kissing someone as old as Herr Schröder seemed unthinkably wrong. I wrinkled my nose. "He's old enough to be our grandfather! What did you do?"

"I told him I'd think about it."

"What? After you gave me such a hard time about Klaus—"

"It's not a romance, Lucie! Everything is falling apart. Josette's in danger. We all are. He's going to start digging—if he hasn't already—he's going to hurt everyone I love."

"Margot, you're making no sense."

"If you knew everything, you would be so scared—" But she cut herself off, shaking her head. "It would take too long to explain. Take the children to the Ravanels'. Go now."

She grabbed my elbow and started steering me towards the boulevard at the end of the street. I stumbled along with the baby carriage, staring at her, trailed by the children and dog. "But why would Herr Schröder want to hurt us? Just because you were out all night? Why is Josette in danger?"

"She won't be for long." My sister faced me, her cheeks pale beneath the dark waves of her long, wild hair now tumbling over her shoulders. "I'm going to the Théâtre Lutèce to save her."

"Margot, you've lost your mind," I said as gently as I could. I put my hand over hers. "Come back to St. Agnes's. We can talk this through with Klaus."

"No!" she nearly yelled.

I took a deep breath, trying to control the rapid beat of my heart. "But he told me he doesn't think we need to go."

"He knows we're planning to leave Paris?" she cried, her face white as a ghost's. "Oh, Lucie—what have you done?"

Panic and shame surged through me, as if I'd accidentally burned everyone's porridge, as I'd done once when I was younger. Berthe had banished me from the kitchen for weeks. My cheeks burned. "I don't understand. Why was it wrong?"

"He's a Nazi, Lucie," she said scornfully, as if I were very stupid indeed. We'd reached the boulevard. "Forget him. You'll never see him again."

I caught my breath. Never see Klaus again?

"Wait—what about Fauve, and Berthe—"

"Berthe is taking Fauve to safety. You mustn't worry."

I gasped. So that was why Berthe had asked the little girl to stay behind. "You made plans for Fauve without me?"

"Berthe's plans, not mine. We have no time for this, Lucie. Just be grateful she's away. Now where's a taxi?" She impatiently looked both ways down the boulevard Beaumarchais.

I looked at the babies and my dog. They all appeared scared

and uncertain, turning between Margot and me. Jeanne started to cry.

My spine snapped straight. "I'm not just running away with them," I told my sister coldly, "without so much as a change of clothes or bottle of milk. I don't know what's happened, but I'm going back to St. Agnes's to talk to Klaus."

Margot's eyes widened as she stared at me. She'd never heard that tone from me before or heard me defy her so strongly.

"Come along, children," I said gently and started to turn back in the direction of St. Agnes's.

Margot grabbed my wrist. Her face was pale and strained. "Herr Schröder found out that someone has been betraying his secrets to Le Lérot." She licked her lips. "Someone... close to him."

"So? How does that...?"

Her eyes met mine.

"Margot," I gasped. "How could you?"

"How could I not?" she hissed.

I looked at my children. "But the risk..."

"It's for them. For all of us." She looked down at baby Louis, somehow still sleeping peacefully in the baby carriage, sucking his thumb. "Do you want them to grow up as beggars in their own country? Watching as the Germans find reasons to send off our citizens to concentration camps, one by one? The soldiers, the Jews, the gypsies, the socialists, the artists, the political exiles... who's next?" She paused. "Motherless children?"

I stared at her, holding my breath.

Margot had been passing secrets to Le Lérot. This changed everything. For all this time, I'd been hurt that my sister had seemed to care more about Herr Schröder's secretarial work instead of caring for these children. But now, at last, I understood.

And I realized how much danger we were in.

"Who is he? Le Lérot?"

"I don't know. I've never met him. I heard a rumor it's..." She snorted; shook her head. "Doesn't matter. I don't believe it."

"What about Josette?"

"I've just learned..." Guiltily, she shook her head. "She might have been doing something similar, too. I think—" She stopped herself.

"For heaven's sake, Margot, don't try to protect me! I've had enough of being in the dark!"

"Otto thinks Le Lérot was creating fake documents at the Théâtre Lutèce. The Germans are going to raid the theater. He thinks Josette might be involved. I need to find her before it's too late."

Fear struck through my heart. "Use the house phone."

"I can't risk going back. He's still in his study. And anyway, you know the German operators listen to every word."

"Oh, Margot, why didn't you tell me sooner?" I cried. Then I clapped my hands and forced myself to smile as I told the children calmly, "All right, everyone, stay close—we're going on an adventure!"

But our so-called adventure was short-lived. We peered up and down the busy boulevard to see no taxis anywhere. With fuel shortages, and most private cars requisitioned by the Germans, and so many of our men away, taxis were often nowhere to be found.

As we waited, my children grew increasingly fidgety from standing in one place on a boring city corner with nothing to do. Only Choupette was patient. She tilted her head, looking at me.

Margot gave a low, slightly hysterical laugh as she finally turned. "You'll have to walk."

My eyes widened. Now I was the one to scoff. "Walk to Belleville? With four toddlers, a baby and a dog?"

"Argh." She rolled her shoulders.

I brightened. "I could ask Klaus if he could—"

"No, Lucie. Don't you get it? You can't trust him. You can't trust any of them."

"I told you—he's different," I said pleadingly. "He's *good*."

Her face was hard. "I wish I could believe that, I really do, but you have a soft heart. I love that about you, but it doesn't make you the best judge of character."

I lifted my chin. "I'm an excellent judge of character. I see people as they wish they could be. Take it back."

"Fine." She threw up her hands. "After this is all over, I'll listen to everything you say about Klaus. I'll give him a chance."

"Oh, thank you—"

"Now just let me think..." She rubbed her chin, then her eyes lit up.

She dragged me back to the rue Froissart, where she knocked on the door of the ground-floor apartment of Jean Pagnier, the orphanage's former mechanic who'd worked as Herr Schröder's driver the last two years.

He opened the door, squinting, a bottle of beer in his hand and a cigarette hanging out of his mouth. It had almost burned down to ash. "Yeah?"

"*Monsieur*," she panted, pushing me forward. "Can you please give them all a ride? Without telling... anyone... about it?"

He looked doubtfully from me, to the baby carriage, to the toddlers now starting to cry and poke each other, and finally my dog, who was sitting patiently.

"Well, now. That sounds a little dodgy, don't it? Take the Métro or walk like every other Frenchman."

But as he started to close the door, Margot said suddenly, "I can pay."

"Pay?" He peeked back around the door. "Marks or francs?"

"Marks." She pulled her German wages out of her bag, and his eyes flickered.

"Fine." He tossed the cigarette to the sidewalk and smashed it with his foot. "But no baby carriage, and the dog costs extra."

Turning, Margot said brightly, "Monsieur Pagnier will take good care of you, Lucie. You remember the address?"

"Of course I do." Did she really think I was such a helpless child as to not remember where the Ravanels lived?

She embraced me. "I'll grab Josette at the theater and join you as fast as I can. But if we're delayed, do whatever Dr. Ravanel says. Leave without us."

"But I don't want to. Not without—"

"Please, Lucie."

She pulled back with tears in her eyes. It startled me. Margot never cried.

"If you ever were in danger again, or hurt, or lost, I don't think I could survive it." She wiped her eyes. "I haven't been a good sister. I know that. I've been selfish and kept secrets. I thought I was keeping you safe, but really, I was scared."

"What are you talking about?"

She took a shuddering breath. "Here's your bag. As soon as I see you again, we'll talk. Really talk." Her voice caught. "About everything." She squeezed my shoulder, then stepped back. "Go now."

"But, Margot—"

She'd already turned away.

As Monsieur Pagnier disappeared to collect the sedan from his back garage, I tried not to burst into tears in front of the children. Even poor Choupette could tell something was wrong, whining against me. I reached down and ruffled her fur.

"What's wong, Wucie? Why aww you sad?" Geneviève put both her chubby hands on my cheeks and stared at me.

I shook my head, trying to smile. "I'm fine, sweet girl." But tears were streaming down my face now. I knew I was leaving St. Agnes's forever, the only home I'd ever known. And worse:

leaving Klaus, without so much as a word. It felt like the hugest betrayal of my life. And I wasn't just betraying him.

I was betraying my own heart and everything in this world I'd ever believed to be true.

"Lucie."

I looked up, blinking back tears. And there, like a miracle, was the love of my life, wearing his German uniform, holding his cap under his arm.

"Klaus." I threw my arms around him with a sob. "I'm so glad you're here."

He pulled back, looking down at me urgently. "We have to talk."

I looked up. "We're leaving Paris. Right now. My sister's in danger—*all of us* are in danger."

He drew back, his handsome face strained. "More than you know," he said grimly.

34

JOSETTE

Tears pricked my eyes as I watched the actors of *La Femme de Machiavelli* take the stage, ready for the curtain to rise. This couldn't be my last time seeing a play from the wings of the Théâtre Lutèce, could it?

I couldn't leave my friends, my place, my purpose, to run away and live safely in the country. No! Absolutely not!

Could I?

I didn't know what to do. My throat ached as the curtain rose and the play began. I watched the lead actress drip, and droop, and then, once the men were off stage, straighten her shoulders and speak boldly. Her costume was perfect. And so was the ingénue's. Not to mention her clever little hat.

No. I was staying.

Margot and Lucie would be fine on their own. They didn't need me to come with them, no matter how much Margot might push. I'd never felt like I was really part of their family, for all my desperate trying.

I'd stay here, where I was wanted. *Needed.*

Surely that was worth a little danger?

I exhaled and realized I'd been holding my breath all day.

But now I could relax. I wasn't going to leave. Let Margot and Lucie go to the country. I'd find somewhere to stay in Paris. I couldn't leave the only place I'd ever felt accepted.

But I'd create travel passes to help Margot and Lucie and the orphans all get to La Ravelle, for that was surely where Margot intended to take them. They wouldn't need to ask Le Lérot. I could just do it. It was lucky I'd found a chance to grab Herr Schröder's stamp that afternoon.

I'd return it to the study tonight, as soon as the forger was done copying it. Schröder must never know it had been compromised. After that, I'd never go back to St. Agnes's. The thought made me sad. Then I pictured Margot's face when I gave her the forged documents and she learned I'd secretly been helping Le Lérot all this time, while she'd been disparaging my devotion to the theater.

I heard a noise behind me then. Turning, I was relieved to see Madame Hébert. "Madame, is the forger here? I was just going down to the basement. Is the key in its usual place? There's an emergency—"

I stopped when I saw her pale, strained face.

"They're coming." Her voice was strangled. "Clothilde saw them gathering outside on the street. The forger's in custody. She and Albert have already fled."

"Who's coming?" I whispered, but I knew.

"If they search, they'll find the basement. Don't hide there. You'd be trapped. You have the stamp?"

Confused, I pulled it from my pocket.

She caught her breath. "Don't let them catch you with it. Escape through the back. Throw it in the river." She looked at me with agonized eyes, her peacock feather sagging, wrinkles showing around her heavily made-up eyes, lined like Cleopatra. "Live, Josette. Then do what you can. Live to save France."

I stared at her, Herr Schröder's stamp still held loosely in my hands. "But I can't just—"

We jumped at the muffled bang of doors being flung against the walls, followed by screams across the audience. On the nearby stage, the actors froze, and the lead actress fell silent as they stared past the spotlights into the darkness.

The house lights turned on, flooding the theater. A voice shouted in German, "This theater is closed. By order of the Reich!"

Madame Hébert turned back to me in a rush, her cheeks flushed, beads of sweat on her forehead, and shoved me towards the backstage hallway. "Go now! Don't wait!"

"But what will happen to—"

"It's all over for me. But maybe not for you. Go!"

She shoved me again—so hard I stumbled back. Then I watched, chilled, as she hurried forward to the front of the stage, her purple silk caftan fluttering, her chin held high, and threw up her hands.

"Stop," she cried, standing between the actors. "This is my theater. If you have a fight, it's with me."

She was sacrificing herself to the Nazis to protect me. I had to get out, or her bravery would be in vain.

And yet I couldn't move.

As everyone in the theater held their breath, staring at the tableau of Madame Hébert on stage beneath the spotlight, a harsh German voice addressed her in heavily accented French. "You are under arrest, *madame*!"

"You Germans are disgusting!" she shouted, tossing her head. She spread her arms wide, her jeweled walking stick glinting in the spotlight. "You have no art or music in your souls! You are no better than... dogs!"

Panting for breath, she shook her fist at them—and collapsed.

Watching from the wings, I took an involuntary step towards her. Then I sucked in my breath. She was creating a spectacle—to give me the chance to escape.

Gripping the hard edges of the rubber stamp in my hands, I grabbed my bag from the back room. Leaving through the stage door would be too obvious, so I climbed out the window in the furthest corner of a lonely storeroom, praying no soldiers would be waiting in the alley.

"Josette!"

Margot's voice. I gasped.

When I turned and fell into her arms, I almost sobbed. "What are you…?"

"Nazi soldiers are blocking the entrance. Otto just told me about the raid, the travel pass forgeries happening here. Were you helping Le Lérot, Josette? Don't lie to me!"

I tossed my head. "Yes, I was. I'm not sorry!"

She exhaled. "I've been helping Le Lérot, too. Passing along the secrets I overhear as a secretary."

I gasped. "For how long?"

Margot gave a small smile. "From the beginning."

"Why didn't you say?"

"Why didn't you?"

We stared at each other in the alley, then burst into laughter.

"Fine spies we are."

"Too good at secrets."

"So good we've really gotten ourselves into a jam." She looked around the alley. "Let's get out of here."

Tears stung my eyes, threatening to spill over my lashes as I followed her. Margot had come for me. As if I were just as important to her as Lucie. Just as much of a sister.

"We'll head for the Ravanels' then get out of—" She blinked fast, looking at me. "Are you crying, Josette?"

"No," I wept.

"Don't be a goose. Did you think I'd just leave you to the Nazis?" Yet she brushed at her own eyes before she grabbed my free hand. "We have to hurry."

But as we hotfooted it out of the back alley, heading towards the river to try to blend in with the rest of the pedestrians coming home from work, two soldiers suddenly blocked our route.

"Halt," one said in German. He glanced behind us. "You are coming from the theater? What was your purpose there? What are your names?"

I sucked in my breath. Margot and I stared at each other, terrified.

"You will come with us now," the other one said in French, his face forbidding.

"Hold." A third figure appeared behind them, and I nearly gasped his name in shock.

Klaus Schröder's face, usually so amiable and bland, was cold; he looked at us blankly, as if we were strangers. No, worse. As if we were enemies.

"*Jawohl, Herr Leutnant.*" They turned to Klaus and saluted. "We are under orders of Standartenführer Becker, sir. To bring in anyone who tries to escape."

"I"—Klaus drew himself up in his uniform, his jaw hard, and I realized that he was quite tall and broad-shouldered, too— "am personal adjutant to the *Reichsbevollmächtigter* himself. Under his direct orders. Do you wish to defy them?"

The soldiers looked at each other nervously.

I stared at Klaus. His affable manner, kind eyes and dull speech had always seemed bland and boring. I'd wondered what Lucie could possibly see in him, what could make her forget the shame of him being a Nazi officer.

But there was something steely in him now that I'd never seen before. Something fierce and dangerous. Was this the real face of him after all?

He said sternly, "The *Reichsbevollmächtigter* wishes to speak to these two directly. I will take them to him at once."

The soldiers looked at him, then at each other. Reluctantly, they nodded.

"*Ja, Herr Leutnant.*"

"*Jawohl.*" The second soldier grabbed our arms. "Do you wish to have help taking these... women"—he spat the word as if it were an insult—"directly to the *Reichsbevollmächtigter?*"

Klaus shook his head. "*Nein.* I can handle these two." He glared at us. "They know to be afraid of me. They won't run."

Margot stiffened, glaring back, and opened her mouth to argue.

I elbowed her hard in the ribs. I wasn't even sure why. Perhaps some memory of the way he'd looked at Lucie when he'd said *my intentions are honorable.* Or maybe it was just that Lucie believed in him so much. She always thought the best of people, but what if, this one time, she was right?

Rubbing her ribs, Margot looked at me, startled, then closed her mouth.

"Now, you two, you're going to face the *Reichsbevollmächtigter,*" Klaus said harshly, yanking painfully on our wrists.

We had no choice but to follow him. My heart was pounding.

But when the soldiers were out of earshot, he exhaled and let us go.

"You have to get out of the city as quickly as possible. I'm taking you to Lucie."

I exhaled in relief. "I knew I wasn't wrong to trust you."

"Oh, you did?" Klaus said mockingly.

My cheeks burned. "Well, I know it now."

"Lucie..." Margot shook her head angrily. "What did my sister tell you?"

"That you're in danger," he said simply.

"She shouldn't—"

"It didn't matter. I already knew. And I'm betraying my country for you."

Margot looked astonished. "What?"

His blue eyes glistened. "My uncle told me to follow you when you left the house, Margot. He wanted to see if you were the mole. If you'd run straight to Le Lérot to tell him about the raid on the theater. He hoped it would either prove your innocence—or flush out the rebel."

"So the arrest of Madame Hébert is just a ruse?" I said, hoping it was true.

He shook his head. "He's going to arrest everyone he suspects of working for Le Lérot." He looked between us. "Didn't you know this day would come? You must have planned what you'd do?"

We were silent. I bit my lip, squirming a little.

He waited, then sighed. "I saw you take Lucie to the chauffeur's house. She told me you were going to save Josette. And that she was supposed to wait with the children at your friends' house in Belleville."

Margot's shoulders sagged a little. Clearly, Lucie had told him everything.

I turned to him. "But you've decided to be on our side."

He exhaled. "You're Lucie's sisters. You're her family. That means," he said in a low voice, "you're my family, too."

I saw what it cost him to say that. His hands were shaking, his shoulders tight. I couldn't even imagine what it would be like, to betray one's country, one's honor, one's blood.

"And your uncle?" I said delicately.

Pain crossed his face. He closed his eyes. "He'll never forgive me. He'll kill me if he ever sees me again," he said bleakly. "And I can only pray my family escapes his wrath." He looked away. "My sister will take my nephews to their grandfather for protection. But my mother..." His voice broke. "When I was conscripted, she begged me to defy the Nazis. She didn't want me to protect her. She said to let the Nazis take her if they must, and let the whole world see their evil."

"She's brave," Josette said.

He wiped his eyes. "Yes. We all must be brave now." He looked between us. "When word gets out that you have been deceiving my uncle for years, right under his nose, and that even his own nephew betrayed him... no one will ever respect him again. His career will be over." He looked away, towards the river. "Maybe his life."

Margot stared at him. Then she snorted. "No. Men like that always manage to get by. But he'll hate us, all right. If he ever finds us, heaven help us."

We took the Métro to Belleville, apparently just a German officer amusing himself with two French girls. But as we sat on the moving underground train, I stared blankly past Klaus, the other passengers, the moving lights.

The theater was closed. My life of purpose and joy was over, and the person I admired most had fallen into German hands, to face prison or worse. I'd only escaped because of her. I looked at the official stamp I'd tucked in my bag. It was all I had left.

That, my life—and my sisters.

35

MARGOT

We found Lucie and the orphans at the Ravanels' cottage, which was in chaos, Choupette running in circles and barking, the older toddlers bickering and whining, the younger two weeping with exhaustion. My father was doing his best to help his wife and daughter pack a couple of overstuffed suitcases. The two women seemed stunned, too shocked to cry. My half-sister had baby Louis against her shoulder. Only he seemed to be placidly sleeping through everything.

"Margot, Josette—Klaus!" With a choking sob, Lucie threw her arms around the young German officer as if she hadn't seen him in months, years, instead of just an hour. "I was so afraid I'd lose you."

"Never," he said, holding her close.

"What is this soldier doing here?" my father demanded, his voice laced with rage as he glared at the Nazi uniform.

"Klaus saved us," Josette said matter-of-factly.

"Schröder ordered him to follow me, to see if I'd lead him to Le Lérot." I looked at Klaus. "He decided to turn against his own uncle and his country because... because of Lucie."

My sister gasped and clung to him all the tighter.

"I see," Dr. Ravanel said grimly.

"The Nazis have taken over the Théâtre Lutèce," Josette said. "So please, Dr. Ravanel, if you know who Le Lérot is, could you please tell him that Madame Hébert is under arrest..."

My father's eyes widened. He looked at me, and I shook my head slightly. I hadn't told Josette anything about him being my contact, but she'd obviously worked it out.

"Let's not discuss Le Lérot." He glanced sideways at Klaus, then turned to his wife. "Don't pack so much, my dear. Just the most important things, I told you."

"But Jean-Luc," she wept, "I don't want to go. Don't make me leave you."

Josette, Lucie and I looked at each other. Josette shrugged with a crooked grin. After our headlong flight from Paris when the Nazis first invaded in June 1940, we'd been through this all before. But this time, we'd had no time to pack our clothes. We had only the money I'd had time to grab from the cookie jar, wages we'd saved over the past two years, along with whatever additional odds and ends we had in our old school bags. We didn't even have extra diapers. Luckily, Lucie had told us the Ravanels had old dishrags we could use, and she'd packed a few bottles of milk for the children. Suzanne's old baby clothes were still at the house in La Ravelle, so the little ones would have changes of clothes once we arrived.

If we arrived.

"Klaus, would you mind checking on our truck?" Dr. Ravanel asked coolly. "It's parked in the alley behind the garden. Make sure there's fuel and the tires have air."

"Of course." After giving Lucie's hand a final squeeze, the young soldier left.

As soon as he was in the garden, my father looked at us. "I don't like him being here. I don't trust him."

The rest of us glanced at each other.

"He saved us," Josette said, but her voice was subdued.

He snorted. "Maybe that's part of the plan. Maybe this is all a trick, and he's still working for his uncle, trying to draw out Le Lérot and catch all of us at once."

"My f— Dr. Ravanel is right." I stopped the truth coming out of my mouth just in time. Lucie still didn't know. I kicked myself for waiting so long. Why had I done this to myself? "We should tell Klaus to leave."

"Perhaps that's safer," Josette allowed.

"No." The voice was so strong and firm it took a moment for me to realize it was Lucie speaking. She stared between me and Josette, her blue eyes like fire, her spine like steel. "He's coming with us."

"Look, Lucie." Josette's voice was gentle. "I know you care for him, but..."

"Klaus was under orders to follow Margot and report back. Instead, he stayed to talk to me. I told him you were going to the Théâtre Lutèce." She turned. "Where he apparently saved you, Josette. And you, Margot."

"We appreciate it," I said soothingly. "But soon, all of Germany will be chasing after him as a traitor. Even if he's trustworthy, he couldn't possibly go with us. He'd bring too much danger."

She stiffened. "He's risked everything for us. Sacrificed everything. And now you want him to die for it?"

"Lucie, surely you have to see—" But she didn't. I tried another tack, shifting my gaze to the orphans. "Think of the children."

"Don't even try," she snapped. She lifted her chin. "If you leave him behind, you'll have to leave me, too."

"Don't be ridiculous!"

"You told me you'd give him a chance, Margot. Were you lying?" Lucie looked at Josette. "Do you care nothing for the fact that he sacrificed his own safety for yours? Because if that's true, then I'd rather be with him than you."

"You can't mean that," I argued. "He's a Nazi—"

"He's not! And the children and I are better off with him. At least he's honorable and doesn't lie, unlike *some*—"

"Oh, for heaven's sake," I said crossly, releasing my arms. I'd had about enough of the hysterics. "We're your family!"

"So is he! I love him, Margot." Her eyes blazed. "I'd do anything to protect him. Just as he would for me." She shook her head, looking between us. "Perhaps I betrayed you, begging him to go to the theater to save you. Sharing our plans to leave Paris." She tossed her blonde hair defiantly. "But I'd do it again! He's a victim of the Nazis—as much as we are! He's sacrificed everything for us. He's a good man. *I love him.*"

We stared at each other, uncertain. Bernadette fell down and started yowling. In Suzanne's arms, baby Louis woke abruptly and started to cry, and he rarely cried.

Lucie swept the infant into her arms, and he immediately quieted, comforted by her presence. Then she kissed Bernadette's soft, dark hair, and the little girl, too, grew calm.

My little sister lifted her chin. "So what's it going to be? Are you going to accept Klaus as one of us? Or am I leaving with him now?"

"Don't weave, Wucie," cried little Geneviève, her big blue eyes gleaming with tears.

"Lucie," sniffed Thérèse, clinging to her dress. "Lucie."

Silence. Then Madame Ravanel said hoarsely, looking between us in horror, "Are you really thinking of allowing him to come home with us? A Nazi soldier?"

My father looked at me. Then, at my expression, he sighed. "Might as well keep him in our sight. Keep an eye on the boy."

Madame Ravanel shook her head, eyes wide. "But—you're all mad! He's a soldier!"

Looking at his wife, he added gruffly, "A soldier who can help us get out of Paris."

His wife set her jaw, clearly having to force herself not to argue further. She turned to her daughter. "Grab that coat."

Lucie frowned at me. "But Berthe and Fauve aren't here yet..."

I hung my head. "They, um, they're not coming."

"Not coming!" She looked at me accusingly.

I took a deep breath. It was hard for me to explain something I knew would upset her. Every word out of my mouth felt difficult.

"Berthe... thinks Roger... can get Fauve to Switzerland."

Hurt flashed in my sister's eyes. "And I didn't even get to say goodbye? To either of them?"

"I..." Anxious to change the subject, I turned to Josette. "Can you make us travel passes with that stamp?"

She shook her head. "I need a printing press. Madame Hébert had an old one in the basement of the theater." She looked away unhappily, and I knew she was thinking of her friends there, now in Nazi custody.

I sighed. "I think Herr Schröder knows it's been stolen." I remembered his earlier questions. "It might not be useful for long. He'll create a new version." I turned to my father. "So how will we make it to La Ravelle without travel passes?"

"Klaus can't do everything," Lucie pointed out.

Outside, twilight was falling. The Ravanels had some money for fuel and food, and we could add to it with our saved wages, but it wouldn't do us much good if we couldn't get past the German checkpoints outside the city. There were checkpoints everywhere.

"We could go ask Roger," I suggested, then added, only half jokingly, "Maybe he can use his black market connections to send us all to Switzerland with Fauve."

"You'd all be caught," my father said quickly.

I frowned. "Perhaps not Switzerland, but he could find somewhere to—"

"No," he said, more harshly, and glared at me. "We're not leading the Germans to Roger."

I felt deflated. I didn't know why he was fighting me so hard when...

Then I slowly lifted my gaze back to him, my eyes wide. Dr. Ravanel saw my face, and he set his jaw, shaking his head slightly.

I was trembling. Was it possible? Could Roger Cochet be...?

I couldn't even think it. My heart pounded. No. Roger had told me outright he cared only about money. He couldn't be Le Lérot. He wouldn't put himself at such great risk, secretly leading the Resistance in Paris. It was too dangerous. He'd be killed—

And in that moment, I suddenly realized just the thought was unbearable. I couldn't lose Roger.

He'd die believing I didn't care.

All this time I'd taken him for granted, like some idiot girl. I'd believed his love would last forever, that he'd always be there if I needed him, even if I pushed him away and ignored my true feelings. How many chances had I wasted out of fear?

I loved him.

I was in love with Roger Cochet.

"I can't believe this is happening," Élisabeth Ravanel muttered. As she pulled clothing out of her suitcase, then put it back again, she darted hard glances at me and Lucie, as if she blamed us for everything. Or maybe just me. I'd burst rudely into their family, the child no one had known about, borne by another woman. I was still wearing a sleek skirt suit and silk stockings purchased by a German officer. She thought the Nazi threat had come only from the girls of St. Agnes's. Madame Ravanel knew nothing about her husband's Resistance activities with Le Lérot. He'd deliberately kept her in the dark. For years now.

Just as Josette and I had done to Lucie—and each other.

Klaus returned from the back garden, his face pale.

"Is the truck in working order?" Dr. Ravanel's voice wasn't exactly friendly, but I could sense he was trying.

"I didn't bring them here," the young man said hoarsely. "I swear. No one followed me."

My father frowned. "What are you—?" Then he saw something through the front window.

"I saw them as I came back through the garden." Klaus came to stand at the window. His pale blue eyes moved to Lucie as he pleaded, "Get out now. I'll stay here, try to delay them—"

My father turned back from the window.

"There seem to be Nazi soldiers gathering in the street."

36

MARGOT

My father's voice was oddly mild, extravagantly calm, just like my mother's when she'd told us something alarming, like, *Oh, the police are here to search our garden for venomous snakes.*

The rest of us rushed to look through the window.

Dr. Ravanel was right. Dozens of Nazi soldiers were massed at the corner. I saw a shadowy figure lurking behind them, walking with a limp and a cane.

"He betrayed us!" Madame Ravanel cried, glaring at Klaus.

"Wait." Josette pointed. "Isn't that Jean Pagnier?"

We all looked and saw the chauffeur, huddling beside the military truck, smoking a cigarette.

"See?" Lucie demanded, glaring at Madame Ravanel. "I told you it wasn't Klaus."

"Sorry," the woman muttered, though she really didn't sound sorry at all.

"That's all right," Klaus said with his typical good humor. Then his smile fled. "But you all must go. Now. Hurry."

"Oh, Klaus, no—I won't leave you—I can't," Lucie gasped, clinging to him, baby Louis held between them.

"No." My father clapped his hand on the German boy's

shoulder. "They're attacking my house. My family. I'll be the one to defend them."

He looked back at me, and my heart twisted. I looked down at the garnet ring sparkling dully on my finger. My mother and father had the same courageous heart, the same history, because they'd worked together for years, across battlefields. They'd loved each other.

I would be strong, too. I was their daughter. They'd always be connected. Through me.

"What? No!" Élisabeth Ravanel cried. "Jean-Luc! You can't go out there!"

He turned fiercely on Klaus. "Get them safely out of Paris. Protect them."

"I won't let you down, sir."

"Good lad." The two shook hands, like a promise. My father had decided to trust him, and he didn't do anything in half measures.

He turned to his wife. His voice became gentle. "Élisabeth, take the suitcases to the truck."

"No!"

"Think of Suzanne," he said softly.

Suddenly uncertain, Madame Ravanel looked across the room at my half-sister. There was fear in her young face.

Dr. Ravanel cupped his wife's cheek. "You have to live, Élisabeth. For her. For me. Remember always that I love you. Forever and ever."

"Jean-Luc," she sobbed, leaning close. Tears streamed down her cheeks.

He took his wife in his arms and kissed her, one last time. "*Adieu*," he whispered.

Then he turned to Suzanne and hugged her. "I love you. I'm so proud of you."

"Love you," she choked out.

Squaring his shoulders, he finally turned to me. "Keep them safe. Promise me."

My throat ached. "I promise."

He nodded, comforted. "Go now. Through the garden."

"I love you... Papa," I blurted—the first time I'd voiced the words I'd felt in my heart for some time now.

He froze. His dark eyes, exactly like my own, glistened suddenly. "And I love you, Margot. You're strong and fearless. Just like your brothers..." His voice choked, and he leaned forward to whisper in my ear, "After you get everyone to safety, you can return to Paris. Le Lérot will find you."

I sucked in my breath. How had he guessed my plans? I yearned to know more. "Is it—"

But before I could ask about Roger, he was already turning away, towards the front door.

"Quickly, children," Lucie said briskly and started towards the back door, holding baby Louis with one arm and Geneviève's hand with the other. Josette had our small canvas bags dangling on one arm as she carried little Jeanne. Suzanne, glancing at her mother, took Bernadette's hand and cajoled her outside, while Klaus lifted Thérèse onto his shoulders. Choupette brought up the rear.

Madame Ravanel and I were last, gathering up the two suitcases. From the back door, she looked back one last time at Jean-Luc. "You'll follow us?"

"Always," he whispered, his dark eyes luminous.

We went out into the garden. Madame Ravanel was blinking back tears. She looked at me bitterly. "How could you bring this on us?"

I caught my breath. Any defense would only point out that her husband had kept—was still keeping—secrets from her. I couldn't bring myself to do that when she was still shocked and hurt over the one secret he hadn't kept: that I was his daughter.

"I'm sorry," I said quietly, not meeting her eyes. "I never meant to hurt anyone."

"I know." She took a deep breath, then forced a smile. "Perhaps once he explains to the Germans he hasn't done anything wrong, they'll let him go."

A lump lifted to my throat as I lied to her. "Perhaps."

We went heavily through the garden and saw the others had already disappeared through the back gate, where the rusty old ambulance truck waited in the unpaved alley.

"I can't." She stopped, dropping her suitcase next to the woodpile. "I have to see he's all right."

"Wait—"

But Madame Ravanel crept quickly through the garden and peeked over the high stone wall. Then she sucked in her breath.

"What is it?" I asked.

She didn't answer, so I left Suzanne's suitcase behind and followed her to the wall. I put my hand on her shoulder, then looked up...

And watched in horror as, on the other side of the stone wall, my father bravely walked out alone into the Belleville street, facing down the Nazi soldiers who'd poured out of the military trucks around the cottage.

Otto Schröder—in his dress uniform and mean little cap with the metal skull and crossbones—limped stiffly forward to meet him, the hard *clack-clack-clack* of his cane against the cobblestones echoing down the street. In the glow of the trucks' headlights, the cane's eagle-head handle glinted, its beak a vicious point.

"So, at last," the German officer said, his eyes narrowing as he looked at my father. "Le Lérot."

Madame Ravanel gasped. I slapped my hand over her mouth, ducking her down to hide behind the cottage's wall.

"Yes," my father said loudly. "I am Le Lérot."

From his wife's big blue eyes, I knew she believed his words because she thought her husband could not lie. Keeping our heads low, we peeked once more over the stone wall, which was shaggy with ivy.

Otto lifted his chin. "Margot has been passing you my secrets for years. How do you know each other? Never mind. I'll soon find out." His lips twisted in a snarl. "I was a fool to be kind to her. And Josette—stealing from me. Even Lucie has turned my own family against me. They all betrayed me. The orphans of St. Agnes have been nothing but an evil to this world, corrupt and vile."

My father glared back. "You are the evil. You are the one who is corrupt and vile. And we French will destroy you soon, drive you from our country like the bullying cowards you are—"

The Nazi officer backhanded him across the face, and I had to clap my hand over Madame Ravanel's mouth once more to muffle her cry.

My father was deliberately sacrificing himself. Distracting the Nazis so we could escape. Anguish gripped my heart; tears burned my eyes, too painful to fall.

I tugged her sleeve. "We have to go," I whispered.

"We must do something to help him," his wife gasped in agony. "What can we do?"

She didn't realize he was already dead. The only question now was how many of us would die with him today.

Keep them safe. Promise me.

I promise.

I grabbed her hand roughly. "We're going. Now."

Her eyes widened. "You would abandon him?"

"He's giving us time. We can't let his sacrifice be in vain."

"How can you be so unfeeling?"

I yanked her hand, hauling her from the stone wall and back through the garden. She struggled, trying to fight me. But I was ruthless.

I left the suitcases behind. It took every bit of fighting skill

I'd ever learned from my father—and my mother—to drag Madame Ravanel to the truck. When one of my high heels broke, I kicked off my shoes, leaving them in the dirt. She begged me to let her go, raging and fighting, calling me cold, even cruel.

But I would save my father's wife, even if she didn't want to be saved.

I was relieved to find Klaus sitting at the wheel of the truck, engine running, Lucie beside him, holding baby Louis. Josette, Suzanne, the older orphans and Choupette were packed in the back, end doors open.

I shoved the older woman into the open back of the ambulance truck with her daughter.

"No!" She fell forward, sobbing. Josette caught her.

"Maman?" Suzanne gasped.

I slammed the ambulance doors shut behind them. Then there was a loud hailstorm of bullets echoing from the other side of the house, and my blood went cold. Madame Ravanel let out a muffled scream.

Klaus called urgently, "We have to go."

Shoeless, I threw myself into the front bench seat beside Lucie, then Klaus stomped on the acceleration, and we drove fast down the unpaved alley.

When we reached the street, he blinked, peering forward. The city was dark, without streetlights, to avoid attracting Allied bombers. The only light came from the blood-red twilight and the headlights of the trucks parked on the nearby cross-street. The one in front of the cottage.

Klaus turned the wheel to drive right past it.

"No," Lucie begged. "Can't we go the other way?"

"We have no choice," he said grimly. "They likely blockaded the other streets so we wouldn't be able to escape. I'm only sure about the way they came."

As we drove past the end of the Ravanels' street, I watched

Nazi soldiers swarming towards the cottage, kicking open the front door.

My father's crumpled body lay bleeding on the street; his eyes stared unseeingly at the sky. He was riddled with bullets, his neck at a strange ninety-degree angle.

Otto Schröder still stood over him—holding his cane high. In the glow of the headlights, I saw the wood was glossy now, the sharp brass handle covered with dark red liquid.

And rage exploded through my soul like a German bomb.

The Nazi officer looked up as the truck passed by the end of the street, and my eyes met his.

Staring at my father's murderer, I slowly drew my finger over my throat. A promise.

Otto's eyes narrowed, and then his vicious lips twisted into an answering challenge of a smile.

37

LUCIE

The ambulance truck was finally quiet. Everyone had cried themselves to sleep.

I swallowed hard. I still couldn't believe what I'd seen—poor Dr. Ravanel lying bloodied in the street. As we'd passed by, I'd tried to tell myself he wasn't dead, just hurt. But I'd seen the unmoving blankness of his staring eyes. Herr Schröder had killed him.

Oh, how could he? *How?*

I felt shaken to the core. For the last two years, I'd convinced myself that Herr Schröder couldn't be *entirely* evil. After all, he was kind to orphan girls and had good manners. Surely he couldn't be as bad as the other Nazis.

But I'd been deceiving myself. I'd raised my children in the home of a murderer. He'd killed poor Dr. Ravanel in cold blood, leaving him dead in the street. There was no reason, none.

Dr. Ravanel had been innocent. We were the ones who were guilty. Margot and Josette of helping the Resistance. Me... of giving his nephew a reason to betray his own country.

It should have been us lying dead, not Dr. Ravanel, who as far as I knew had only done good in the world, healing the sick and injured. He'd taught me first aid, when I hadn't wanted to learn how to fight like the other girls. He'd tried to help us. He should have been rewarded. Praised.

Instead, he'd been shot and bludgeoned in the street.

I'd wept, holding baby Louis in my lap. He'd fallen asleep easily, unlike the little girls in the back of the truck, who'd cried themselves to sleep, following the example of everyone else. We'd heard the muffled sounds of Suzanne and Madame Ravanel sobbing for hours, before they too had gone silent. Even Klaus, driving, had had tears in his eyes.

Only Margot, beside me, had remained dry-eyed.

Using back alleys, we'd driven slowly out of the city without headlights, stealing through the dark of night as Klaus avoided German checkpoints.

My sister had demanded we go to Roger's flat, but Klaus had refused. "He's a known collaborator."

"You don't know what you're talking about," she'd snapped.

"It could be a rumor," he'd allowed. "But we don't have time to find out. Don't underestimate my uncle. They're likely right behind us."

"But Roger could help us escape," she'd argued. "He might even be—"

"If he's not a collaborator, your friend won't even be able to help himself, not if we bring trouble right to his door," he'd told her firmly.

"But you don't understand. I think he might be—"

"What?"

She'd stared at him, then set her jaw and looked away. "Nothing."

And he'd returned his focus to the road.

It was only when we were well past the northern outskirts and out in the country that Klaus finally pulled off the slender track of backroad into a small copse. We opened the back doors of the truck.

Woken abruptly from her exhaustion and tears, Madame Ravanel stumbled out. "Where have you taken us? What have you done?"

"Gotten you to safety, *madame*," Margot said.

I started to explain, "We're north of Paris—"

"We need to go back!" Madame Ravanel cried.

"We cannot," Klaus said.

"Oh, shut up, you Nazi! I wasn't speaking to you."

I stiffened, bouncing the baby in my arms as he started to stir and squawk. "Madame Ravanel, I'm so sorry. But it's not Klaus's fault. He saved us."

By now, all the children in the back of the ambulance had woken up and were starting to cry that they were hungry, that they were thirsty, that they wanted to go home.

Madame Ravanel hugged her teenage daughter tight—her eyes feverish, her blonde hair, streaked with gray, falling out of her untidy chignon—then lifted her chin.

"I will forgive everything if we go back," she said stiffly. "Perhaps he's in custody! Please. We can still save him."

I sucked in my breath and put my hand to my mouth. She was still in denial. She must have heard the gunshots, but the back of the ambulance had no windows. She hadn't actually seen her husband's body in the street. I didn't know what to do. Then—

"He's dead," Margot told her flatly.

Madame Ravanel's ragged intake of breath ended in a scream. "Dead!"

Did my sister have to be so blunt about it? Tossing her a frown, I put my hand gently on the woman's shoulder. "I'm sorry, *madame*. We saw him in the street when we drove away. The Nazis—"

Cursing, the older woman pulled away and turned on Margot. "You left my husband to die! You brought the Nazis to our door! This is all your fault—you killed my husband!"

And she slapped my sister's face.

It fell loudly, echoing in the night. Shocked, Margot lifted her hand to her cheek.

Geneviève started wailing. Lowering myself to one knee, still holding baby Louis, I tried to comfort all five children at once as they cried and clung to me. I felt overwhelmed by their feelings—and my own.

Then I felt Klaus's hand on my shoulder. He lifted two of the children, and I looked up at him gratefully. Behind his strong silhouette, stars were strewn like silver cat's-eye marbles across the velvety purple sky. I felt his quiet strength. His love.

Her hand still on her cheek, Margot took a deep breath. The sister I'd known would have retorted with hot words or perhaps even hit back. But faced with the grief of Dr. Ravanel's widow, she just bowed her head and whispered, "I'm sorry."

"I can't believe we lost him," Madame Ravanel choked out, holding her daughter close.

"Papa," Suzanne wept in her arms.

Something nagged at me. Some bit of memory.

Margot had called Dr. Ravanel *Papa*, too.

As the Ravanels' sobs grew quieter, Klaus caught the older woman's gaze. "*Madame*," he said awkwardly, "I need somewhere to drive to."

"What difference does it make when Jean-Luc is dead?" She wiped her eyes, visibly shaking. "Who cares if the Nazis catch us now?"

"He knew what he was doing," Margot said quietly. "He sacrificed himself to save you—both of you. All of us." She looked at Suzanne. "Are you going to waste it?"

Madame Ravanel glared, then her expression dissolved to despair.

Her daughter looked at us. "Can we still go to La Ravelle?" Suzanne said slowly.

Klaus shook his head. "Not now they are sure Dr. Ravanel is involved."

"He was Le Lérot! All along!" Madame Ravanel wailed. She covered her face with her hands. "Oh, Jean-Luc. Why did you never tell me?"

Josette, Klaus and I looked at each other, startled.

"Dr. Ravanel was Le Lérot?" he asked.

"It can't be true," Josette said.

Madame Ravanel sniffed. "He said he was. To the Germans. Why would he lie?"

"My uncle will ponder the same question," Klaus said. "He will be desperate to question us."

I shivered at the expression on his face. Any questioning his uncle would do, should he find us, would be very painful.

"He'll send soldiers, *madame*," he continued, "to any known address or connection of your husband's—or yours. We need a destination they won't know about. And we'll never get through the demarcation line now. So it needs to be within occupied France."

As I shushed and calmed the orphans, leading them back to the truck, Madame Ravanel paced in front of the shadowy trees. Finally, she turned to us in the moonlight. "I have a friend who lives on a farm up north. Perhaps we can go to her."

"Is she known to be your friend?"

"She was my favorite teacher at my *lycée*, but she left when her mother got sick. I haven't seen her in decades. We haven't so much as exchanged letters since Suzanne was born. But I know... I know she wouldn't leave their farm." She bit her lip. "At least I don't think so. But she was like my big sister back then." Her shoulders sagged as she looked down at her hands. "I always meant to keep in touch, but after I became a wife... a mother... There never seemed to be enough time to write."

"Would she really take us all in?" I asked doubtfully.

She hesitated. "I think so. At least for a night or two. Enough to have space to think about what to do next."

Klaus nodded. "All right. Come sit in front with me, *madame*, if you please, and help me find the way. The rest of you, sit in the back."

Madame Ravanel wiped her eyes. "There's a map beneath the driver's seat. It only has the main roads of France. But it should at least get you close."

Turning to me, Klaus said in a low voice, "The children need to be kept quiet in back. They'll attract too much attention if we get pulled over. Can you keep an eye on them?"

"Yes." I suddenly clutched his hand. "Thank you for saving us."

He looked at me, then kissed the top of my head tenderly. "You saved me, too. Loving you gave me the strength to pull away from everything I know is wrong, no matter how many times my uncle and the others told me it was my duty. You gave me back my soul, Lucie." He cupped my face. "We'll get through this. And then—"

"Yes." Smiling, I touched his rough cheek. "And then."

I'd known I was betraying my sisters by telling him everything. But I'd put my trust in Klaus, as he'd done for me; I loved him, and he loved me. We were meant to be together.

Until death parted us.

3 8

LUCIE

We tumbled out of the truck a couple of hours later to find a dark country road lit only by moonlight, many kilometers from the nearest town.

The children were hungry and cranky. Most of them had slept, and fortunately, the one time the truck had been stopped, I'd managed to keep them quiet. We'd held our breath, waiting for the back door to be flung open by angry Nazi soldiers, but instead, the engine had restarted and we'd carried on.

Now, I saw a dark forest beyond softly rolling farmland. Nearby, a single light glowed in a farmhouse window. But other than that small candle, the darkness seemed to stretch on forever, modern Paris nothing but a distant memory—or perhaps even a myth.

I looked at the uncovered farmhouse window and realized how much I'd missed that. In Paris, every window was covered, by decree. No lights were allowed at night—or people either. Nazi soldiers were just waiting for the chance to break any defiance, and break heads too. I hadn't realized till now just how oppressive Paris had become, and how desperate and scared I'd been, trying to protect the little children and find the silver lining to living in an open-air prison.

Here, I could breathe the fresh country air.

Klaus had parked in the gravel in front of the farmhouse. A big shaggy dog suddenly appeared on the porch, barking wildly. Choupette turned her head in surprise.

A gray-haired woman peeked out the front door, her expression wary. "What do you want?" Then she saw Madame Ravanel, and her fists unclenched. She squinted. "Élisabeth...? Is that you?"

She moved forward, and the two women fell into each other's arms. Madame Ravanel wept against the older woman's shoulder, and a few moments later, we were all welcomed into the farmhouse, even Choupette, who'd quickly made friends with the woman's dog, Médor.

We soon learned that Madame Brunner's husband had been killed in the previous war, and their two grown sons had died in Germany's most recent invasion. She'd been left with only Médor to help her.

Madame Brunner hugged the children close, calling them *les pauvres petits*, then quickly warmed up broth and milk, and made sandwiches for the rest of us. But even in her courtesy, the widow kept giving Klaus scared sideways glances.

"Don't be nervous, Aurélie. He's not a Nazi," Madame Ravanel told her earnestly, then looked at Klaus. "Not anymore. He saved us, after the Germans murdered my husband. He's one of us now. *Le bon Dieu* help him."

Of course the older woman had questions. But after Klaus explained, she looked at me dreamily. "So you betrayed your country for love."

"I had no choice." His voice was low and sad.

Madame Brunner looked wistful. "My own husband was German by birth, from Alsace. He became a French citizen when he married me, and fought for France in the Great War. In the Foreign Legion, against Germany. Because he loved me."

Warmth filled my heart as I reached for Klaus's hand. We smiled at her shyly.

"So you understand, *madame*?" he said.

She nodded, then sighed. "But it's different now. France is under occupation." Her expression became worried. "Everyone will be hunting you. The Germans won't rest until they punish you, Klaus. And even you, Lucie." She turned to me. "And not just the Germans. Your own countrymen will see you as a collaborator and traitor."

"But surely..." I started to argue, then noticed the children drowsing. They'd been too exhausted to eat much. As Jeanne slept in my lap, I stroked her hair. "Is there somewhere I can take the children to sleep, Madame Brunner?"

"My sons' old bedroom upstairs." She looked at baby Louis, now tucked with blankets into a corner of the sofa. "Wait—I still have the old crib in the attic. Let me find it..."

And so an hour later, all my babies were asleep and cozy and warm, the toddlers sharing beds, the baby in a nearby antique crib a hundred years old. The bedding was clean, and thanks to a nearby fire, the rooms were comfortable.

Klaus helped me settle them down, rocking Geneviève in a chair by the bedroom fire. The rosy-cheeked blonde, who wasn't quite three, was exhausted and bewildered, but finally, even she managed to drop off to sleep. He placed her in the small bed next to dark-haired Thérèse, then we held our breath and slipped out, closing the bedroom door behind us.

Alone together in the hallway, my beloved kissed me softly, holding me in his strong arms. I closed my eyes, leaning against him, feeling safe, in spite of everything.

Finally, he drew away and reached out to lift my chin. "Lucie."

I opened my eyes reluctantly. "Yes?"

Worry flashed in his eyes, then he exhaled. "Never mind. Let's go downstairs."

But I held on to his hand. "What were you going to say?"

His gaze shifted to the floor. "I don't have the right."

"Say it anyway. Isn't that what we promised each other? No secrets?"

Closing his eyes, he took a deep breath. When he opened them, he took both my hands in his own and kissed them softly, one by one. Electricity raced through me, so strong that it curled my toes.

"Lucie... Madame Brunner is right. I'm going to be a hunted man. And because I love you, I want you a million kilometers from me, to protect you..."

"Never," I said, holding his hands tight.

"*Liebchen*," he whispered and kissed me once more.

He finally pulled away with a low laugh. "I have no right to ask." He lifted his gaze to mine. "But I must. Because every moment I look at you, I think I'll explode if I don't. Because I want you to say yes so badly. And yet I don't."

"For heaven's sake—what is it?"

He looked at me. Then slowly, right there in the dark hallway, he lowered himself to one knee.

I goggled down at him.

"Lucie Vashon," he said in a low voice, "will you marry me?"

My breath caught.

"Yes," I whispered, and his face lit up in a wild smile that I felt from my scalp to the very tips of my toes. "Yes!"

He jumped up, his handsome face alight with joy—but also the merest shadow of sorrow. I threw my arms around him, crying with happiness but sadness too, because I knew now that we were living on borrowed time. We had to make every moment count. He caressed my cheeks, my forehead, with butterfly kisses, saying he didn't deserve me but would spend every moment of the rest of his life trying to, as I said the same.

Later, when we went down to the dining room to join the adults next to the fire, we did so hand in hand.

Margot looked up when we entered, her eyes widening as she took us in. "What is it? What's happened?"

Klaus and I blushed as we glanced at each other. My hand gripped his tightly, and his mine. But he waited, nodding at me, and I smiled, feeling like my heart was about to burst.

"We're engaged."

"How lovely," Madame Brunner said warmly. "*Félicitations!*"

But she was the only one to congratulate us. Margot, Josette, Madame Ravanel and even Suzanne just stared at us blankly from where they were sitting around the worn dining table.

"You're engaged," Madame Ravanel said faintly. "On the day we've lost everything. The day my husband was murdered." She looked at Klaus. "By your uncle."

Shame surged through me. She was right—how dare I reach for happiness amid such misery? How could I be so selfish? I hung my head.

Klaus's hand tightened on mine.

"In a world like this, *madame*," he told her steadily, "we must celebrate anything good when we can. While we can."

She stared at him for a moment, then her eyes welled with tears. "You're right," she whispered. "Jean-Luc would say the same."

Madame Ravanel exhaled, and some of the tension left the table, as everyone hugged her and Suzanne, offering words of comfort. The teenager reached for Margot to include her in the center of the circle, as if she too had the right to grieve. Only Madame Ravanel seemed to resist—and didn't hug Margot back.

I love you, Papa. The last few hours, I'd tried to tell myself I must have misheard, misunderstood. But now...

A chill crept through me. It seemed such a strange thing. Why would my sister have said that to Dr. Ravanel right before he died? Just as a mark of respect?

Ever since she and Josette had returned to Paris nearly two years ago, I'd had the feeling Margot was keeping something from me. And now, as I looked at her being hugged so fiercely by Suzanne, I had the unnerving feeling that everyone knew the secret but me.

I love you, Papa.

Surely my big sister, the protector of my childhood, whom I'd idolized and adored all my life—she wouldn't have lied to me. Not to my face. Not for years. She loved me too much for that. Respected me too much.

Didn't she?

I blinked, staring at the ragged silk stockings covering her feet. Where were her shoes?

"Jean-Luc would want you both to be happy," Madame Ravanel was saying now, her voice a little stiff. Turning her back on Margot, she shook Klaus's hand, then kissed my cheek. As brief and strained as it was, I was touched by her effort.

"Thank you, *madame.*"

Madame Brunner poured her former pupil a small glass of brandy and held it out without a word. Madame Ravanel gulped it down.

"What will you do?" her friend asked.

"I don't know." Madame Ravanel wiped her mouth and shook her head, staring blankly at the fire. "I can't bear to think of my husband's body being picked up by the authorities, tossed in an unmarked grave."

"Was Papa really Le Lérot?" Suzanne asked.

Her mother just continued to stare at the fire, so her daughter patted her arm. "He must have been, if he said he was.

The Germans thought so, too. We should hold our heads high. Papa died for his family. He died for France. He's a hero—just like Daniel. Just like Paul."

Madame Ravanel lifted her head then and stared at her daughter, but almost as if she wasn't really seeing her.

"Paul," she whispered. Then she blinked and turned suddenly towards Margot, the simmering tension she'd had towards my sister suddenly evaporating for no reason I could see.

Blinking back tears, the widow held out her arms. "*Ma petite*," she said hoarsely. "Forgive me. It was not your fault. I'm so sorry."

With a stifled sob, Margot went into the other woman's arms. As I watched them embrace, I almost wanted to cry, too.

"You're welcome to stay here as long as you like," Madame Brunner told her, sipping a little brandy herself. "You and the children." Then she frowned, staring at Margot's feet. "What happened to your shoes?"

"They were Nazi shoes, so I kicked them off," she said, tossing her head. She looked down at her fancy skirt suit with a frown. "These are, too." She looked up. "I don't suppose you have any old clothes you can spare?"

"Of course."

"You really want us to stay, Aurélie?" Madame Ravanel gave a half hysterical laugh. "A bunch of babies, some wild teenagers, a German deserter and a broken-down widow like me? Didn't you hear the Nazis are looking for us?"

"Well, when you put it like that..." The older woman gave a low laugh. Then she sobered. "It's been nice to have company in the house again. It was a little lonely, just Médor and me." She glanced at Klaus and us three older girls. "Plus, I could really use help with the harvest this year. I have a greedy neighbor already circling if I can't manage to give the Germans their requisition of wheat."

Klaus and I looked at each other in hope.

Madame Brunner smiled, crinkling her warm eyes. "We're so remote out here, the Germans mostly ignore us, as long as we keep up our quotas of food to the city. Plus, my brother is the mayor. We keep to our own. You'd be safe enough. Safe as you can be anywhere in France." She glanced at the ceiling, towards where the children were sleeping. "And so will they. Poor little things." She looked around, her voice almost pleading. "Won't you stay?"

"We'd love to," said Suzanne suddenly. She glanced at her mother. "Wouldn't we, Maman?"

Madame Ravanel looked at her daughter, then exhaled. "Thank you, Aurélie. I think we would."

"And don't worry, I'll help with the harvest," said Suzanne stoutly. "I'm stronger than I look."

"I'm used to farm work," Klaus said. "But, *madame*... do you think your brother would be willing to marry us? Soon?" He smiled at me.

I blushed, ducking my head—but not before I'd seen my sister flinch at the word *marry*.

"You all can stay. I'm going back to Paris," Margot said, her jaw tight.

"So am I," said Josette.

They glared at each other, as if they didn't approve of the other one doing anything so dangerous.

"If you're sure that's wise," Madame Brunner said diplomatically, "I could probably find you a ride. Though of course you have your truck—"

"*Our* truck," Madame Ravanel murmured before drinking more brandy.

"Anyway, the Germans will be looking for it," Klaus pointed out.

"But you can't go back to Paris!" I cried, since no one else was saying it. Who cared about the truck? "Herr Schröder will arrest you the moment you return. And torture out any information you might have about Dr. Ravanel."

As Josette lifted a pointed eyebrow at Margot, I looked between them, and I suddenly knew the secret they'd been keeping. All those little clues I hadn't wanted to see. All those signs I'd done my best to ignore.

Heartsick, I looked at my sister. "How long have you been lying to me?" I whispered.

Margot's cheeks went pale. "Lucie, I swear, I was trying to protect you—"

"Oh, stop it," Josette snapped. "For heaven's sake! You've kept her in the dark long enough."

"She doesn't know?" Suzanne said, astonished.

My cheeks burned as I stared at my sister. I felt an ache in my throat. "I want to hear you admit it."

But Margot was glaring at Josette, her hands tightening into fists. "You always ruin everything! Stay out of my life!"

"I *have* stayed out of it. For years. *Enough.* I can see you're never going to tell her." Josette turned to me. "Margot's not actually your sister. She's the secret love child of Dr. Ravanel... and Sister Helen!"

All the air seemed to rush from my lungs, and my limbs went numb. I stared at Josette, feeling everyone else's pitying eyes as they watched with shocked fascination.

"Josette, you—" Margot swore at her; she looked as if she would have loved to drop the redhead in a vat of boiling oil.

Then she turned to me and took my numb hands in her own. "Lucie, dear. I was scared the secret would be dangerous to you if you knew. And I didn't want to hurt you."

"You... aren't my sister?"

She squeezed my hands. "I'm your sister in all the ways that matter. But before Helen left for America, she told me she was my mother. She left me with the Vashons before you were born. She and Dr. Ravanel, they..." She glanced at Madame Ravanel out the corner of her eye. "They worked together for many years. And they had... a single night. This was before he married," she rushed to say. "And he didn't even know about me. Not until recently."

I looked at Madame Ravanel and Suzanne. There was no surprise in their faces, only pity for me, obviously the last to know. It seemed everyone still thought of me as a helpless, naïve child, the one who couldn't walk to the *pharmacie* halfway down the street without getting lost, or cook porridge without nearly setting the kitchen on fire.

They didn't see how much I'd learned and grown over the last two years. How I'd been forced to struggle and survive on my own. How I'd managed to do just that, as well as take care of six tiny orphans in the bargain.

They didn't see me at all.

I ripped my hands away. "You're not my sister," I choked out to Margot. Then I turned to Josette, who was looking at her smugly. "You're not my sister, either." Her eyes went wide. Turning away, I blinked back tears, my throat aching. "If you were my sisters, you wouldn't have lied to me all this time. You would have seen who I've become." I lifted my chin. "I'm just as strong as either of you. I'm—"

My proud words were wrecked by a sob. My cheeks flamed with humiliation and rage I didn't know how to deal with—I'd never felt anything like it before.

Turning on my heel, with Choupette hugging me like a shadow, I fled the farmhouse, away from all their pitying eyes, and out into the haunted summer night.

39

JOSETTE

Telling Lucie, I'd felt a rush of relief, like an oppressive cloud of hot air had been suddenly released by an open window.

I'd done it. At last. It was ridiculous, not to mention cruel, that Margot had kept Lucie in the dark this long. I was sick of covering for her. For two years, I'd been burdened by this secret. But the fierce joy sparked by its release had lasted only a few seconds. Then I'd seen Margot's face; the horrified looks of all the others. And Lucie had turned on me.

You're not my sister, either.

I'd never seen Lucie so angry, never even known it was possible. Now, I gaped after her as the front door banged hard against the frame and she disappeared out into the night with her dog.

Klaus stepped forward apologetically. "I'll go—"

"No." Margot stopped him with a gesture. "It's me she's mad at. It has to be me."

Without even a glance in my direction, she stalked outside, still shoeless. I felt Madame Ravanel, Madame Brunner, Klaus and Suzanne staring at me. My cheeks burned.

"So?" I said, lifting my chin defensively. "Lucie deserved to know."

The others looked at each other. They said nothing, but I felt their silent judgment. They clearly thought I was the cruel one. That I hadn't blurted out the secret just for Lucie's benefit but to hurt Margot.

They were so wrong. I clenched my hands. I didn't resent Margot. Not anymore. I'd forgiven her for taking Roger's love, for being so bossy all the time, for criticizing and demeaning me for years. I'd forgiven her for being adored from the day she was born while I'd had to fight and scratch for every little crumb of love.

Hadn't I?

Closing my eyes, I exhaled. Now that I thought of it, wasn't I still keeping my own secret, too?

I looked at them wanly. "I'll go apologize," I mumbled and followed them outside.

The summer night was dark and quiet, the stars bright. Margot and Lucie stood together in the shadows by the trees, frosted by moonlight, arguing. The two people I loved most in the world.

I'd come out to apologize. So why did I suddenly feel so angry at both of them? For keeping their secrets—for taking me away from my home at the Théâtre Lutèce—for caring only about Dr. Ravanel's death and not Madame Hébert's arrest.

And more.

For being loved. For being adored. For being so certain of it.

"I should have told you, Lucie." Margot's voice was unusually humble.

"You kept it from me for *two years*." Lucie sounded tearful. "How could you? Why didn't you tell me when you first found out?"

"I didn't know until after you were gone."

Lucie's jaw hardened. "After you left me, you mean. Abandoned me in Boulins with those awful people so you could traipse off to Marseille."

She looked stricken. "How many times can I tell you I'm sorry—"

"Margot felt awful about it," I said, moving closer. "She spent every hour of every day looking for you after you went missing."

Lucie looked between us, her expression wretched.

"It's why we came to Paris to find you," Margot said, "instead of going to America to be safe."

"Margot could have gone to college in Los Angeles," I added. "I could have gone to Hollywood. But we stayed for you."

"So it's my fault, is it?" Lucie said quietly, her cheeks red. "I kept you from running off to America with your mother, Margot. And I kept you from being a big star, Josette. Just because I was stupid enough to stay in Paris to take care of homeless babies. I'm so sorry."

I hadn't known Lucie had it in her to be sarcastic. And just because I was trying to be honest, like she'd said she wanted!

"Well, we did give some things up," I told her, folding my arms. "You might as well know. We stayed for you. We tried to help you."

"Help me!" She threw up her hands. "Neither of you helped. You were both focused on your own selfish plans."

"Selfish?" Margot said, her ire raising in turn. "I was trapped into being a secretary for a Nazi. It brought me nothing but shame. So when Dr. Ravanel asked if I could pass secrets on to Le Lérot, what could I say but yes?"

"And I had to help Jews escape France by getting them forged papers," I said. "I had to."

Lucie glared at each of us. "No, you didn't. We could have stayed quiet and kept our heads down in Paris and tried to just survive and protect the ones we loved—the ones we were actually responsible for. The helpless children who had no one else to save them. But you didn't care if you risked their lives, along with mine, and Berthe's… just so you could feel brave and strong! Well, there are all kinds of strength. Sometimes it's knowing which battles to fight and which not to."

"You're saying this, Lucie?" Margot scoffed. "After all your years of trying to protect every single person you met?"

Lucie's nostrils flared. Wrapping her arms around herself, she said quietly, "I've been forced to change. In this war. As you would know, if you'd paid attention."

"And when have either of you ever paid attention to me—or how I might be feeling?" I demanded. "I didn't forge travel documents because I was trying to be brave. I did it because I felt *guilty*."

"What do you mean?"

I didn't want to tell them. I especially didn't want to tell Margot. After all the fuss I'd made over her own secret, she would eviscerate me. But it was time to grow up. Maybe it had just been about being brave to keep one's own self-respect, just as Lucie had said. I took a deep breath.

"Sister Helen found out who left me as a foundling. My mother was only eighteen when she had me. She was working as a maid in Paris when her boss's son seduced her—or raped her." I was forced to admit the possibility out loud. "He tossed her aside when she became pregnant. She was Jewish, a refugee from Poland. She couldn't return to her family with a baby in her arms. So she left me at St. Agnes's door."

But if I'd thought being vulnerable would make them kind, I was wrong.

Margot stared at me incredulously. "So what are you saying? That we should feel sorry for you? That you've been persecuted, like the ones forced to wear gold stars on their clothes, who're getting pushed into concentration camps?"

"No! That's not—"

"I'm sorry about your parents, Josette," Lucie said sadly. "I can't even imagine what it would be like to have your parents give you up." Then her young face hardened as she turned to Margot. "But I do know how it feels to have your only family abandon you."

Margot flinched. Then her eyes narrowed.

"Well, try and imagine it," she said shortly. "Because Claude Vashon isn't your father, either. He was dead before you were born. Your mother became a prostitute, and no one even knows who your father is."

I gasped. So much for the more mature version of Margot. Feeling hurt, she'd launched a vicious counter-attack. She'd done it to me for years, but never with Lucie. Never before now.

Lucie looked stunned.

Then she gave Margot a hard shove. "Take that back!"

"I won't, and you're a hypocrite for getting angry about me telling you the truth! You said you didn't want any more secrets... well here you go!"

"You can be so horrible, Margot! I can't believe I ever admired you!"

"Good," Margot ground out, tossing her dark curly hair. "I'm glad you've stopped admiring me. I guess that means I can stop pretending it's anything but stupid for you to marry a Nazi!"

"She's right, Lucie," I said in a low voice. "They'll say you lured him into betraying his duty and country and family. You'd both be hunted as traitors."

"Stupid?" she repeated incredulously to Margot. "At least Klaus is on our side. You worked overtime to get Otto Schröder to fall in love with you—even knowing he was a monster!"

"I was trying to get him to trust me!"

"*Trust* you? You flirted with him night and day. As you once accused Josette of doing with Roger—you did everything but grease yourself down and put yourself on a spit to be cooked for his dinner!"

"How dare you!"

"You push everyone away, Margot," she persisted. "Roger. Sister Helen. Josette. Even me. You pretend to care, while lying about everything that matters. You can't bear to be vulnerable. To risk anyone actually knowing you."

"It's not true," whispered Margot. She took a breath. "I never meant to... I was going to tell you, Lucie. I *was*."

"But you didn't," I pointed out.

She turned on me with glittering eyes. "Are you making yourself out to be some kind of hero, Josette? After the brutal way you told her?"

"Someone had to do it," I replied coldly. I tilted my head. "I'm amazed you finally told Dr. Ravanel."

"I..." She stopped, biting her lip.

I stared at her. "He guessed, didn't he? And I bet it only happened recently. If he'd known, he would never have let you put yourself in danger. He would have tried to protect you, like he did his wife and Suzanne."

Margot glared at me. "You're just bitter because no one will ever love you, Josette. You're still so jealous of Roger and me, you're dying of it!"

It felt like a slap. I drew back with a gasp.

Then I saw what she was doing. I'd cut too close to the bone. Once, I would have been distracted by her accusation, and dissolved into misery and anguish. Now, I saw the manipulation for what it was.

I narrowed my eyes. "You lied to your father's face. For *years*."

"It was my only chance to get to know him." Margot's voice was high. "I knew what I was doing—"

"Oh, you knew, did you?" I interrupted silkily, heart

pounding in fury. "So you were planning all along for him to be shot dead in the street, while we fled for our lives?"

Silence fell in the cool summer night, amid the darkness of the farm's rolling hills, lit only by moonlight and the glow of the candle in the house's window—broken only by the sudden, plaintive wail of an unseen night bird.

"Take that back," Margot whispered. "His death wasn't my fault."

"Wasn't it?" Something ugly in my soul wouldn't let me turn back. "You're the one who made it personal with Otto Schröder. You made a fool of him. I bet you even kissed him, didn't you?"

"She did," confirmed Lucie. "Just today."

My nose wrinkled as I looked at Margot. "You're disgusting."

She looked between us wildly, raking back her dark curly hair. "I never wanted him to kiss me—I hate him! He deserves to die for what he's done!"

"So that's why you're going back to Paris?" Lucie said quietly. "Revenge? You'd rather commit suicide in some insane vendetta than take care of the people you love?"

Margot looked anguished. "I can't leave Le Lérot to fight alone—"

"So Dr. Ravanel wasn't Le Lérot?" I gasped. "Then who is?"

She flashed me a troubled look, then said in a halting voice, "All I know for sure is... it wasn't Dr. Ravanel." She added, "And I know he needs my help."

"As Madame Hébert needs mine." I straightened. "And so does everyone trying to escape Paris."

"Please, Margot. Please, Josette." Lucie looked ethereal in the moonlight as she looked between us with tears in her eyes. "You'll die if you return to Paris, die for nothing. Please don't go." Her voice cracked. "Stay with me."

40

MARGOT

I couldn't believe Lucie was asking me to let my father's murderer walk free; to let the Germans continue to rain terror down on our country.

I lifted my chin. "You can stay here and hide if you want, Lucie. I'm going to fight."

"Me too," said Josette, tossing her red hair.

Lucie's face turned very cold.

"I'm sick of you," she whispered. "Both of you. Taking such foolhardy risks. You both think you're so important. And you scorn what I've done, raising six children without your help." She straightened. "Go, then. Go get yourselves killed."

The ground felt cold beneath my feet. What had I said? What had I done?

My mouth was always getting me into trouble. Especially when I felt scared or attacked. My brain just went blank, and before I knew it, I was saying horrible things, trying to push people away.

Maybe they were right...

"Lucie, I didn't mean—"

"You meant every word." My sister's voice was flat. "As far as you're concerned, I'm a coward. A useless burden." She set her jaw. "So it's good you won't have to take care of me anymore. You won't have to come up with excuses every time I ask for help. Go back to Paris and get yourself killed helping strangers. You've never even met Le Lérot, but I can tell he means more to you than I do."

"Lucie..."

"And you." She turned to Josette. "Our whole lives, you've complained about not getting enough love or appreciation or attention. You've felt so very sorry for yourself. Poor Josette, left at the orphanage gate. Poor Josette, who doesn't get as much attention as Margot. Poor Josette, who threw herself at the first man who showed any interest and fell apart when he didn't reciprocate. But the truth is, all this time," she said slowly, "you *loved* it. You loved being a martyr. The world treated you badly. That meant you were off the hook. How lucky you are. Everyone's to blame but you."

Josette was pale. She clenched her hands into fists. "You don't know what you're talking about."

"Don't I?"

She sucked in her breath. "Fine. Maybe you're right. Maybe I spent my whole life yearning for love. But now I know there's something more." She lifted her chin. "I'm not going to let people die. Not if I can save them." Looking between us, she said quietly, "I need to save them. More than I need to be loved by you."

"Fine by me," Lucie said coldly. "I don't need you, either."

Staring between my two sisters, I felt sick. I'd done everything I could. I'd let my mother go to America alone and traveled across France with Josette to save Lucie; I'd killed myself trying to protect them, putting up with Otto Schröder's gifts and attentions, though they made my skin crawl; I'd managed to lead them to safety even after I'd seen my father murdered in front of my eyes. And it still wasn't enough. All my sacrifice and effort meant nothing.

The three of us stared at each other bitterly.

Three sisters, now enemies.

We all seemed shell-shocked, as if none of us could believe everything that had been said. But it was too late to take it back. I couldn't back down, not after all their hurtful words. *Let them be the ones to apologize*, I thought.

But they didn't, so neither did I.

"Take this," I choked out, pulling my mother's garnet ring off my finger, then pressing it into Lucie's hands. "You'll need something if you're so determined to wreck your life."

She frowned at it. "Where'd it come from?"

"My father gave it to my mother once," I whispered. My eyes were burning, and I blinked fast, determined not to let them see me cry. "Now I'm giving it to you."

She frowned, confused. Then she tightened her fingers around the ring. "A bad-luck, hand-me-down ring. *Merci.*"

Her tone was sarcastic. I turned away to hide my tears.

We returned to the farmhouse in silence, none of us meeting each other's eyes. Lucie went straight to Klaus, and the two of them disappeared to talk alone.

Josette and I had only each other, which meant we had no one.

"Madame Brunner," I said, lifting my chin. "Did you say you could find us a ride to Paris?"

And so it was that just a short while later, in the darkness before dawn, I climbed behind metal canisters in the back of a milk truck traveling to the capital city, now wearing Madame Brunner's old dress and shoes. As Josette and I sat across from each other in the dark, rattling and bumping over the road, I could feel her gaze on me. But I didn't need to wonder what she was thinking. I knew now.

She and Lucie blamed me for everything.

I didn't look in her direction. I was done trying to take care of them. I'd done everything I could, and I was done trying to explain myself or make them appreciate how hard I'd tried. Done.

I'd left half my money hidden in the widow's breadbox, just in case. And I'd pilfered a knife from the kitchen, for self-protection. From now on, they were on their own. And so was I.

Le Lérot will find you, my father had told me.

I'd just have to trust he would. Whoever Le Lérot was, whether he was Roger or not, I'd help him get the Germans out of my city, out of my country.

And most of all, I would get justice against Otto Schröder.

I had nothing to fear anymore. Nothing to lose.

As faint light crept through the edges of the back doors, the milk truck slowed at a crossroads. I heard the sounds of a city and guessed we were approaching the outskirts of Paris. When the truck stopped, on impulse I opened the back doors and jumped out.

Josette blurted, "Wait, Margot—"

But I didn't need to hear more insults and blame. I felt awful enough.

Without pausing, I shut the doors behind me. I had one last glimpse of her agonized face, and then the milk truck sped down the road.

Dawn was pink over the eastern sky. I'd been right—I was on the edge of Paris. I took a deep breath, then started the long walk on foot. I still had the paper with Roger's address. I prayed he would be there. That he'd forgive me for treating him so badly for so long.

You push everyone away.

No. I wouldn't let myself think of love. Or what I'd lost.

My sisters...

The Nazis' fault. One Nazi in particular.

I hefted my bag higher on my shoulder, then lifted glittering eyes towards the long road that led straight to the heart of the darkened city of light. The Nazis were to blame for everything.

And I would get my revenge.

EPILOGUE

LUCIE

Klaus and I were married a week later, in the widow's ruined barn on the edge of the farm, half hidden by the trees.

As the sun rose in the sky, we were wed in secret by Madame Brunner's sympathetic brother, the mayor. She was our only other witness. Madame Ravanel and Suzanne diplomatically begged off, staying at the farmhouse to watch the children.

To anyone who asked, Klaus was a French citizen from Alsace, the region that had been handed back and forth between Germany and France for decades. Just another war refugee who'd lost his papers, and supposedly with flat feet, so he'd been given an agricultural referral rather than being conscripted. It hurt to tell the babies the lie, to pretend everything they'd thought about Klaus—the truth—had been just a dream. But since they were so little, their memories were fortunately short.

But my sisters had been right about one thing—if the Gestapo ever found Klaus, they would destroy him, and me and everyone we loved.

So we'd now be Klaus and Lucie Brunner, supposedly

distant relatives of Madame Brunner's dead husband. We would stay at this remote place, raise the children and help work her farm. We would take care of each other and try to ride out the waves of war.

As the mayor spoke the words of the civil ceremony, I trembled beneath my yellowing tulle veil, the widow's old-fashioned wedding gown enveloping me in white satin. I held sunflowers from her garden for my bouquet. We'd made our cake with honey and cheap brown flour.

"You're now husband and wife." The *maire* beamed at us. He turned to Klaus. "You may kiss the bride."

My husband looked down at me tenderly. "*Liebchen.*"

My heart felt like it might explode, it was beating so hard and fast. I looked up at the sunlight gleaming against the green leaves of the trees, hearing the birdsong in the soft country air. I knew the danger now I was married to the enemy. But I didn't care. He was mine.

He lowered his head to kiss me, and I felt so happy I almost wept. What had I ever done to deserve such joy?

But when he finally pulled away, I looked down at my newly adorned left hand. The garnet and gold ring gleamed, foreign and strange in spite of its beauty, and I felt suddenly cold. I'd been so rude to Margot. What had possessed me to say such terrible things to her and Josette? What had possessed *them*? What fool had ever been so cruel as to say honesty was the best policy?

It felt wrong not to have them at my wedding, sharing my joy. And terrifying to think I might never see them again.

I suddenly wondered how the war would end—for all of us.

But Margot and Josette were gone now, disappeared in the night, beyond the reach of my love and care. We'd each made our choice.

And there was no going back.

A LETTER FROM JENNA

I want to say a huge thank you for choosing to read *The Last War Orphan*. If you did enjoy it, and want to keep up to date with all my latest releases, just sign up at the following link. Your email address will never be shared, and you can unsubscribe at any time!

www.bookouture.com/jenna-ness

By the way, Lucie's habit of burning the orphanage's porridge was entirely inspired by life. I can't tell you how many dinners I burned while writing this book. (It's surely a coincidence my family seems to prefer takeaway lately?)

Growing up is hard. When you're young, you wonder what kind of person you'll turn out to be, what kind of life you'll have. You decide whether to conform to people's expectations—or defy them. That's the battle Margot, Josette and Lucie face in *The Last War Orphan*.

But growing up doesn't only happen when you're young. The griefs of youth are usually just the start, unfortunately. Heartbreak builds over a lifetime. The truth is, at any age, we're all fighting some kind of war. I think the only way to get through it is to hold on to our friends and family with every bit of love we can give.

As World War II finally draws to a close, that's what Margot, Lucie and Josette will have to do. I'm working on the last book of the Orphans of St. Agnes trilogy now. If the girls want a chance to survive, they'll have to face their final battle together, in the greatest test of their lives. Will their hearts be brave enough to endure it?

I hope you loved *The Last War Orphan*, and if you did I would be very grateful if you could write a review. I'd love to hear what you think, and as a new historical author, reviews make such a difference helping new readers discover my books for the first time.

And I'm always happy to hear from readers. Please feel free to get in touch through social media or my website. As always, I'm so grateful to have you here with me.

Love, Jenna x

www.jennaness.com

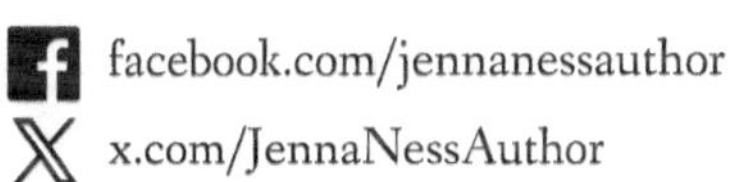

PUBLISHING TEAM

Turning a manuscript into a book requires the efforts of many people. The publishing team at Bookouture would like to acknowledge everyone who contributed to this publication.

Commercial

Lauren Morrissette

Hannah Richmond

Imogen Allport

Cover design

Ami Smithson

Data and analysis

Mark Alder

Mohamed Bussuri

Editorial

Lizzie Brien

Hannah Wilson

Copyeditor

Laura Kincaid

Proofreader

Liz Hatherell

Marketing
Alex Crow
Melanie Price
Occy Carr
Cíara Rosney
Martyna Młynarska

Operations and distribution
Marina Valles
Stephanie Straub
Joe Morris

Production
Hannah Snetsinger
Mandy Kullar
Nadia Michael
Charlotte Hegley

Publicity
Kim Nash
Noelle Holten
Jess Readett
Sarah Hardy

Rights and contracts
Peta Nightingale
Richard King
Saidah Graham